HARBOUR

ALSO BY JOHN AJVIDE LINDQVIST

Let the Right One In

Handling the Undead

HARBOUR

John Ajvide Lindqvist

TRANSLATED FROM THE SWEDISH BY MARLAINE DELARGY

Quercus

First published in Great Britain in 2010 by

Quercus
21 Bloomsbury Square
London
WC1A 2NS

Published by agreement with Ordfronts Förlag, Stockholm,
and Loenhardt & Høier Literary Agency aps, Copenhagen.

First published in Sweden as *Människohamn* by Ordfront in 2008

A CIP catalogue record for this book is available
from the British Library.

ISBN (HB) 978 1 84916 511 2
ISBN (TPB) 978 1 84916 512 9

10 9 8 7 6 5 4 3 2 1

Printed and bound in Great Britain by
Clays Ltd, St Ives Plc.

To my father
Ingemar Pettersson (1938–1998)

He gave me the sea
The sea took him from me

Welcome to Domarö.

It's a place you won't find on any maritime chart, unless you look really carefully. It lies just about two nautical miles east of Refsnäs in the archipelago in southern Roslagen, a considerable distance in from Söderarm and Tjärven.

You will need to move some of the islands out of the way, create empty expanses of water between them in order to catch sight of Domarö. Then you will also be able to see the lighthouse at Gåvasten, and all the other landmarks that arise in this story.

Arise, yes. That's the right word. We will be in a place that is new to people. For tens of thousands of years it has been lying beneath the water. But then the islands rise up and to the islands come the people, and with the people come the stories.

Let us begin.

I

Banished

Where the waves thunder and the storms cry.
Where the breakers crash and the salt water whirls,
that is where the place that is ours rises from the sea.
The legacy that passes from father to son.

LENNART ALBINSSON — RÅDMANSÖ

The sea has given and the sea has taken away

Who flies there in the feather-harbour, who climbs
up there out of the black, shining waters?

Gunnar Ekelöf — Tjärven

Sea buckthorn

*Three thousand years ago, Domarö was nothing but a large, flat rock
sticking up out of the water, crowned by an erratic boulder the ice had
left behind. One nautical mile to the east it was possible to glimpse the
round shape that would later rise out of the sea and be given the name
Gåvasten. Apart from that, there was nothing. It would be another
thousand years before the surrounding islets and islands dared to poke
their heads above the water, beginning the formation of the archipelago that goes under the name of Domarö archipelago today.*

By that time the sea buckthorn had already arrived on Domarö.

*Down below the enormous block left by the ice, a shoreline had
formed. There in the scree the sea buckthorn worked its way along
with its creeping roots, the hardy shrub finding nourishment in the
rotting seaweed, growing where there was nothing to grow in, clinging
to the rocks. Sea buckthorn. Toughest of the tough.*

And the sea buckthorn produced new roots, crept up over the water's edge and grew on the slopes until a metallic-green border surrounded the uninhabited shores of Domarö like a fringe. Birds snatched the fiery yellow berries that tasted of bitter oranges and flew with them to other islands, spreading the gospel of the sea buckthorn to new shores, and within a few hundred years the green fringe could be seen in all directions.

But the sea buckthorn was preparing its own destruction.

The humus formed by its rotting leaves was richer than anything the stony shores could offer, and the alder saw its chance. It set its seeds in the mulch left by the sea buckthorn, and it grew stronger and stronger. The sea buckthorn was unable to tolerate either the nitrogen-rich soil produced by the alder, or the shade from its leaves, and it withdrew down towards the water.

With the alder came other plants that needed a higher level of nutrition, competing for the available space. The sea buckthorn was relegated to a shoreline that grew far too slowly, just half a metre in a hundred years. Despite the fact that it had given birth to the other plants, the sea buckthorn was displaced and set aside.

And so it sits there at the edge of the shore, biding its time. Beneath the slender, silky green leaves there are thorns. Big thorns.

Two small people and a large rock (July 1984)

They were holding hands.

He was thirteen and she was twelve. If anyone in the gang caught sight of them, they would just die right there on the spot. They crept through the fir trees, alert to every sound and every movement as if they were on some secret mission. In a way they were: they were going to be together, but they didn't know that yet.

It was almost ten o'clock at night, but there was still enough light in the sky for them to see each other's arms and legs as pale movements over the carpet of grass and earth still holding the warmth

6

of the day. They didn't dare look at each other's faces. If they did, something would have to be said, and there were no words.

They had decided to go up to the rock. A little way along the track between the fir trees their hands had brushed against each other's, and one of them had taken hold, and that was it. Now they were holding hands. If anything was said, something straightforward would become difficult.

Anders' skin felt as if he had been out in the sun all day. It was hot and painful all over, and he felt dizzy, as if he had sunstroke; he was afraid of tripping over a root, afraid of his hand becoming sweaty, afraid that what he was doing was *out of order* in some way.

There were couples in the gang. Martin and Malin were together now. Malin had gone out with Joel for a while. It was OK for them to lie there kissing when everybody could see them, and Martin said he and Malin had got as far as petting down by the boathouses. Whether or not it was true, it was OK for them to say—and do—that kind of thing. Partly because they were a year older, partly because they were good-looking. Cool. It gave them licence to do a lot of things, and to use a different language too. There was no point in trying to keep up, that would be embarrassing. You just had to sit there staring, trying to laugh in the right places. That's just how it was.

Neither Anders nor Cecilia was a loser. They weren't outsiders like Henrik and Björn—Hubba and Bubba—but they weren't part of the clique that made the rules and decided which jokes were funny, either.

For Anders and Cecilia to be walking along holding hands was utterly ridiculous. They knew this. Anders was short and borderline spindly, his brown hair too thin for him to give it any kind of style. He didn't understand how Martin and Joel did it. He'd tried slicking his hair back with gel once, but it looked weird and he'd rinsed it out before anyone saw it.

There was something flat about Cecilia. Her body was angular and her shoulders were broad, despite the fact that she was slim. Virtually no hips or breasts. Her face looked small between those broad shoulders. She had medium-length fair hair and an unusually small nose dusted with freckles. When she put her hair up in a ponytail, Anders thought she looked really pretty. Her blue eyes always looked just a little bit sad, and Anders liked that. She looked as if she knew.

Martin and Joel didn't know. Malin and Elin didn't know. They had the feeling, said the right things and were able to wear sandals without looking stupid. But they didn't know. They just did things. Sandra read books and was clever, but there was nothing in her eyes to indicate that she knew.

Cecilia knew, and Anders could see that she knew, which proved that he knew as well. They recognised one another. He couldn't explain what it *was* that they knew, but it was something. Something about life, about how things really were.

The terrain grew steeper, and as they made their way up towards the rock the trees thinned out. In a minute or two they would have to let go of one another's hands so they'd be able to climb.

Anders stole a glance at Cecilia. She was wearing a yellow and white striped T-shirt with a wide neckline that revealed her collarbone. It was just unbelievable that she had been linked to him for what must be five minutes, that her skin had been touching his.

That she'd been his.

She had been his for five minutes. Soon they would let go, move apart and become ordinary people again. What would they say then?

Anders looked down. The ground was starting to become stony, he had to watch where he was putting his feet. Every second he was expecting Cecilia to let go, but she didn't. He thought perhaps he was holding on so tightly that she *couldn't* let go. It was an embarrassing thought, so he loosened his grip slightly. Then she let go.

He spent the two minutes it took to climb up the rock analysing whether he had, in fact, been holding her hand too tightly, or whether loosening his grip had made her think *he* was about to let go, and so she let go first.

Regardless of what he knew or did not know, he was convinced that Joel and Martin never had this kind of problem. He wiped his hand furtively on his trousers. It was slightly stiff and sweaty.

When they reached the top of the rock, his head felt bigger than usual. The blood was humming in his ears and he was sure his face was bright red. He stared down at his chest where a little ghost looked out from a circle with a red line through it. *Ghostbusters*. It was his favourite top, and it had been washed so many times that the outline of the ghost was becoming blurred.

'It's so beautiful.'

Cecilia was standing at the edge of the rock looking out over the sea. They were up above the tops of the trees. Far below they could see the holiday village where almost all their friends lived. Out at sea the ferry to Finland was sailing along, a cluster of lights moving across the water. Further away and further out there were other archipelagos whose names Anders didn't know.

He stood as close to her as he dared and said, 'I think it's the most beautiful thing in the world,' and regretted it as soon as the words were out of his mouth. It was a stupid thing to say, and he tried to improve matters by adding, 'That's one way of looking at it', but that wasn't right either. He moved away from her, following the edge of the rock.

When he had walked all the way round, a distance of perhaps thirty metres, and was almost back with her, she said, 'It's odd, isn't it? This rock, I mean?'

He had an answer to that. 'It's an erratic boulder. According to my dad, anyway.'

'What's that?'

He gazed out across the sea, fixed his eyes on the Gåvasten lighthouse and tried to remember what his father had told him. Anders made a sweeping movement with his arm, taking in the surrounding area. The old village, the mission, the alarm bell next to the shop.

'Well…when there was ice. Covering everything here. The ice age. The ice picked up rocks. And when it melted, these rocks ended up all over the place.'

9

'So where did they come from? Originally?'

His father had told him that as well, but he couldn't remember what he'd said. Where could the stones have come from? He shrugged his shoulders.

'From the north, I suppose. From the mountains. I mean, there are lots of rocks there…'

Cecilia peered over the edge. The top was almost flat, but it must have been at least ten metres deep. She said, 'There must have been a lot of ice.'

Anders remembered a fact. He made a movement up towards the sky. 'One kilometre. Thick.'

Cecilia wrinkled her nose, and Anders felt as if he had been stabbed in the chest. 'Never!' she said. 'You're joking?'

'That's what my dad says.'

'A *kilometre*?'

'Yes, and…you know how the islands and everything, they kind of keep on coming up out of the sea a little bit more each year?' Cecilia nodded. 'That's because the ice was so heavy it kind of pushed everything down and it's still…coming back up. Just a little bit, all the time.'

He was on a roll now. He remembered. As Cecilia was still looking at him with an interested expression, he carried on. He pointed over towards Gåvasten.

'Two thousand years or so ago, there was only water here. The only thing that was sticking up was the lighthouse. Or the rock, I mean. The rock the lighthouse is standing on. There was no lighthouse then, of course. And this rock. Everything else was under water. In those days.'

He looked at his feet, kicking at the thin covering of moss and lichen growing on the rock. When he looked up, Cecilia was gazing out across the sea, the mainland, Domarö. She put her hand on her collarbone as if she was suddenly afraid, and said, 'Is that *true*?'

'I think so.'

Something altered inside his head. He started to see the same thing as Cecilia. When he and his dad had been up here the previous summer, the words had just gone into his head as facts, and even though he'd thought it was exciting, he hadn't really *thought* about it. Seen it.

Now he could see. How *new* everything was. It had only been here for a short time. Their island, the ground on which their houses sat, even the ancient wooden boathouses down in the harbour were just pieces of Lego on the primeval mountain. His stomach contracted as if he were about to faint, vertigo from gazing down into the depths of time. He wrapped his arms around his body and suddenly he felt completely alone in the world. His eyes sought the horizon and found no comfort there. It was silent and endless.

Then he heard a sound to his left. Breathing. He turned his head and found Cecilia's face only a fraction away from his own. She looked into his eyes. And breathed. Her mouth was so close to his that he could feel her warm breath on his lips as she exhaled, a faint hint of Juicy Fruit in his nostrils.

Afterwards he would find it difficult to understand, but that's what happened: he didn't hesitate. He leaned forward and kissed her without giving it a thought. He just did it.

Her lips were tense and slightly firm. With the same inexplicable decisiveness he pushed his tongue between them. Her tongue came to meet his. It was warm and soft and he licked it. It was a completely new experience, licking something that was the same as the object doing the licking. He didn't exactly think that, but he thought something like it, and at that moment everything became uncertain and strange and he didn't know what to do.

He licked her tongue a little bit more, and part of him was enjoying it and thinking it was fantastic, while another part was thinking: *Is this what you're supposed to do? Is this right?* It couldn't be, and he suspected this was where you moved on to petting. But even though his cock was beginning to stiffen as his tongue slid over hers, there was no possibility, *not a chance*, that he was going to start…touching her like that. Not a chance. He couldn't, he didn't know how, and… no, he didn't even *want* to.

Preoccupied with these thoughts he had stopped moving his tongue without noticing. Now she was the one doing the licking. He accepted this with gratitude, the enjoyment increased slightly, the doubts faded away. When she withdrew her tongue and kissed him in the normal way before their faces moved apart, he decided: *that went quite well.*

He had kissed a girl for the first time and it had gone well. His face was red and his legs felt weak, but it was OK. He glanced at her and she seemed to share his opinion. When he saw that she was smiling slightly, he smiled too. She noticed and her smile broadened.

For a second they gazed into each other's eyes, both smiling. Then it all got too much and they looked out to sea once again. Anders no longer thought it looked frightening in the least, he couldn't understand how he could have thought it did.

I think it's the most beautiful thing in the world.

That's what he'd said. And now it was true.

They made their way back down. When they had got past the stoniest part, they held hands again. Anders wanted to scream, he wanted to jump and smash dried-up branches against the tree trunks, something wanted to come out.

He held her hand, a happiness so enormous that it hurt bubbling away inside him.

We're together. Cecilia and me. We're together now.

Gåvasten (February 2004)

'What a day. It's incredible.'

Cecilia and Anders were standing by the window in the living room, looking towards the bay. The ice was covered with virgin snow, and the sun shone from a cloudless sky, eating away the contours of the inlet, the jetty and the shore like an over-exposed photograph.

'Let me see, let me see!'

Maja came racing in from the kitchen, and Anders barely had time to open his mouth to warn her for the hundredth time. Then her thick socks skidded on the polished wooden floor and she landed flat on her back at his feet.

In a reflex action he bent down to comfort her, but Maja immediately rolled to one side and wriggled back a metre. Tears sprang to her eyes. She screamed, 'Stupid stupid things!' then tore off the socks and hurled them at the wall. Then she got up and ran back into the kitchen.

Anders and Cecilia looked at each other and sighed. They could hear Maja rummaging in the kitchen drawers.

Whose turn?

Cecilia winked and took on the task of intervening before Maja tipped the entire contents of the drawers on to the floor, or broke something. She went into the kitchen and Anders turned back to the glorious day.

'No, Maja! Wait!'

Maja came running in from the kitchen with a pair of scissors in her hand, Cecilia right behind her. Before either of them could stop her, Maja had grabbed one of the socks and started hacking at it.

Anders seized her arms and managed to get her to drop the scissors. Her whole body was trembling with rage as she kicked out at the sock. 'I hate you, you stupid thing!'

Anders hugged her, holding her flailing arms fast with his own. 'Maja, that doesn't help. The socks don't understand.'

Maja was a quivering bundle in his arms. 'I hate them!'

'I know, but that doesn't mean you have to...'

'I'm going to chop them up and burn them!'

'Calm down, little one. Calm down.'

Anders sat down on the sofa without loosening his grip on Maja. Cecilia sat down next to him. They spoke softly and stroked her hair and the blue velour tracksuit that was the only thing she would consent to wear. After a couple of minutes she stopped shaking, her heartbeat slowed and she relaxed in Anders' arms. He said, 'You can wear shoes instead, if you like.'

'I want to go barefoot.'

'You can't. The floor's too cold.'

'Barefoot.'

Cecilia shrugged her shoulders. Maja rarely felt cold. Even when the temperature was close to freezing she would run around outdoors in a T-shirt unless somebody said something to her. She slept eight hours a night at the most, and yet it was rare for her to fall ill or feel tired.

Cecilia held Maja's feet in her hands and blew on them. 'Well, you need to put some socks on now. We're going out.'

Maja sat upright on Anders' knee. 'Where to?'

Cecilia pointed out of the window, towards the north-east.

'To Gåvasten. To the lighthouse.'

Maja leaned forward, screwing her eyes up into the sunlight. The old stone lighthouse was visible only as a vague rift in the sky where it met the horizon. It was about two kilometres away, and they had been waiting for a day like this so they could make the trip they had been talking about all winter.

Maja's shoulders drooped. 'Are we going to *walk* all that way?'

'We thought we might ski,' said Anders, and the words were hardly out of his mouth before Maja shot off his knee and raced into the hallway. She had been given her first pair of skis on her sixth birthday two weeks earlier, and on only her second practice outing she had done really well. She had a natural talent. Two minutes later she was back, dressed in her snowsuit, hat and gloves.

'Come on then!'

They ignored Maja's protests and made a picnic to eat out by the lighthouse. Coffee, chocolate and sandwiches. Then they gathered up their skiing equipment and went down to the inlet. The light was dazzling. There had been no wind for several days, and fresh snow still covered the branches of the trees. Wherever you turned there was whiteness, blinding whiteness. It was impossible to imagine that there could be warmth and greenness anywhere. Even from space the earth must look like a perfectly formed snowball, white and round.

It took a while to get Maja's skis on because she was so excited she couldn't stand still. Once the bindings were tight and the straps of the poles wrapped around her hands, she immediately slid out on to the ice, shouting, 'Look at me! Look at me!'

For once they didn't need to worry as she set off on her own. Despite the fact that she had travelled a hundred metres from the jetty before Anders and Cecilia had even got their skis on, she was clearly visible as a bright red patch in the middle of all the whiteness.

It was different in the city. Maja had run off on her own several times because she had seen something or thought of something, and they had joked about fitting her with a GPS transmitter. Not that it was all that much of a joke, really; they had given it serious consideration, but it felt like overkill.

They set off. Far out on the ice Maja fell over, but she was back on her feet in no time and whizzing along. Anders and Cecilia followed in her tracks. When they had travelled about fifty metres, Anders turned around.

Their house, generally known as the Shack, lay at the edge of the point. Plumes of smoke were rising from both chimneys. Two pine trees, weighed down with snow, framed it on either side. It was a complete dump, badly built and poorly maintained, but right now, from this distance, it looked like a little paradise.

Anders struggled to get his old Nikon out of his rucksack, zoomed in and took a picture. Something to remind him when he was cursing the ill-fitting walls and sloping floors. That it was a little paradise. As well. He put the camera away and followed his family.

After a couple of minutes he caught up with them. He had intended to lead the way, making it easier for Maja and Cecilia as they followed in his tracks through the thick covering of snow, but Maja refused. She was the guide and group leader, and they were to follow her.

The ice was nothing to worry about; this was confirmed when they heard a roaring sound from the direction of the mainland. A car was heading for Domarö from the steamboat jetty in Nåten. From this distance it was no bigger than a fly. Maja stopped and stared at it.

'Is that a *real* car?'

'Yes,' said Anders. 'What else would it be?'

Maja didn't reply, but carried on looking at the car, which was on its way towards the point on the opposite side of the island.

'Who's driving?'

'Holidaymakers, probably. Wanting to go for a swim.'

Maja grinned and looked at him with that supercilious expression she sometimes wore, and said, 'Daddy. Wanting to go for a swim? *Now?*'

Anders and Cecilia laughed. The car disappeared behind the point, leaving a thin cloud of whirling snow behind it.

'People from Stockholm, then. I expect they're on their way to their summer cottage to…look at the ice, or something.'

Maja seemed satisfied with this response, and turned to set off again. Then she thought of something and turned back.

'Why aren't we people from Stockholm, then? We live in Stockholm, after all.'

Cecilia said, 'You and I are from Stockholm, but Daddy isn't, not really, because his daddy wasn't from Stockholm.'

'My grandad?'

'Yes.'

'What was he, then?'

Cecilia made a vague movement with her lips and looked at Anders, who said, 'An old fisherman.'

Maja nodded and set off towards the lighthouse, which had now become an extended blot against the bright sky.

Simon was standing on the veranda, tracking their progress through his telescope. He saw them stop and talk, saw them set off again with Maja in the lead. He smiled to himself. That was just typical of Maja. Trying so hard, working, wearing herself out. The child had a dynamo inside her, a little motor spinning away, constantly charging itself. The energy had to go somewhere.

In everything but blood he was her great-grandfather, just as he was grandfather to Anders. He had known them both before their eyes were able to focus on his face. He was an outsider, absorbed into this family that was not his own.

While he was filling the coffee machine he glanced up, from habit, at Anna-Greta's house. He knew she had gone over to mainland to do some shopping and wouldn't be back until the afternoon but he looked anyway, and caught himself missing her already.

More than forty years together, and he still longed to see her. That was a good thing. Perhaps it had something to do with living apart. At first he had been hurt when Anna-Greta said yes, she loved him, but no, she had no intention of moving in with him. He could carry on renting his house from her as before, and if the situation didn't suit him it was unfortunate, but so be it.

He had gone along with it, hoping that things would change in time. They did, but not in the way he had thought. Instead he was the one who changed his point of view and after about ten years he'd come to the conclusion that everything worked extremely well. The rent he paid was token. It hadn't gone up by a single krona since he first moved into the house in 1955. One thousand kronor per year. They would spend the money on a trip on the ferry to Finland, eating and drinking nothing but the best. It was a small ritual.

They weren't married—Anna-Greta felt that her marriage to Erik had been one too many—but to all intents and purposes, Simon was her husband and the children's grandfather and great-grandfather.

He went out on to the glassed-in veranda and picked up the telescope. They were still ploughing on out there, they had almost reached the lighthouse now. They had stopped, and he couldn't make out what they were doing. He was trying to adjust the focus so that he could see what they were up to, when the outside door opened.

'Hello there!'

Simon smiled. It had taken him a few years to get used to the fact that those who lived here all year round simply came stomping into each other's houses without knocking. In the beginning he would knock on people's doors and be rewarded with a long wait. When the door finally opened, the look on the resident's face clearly said, *Why are you standing out here putting on airs and graces? Come inside.*

Boots were removed, there was the sound of throat-clearing in the porch, and Elof Lundberg walked in, wearing his cap as usual, and nodded to Simon.

'Good morning to you, sir.'

'And good morning to you.'

Elof licked his lips, which were dry from the cold, and looked around the room. What he saw didn't appear to provide him with anything worth commenting on, and he said, 'So. Any news?'

Simon shook his head. 'No. The usual aches and pains.'

Sometimes he found it amusing, but today he wasn't in the mood to stand there exchanging pleasantries with Elof until they got down to business, so he decided to flout convention. 'Is it the drill you're after?' he asked.

Elof's eyes narrowed as if this was a completely unexpected question that needed some consideration, but after thinking for a couple of seconds he said, 'The drill. Yes. I thought I might...' he nodded in the direction of the ice, '...go out and see if I have any luck.'

'It's under the steps as usual.'

The last time they had had a really icy winter, three years ago, Elof had come to borrow Simon's ice drill a couple of times a week. Simon had said Elof was welcome to come and fetch it whenever he needed it and just put it back when he was finished. Elof had made noises indicating agreement, and had continued to come in and ask every single time.

On this occasion, his mission seemingly accomplished, Elof showed no signs of leaving. Perhaps he wanted to get warm before he set off. He nodded at the telescope in Simon's hand.

'So what are you looking at?'

Simon pointed towards the lighthouse. 'The family's out on the ice, I'm just...keeping an eye on them.'

Elof looked out of the window, but of course he couldn't see anything. 'Whereabouts are they?'

'Out by the lighthouse.'

'Out by the lighthouse?'

'Yes.'

Elof was still looking out of the window, his jaws working as if he were chewing on something invisible. Simon wanted an end to this before Elof caught the aroma of the coffee and invited himself to stay for a cup. He wanted to be left in peace. Elof pursed his lips and suddenly asked, 'Has Anders got one of those…mobile phones?'

'Yes, why?'

Elof was breathing heavily as he gazed out of the window, looking for something it was impossible to see. Simon couldn't understand what he was getting at, so he asked again.

'Why do you want to know if he's got a mobile?'

There was silence for a few seconds. Simon could hear the last of the water bubbling through the coffee machine. Elof turned away from the window and gazed at the floor as he said, 'I think you should ring him and tell him…he ought to come home now.'

'Why?'

Silence fell once again, and Simon could smell the aroma of the coffee drifting from the kitchen. Elof didn't seem to notice. He sighed and said, 'The ice can be unsafe out there.'

Simon snorted. 'But it's half a metre thick right across the bay!'

Elof sighed even more deeply and studied the pattern on the carpet. Then he did something unexpected. He raised his head, looked Simon straight in the eye and said, 'Do as I say. Ring the boy. And tell him to gather up his family. And go home.'

Simon looked into Elof's watery blue eyes. Their expression was deadly serious. Simon didn't understand what this was all about, but he had never encountered this level of seriousness, this kind of authority from Elof before. Something passed between them that he couldn't put his finger on, but it made him go over to the phone and key in the number of Anders' mobile.

'Hi, this is Anders. Leave a message after the tone.'

Simon hung up.

'He's not answering. It's probably switched off. What's this all about?'

Elof looked out across the bay once more. Then he pursed his lips and nodded, as if he'd come to a decision. 'I expect it'll be fine.' He turned towards the hallway and said, 'I'll take the drill for a couple of hours, then.'

Simon heard the outside door open and close. A cold draught whirled around his feet. He picked up the telescope and looked out towards the lighthouse. Three little ants were just clambering up on to the rocks.

'Hang on a minute!'

Anders waved to Maja and Cecilia to get them in the right position and took a picture, two pictures, three pictures with different degrees of zoom. Maja was struggling to get away the whole time, but Cecilia held her close. It looked fantastic with the two small figures in the snow and the lighthouse towering up behind them. Anders gave them the thumbs up and stowed the camera in his rucksack once again.

Maja and Cecilia headed for the bright red door in the lighthouse wall. Anders stayed where he was with his hands in his pockets, gazing at the twenty-metre-high tower. It was built of stone. Not brick, but ordinary grey stone. A building that looked as if it could withstand just about anything.

What a job it must have been. Transporting all that stone here, lifting it, putting it in place...

'Daddy! Daddy, come on!'

Maja was standing next to the lighthouse door jumping up and down with excitement, waving her gloves in the air.

'What is it?' asked Anders as he walked towards them.

'It's open!'

Indeed it was. Just inside the door were a collection box and a stand containing brochures. There was a sign saying that the Archipelago Foundation welcomed visitors to Gåvasten lighthouse.

Please take an information leaflet and continue up into the lighthouse, all contributions gratefully received.

Anders rooted in his pockets and found a crumpled fifty-kronor note, which he happily pushed into the empty collection box. This was better than he could have hoped for. He had never expected the lighthouse to be open, particularly in the winter.

Maja was already on her way up the stairs, Anders and Cecilia following. The worn spiral staircase was so narrow that it was impossible for two people to walk abreast. Iron shutters fastened with wing nuts covered the window openings.

Cecilia stopped. Anders could hear that she was breathing heavily. She reached out behind her back with one hand. Anders took it and asked, 'How are you doing?'

'OK.'

Cecilia carried on upwards as she squeezed Anders' hand. She had a tendency towards claustrophobia, and from that point of view the lighthouse was an absolute nightmare. The thick stone walls rising up so close together swallowed every sound, and the only light came from the open door down at the bottom and a fainter source of light higher up.

After another forty or so steps it was completely dark behind them, while the light above them had grown stronger. From somewhere up above they could hear Maja's voice, 'Hurry up! Come and see!'

The staircase ended at an open space in a wooden floor. They were standing in a circular room where a number of small windows made of thick glass let in a limited amount of light. In the middle of the room was another open door in a tower within the tower, with light pouring out.

Cecilia sat down on the floor and rubbed her hands over her face. When Anders crouched down beside her she waved dismissively. 'I'm fine. I just need to...'

Maja was shouting from inside the tower and Cecilia told him to go, she would follow shortly. Anders stroked her hair and went over to the open door, which led to another spiral staircase, this one made of iron. The light hurt his eyes as he climbed the twenty or so steps up to the heart and the brain of the lighthouse, the reflector.

Anders stopped and gazed open-mouthed. It was so beautiful.

From the darkness we ascend towards the light. He made his way up the dark staircase, and it was a shock to reach the top. Apart from a whitewashed border right at the bottom, the circular walls were made entirely of glass, and everything was sky and light. In the middle of the room stood the reflector, an obelisk made up of prisms and different coloured, geometrically precise pieces of glass. A shrine to the light.

Maja was standing with her nose and hands pressed against the glass wall. When she heard Anders coming, she pointed out across the ice, towards the north-east.

'Daddy, what's that?'

Anders screwed his eyes up against the brightness and looked out over the ice. He couldn't see anything apart from the white covering, and far away on the horizon just a hint of Ledinge archipelago.

'What do you mean?'

Maja pointed. 'There. On the ice.'

A gust of wind made the powdery snow whirl up, moving like a spirit across the pristine surface. Anders shook his head and turned back to face the room.

'Have you seen this?'

They examined the reflector and Anders took some pictures of Maja through the reflector, behind the reflector, in front of the reflector. The little girl and the kaleidoscope of light, refracted in all directions. When they had finished Cecilia came up the stairs, and she too was amazed.

They ate their picnic in the light room looking out across the archipelago, trying to spot familiar landmarks. Maja was interested in the graffiti on the white wall, but since some of it required explanations unsuitable for the ears of a six-year-old, Anders took out the information leaflet and started reading aloud.

The lower parts of the lighthouse had been built as early as the sixteenth century, as a platform for the beacons lit to mark the navigable channel into Stockholm. Later the tower was added and a primitive reflector was installed; at first it was illuminated using oil, then kerosene.

That was enough for Maja, and she was off down the stairs. Anders grabbed hold of her snowsuit.

'Just hang on, sunshine. Where are you off to?'

'I'm going to look at that thing I said I could see.'

'You're not to go too far.'

'I won't.'

Anders let go and Maja carried on down the stairs. Cecilia watched her disappear.

'Shouldn't we...?'

'Well yes. But where can she go?'

They spent a couple of minutes reading the rest of the leaflet, and learned that the Aga aggregate had eventually been installed, that the lighthouse had been decommissioned in 1973 and had then been taken over by the Archipelago Foundation, which had put in a symbolic hundred-watt bulb. These days it ran on solar cells.

They looked at the graffiti and established that at least one instance of sexual intercourse must have taken place on this floor, unless of course it was just a case of wishful thinking on the part of the writer. Then they gathered their things together and set off down the stairs. Cecilia had to take her time because of the palpitations, the pressure on her chest, and Anders waited for her.

When they got outside there was no sign of Maja. The wind had started to get up and the snow was swirling through the air in thin veils, glittering in the sunlight. Anders closed his eyes and inhaled deeply. It had been a fantastic outing, but now it was time to go home.

'Maaaja,' he shouted. No reply. They walked around the lighthouse, looking out for her. The rock itself was only small, perhaps a hundred metres in circumference. There was no sign of Maja anywhere, and Anders gazed out across the ice. No small red figure.

'*Maaaja!*'

This time he shouted a little more loudly, and his heart began to beat a little more quickly. It was foolish, of course. There was no chance that she could have got lost here. He felt Cecilia's hand on his shoulder. She was pointing down at the snow.

'There are no tracks here.'

There was a hint of unease in her voice too. Anders nodded. Of course. All they had to do was follow Maja's tracks.

They went back to where they'd started from, by the lighthouse door. Anders poked his head inside and shouted up the stairs, just in case Maja had come back and they hadn't heard her. No reply.

The area around the door was covered in footprints made by all of them, but there were no tracks leading off to the right or left. Anders took a few steps down the rock. He could see their own tracks leading up towards the lighthouse from the ice, and Maja's footprints heading off in the opposite direction.

He stared out over the ice. No Maja. He blinked, rubbed his eyes. She couldn't have gone far enough to be out of sight. The contours of Domarö merged with those of the mainland, a thicker line of charcoal above a thinner one. He turned to face the other way, catching Cecilia's expression: concentrated, tense.

There was no sign of their daughter in the opposite direction either.

Cecilia passed him on her way out on to the ice. She was walking with her head down, following the tracks with her eyes.

'I'll check inside the lighthouse,' Anders shouted. 'She must be hiding or something.'

He ran over to the door and up the stairs, shouting for Maja but getting no reply. His heart was pounding now and he tried to calm himself down, to be cool and clear-headed.

It just isn't possible.

It's always possible.

No, it isn't. Not here. There's nowhere she can be.

Exactly.

Stop it. Stop it.

Hide and seek was Maja's favourite game. She was good at finding places to hide. Although she could be over-excited and eager in other situations, when she was playing hide and seek she could keep quiet and still for any length of time.

He walked up the stairs with his arms outstretched, stooping like a monkey so that his fingers brushed the edges where the staircase met the wall. In case she'd fallen. In case she was lying in the darkness where he couldn't see her.

In case she'd fallen and banged her head, in case she...

But he felt nothing, saw nothing.

He searched the room at the top of the stairs, found two cupboards that were too narrow for Maja to be able to hide in. Opened them anyway. Inside were rusty, unidentifiable metal parts, bottles with hand-written labels. No Maja.

He went over to the door leading to the upper tower, closed his eyes for a couple of seconds before he went inside.

She's up there now. That's where she is. We'll go home and we'll file this with all those other times she's disappeared for a while and then come back.

Next to the staircase was a system of weights and chains, the cupboard containing the light's mechanism secured with a padlock. He tugged at it and established that it was locked, that Maja couldn't be in there. He went slowly up the stairs, calling her name. No reply. There was a rushing sound in his ears now, and his legs felt weak.

He reached the room containing the reflector. No Maja.

Barely half an hour ago he had photographed her here. Now there was no trace of her. Nothing. He screamed, *'Maaaajaaaa!* Out you come! This isn't funny any more!'

The sound was absorbed by the narrow room, making the glass vibrate.

He walked all the way around the room, looked out across the ice. Far below he could see Cecilia following the track that had led them here. But the red snowsuit was nowhere to be seen. He was gasping for air. His tongue was sticking to his palate. This was impossible. This couldn't be happening. Desperately he stared out across the ice in every direction.

Where is she? Where is she?

He could just hear the sound of Cecilia's voice shouting the same thing as he had shouted so many times. She got no reply either.

Think, you idiot. Think.

He looked out across the ice again. There was nothing to interrupt his gaze, no cover at all. If there had been holes in the ice, they would have been visible. However good you are at hiding, you still have to have a *place* to hide.

He stopped. His eyes narrowed. He could hear Maja's voice inside his head.

Daddy, what's that?

He went over to the spot where she had been standing when she asked the question, looked in the direction where she had pointed. Nothing. Only ice and snow.

What was it that she saw?

He strained to try and see something, then realised he was still wearing his rucksack. He pulled out the camera and looked through the viewfinder, zoomed in and panned across the area where she had been pointing. Nothing. Not a hint of another colour, not the slightest nuance in the whiteness, nothing.

His hands were shaking as he dropped the camera back in his rucksack. Out on the ice there was only white, white, but the sky had grown a little darker. It would soon be afternoon, it would be dark in a couple of hours.

He put his hands to his mouth, stared out into the vast emptiness, heard Cecilia's distant cries. Maja was gone. She was gone.

Stop it, stop it.

And yet a part of him knew that it was so.

It was just after two when Simon's telephone rang. He had spent the last hour fiddling with old conjuring props that his hands, stiff with rheumatism, could no longer use. He had considered selling them, but had decided to keep them as a little family treasure.

He answered the telephone on the second ring. He'd hardly managed to say hello before Anders interrupted.

'Hi, it's Anders. Have you seen Maja?'

'But surely she's with you?'

A brief pause. A quivering exhalation at the other end of the line. Simon sensed that he had just extinguished a hope. 'What's wrong?'

'She's gone. I knew she couldn't have got back to the land, but I thought—I don't know, Simon, she's gone. She's gone.'

'Are you at the lighthouse?'

'Yes. And she can't…it's just not…there's nowhere…but she isn't here. Where is she? Where is she?'

Two minutes later Simon had pulled on his outdoor clothes and kicked the moped into life. He rode out on to the ice where Elof was sitting on a folding chair, gazing down into the hole he had made with Simon's drill. He looked up as he heard the moped approaching. Simon braked.

'Elof—have you seen Maja, Anders' daughter?'

'No—what, here? Now?'

'Yes. In the last hour or so.'

'No, I haven't seen a soul. Or a fish, come to that. Why?'

'She's disappeared. Out by the lighthouse.'

Elof turned his head towards the lighthouse, kept his eyes fixed in that direction for a few seconds and scratched his forehead.

'Can't they find her?'

Simon clenched his teeth so tightly that his jaw muscles tensed. This bloody long-winded way of going about things. Elof nodded and started reeling in his line.

'I'd better…get a few people together then. We'll come over.'

Simon thanked him and set off towards the lighthouse. When he turned to look back after fifty metres or so, Elof was still fiddling about with his fishing gear, making sure it was all neatly packed away before he set off. Simon ground his teeth and rode so that the snow whirled up around his wheels as twilight fell.

Five minutes later Simon was out by the lighthouse helping to search, despite the fact that there was nowhere to look. He concentrated on riding around on the ice to check if Elof had been right, that there could be weak spots. He didn't find any.

After another quarter of an hour a number of dots could be seen approaching from Domarö. Four mopeds. Elof and his brother Johan. Mats, who owned the shop, had his wife Ingrid on the back. Bringing up the rear, Margareta Bergwall, one of the few women in the village who had their own moped.

They rode around the lighthouse in ever-widening circles, searching every square metre of the ice. Anders and Cecilia wandered aimlessly around on the lighthouse rock itself, saying nothing. After an hour it was so dark that the moonlight was stronger than the small amount of sunlight that remained.

Simon went up to Anders and Cecilia, who were now sitting by the lighthouse door, head in hands. Far out on the ice the faint lights of the four mopeds were just visible, still circling round and round like satellites of a desolate planet. A police helicopter with a searchlight had arrived to extend the search area.

Simon's joints creaked as he crouched down in front of them. Their eyes were empty. Simon stroked Cecilia's knee.

'What did you say about the tracks?'

Cecilia waved feebly in the direction of Domarö. Her voice was so weak that Simon had to lean forward in order to hear.

'There weren't any.'

'You mean they didn't go off in a different direction?'

'They stopped. As if…as if she'd been lifted up into the sky.'

Anders whimpered. 'This can't be happening. How can this be happening?'

He looked into Simon, right through Simon, as if he were looking for the answer in a knowledge that lay somewhere behind Simon's retina.

Simon got up and went back down on to the ice, sat on the back of his moped and looked around.

If only there were somewhere to start.

A nuance, a shadow, anything that could serve as a loose edge where they could begin tearing away. He pushed his hand down into his jacket pocket and closed it around the matchbox that lay there. Then he placed the fingertips of his other hand on the ice and asked it to melt.

First the snow melted, then a deepening hollow appeared, filling up with water. After perhaps twenty seconds there was a black hole in the ice, perhaps as big as a clenched fist. He let go of the matchbox and, with some difficulty, lowered his arm into the cold water. The surface of the ice was just above his elbow before he was able to grip the lower edge.

The ice was thick. There was absolutely no chance that Maja had fallen through somewhere.

So what has happened?

There was no loose edge. Nowhere for his thoughts to poke and prod, widen the crack, work things out. It was just impossible. He went up and sat down with Anders and Cecilia, giving them a hug and saying a few words from time to time, until in the end it was completely dark and the mopeds began to spiral their way back towards the lighthouse.

Domarö and time

During the course of this story it will be necessary occasionally to jump back in time in order to explain something in the present. This is regrettable but unavoidable.

Domarö is not a large island. Everything that has happened

29

remains here and influences the present. Places and objects are charged
with meanings that are not easily forgotten. We cannot escape.

In the scheme of things, this is a very small story. You could say it
would fit in a matchbox.

What the cat dragged in (May 1996)

It was the last week in May and the perch were plentiful. Simon
had a simple method of fishing. He had spent several years experi-
menting with his nets, laying them out in different places, and had
come to the conclusion that all this travelling around was unnecessary. It worked just as well if he tied one end of the net to the
jetty and towed the other end out with the boat. Easy to lay and
even easier to empty. He hauled the net in from the jetty, and could
usually disentangle the fish he didn't want on the spot and throw
them back in the sea.

This morning's seven perch were in the fridge, cleaned and ready,
and the dace he had released had swum off. Simon was standing by
the drying rack picking bits of seaweed out of the nets, while the gulls
finished their meal of fish guts. It was a bright, warm morning, the
sun was beating down on the back of his neck and he was sweating
in his overalls.

Dante the cat had been following him all morning; he never
seemed to learn how extremely unusual it was to find herring in the
net. The odd herring he had been given was sufficient to keep the
flame of hope burning in his head, and he always followed Simon
down to the jetty.

Once Dante realised that no herring had managed to entangle
themselves in the net this morning either, he had settled down on the
jetty to glower at the gulls fighting over the fish guts. He would never
dare to attack a gull but no doubt he had his fantasies, just like every
other living creature.

Simon unhooked the net and rolled it up so that it wouldn't become brittle in the sun. As he made his way down to the boathouse to hang it up, he could see that the cat was busy with something out on the jetty.

Or rather, fighting with something. Dante was jumping back and forth, up in the air, batting with his paws at something Simon couldn't see. It looked as if the cat was dancing, but Simon had seen him play with mice in the same way. And yet this was different. The game with mice and frogs really was a game, in which the cat pretended his prey was harder to catch than it actually was. This time it looked as if the cat was genuinely...afraid?

The fur on his back was standing up, and his jumps and tentative attacks could only be interpreted as an indication that he was dealing with something worthy of respect. Which was difficult to understand, since nothing was visible from a distance of twenty metres, and Simon's eyesight was good.

He twisted the net to avoid tangles, laid it down on the ground and went to see what the cat was doing.

When he got out on to the jetty, he still couldn't see what was making the cat so agitated. Or...yes, the cat was circling around a bit of rope that was lying there. This wasn't like Dante at all; he was eleven years old and no longer deigned to play with balls or bits of paper. But obviously this piece of rope was great fun.

Dante made a sudden attack and got both paws on the piece of rope, but was hurled backwards with a jerk, as if the rope had given him an electric shock. He swayed and fell sideways, then flopped down on the jetty.

When Simon got there the cat was lying motionless next to the furthest bollard. The thing he had been playing with wasn't a piece of rope, because it was moving. It was some kind of insect, it looked like a worm of some sort. Simon ignored it and crouched down next to the cat.

'Dante, old friend, what's wrong?'

The cat's eyes were wide open and his body shuddered a couple of times as if racked by sobs. Something trickled from his mouth. Simon lifted the cat's head and saw that it was water. A stream of water was trickling out of the cat's mouth. Dante coughed and water spurted out. Then he lay still. His eyes stared blankly.

A movement in Simon's peripheral vision. The insect was crawling along the jetty. He bent over it, studying it more closely. It was completely black, the thickness of a pencil and about the same length as a little finger. Its skin shone in the sunlight. Dante's claws had made a scratch in one place, revealing pinkish flesh.

Simon gasped; looked around to see a coffee cup that had been left behind on the jetty. He grabbed it and upended it on the insect. He blinked a couple of times and ran his hands over his face.

It's not possible. It can't be...

This insect was not to be found in any insect book, and Simon was probably the only person for miles around who knew what it was. He had seen one before, in California forty years earlier. But that one had been dead, dried. If it hadn't been for what had happened to the cat, it would never even have occurred to him.

Dante.

The original Dante, the one after whom all Simon's cats were named. The magician, the greatest of them all. After decades spent touring and making films, he had settled down on a ranch in California. Simon had been granted an audience with him there when he was twenty-four years old and a promising talent.

Dante had shown him around his museum. Handmade props from different eras: the Chinese fountains that were his star turn for some years, the substitution trunk in several different versions, water-filled chests and cupboards from which Dante had escaped in circus rings all over the world.

When the guided tour was over, Simon had pointed to a small glass display case standing in a corner. There was a pedestal in the middle of the case, and on it lay something that looked like a piece of a leather shoelace. He asked what it was.

Dante had raised one eyebrow dramatically in a well-practised gesture and had asked Simon, in the Danish of his childhood, to what extent he believed in magic.

'You mean…real magic?'

Dante nodded.

'I would have to say that I am…an agnostic, in that case. I haven't seen any proof, but I don't discount the possibility. Does that sound reasonable?'

Dante seemed happy with the answer, and removed the glass top from the case. Simon realised he was expected to take a closer look, and did so. He was able to see that the leather shoelace was in fact a dried-out insect that resembled a centipede, apart from the fact that it had only a small number of legs.

'What exactly is it?'

Dante looked at Simon for so long that it began to feel awkward. Then the magician nodded as if he had reached a tacit decision, replaced the glass cover, took out a leather-bound book and began to leaf through it. Brightly coloured pictures flickered before Simon's eyes until eventually Dante stopped at a particular page and held out the book.

The picture, which covered the entire page, was hand painted. It depicted a worm-like insect, skilfully painted so that the light shimmered on its black, shiny skin. Simon shook his head and Dante sighed before closing the book.

'It's a Spiritus, or *spertus* as you say in Sweden,' he said.

Simon looked at the glass case, at the magician, at the case once again. Then he said, 'A real one?'

'Yes.'

Simon leaned closer to the glass. The dried-out creature inside certainly didn't look as if it possessed any extraordinary powers. Simon looked at it for a long time.

'How can it be dead? I mean, it is dead, isn't it?'

'I don't know, in answer to both your questions. It was in this condition when I received it.'

'How did that come about?'

'I'd prefer not to go into all that.'

Dante made a gesture, indicating that the audience in the museum was over. Before dragging himself away from the display case, Simon asked, 'Which element?'

The magician gave a wry smile. 'Water. Naturally.'

Coffee was consumed, polite phrases were exchanged, then Simon left the ranch. Two years later Dante was dead, and Simon read in the paper that his belongings were to be auctioned. He considered a trip to California to bid for the object in the glass case, but for one thing he was in the middle of a tour performing at outdoor venues, and for another it would be too expensive, once you factored in the cost of the journey. He decided not to bother.

During the years that followed he sometimes thought about that meeting. Colleagues who heard that he had met Dante wanted to know everything. Simon told them stories, but left out the thing he remembered most clearly: Dante's Spiritus.

It could have been a joke, of course. The magician had been famous not only for his magic skills, but also for his clever way of marketing himself with crowd-stopping public performances. He had created an aura of mystery around himself. His appearance, the goatee and the dark eyes, had for several decades been the accepted image of a magician. The whole thing could be a lie.

One thing that suggested this was not the case was the fact that Dante had never stated publicly that he owned a Spiritus; Simon had never heard anyone mention it. Dante was happy to add fuel to speculation that he had entered into a pact with the Devil, that he had formed an alliance with the powers of darkness. All good PR, of course, and utter nonsense. But the magician's final reply that day in the museum had guided Simon's speculations towards a different version, one which made a liar of Dante in a different way.

Simon believed Dante had been lying when he said that the Spiritus was already dead when it came to him.

Water. Naturally.

Dante was most acclaimed for his magic involving water. He was a match for Houdini in his ability to escape from various water-filled vessels and containers. It was said that he could hold his breath for five minutes—at least. He was able to move water from one place to another, a trick that involved a large amount of water appearing where none had been a second before.

Water. Naturally

If Dante had owned a Spiritus of the element water, everything was easy to explain: genuine magic, which Dante had merely limited to prevent people suspecting what was really going on.

Or perhaps the powers of the Spiritus were limited? Simon did some reading around the subject.

His agnostic inclination gradually gave way to a belief in the fantastical, at least when it came to the Spiritus. It seemed as if a few people, over the course of history, had actually owned the genuine article. Always a black insect of the kind he had seen in Dante's museum, whether it was a question of earth, fire, air or water.

He tried to find out what had happened to the Spiritus he had seen but he got nowhere. He bitterly regretted that he hadn't taken the chance to travel over while the opportunity was still there. He would never get to see a Spiritus again.

Or so he thought.

His gaze moved between the dead cat and the coffee cup. It was an ironic twist of fate that *Dante* should find a Spiritus for him, and die as a result.

A few hours later Simon had put together a wooden box, placed Dante inside and buried it by the hazel thicket where the cat used to sit watching the birds. Only then did his excitement over the Spiritus begin to give way to a slight sense of sorrow. He was not a sentimental man, he had had four different cats with the same name, but still an epoch was going to the grave with this fourth Dante. A small witness who had wound his way around Simon's legs for eleven years.

'Goodbye, my friend. Thank you for all those years. You were a fine cat. I hope you'll be happy wherever you end up. I hope there'll be herring for you to fish out with your paws. And someone who… is fond of you.'

Simon felt a lump in his throat, and wiped a tear from his eye. He nodded and said, 'Amen,' then turned and went into the house.

There was a matchbox on the kitchen table. Simon had managed to get the insect inside without touching it. Now he approached the matchbox cautiously, placed his ear against it. There was no sound.

He had read up on this. He knew what was expected of him. The question was, how much did he really want to do it? It wasn't easy to work out from the books what was speculation and what was fact, but one thing he thought he knew: pledging oneself to a Spiritus carried with it an obligation. A promise to the power that had relinquished it.

Is it worth it?

No, not really.

As a young man he would have gone crazy at the very possibility, but he was now seventy-three years old. He had put his magic props on the shelf two years ago. These days he performed only at home, when friends asked him. Party tricks. The cigarette in the jacket, the salt cellar passing through the table. Nothing special. So he had no real need for genuine magic.

He could argue back and forth until the cows came home, but he knew he was going to do it. He had spent a lifetime in the service of drawing-room magic. Was he likely to back out now, when the very essence of the thing was at his fingertips?

Idiot. Idiot. You're going to do it, aren't you?

Cautiously he pushed open the box and looked at the insect. There was nothing about it to indicate that it was a link between the human world and the insane beauty of magic. It was fairly disgusting, in fact. Like an internal organ that had been cut out and had turned black.

Simon cleared his throat, gathering saliva in his mouth.

Then he did it.

The globule of spittle emerged between his lips. He lowered his head over the box and saw the stringy phlegm finding its way down towards the insect. A thread was still connected to his lips when the saliva reached its goal and spread out over the shining skin.

As if the thin string of saliva connecting them had been a needle, a taste reached Simon via his lips. It immediately shot into his body, and it was a taste like nothing else. It most closely resembled the taste of a nut that had gone bad in its shell. Rotten wood, but sweet and bitter at the same time. A disgusting taste.

Simon swallowed, but there was nothing to lubricate his throat, and he smacked his tongue against his palate. The thin string broke, but the taste continued to grow in his body. The insect twitched and the sore on its skin began to heal. Simon stood up, his whole body nauseated.

This was a mistake.

He managed to get a beer out of the fridge, opened it and took a couple of gulps, swilling the liquid around his mouth. A little better, but the nausea in his body was still there, and the vomit began to rise in his throat.

The insect had recovered and was now crawling out of the box, on to the kitchen table, and heading in Simon's direction. He backed away towards the sink, staring at the black clump as it crawled towards the edge of the table, then fell to the floor with a soft, moist thud.

Simon moved to the side, towards the cooker. The insect changed direction, following him. Simon could feel that he was about to be sick. He took a couple of deep breaths and rubbed his eyes with the tips of his fingers.

Calm down. You knew about this.

And yet he couldn't make himself stand still when the insect was almost up to his foot. He fled into the hallway and sat down on the seaman's chest where he kept wet weather gear, pressing his hands to his temples and trying to see the situation clearly. The nausea was beginning to subside, the taste was no longer as intense.

The insect crawled across the kitchen doorway, heading in his direction. It left a faint trace of slime behind it. Simon knew things now that he had not known five minutes ago. Knowledge had been injected into him.

What he was experiencing as a taste within his body, the insect was experiencing as a smell. It would trail him, follow him until it was allowed to be with him. That was its sole aim. To be with him—

till death do us part

—to share its power with him. He knew. With the saliva he had formed a bond that could not be broken.

Unless…

There was a way out. But it wasn't relevant at the moment, with the insect on its way towards his foot once again. It was his now. Forever, until further notice.

He took a few rapid steps past the insect, which immediately changed direction, and picked up the matchbox from the kitchen table. He placed the box over the crawling black body and slid the cover over it. The boy on the label was marching towards a bright future as Simon weighed the box in his hand.

He clamped his lips together, suppressing the sickly feeling as the insect moved around in the box, and he felt its warmth against the palm of his hand. Yes. It was warm. It was feeling fine now, it had been fed and it had acquired an owner.

He put it in his pocket.

About the Shack

For such steeds find life difficult, those who cannot
tolerate either the spur or the whip. With every pain that
befalls them, they take fright and flee in terror towards the
gaping abyss.

SELMA LAGERLÖF — THE STORY OF GÖSTA BERLING

The fern (October 2006)

It was the fern that clinched it.

Anders had been sitting and staring at it for twenty minutes,
during which time he had smoked two cigarettes. He was looking at
the fern through a veil of smoke and dust particles, drifting around in
grubby sunlight. The window had not been cleaned for a long time,
and its surface was marked with uneven greasy patches, a legacy of
all those evenings when Anders had stood with his forehead resting on the glass, gazing down into the car park and waiting for
something to happen, something that could change things. Something,
anything, a miracle.

The fern was on the windowsill above the radiator. A long frond
waved in the rising heat. The leaves were small and brown, withered.

Anders lit another cigarette to sharpen his thoughts, or perhaps as a reward for the fact that he had had a real thought, a clear thought. The smoke made his eyes smart, he coughed and kept looking at the fern.

It's dead.

Most of its fronds were plastered against the side of the pot, pale brown against the red. The compost in which it had been planted was so dry it was almost white. Anders took a deep drag and tried to remember: how long had the fern looked like that, how long had it been dead?

He searched his memory for days and evenings in the past when he had sat on the sofa or wandered around the apartment or stood by the window. They drifted together to form a fog, and he couldn't see a wilting fern through the mist. When he thought about it more closely, he couldn't even remember when he had acquired the fern, why he had ever got the idea of buying a living plant.

Had someone given it to him?

Possibly.

He got up from the sofa, and his legs wouldn't carry him properly. He thought about filling a bottle with water and giving it to the fern, but he knew there were so many dishes in the sink that he wouldn't be able to get the bottle under the tap. In the bathroom it was impossible to get the bottle at the right angle for the water to run in. So he would have to unscrew the shower head and…

It's dead anyway.

Besides which, he just didn't have the strength.

In the pot he found eight cigarette stubs. Some were half-pushed down into the hard compost. So he must have stood here smoking. He didn't remember that. As he ran his fingers over the dry fronds, some of the leaves came off and drifted down to the floor.

Where did you come from?

He got the idea that the plant had simply tumbled into the material world in the same way as Maja had tumbled out of it. Through a gap in time and space it had suddenly been there, just as his daughter had suddenly not been there. Gone.

What was it Simon used to say when he was doing tricks for them?

*Nothing here, nothing there…*then he would point to his head… *and absolutely nothing here.*

Anders smiled as he remembered the look on Maja's face the first time Simon had done some magic tricks for her, just a couple of months before she disappeared. A rubber ball in one hand went up in smoke, and the ball Maja had just been holding suddenly became two. Maja had carried on looking at Simon with the same expectant expression: *OK, what's next?*

Magic is not the same miracle when you're five years old. It's more like something natural.

Anders stubbed out his cigarette in the pot, making the eight cigarette ends nine, and at the same moment he remembered: *Mum.*

It was his mother who had brought the plant when she came to visit him four months earlier. She had cleaned the apartment for him and placed the fern there. He had been in the middle of a period of apathy, and had just lain on the bed watching her. Then she had disappeared, back to her own life in Gothenburg.

The fern had not been among the things he needed, and so he had forgotten it, paying it no more heed than a mark on the wallpaper.

But he was seeing it now. He was looking at it. He was thinking the thought once again.

That's the ugliest thing I've ever seen.

Yes. That was what had occurred to him when he finally caught sight of it. The lonely, dead fern on the dusty windowsill against a background of dirty sunlight through an unwashed window. That it was the ugliest thing he'd ever seen.

For once the thought didn't stop there, but continued and swept across the life that could end up producing such a monster, and it was an ugly life.

He could cope with that, the idea that his life was ugly. He knew that, he had arranged things that way, he had got used to it and was ready to die within a few years as a result of his ugly life.

But the fern…

The fern was too much. It was intolerable.

Anders coughed and dragged himself into the bedroom. It felt as if his lungs had shrunk to the size of a fist. A tightly clenched fist. From the bedside table he picked up the photograph of Maja and took it over to the window.

The photograph had been taken on her sixth birthday, two weeks before she disappeared. She had a mask pushed up on her forehead; she had made it at nursery, and called it the devil troll. He had caught her just as she had pushed up the mask and was looking at him with expectant eyes to see what effect her 'scary face' had had.

The dimples in her cheeks showed up beautifully, her thin brown hair was pushed back by the mask revealing her ears, which stuck out slightly. Her eyes, which were actually unusually small, were wide open and staring straight into his.

He knew the picture by heart, every minute particle that had got stuck to the lens and remained as a white dot, every downy hair on her upper lip. He could take it out whenever he wanted.

'Maja,' he said. 'I can't do this any more. Here. Look.'

He turned the photograph so that Maja's eyes were looking at the fern.

'Enough.'

He put the photo down next to the fern and opened the window. His apartment was on the fourth floor, and when he leaned out he could see over towards Haninge Centrum, the station for the commuter trains. He looked down. It was about ten metres to the tarmac of the car park, there wasn't a soul in sight.

He picked the photograph up again, pressed it to his heart. Curls of smoke found their way out into the sunlight, drifting upwards.

'I've had enough.'

He grabbed the edge of the pot and lifted the fern out of the window. Then he let go. A second later he heard the distant crash as the pot shattered on the ground. He turned his face to the sun and closed his eyes.

'This has to stop.'

The anchor

Beside the shore in the churchyard at Nåten there is an anchor. A huge anchor made of cast iron, with a stock of tarred wood. It is bigger than any gravestone, bigger than anything else in the churchyard, with the exception of the church itself. Almost all those who visit the churchyard come to the anchor sooner or later; they stop and look at it for a while before moving on.

At eye level on the anchor-stock is a plaque. It says, 'In memory of those lost at sea.' The anchor, then, is a memorial to those whose bodies could not be interred in the ground, whose ashes could not be scattered beneath the trees. Those who went out and never came home.

The anchor is four and a half metres long, and weighs approximately nine hundred kilos.

Just imagine the ship it came from! Where is it now?

Perhaps an invisible chain runs from the anchor in the churchyard at Nåten. It goes up into the sky, down into the ground or out to sea. And there, at the other end of the chain, we will find the ship. The passengers and crew are those who have disappeared. They wander around on deck, gazing out at the empty horizon.

They are waiting for someone to find them. The sound of a diesel engine, or the top of a mast far away in the distance. A pair of eyes that will come along and see them.

They want to continue their journey, to arrive at last, they want to go down into the grave, they want to burn. But they are fastened to the earth by an invisible chain, and can only stare out across a desolate sea, forever becalmed.

Back

As the tender reversed away from the jetty, Anders raised a hand in farewell to Roger in the driving seat. They were almost the same age, but had never hung out together. They always said hello, however, as everyone on the island did when they met. Except perhaps for some of the summer visitors.

He sat down on his suitcase and watched the tender as it moved backwards, turned and set its course for the southern point on its way back to Nåten. He unbuttoned his jacket. It was a couple of degrees warmer here than in the city; the sea water still retained some of the heat of summer.

For him, arriving on Domarö had always been associated with a particular smell: a mixture of salt water, seaweed, pine trees and diesel from the tank by the steamboat jetty. He breathed in deeply through his nose. He could smell virtually nothing. Two years of heavy smoking had sabotaged his mucous membranes. He pulled a packet of Marlboros out of his pocket, lit a cigarette and watched the tender as it rounded North Point, looking to the untrained eye as if it were dangerously close.

He hadn't been here since Maja disappeared, and he still didn't know whether it was a mistake to come back. So far he felt only the quiet, melancholy pleasure of coming home. To a place where you know the location of every single stone.

The thicket of sea buckthorn next to the jetty looked just the same as it always had, neither bigger nor smaller. Like everything else on the island, the sea buckthorn was eternal, it had always been there. He'd used the thicket as a hiding place when they were playing hide and seek, and later as a place to stash booze from the Åland ferry when he didn't want his father to see it.

Anders picked up his suitcase and walked down on to the southern village road. The buildings in the area around the harbour consisted mainly of old pilots' houses, now renovated or rebuilt. Pilot boats had formed the basis of Domarö's relative prosperity during the nineteenth and early twentieth century.

Anders didn't want to meet anyone so he took the short cut along the cliffs up towards the ramblers' hostel, which was closed for the season. The track narrowed and split in two. The left-hand fork led to his grandmother's house and to Simon's house, the right fork to the Shack. After some consideration he took the left fork.

Simon was the only person with whom he had kept in regular touch over the last few years, the only one he had felt able to ring even when there was nothing to say. Anders' grandmother rang sometimes, his mother less often, but Simon was the only one whose number Anders would key in himself when he needed to hear another person's voice.

Simon was digging his patch ready for the autumn, and he didn't appear to have aged noticeably since Anders last saw him, the winter when Maja disappeared. He was probably at the age when it no longer matters. Besides, he had always seemed to Anders to be the same age, which is to say really, really old. It was only when he looked at photographs from his childhood, where Simon was around sixty, that he could see the difference twenty years had made.

Simon put his arms around him and rubbed his back.

'Welcome home, Anders.'

The medium-length white hair that was Simon's pride and joy tickled Anders' forehead as he rested his cheek on Simon's shoulder and closed his eyes. Those brief moments when you don't have to be a responsible, grown-up person. You have to make the most of them.

They went into the house and Simon put the coffee on. Not much had changed in the kitchen since Anders used to sit there during the summer when he was a little boy. A water heater had been installed above the sink, and a microwave oven. But the fire in the cast iron stove was crackling as it had always done, spreading its warmth over the same wallpaper, the same furniture. Anders' shoulders dropped slightly, relaxing. He had a history and a home. They hadn't disappeared just because everything else had gone to hell. Perhaps his memories gave him a licence, permission to exist here.

Simon placed a plastic box of biscuits on the table and poured the coffee. Anders picked up his cup.

'I remember when you...what was it you did? You had three of these and a piece of paper that moved back and forth. Then in the end...there was a toffee under each cup. Which I got. How did you do that?'

Simon shook his head and pushed back his hair. 'Practice, practice and more practice.'

Nothing had changed there either. Simon had never revealed any of his secrets. He had, however, recommended a book called *Magic as a Hobby*. Anders had read it when he was ten years old, and hadn't really understood any of it. It did describe how to do different tricks, and Anders tried a couple of them. But it wasn't the same as what Simon did. That was *magic*.

Simon sighed. 'I wouldn't be able to do that today.' He held up his fingers, stiff and crooked as they held the coffee spoon. 'I only have the simple things left now.'

He pressed his hands together and rubbed them against each other before opening them again. The coffee spoon was gone.

Anders smiled and Simon, who had appeared on the world's greatest stages, performed for kings and queens, leaned back on his chair and looked insufferably pleased with himself. Anders looked at Simon's hands, on the table, on the floor.

'So where is it, then?'

When he looked up, Simon was already sitting there stirring his coffee with the spoon. Anders snorted. 'Misdirection, I presume?'

'Indeed. Misdirection.'

That was the only important thing he had learned from the book. That a great deal of magic was a question of misdirection. Pointing in the wrong direction. Getting the observer to look where it isn't happening, getting them to look back when it's already happened. Like the business with the coffee spoon. But it was merely a theoretical knowledge. It didn't help Anders. He took a sip of his coffee and listened to the crackling of the stove. Simon rested his arms on the table. 'How's it going?'

'Really?'

'Really.'

Anders looked down into his coffee. The light from the window was reflected as a bobbing rectangle. He looked at it and waited for it to stop. When the rectangle was completely still he said, 'I've decided to live. After all. I thought I wanted to disappear as well. But…it turned out that isn't the case. So now I intend to try…I'm at rock bottom. I've reached the lowest point and…that's when it becomes possible to move on. Upwards.'

'Hmm,' said Simon, and waited. When nothing more was forthcoming, he asked, 'Are you still drinking as much?'

'Why?'

'I just thought…it can be difficult to stop.'

A muscle twitched in Anders' cheek. He wasn't keen on discussing this. He and Cecilia had drunk in moderation when they had Maja. One wine cask a week, approximately. After Maja's disappearance Cecilia had stopped altogether; she said that even one glass of wine messed up her head. Anders had drunk enough for both of them, and then some. Silent evenings in front of the TV. Glass after glass of wine, and then spirits. To avoid thinking at all.

He didn't know how much his drinking had to do with the fact that after six months she had said she couldn't cope any more, that their relationship was like a lead weight around her feet, dragging her deeper and deeper into the darkness.

After that, the drinking had become central to his life. He had set a boundary for himself: not to start before eight o'clock in the evening. After a week, he had moved the boundary to seven. And so on. In the end he was drinking whenever he felt like it, which was almost all the time.

During the three weeks that had passed since the incident with the fern, he had once again set the boundary at eight o'clock, with an enormous effort of will, and had managed to stick to it. His face and eyes had regained at least some of their normal colour, after a year of being red from burst blood vessels.

Anders ran his hand over his face and said, 'I've got it under control.'

'Have you?'

'Yes. What the hell do you want me to say?'

Simon didn't move a muscle in response to this outburst. Anders blinked a couple of times, feeling ashamed of himself, and said, 'I'm working on it. I really am.'

Silence fell once more. Anders had nothing to add. The problem was his, and his alone. Part of the idea of returning to Domarö had been to get away from the destructive routines he had fallen into. He could only hope it would work. There was nothing more to say.

Simon asked if he had heard anything from Cecilia, and Anders shrugged.

'Haven't heard from her in six months. Strange, isn't it? You share everything, and then…pouff. Gone. But I suppose that's just the way it is.'

He felt the bitterness come creeping in. That wasn't good. If he sat here for a while longer he would probably start crying. Not good. It wasn't a question of suppressing his emotions, he'd wept bucketfuls.

Bucketfuls?

Well. One bucketful, perhaps. An entire fucking ten-litre bucket full of tears. Absorbed by tissues, sleeves, dripping on to the sofa, on to the sheets, rising like steam from his face during the night. Salt in his mouth, snot in his nose. A bucket. A blue plastic bucket filled with tears. He had cried.

But he wasn't going to cry now. He had no intention of starting his new life bemoaning everything that had vanished.

He finished his coffee and stood up.

'Thank you. I'll go down and see if the house is still standing.'

'It is,' said Simon. 'Oddly enough. You'll call and see Anna-Greta, won't you?'

'Tomorrow. Definitely.'

48

When Anders got back to the point where the track forked in two different directions, he thought: *A new life? There's no such thing.*

It was only in the magazine headlines that people got a new life. Stopped drinking or taking drugs, found a new love. But the same life.

Anders looked along the track towards the Shack. He could buy new furniture, paint it blue and change the windows. It would still be the same horrible house, the same poor basic construction. He could of course tear the whole thing down and build a new house, but how do you do that with a life?

Can't be done. When it comes to a life, all you can change is the equivalent of furniture, paint and windows. Doors, maybe. Change the things that are in too bad a state and hope the core holds. Despite everything.

Anders gripped the handle of his suitcase firmly and set off along the track to the Shack.

The Shack

A curious name. The Shack. Not the sort of thing you put up on a poker-work sign, like *Sjösala* or *Fridlunda*.

But then the Shack wasn't the name its builder had given it, or the name on the insurance documents. It was actually called Rock Cottage. But the Shack was what everybody on Domarö called it, even Anders, because it was a shack.

Anders' great-great-grandfather had been the last pilot in the Ivarsson family. When his son Torgny inherited the pilot's cottage, he extended it and made it into a fine two-storey house. Inspired by his success, he also built Seaview Cottage, the house Simon now rented on a permanent basis.

When the first summer visitors arrived on the Vaxholm ferries at the beginning of the twentieth century, several of the islanders wanted to add extensions to their houses, or rebuild them completely.

The brothers fitted out old hen houses as small summer cottages, extended and re-roofed boathouses, even built new properties in some instances. The building that later became the ramblers' hostel was built to order for a textile factory owner from Stockholm.

When the son, Anders' grandfather Erik, needed a place of his own in the mid-1930s, he was allocated the empty plot out on the cliffs. People probably had their doubts. Erik had accompanied his father on various building projects, lending a hand and carrying out some of the simpler work. He showed no particular talent. But he knew the basics.

His father offered to help, but Erik was determined to build the house himself. He was a hot-headed boy who couldn't bear to be contradicted; he swung between periods of intense activity and gloomy introspection. Building the house was to be the proof that he could stand on his own two feet and make his own way in the world.

Timber was transported from a forestry company on the mainland; it was cut at the sawmill in Nåten and shipped across to Domarö. So far, everything was going well. In the summer of 1938, Erik began to lay the foundations. With autumn approaching he had finished the joists and the roof ridges, and the roof trusses were in place. He never once asked his father for advice, and wouldn't even allow him to visit the site.

And so the inevitable happened. One Saturday in the middle of September Erik went across to Nåten. He and his fiancée Anna-Greta were going to go into Norrtälje to look at wedding rings. They were planning to marry in the spring, and the young couple hadn't seen much of each other during the summer, as Erik had been so busy working on the house. The idea was that he and his wife-to-be would move into the completed house after the wedding.

Once Erik's boat had disappeared from view around the southern point, his father sneaked down to the building site with a plumb line and a spirit level.

He came out onto the cliffs and stopped to look at the wooden framework. It looked reasonable, but weren't the gaps between the upright posts for the walls a little too wide? He knew that the pine tree outside the front door grew at an angle of exactly ninety degrees to the ground. He crouched down, closed one eye and squinted. Either the tree had started to grow crooked during the summer, or...

He had a bad feeling in the pit of his stomach as he took out his folding rule and measured the distance between the posts. They were too far apart, and there wasn't even the same distance between them everywhere. In some places it was seventy centimetres, in others a little over eighty. He always went for fifty, sixty at the most. And there weren't enough horizontal supports.

He went to look at the stock of wood. It was as he had suspected: there wasn't a single whole piece of timber left. Erik had scrimped on the wood.

The bad feeling in his stomach moved up to his chest as he went around the building with the plumb line and spirit level. The foundations inclined slightly towards the east, and the framework inclined more strongly towards the west. Presumably Erik had realised that he hadn't got the foundations right, and had tried to compensate by making the house lean in the opposite direction.

Torgny walked around the foundations tapping them with a stone. It wasn't a disaster, but in places it sounded hollow. Erik had got air bubbles in the mortar. And there were no air vents either. If Erik put a slate roof on the crooked frame, it was only a question of whether the damp from underneath or the weight from above would wreck the house first.

Torgny slumped down on the threshold and noted in passing that the door measurements were wrong. And he was the first person to think what so many people would say in the future: *What a bloody shack.*

What could he do?

If it had been in his power, he would have pulled the whole lot down immediately and put up a new framework before Erik came home, confronting him with a fait accompli. He did actually consider for a moment whether he could keep Erik away from home for a week on some wild pretext, get together every single person he knew and do just that. But it wasn't that simple. Just to redo the foundations…

He teetered across the sparse floor joists and inspected the internal layout of the house. That was peculiar as well. A long, narrow hall ran through the house, with the incorrectly proportioned bedrooms and kitchen scattered along its edges. It was as if Erik had started with the living room, which did actually appear to be normal, then added each of the other rooms as they occurred to him, until he ran out of wood.

Torgny stood with his legs apart, balancing on two joists in the middle of what would be the living room. And he was ashamed. It wasn't so much that it was his son who had built this, but more that he would have to spend the rest of his days with this monstrosity close by, on his property. That it would, so to speak, become a part of the family.

Torgny gathered up his things and left Erik's house without looking back. Once he was home, he put a decent slug of spirits in his coffee and a great gloom settled over him as he sat out on his balcony in the autumn sunshine.

His wife Maja came out and sat beside him with a pail of apples to be peeled and puréed.

'How was it?' she asked, as she produced a serpentine curl of peel from the first apple.

'How was what?'

'The house. Erik's house.'

'Well, let's hope it'll keep the wind off them.'

Maja's knife slipped and the serpent fell to the ground before she made it to the end. 'Is it that bad?'

Torgny nodded and gazed into the dregs of his coffee. He thought he could see the Tower of Babel, crashing down on to the screaming crowd. You didn't have to be clairvoyant to understand what that meant.

'Isn't there anything you can do?'

Torgny shook his cup so that the tower disappeared, and shrugged his shoulders.

'I could go up there with a can of kerosene and a match, of course, but…he might take it the wrong way.'

Erik came home that evening in an excellent mood. He and Anna-Greta were agreed on plain, simple rings, so that matter had been more or less a formality. But they had had a lovely day in Norrtälje, sitting by the canal and professing their love for each other while planning their wedding.

Torgny was sitting at the kitchen table mending nets; he listened to his son's unusual talkativeness, nodding and making the right noises as he agreed that Erik had got himself a fine girl there.

Maja stood at the stove stirring the apple purée, making little contribution to the conversation. After a while, Erik noticed that something was wrong. He looked from one to the other.

'Has something happened?'

Torgny looped the yarn through a hole, pulled it tight and knotted it; he didn't look up from his work as he asked, 'What were you thinking of doing about the slates?'

'What slates?'

'For your…house.'

'What do you mean?'

'I'm allowed to ask a question.'

Erik looked at his mother, who was stirring the apple with great concentration, keeping her back to both of them. His father still had his eyes entangled in the torn mesh of the net. After a short silence Erik asked, 'Isn't it right?' When his father didn't reply, he added, 'So what's wrong with it, then?'

Torgny cut off the loose ends with his penknife and rolled them into a little ball.

'Well, if I can put it like this…you ought to consider using sheet metal. If you're planning on having people actually living in that house.' Erik just stared at him. He went on, 'If we could just go through it together, there are a few things I think need taking care of, and perhaps we could…'

Erik interrupted him. 'You think I ought to pull it down, don't you? The whole thing?' Torgny opened his mouth to reply, but Erik slammed his hand down on the table and yelled, 'Fuck you!'

Maja spun around from the stove so quickly that a few drops of apple purée flew off the wooden spoon in her hand and landed on the front of Erik's shirt as he got up from the table.

'Erik!' she said. 'That's no way to speak to your father!'

Erik glared at her as if he were thinking of hitting her, then his gaze dropped to the warm amber drops on his chest.

'Two things,' said Torgny as Erik stood there with his head down. 'Two things. Then you can go wherever you want, and you can get as angry as you want. You are not putting slates on that roof. And you will put air vents in the foundations. After that you can do what you like.'

Torgny cut a piece of yarn to begin darning the next tear. But his hands were shaking and he cut his thumb. It wasn't a deep gash, but a few drops of blood oozed out.

He looked at the blood. Erik looked at the blobs of apple purée on his shirt. Maja was still standing there with the wooden spoon half-raised. A couple of seconds went by and something that was not a house collapsed between them, there was the sound of splintering wood, the squeal of protest as nails were ripped out.

Then Erik walked out of the kitchen. They heard his footsteps thundering up the stairs, the door of his room slamming behind him. Torgny sucked the blood off his thumb. Maja stirred the pan a few times.

Something had collapsed.

After that evening Erik lost all his enthusiasm. He carried on with his carpentry during the autumn and had the panels finished before the winter came, and he fitted a metal roof. He drilled air vents that were misshapen and ugly, but at least they let some air into the foundations.

He did all of this, but he did it without pleasure, without energy. He ate his dinner in silence and gave monosyllabic answers to his parents' questions. Sometimes he went to Nåten to meet Anna-Greta, and he must have made a bit of an effort on those occasions, because the wedding was still on.

Torgny never went to the house again while it was being built. When people asked how the lad was getting on with his house, he said he wasn't interfering at all, it was Erik's business. He had said his piece, had saved what could be saved. He could do no more.

Winter came late. Apart from the usual cold snap at the beginning of November, it was mild with no sign of snow until well into January. Erik had put the windows in and was now spending the afternoons and evenings in his house. A large kerosene lamp spread its light across the cliffs, and from a distance it looked really cosy.

In the middle of January, Erik moved his bed and basic household equipment down to the house. Torgny and Maja stood at the kitchen window secretly watching as he carried his bed on his back down the hill. Maja placed her hand on Torgny's shoulder.

'Our boy is leaving home.'

'Yes,' said Torgny, turning away as tears began to prick at his eyes. He sat down at the kitchen table and filled his pipe. Maja stayed at the window, watching Erik as he disappeared behind Seaview Cottage.

'He's got a mind of his own, anyway,' she said. 'Nobody can take that away from him.'

The house was finished at the beginning of May. The wedding took place two weeks later. The ceremony was to take place outdoors, on the cliffs at North Point, and afterwards everyone was invited to a combined wedding reception and topping-out ceremony in Erik's house on the point.

It was a windy day. People had to hold on to their hats, and when the bride threw her bouquet it was swept out to sea before anyone had the chance to catch it. The party made its way to the couple's house with their clothes flapping and tears in their eyes due to both the wind and the emotion of the occasion.

Anna-Greta thought Erik was holding her hand far too tightly as they passed the harbour and continued towards his home, leading the procession. He was probably just nervous and excited. She herself had butterflies in her stomach, because Erik had yet to show her the house where they were to live together as a married couple, for better or worse, till death did them part. However, his grip was actually so tight that she couldn't give his hand a consoling squeeze in return; she couldn't move her hand at all.

Erik's mother and her friends had set up the tables outside that morning, but when the wind got up an hour before the wedding, they had moved everything inside. The tables were already laid when the guests walked in, and Maja and her helpers immediately started setting out the food.

Erik let go of Anna-Greta's hand and gave a short speech welcoming everyone. This gave her the opportunity to look around. It all looked lovely, but there was one detail she couldn't help noticing: in spite of the fact that the windows were closed, the curtains were billowing out. And…

What is it? There's something…

Her eyes moved from the hallway to the kitchen and living room. The windows, the doors, the ceiling. Something was making her feel slightly seasick, as if a weight were shifting in her stomach. There was no time to reflect on the matter. Erik had finished speaking, and the guests were taking their seats. She put the whole thing down to her own nervousness.

Erik grew more and more morose as the afternoon and evening progressed. There were discussions about fishing and summer visitors, about Hitler and the possible occupation of Åland, but in the corners and barely out of earshot people were tapping on the walls and pointing at corners and angles. Heads were shaken, and certain comments reached Erik's ears.

Anna-Greta noticed that Erik was pouring himself generous measures of schnapps. She tried to distract his attention from the alcohol, but once Erik had passed a certain point, it was as if he became nothing more than a pair of listening ears and a drinking mouth. Later in the evening, when several of the guests were talking quite openly about things they had only whispered earlier, she found him sitting on a chair, staring at one of the walls.

Three of the children were playing a game. They had some hard-boiled eggs left over from the meal, and they were having a competition to see who could get their egg to roll the furthest, simply by putting it down on the floor and letting go of it.

Suddenly Erik stood up and cleared his throat loudly. There was a party atmosphere in the funny house, and only a few conversations were broken off. Erik didn't seem to care. He leaned against the back of the chair so that he wouldn't fall over, and said loudly, 'There's been a lot of talk one way and another, so I thought it was time *I* said what *I* think about this Hitler bloke.'

He gave a highly inflammatory speech, but a very strange one. His argument was muddled and vaguely incomprehensible. At any rate, the main thrust was that people like Hitler should be eradicated from the face of the earth, and why? Well, because they poked their noses into other people's business and crushed the freedom of others with their authority. Hitler was one of those people who always thought he knew best, and therefore other people were crushed beneath his feet.

Erik ended by saying, 'We can bloody well do without these know-alls. That's what I think, anyway.'

It was only when Torgny stood up a little while later, made his excuses and took Maja with him, that Anna-Greta realised the speech had been about something else entirely.

No, it wasn't exactly a successful wedding reception. Nor was the wedding night, for that matter. Erik was too drunk to do anything at all, and towards morning Anna-Greta went out and sought consolation with the gulls, who had begun to circle above the cliffs.

What kind of life was it going to be, here in this house?

Plastic beads

The pine tree was still standing by the porch, as tall and straight as ever. Anders put his case down beside it and contemplated the Shack. The sheet metal roof had been changed to corrugated tin, and its corrugations were full of pine needles. The gutters were probably blocked.

The rickety jetty extended out into the water from the wormwood meadow on the shoreline. Anders' grandmother had brought a plant with her from Stora Korset many years earlier, and it had spread, very slowly, until the swaying blanket of leaves and naked stems surrounded the old plastic-hulled boat lying upturned on a couple of blocks of wood.

He took a walk around the outside of the house. On the side facing inland it looked OK, but on the side facing out to sea the red paint had faded, and some of the planks of wood in the walls had split. The TV aerial had disappeared. When he went up on to the patio he could see the antenna lying there like an injured spider.

He was in pain all the time. All the time there was a weight on his chest and pain that felt like a scream. As he made his way around the corner of the house he caught sight of something red among the dog roses. Maja's little boat. A cheap inflatable thing they had played with together that last summer. He and Maja and Cecilia.

Now it was lying there, torn and deflated among the rose bushes. He remembered telling Maja not to drag it across any sharp stones, not to…now it was impaled on hundreds of thorns and everything was gone and it was too late.

It was because of the boat he hadn't come back to Domarö for almost three years. Because of the boat and other memories like it, other traces of the past. Things that contemptuously continued to exist, despite the fact that they should no longer be here because the significance they'd held was gone.

He had expected this. He had steeled himself. He didn't cry. He could see the red glow of the boat from the corner of his eye as he carried on around the house on legs that were moving only because he told them to move. He turned the corner and found his way to the table in the garden, slumped down on the bench. He was finding it difficult to breathe, small hands were squeezing his windpipe and black dots danced before his eyes.

What the hell did I come here for?

When the worst of the cramps in his throat had passed, he got up and kicked away the stone by the gooseberry bush. A few woodlice scuttled over the plastic bag containing the door key. He waited until they had gone, then bent down and picked up the bag. As he straightened up he suddenly felt dizzy. He went over to the front door as if he were drunk, unlocked it, dragged himself to the bathroom and drank several gulps of rusty-tasting water straight from the tap. Breathed, took a few more gulps. The dizziness was still there.

The door from the hallway into the living room was open, and the light from the sea and sky cast a white lustre over the sofa under the window. He saw it through a tunnel, staggered over and collapsed on to it.

Time passed.

He lay on the sofa with his eyes open or his eyes closed, and realised he was freezing. But it was merely a fact, it was unimportant. He looked at the blank television screen, the soot-covered doors of the Roslagen stove.

He recognised everything, and everything was unfamiliar to him. He had thought there would be some sense of homecoming, a sense of returning to something that still belonged to him. There wasn't. He felt like a burglar in someone else's memories. All this belonged to a stranger, someone he had been a long time ago and no longer knew.

It had grown darker outside the window and the sea was lapping against the rocks. He crawled off the sofa and fetched a tin, which he filled with chimney-cleaning fluid; he placed it in the open hearth and lit it to get rid of the cold air in the chimney. Then he lit a fire and went to open the bedroom door, to spread the warmth through the house. He stopped halfway.

The door.

The door was closed.

Someone had closed the door.

Anders stood still, breathing through his nose. Faster and faster, like an animal scenting danger. He stared at the door. It was an ordinary door. Pale pine, the cheapest kind. He had bought it himself from the sawmill in Nåten and spent a day taking out the old, crooked frame and fitting the new door. A perfectly ordinary door. But it was closed.

He was absolutely certain it had not been closed when he and Cecilia left here for the last time, exhausted, empty, all cried out.

Calm down. Simon has closed it.

But why would he have done that? There were no other signs that anyone had been in the house. Why would Simon have come in just to close the bedroom door?

So the door must have been closed when they left. He must have got it wrong.

But I haven't.

He remembered all too clearly. How Cecilia had gone out to the car with the last thing, a case containing Maja's summer clothes. How he had stood there looking back into the house for one last time before he closed and locked the front door. He had known he was saying goodbye, that none of the things they had imagined were ever going to happen, that he might never see this place again. The image had been seared into his brain.

And the door to the bedroom had been open.

He reached out for the handle. It was cold. His heart was pounding in his chest. Carefully he pushed down the handle and pulled. The door swung open. Despite the chill pouring out from the bedroom, he felt a drop of sweat trickle from his armpit.

Nothing.

There was nothing, of course. The beam of the lighthouse flashed across the double bed opposite the door. Everything was as it should be. And yet he groped for the switch and put the light on before he went in.

The double bed was made, the white satin quilt cover shone and spread light across the pale blue wood-panelled walls, the cheap painting of a ship in danger on a stormy sea above the bed.

He walked over to the window. The lighthouse at North Point was flashing out across the bay. A single floodlight in the harbour illuminated the steamboat jetty and the boats bobbing by the jetties. There wasn't a soul out there. In the brief intervals of darkness he could see short flashes from Gåvasten, the hated lighthouse at Gåvasten.

He could see the opposite wall reflected in the dark window pane. The wardrobe, Maja's bed. It was unmade, the way they had left it. Neither he nor Cecilia could bring themselves to smooth out the quilt and eradicate the last traces of the child who used to lie there. Anders shuddered. The chaotic covers looked as if they might be hiding a body. He turned around.

A bed. An unmade bed. Nothing else. A small, unmade bed. The pillowcase with its picture of Bamse the Bear carrying a pile of jars of honey. She had had a subscription, and the comics had kept on coming. He had read them. Read them aloud, the way he used to, even though no one was listening.

He went and sat down on her bed, gazed around the room. He curled up. Curled up a little more. He had a pain in his chest, a lump was growing. He saw the room through her eyes, the way she had seen it.

There's the big bed, that's where Mummy and Daddy sleep, I can go over there if I'm scared. This is my beautiful bed, there's Bamse. I am six years old. My name is Maja. I know that I am loved.

'Maja...Maja...'

The lump in his chest was so big it couldn't be dissolved with tears, and he was being sucked down towards it. He had no grave to visit, nothing that meant Maja. Except for this. This place. He hadn't

61

understood that until now. He was sitting on her grave, her resting place. His head was drawn down towards the floor, down between his knees.

Strewn across the floor by the bed were a number of her plastic beads. Twenty or thirty of them. She had made necklaces, bead pictures, it had been her favourite pastime. She had had a whole bucketful of beads in every colour you could think of, and it was under her bed.

Except for those that were strewn across the floor.

Anders picked up a few of the beads, looked at them as they lay there in the palm of his hand. One red, one yellow, three blue.

Another memory from the last day, kneeling beside her bed, leaning his head on the mattress, searching for the smell of her in the sheets and finding it, the fabric soaking up his tears.

He had been on his knees. He had moved around the bed on his knees, searching for the smell of her. Yes. But there had been no beads under his knees then. He had forgotten much of his life in the years that followed, much lay in a fog, but that last day out here burned brightly. Clearly. No beads pressing into his skin.

Are you sure?

Yes. I'm sure.

He slid down on to the floor and looked under the bed. The transparent bucket that held the beads was near the edge. It was two-thirds full. He pushed his hand in and allowed it to be surrounded by beads, stirred it around. When he pulled out his hand, a number of beads were stuck to his skin.

Rats. Mice.

He buried both hands in the bucket, filled his cupped hands with beads and allowed them to pour back in. No droppings. Mice couldn't even walk through a kitchen cupboard without leaving droppings behind.

He pushed the bucket back under the bed and looked around the floor. The twenty or thirty beads were all close to the bed. He crawled across the floor, looked in the corners, along the edges. No beads.

Under the double bed there were big balls of fluff, nothing else.

Just a minute…

He moved back to Maja's bed and looked underneath.

A box with no lid containing Duplo Lego was behind the bucket of beads, next to Bamse. He pulled it out. A layer of dust covered the multi-coloured blocks. He couldn't check because he had moved his hands around in the bucket, but had there been any dust on the beads?

He sat on the floor with his back against Maja's bed. His eyes focused on the wardrobe. It was a clumsy object fixed to the wall, built by Anders' grandfather with the same lack of skill that characterised the rest of the house. It was approximately a metre wide, made from rough left-over wood. The key was in the lock.

His heart began palpitating once again, and a cold sweat broke out on his palms. He knew the wardrobe had a handle on the inside. Maja liked to sit inside underneath the clothes and pretend she…

Stop it. Stop it right now.

He clamped his lips together, stopped breathing. Listened. There was not a sound apart from the rushing of the sea against the rocks, the wind soughing through the pine trees, his own heart pounding in his ears. He looked at the wardrobe door, at the key. It was moving.

Anders leapt to his feet and pressed his hands against his temples. His lower jaw had begun to tremble.

The key was not moving. Of course it wasn't moving.

Stop it. Stop it.

Without looking back he walked out of the room, turned the light off and closed the door. His fingers were ice-cold, his teeth chattering. He placed a few logs on the fire, then sat for a long time warming his hands, his body.

When he felt calmer he opened his suitcase and took out one of the litre casks of red wine, tore it open and knocked back a third of the contents. He looked at the bedroom door. He was still just as frightened.

The fire in the kitchen stove had gone out. He didn't bother with it, he just picked up his cigarettes and a glass and went back to the safe circle of warmth by the fire, where he finished off the wine cask. When it was empty he threw it on the fire and fetched another.

The wine did its job. The knots in his muscles loosened and his thoughts drifted off aimlessly without alighting anywhere in particular. Halfway through the second box he got up and looked out across the sea, glass in hand. The lighthouse at Gåvasten was flashing in the distance.

'Cheers, you bastard. Cheers, you fucking bastard.'

He emptied the glass and began to sway in time with the flashing light.

The sea. And us poor bastards with our little flashing lights.

Something bad is coming

At half-past three Anders was woken by someone banging on the door. He opened his eyes and lay motionless on the sofa, pulling the blanket more tightly around him. The room was in darkness. The beam of the lighthouse swept through and the floor swayed. His head felt heavy.

He lay there with his eyes wide open wondering if he had misheard, if it had been a dream. The lighthouse beam swept by once again. This time the floor remained still. Behind him he could hear that the wind was getting up. The sea was hurling itself against the rocks and a cold draught whistled through the gaps in the house.

He had just closed his eyes to try and go back to sleep when the pounding started again. Three powerful blows on the outside door. He sat up quickly on the sofa and looked around instinctively for a weapon. There was something horrible about those short, hard blows.

As if...as if...

As if someone had come to get him. Someone following an order. Someone who had the right to take him. His legs were ready for flight as he slipped off the sofa, shuffled across to the fire and seized the poker.

He stood there with the poker held aloft, waiting for the pounding to come again. There was no sound apart from the growing fury of the sea, the creaking as a half-broken branch twisted in the wind.

Calm down. Perhaps it's just...

Just what? An accident, someone needing help? Yes, that was probably the most likely scenario, and here he was looking as if he was expecting an alien invasion. He took a few steps towards the outside door, still holding the poker in his hand.

'Hello?' he shouted. 'Who's there?'

His heart was pounding and it felt as if something was tightening around his head.

There's something wrong with me.

Someone had run aground in their boat, their engine had failed in the strong wind and they had made their way up the rocks to his door, perhaps they were standing there now, soaked to the skin and freezing.

But why are they hammering on the door like that?

Without switching on any of the lights that might dazzle him, Anders crept over to the hall window and peeped out. Nobody was standing on the porch, as far as he could see. He switched on the outside light. There was nobody there. He opened the door and looked out.

'Hello? Is anyone there?'

Maja's swing was flying wildly to and fro in the wind, dry leaves whirled around the yard. He put the door on the latch and stepped out on to the porch, closed the door behind him and glanced around, listening intently.

He thought he could hear the sound of an engine from the direction of the village. A small outboard motor or a chainsaw. But who would take a boat out at this hour, who would be cutting trees in the middle of the night? It could be a moped, of course, but the same question applied.

Maja's swing was disconcerting. The way it was moving it looked as if someone was sitting on it and swinging, someone he couldn't see. A cold blast of wind swept across his chest and stomach as he took a few steps away from the door and called 'Maja?' out into the empty air.

No reply. No change in the frantic movement of the swing. He lowered the poker and ran his free hand over his face. He was still drunk. Drunk and wide awake. The sound of the engine—if that's what it was—had stopped. All he could hear was the creaking of the broken branch.

He went back to the door and examined the outside. No damage from the knocking. The corners of his mouth twitched.

I know what this means.

His grandmother had told him about one occasion when her father had spent the night in a hut on one of the little islands out in the archipelago. He had been on 'an errand', which at the time was the euphemism for smuggling spirits. He had probably arranged to meet some Estonian cargo boat outside the three-mile limit towards dawn, and had decided it would be safest to spend the night out in the archipelago.

In the middle of the night he is woken by the sound of hammering on the door. It's a simple cottage door, and the heavy blows are making the latch jump. He thinks it's customs that are on his trail, but this time they have made their move too early. He has nothing they can confiscate, and he is perfectly happy to explain why he is spending the night here—he has brought his fowling piece with him for appearance's sake. He is quite happy to open the door.

No one is there. There is not a soul in sight, and only his own fishing boat is moored by the jetty. However, to be on the safe side he picks up the money he is going to use to pay for the contraband and takes a walk around the island with the gun in his hand. He manages to frighten a couple of eider ducks out of a clump of reeds, but nothing else.

As dawn breaks he sets off for the meeting place. After a few nautical miles he catches sight of the cargo ship at anchor just beyond the limit.

Then he hears an explosion.

At first he thinks it might be his own compression ignition engine, but he realises that the resonance of the explosion is too deep, that it has come from outside his boat. He picks up the telescope and looks over at the cargo boat he is to meet.

Something has happened to it. At first he can't make out what it is, but as he gets closer he can see that it is listing and beginning to sink. By the time he reaches it there is no longer anything to reach. He scans the surface of the sea with the telescope, but there is nothing to be seen.

'Four men and at least a thousand litres of schnapps went down that day,' his grandmother's father told her later. 'That was what it wanted to tell me, whatever was banging on the door. That something bad was coming.'

Anders' grandmother had retold the story using exactly the same words, and ever since it had been an expression that came into his mind from time to time when he wanted to describe something. It came to him now, as he examined the door and found not a trace of whoever had been hammering on it.

Something bad is coming.

He looked up at the pine trees, their swaying tops invisible in the darkness outside the circle of light from the outdoor lamp. A loose piece of metal on the woodshed banged once, as if to underline the point.

Something bad is coming.

It was impossible to go back to sleep. Anders lit the kitchen stove, then sat at the kitchen table staring at the wall. His head felt as if it were full of lukewarm porridge, enclosed in a perverse membrane of clarity. He was able to think clearly, but not deeply.

The wind was howling around the walls, and Anders shivered. He suddenly felt *exposed*. Like an unwanted child left out in the forest.

Exposed. His fragile little house stood alone, exposed on the point. The deep sea was forcing its way upward, reaching out its arms. The wind was curling itself around the house, flexing its muscles and trying to find a way in.

Something bad is coming. It's after me.

What 'it' was, he had no idea. Just that it was big and strong, and it was after him. That his fortifications were inadequate.

The old wine tasted like rotten fruit in his mouth; he drank half a litre of water straight from the tap to rinse away the taste. The water wasn't much better. Salt water had probably got into the well—the tap water had a thick, metallic taste. Anders rinsed his face and dried it with a tea towel.

Without thinking about it, he went into the bedroom and fetched the bucket of plastic beads, then sat down at the kitchen table and started picking them out, pushing them together. First of all he made a heart in red. Then a blue heart outside the red one. Then a yellow one, and so on. Like a Russian doll, the hearts surrounding one another. When he got to the edge he got up and put some more wood in the stove.

The beads he had taken to make his heart design hadn't made any noticeable difference to the level in the bucket. He had plenty of beads and plenty of tiles. He would really have liked a bigger tile. So that he could make an entire picture.

If you stick them together…

He dug a hacksaw out of his toolbox and set to work. When he had sawn the edges off nine tiles, he smoothed them down with sandpaper to make an even surface for the glue to stick to. The work took up all of his attention and he didn't even notice as the dawn came creeping across the sea.

Only when all the edges were smooth and he got up to look for the unopened tube of araldite that he knew should be somewhere did he glance out of the window and realise that the morning sun had leached the brightness from the beam of the North Point lighthouse.

Morning. Coffee.

He washed away the worst of the limescale from the pot and poured water into the coffee machine. In the larder there was an open packet of coffee, which had doubtless lost all its flavour. He compensated by using twice as much as usual, and switched on the machine.

He found the glue and spent another half-hour smoothing down any slight imperfections and sticking the tiles together. The morning sun was slanting in through the kitchen window as he stood back to admire his work.

Nine tiles with room for four hundred beads on each one, all stuck together. A white, knobbly surface just waiting for three thousand six hundred coloured dots. Anders nodded. He was pleased with himself. He could get going now.

But what shall I make?

As he smoked a cigarette and sipped at the warm liquid, which did indeed taste more like the ghost of a cup of coffee, he contemplated the white surface and tried to come up with a picture that he would create there.

One of Strindberg's wild sea paintings in beads. Yes. But there probably weren't enough nuances for that. Something more naïve, like a child's picture. Cows and horses, a house with a chimney. No, that was no challenge.

A child's picture…

He glowered at the lighthouse on North Point and searched his memory. Then he pushed away his coffee cup and started rummaging in drawers. He hadn't a clue what had become of the camera.

He found it in the junk drawer, where everything that might just be worth keeping ended up. The counter showed that twelve pictures had been taken. He used the point of a pencil to push in the rewind button, and the motor began to turn, slowly and with much complaining. The batteries were more or less dead. There was a click and the motor speeded up: nothing more to rewind. Anders removed the roll of film and sat down at the kitchen table again.

He closed his hand around the small metal cylinder; it felt cool after lying in the drawer. They were in there. The last pictures of a family. He warmed it in his hand, warmed the tiny people on the ice who would soon be struck by something dreadful.

He took the roll of film between his thumb and index finger, studying it as if he might be able to see something of what was inside. An impulse told him to leave it alone, to let that family stay in there, forever unaware of what was to come. Not to let it out to trample in the sludge that life had become. To let that family stay in its little time capsule.

Someone hates us

With the morning's first cup of coffee by his side, Simon was sitting at the kitchen table staring down into the half-open matchbox. The black larva lay there motionless, but Simon knew it was alive.

He sat with his lips clamped firmly together, gathering saliva in his mouth. When he had enough he allowed it to trickle out between his lips and down into the box. The larva moved slightly when the spit landed on its shiny skin, as if it were sleepy; Simon watched as the saliva was slowly absorbed and disappeared.

It was a morning ritual that was every bit as necessary as going for a pee and having a cup of coffee, he had come to realise.

A week or so after Spiritus came into his care, he had left the box in the kitchen drawer one morning without spitting into it, and taken the boat over to the mainland to do some shopping. As he set off in the boat he already had the taste in his mouth. It grew stronger during the crossing. The taste of old wood, of rancid nuts, expanded out of his mouth, into his blood and through his muscles.

As he was slowing down ready to moor the boat by the jetty in Nåten, he threw up all over the floor. He knew the reason, but refused to give in and carried on towards the jetty, moving as slowly as possible. When the boat hit a post, it was as if his body was being wrenched inside out. He threw up until there was nothing left but bile.

This was a nausea much greater than the body itself can produce, a septic shock similar to acute poisoning. Simon curled up in the stern as his stomach contorted in cramps, and managed to swing the boat around so that it was heading back to Domarö.

He was convinced that he was going to die, and all the way back he remained curled up in the foetal position as deep, wet belches forced their way out of him and his body rotted.

He didn't manage to moor the boat properly, but ran it up on the shoreline and crawled on his knees through the shallow water, across the pebbles on the shore, the lawn and into the house. By the time he got the matchbox out of the drawer, his mouth was so dry from all the vomiting that it took him a couple of minutes to collect enough saliva to enable him to give Spiritus what Spiritus craved. It took several days before he was fully recovered, before his body felt strong once again.

Since then he had been careful to spit into the matchbox every morning. He didn't know what was waiting at the end of this pact he had entered into, but he knew he had to fulfil its terms for as long as he lived.

And then?

He didn't know. But he feared the worst, in some form. And he regretted the fact that he hadn't swept Spiritus off the jetty that day. Down into the sea where it belonged. He regretted that. But it was too late now.

He took a sip of his coffee and looked out of the window. The sky was high and clear, the way it looks only in the autumn, with a few yellow birch leaves drifting down. There was nothing to indicate that a storm was on its way, which Simon knew it was, just as he knew many other things. Where to find water under the ground, when the ice would form, how much rain would fall.

When he had finished his coffee and rinsed the cup, Simon put on his knee-high boots and went out. This was one of the islanders' habits that he had adopted: knee-high boots in every situation. You never knew what you might end up squelching through, and it was best to be prepared.

Perhaps the post and newspapers might have arrived on the early boat today, and if they hadn't there were always some old men by the mailboxes who, like Simon, had nothing better to do than to go and see if the post had come on the early boat. Which it almost never had.

On the way up to the mailboxes he glanced along the track to the Shack. There was plenty to do there, and perhaps that was a good thing for Anders. Something to occupy the hands is an excellent cure for gloomy thoughts, he knew that from personal experience. During the worst periods with Marita, his first wife, it was practising with packs of cards, handkerchiefs and other things that had stood between him and panic-stricken terror.

With Anna-Greta things were very different, of course. In that relationship it was mostly melancholy he had driven away with sleight of hand and miscalculations.

As far as he knew, Anders had no particular hobby to occupy his mind, so undergrowth that needed clearing, flaking paint and wood that needed chopping could well do him some good.

From a distance of a hundred metres away, he could already see that today's conversation group by the mailboxes consisted of Holger and Göran. They were instantly recognisable. Holger stooped and miserable from disappointments that had started when he was only young, Göran still straight-backed after forty years in the police service.

But what the...?

The two men were deep in an intense discussion. Holger was shaking his head and waving one arm in the direction of the sea, while Göran was kicking at the ground as if he were annoyed. But that wasn't what was peculiar.

The mailboxes were gone.

The wall of the shop, closed for the season, was completely empty. Only the yellow box for outgoing post was still hanging there, and that looked odd as well.

Have they stopped the postal service?

As Simon got closer he realised that wasn't the problem. Ten metres away from the shop he stood on the first splinters. Splinters of plastic and splinters of wood, bits of the mailboxes that had been hanging on the wall only yesterday. The yellow metal box for outgoing post was dented and crooked.

Holger caught sight of him and burst out, 'Oh, here comes the Stockholmer. We're not likely to get much sympathy there.'

Simon stepped into the mosaic of shattered, multi-coloured plastic. 'What's happened?'

'What's happened?' said Holger. 'I'll tell you what's happened. Last night when we were fast asleep some bastards from Stockholm came over here in a boat and smashed our mailboxes for the hell of it.'

'Why?'

Holger looked as if he couldn't believe his ears. That was his normal reaction to anything he perceived as a challenge to his theories, and as usual he embarked on his reply by repeating the question, just to show how completely stupid it was.

'Why? Do you think they actually need a *reason*? Maybe they couldn't get a mooring in the harbour, maybe they weren't happy with the number of hours of sunshine last summer, or maybe they just think the most fun you can have is destroying something, and if you ask me I'd go for the last option. It makes me so bloody furious.'

Holger turned on his heel and limped down to the steamboat jetty, where Simon could see Mats, the owner of the shop, waiting for the tender.

Simon turned to Göran and asked, 'Is that what you think?'

Göran looked at the devastation around them and shook his head. 'I think we have no idea who did this. Could be anybody.'

'Someone on the island?'

'No one I can think of. But you never know.'

'Did nobody hear anything?'

Göran nodded in the direction of the jetty. 'Mats heard something, and then he heard an engine start up. But he didn't know if it was an outboard motor or a moped. The wind was in the wrong direction.'

'They must have made…a hell of a noise.'

'I don't know,' said Göran, scooping up some green and grey pieces and showing them to Simon. 'Look at these. What do you think?'

The pieces in Göran's hand, shark fins and rhomboids, all had sharp edges where they had broken off. The pieces on the ground were quite big too. No little bits.

'It doesn't look as if they were smashed.'

'No, it doesn't, does it? More as if they've been *cut*. With a box cutter or something. And look at this.'

Göran pointed at the metal box. It was dented and crooked, but the dents had sharp angles in the middle where the bare metal showed through. It was not blows that had created the dents, but a stabbing action. Someone had stood there stabbing at the mailbox with a big knife.

Simons shook his head. 'Why would someone do that?'

Göran hesitated before replying, as if he wanted to be sure that he was choosing the right words. Eventually he said, 'My experience of this sort of thing…is that people do this because they feel hate.'

'And what is it they—or he—hate in cases like this?'

'Us.'

Simon looked at the debris on the ground again, at the dented metal box. Rage. All the mailboxes represented the people on the island. Every box was an extension of the person to whom it belonged. A name.

Göran shrugged. 'Or else it's the simple urge to destroy things. How should I know. Sometimes that's what it is. But usually it isn't. So what are we going to do about this lot?'

Any kind of outrage or violent deviation from the norm has a tendency to create gaps in the chain of responsibility: no one guilty, no one responsible. In which case two old men who just happened to be passing can easily end up clearing up the mess. Göran crouched down and started picking up pieces, Simon fetched the rubbish bin from the steps leading to the shop. Then they worked together to gather up the wreckage. When the bin was full, Göran went down to the harbour for an empty barrel, while Simon sat down on the steps and wiped the sweat from his brow.

So bloody unnecessary. All this trouble just because someone… hates.

He pulled a face and rubbed his eyes.

Ha. There's no end to how much trouble there can be if someone hates hard enough. In fact, we ought to be grateful if it stops at mailboxes.

'Simon?'

Simon looked up. Anders was standing in front of him with a letter in his hand, looking around. 'Where are the mailboxes?'

Simon explained what had happened, and told Anders to give his letter directly to Mats, who was in fact just on his way up from the harbour with the blue mail crate in his arms. Göran and Holger were following behind.

Göran had got hold of a roll of black plastic sacks, and started putting the pieces in one of them. Holger pushed his hands into his pockets and stared at Anders.

'So,' he said. 'We've got a visitor. When did you get here?'

'Yesterday.'

Holger nodded over this nugget of information for a long time. He looked at the others for support, first at Mats and then at Göran, but no support was forthcoming. When the look he got in return from Göran was more annoyed than anything, Holger seemed to remember what the situation was.

'My condolences on your loss, by the way,' he managed to squeeze out.

They talked for a while about what to do about the post. For today, Mats would wait and explain to everyone what had happened. They would all need to get themselves a new mailbox as soon as possible. Meanwhile a plastic bucket with a lid would do instead, or even a bag. As long as everyone put his or her mailbox number on it.

Anders waved his letter. 'So what shall I do with this, then? It's a film to be developed. I wouldn't like it to get lost.'

Mats took the letter and promised he would make sure it was sent. Then he gave out the post to those who were there. No letters for Simon, just a newspaper, *Norrtelje Tidning*, and an advert for some pension fund.

As Simon and Anders set off home, Göran said, 'You won't forget, will you?'

'No,' said Simon. 'I'll call round one day.'

They took the route along the shoreline. The jetties belonging to the summer visitors were more or less empty. The odd individual would probably come out at the weekend, but otherwise the season was over for this year.

'What is it he doesn't want you to forget?' asked Anders.

'Göran moved back here a while ago, when he retired. But he hasn't got a well, so he wanted me to go over with my divining rod to find him some water.'

'How do you actually do that?'

'Practice, practice and more practice.'

Anders punched Simon playfully on the shoulder. 'Stop it. That isn't magic. I really am interested.'

'Well, it is a kind of magic, you know. Are you coming in to see Anna-Greta?'

Anders dropped the subject. For a number of years Simon had been the local water diviner. Whenever anyone needed to sink a well, it was to Simon they turned to find a spring. Simon would come, walk around with the rowan twig that was his divining rod, and eventually point out a suitable spot. He hadn't been wrong yet.

Anders snorted. 'Holger seemed to think I was the one who smashed up the mailboxes.'

'You know his wife drowned last year?'

'Sigrid? No, I didn't know that.'

'Went out in the boat to check the nets and never came back. They found the boat a few days later, but not Sigrid.'

Sigrid. One of the few people Anders had been genuinely frightened of when he was little. An overfilled cup just waiting for the drop that would make it run over. It could be anything. The weather, the sound of bicycles, a wasp that came too close to her ice cream. Whenever Anders sold her some herring he would make a point of picking out the biggest and best, and preferred to give her too much rather than a single gram too little.

'Did she drown herself?'

Simon shrugged his shoulders. 'I suppose some people think so, but...'

'But what?'

'Others think Holger did it.'

'Is that what you think?'

'No. No, no. He was much too frightened of her.'

'So now he's only got the Stockholmers left to hate?'

'That's right. But he can put even more energy into it now.'

Holger's thesis

This aversion towards people from the capital is not unique to Domarö, or even to Sweden. It exists everywhere, and sometimes with good reason. Holger's story is representative of what has happened in the Stockholm archipelago generally, and on Domarö in particular.

Just like Anders and many others on Domarö, Holger came from a family of pilots. Through a series of clever acquisitions, marriages and other manoeuvres, the Persson family eventually ended up owning the entire north-eastern part of Domarö, an area covering some thirty hectares, measured from the shoreline inland, and comprising forest, meadows and arable fields.

This was what Holger's father had to look after when he came of age at the beginning of the 1930s. Summer visitors had begun to come, and like many others on the island he had a couple of boathouses done up and extended so that he could rent them out.

To cut a long story short, however, there were debts in the family, and Holger's father had an unfortunate tendency to hit the bottle when things were not going well. One summer he got to know a broker from Stockholm. Generous amounts of alcohol were proffered, and fraternal toasts shared. There was even talk of Holger's father becoming a member of the Order of the Knights Templar, the legendary masonic lodge headed by Carl von Schewen.

Well. Somehow the whole thing ended up with Holger's father selling Kattudden to the broker. A piece of land measuring about fifteen hectares where no trees grew and the grazing was poor. He got a price that was rather more than he would have expected if he'd sold the land to another islander.

But of course the broker was not interested in either grazing or forestry. Within a couple of years he had divided Kattudden into thirty separate plots, which he then sold to prospective summer visitors. Each plot went for a sum approximately half what he had paid for the whole piece of land.

When Holger's father realised what had happened, how thoroughly deceived he had been by the broker, the bottle was waiting to console him. At this point Holger was seven years old, and was forced to watch as his father drank himself into a morass of self-pity, while the Stockholmers happily erected their 'summer cottage' kit homes on land that had belonged to his family for generations.

A couple of years later his father took his shotgun out into the forest they still owned, and didn't come back.

Different versions of this story are told on many of the islands in the archipelago, but this was the Persson family's version, and it is undeniably one of the uglier tales. These transactions have given rise to a great deal of bitterness everywhere, and Holger was the most bitter of all.

His basic thesis was simple: Stockholmers were the root of all evil; some were guiltier than the rest, and the biggest villains of them all were Evert Taube and Astrid Lindgren.

Holger never tired of explaining his thesis to anyone who was prepared to listen: the archipelago had been a living community with a hard-working population, until Evert Taube came along and romanticised the whole thing, with his 'Rönnerdahl' and 'Calle Schewen's Waltz'. The real Carl von Schewen had become something of a recluse in his old age, thanks to all the curious Stockholmers who took a trip out to his jetty or lay there spying on him through telescopes from their boats to see if Calle might be busy building a haystack or dancing with the rose of Roslagen.

But this was merely a boring detail under the circumstances. The worst thing was that Taube's romantic portrayal opened the eyes of the Stockholmers to the archipelago, where people wore flowers in their hair, danced to the sound of the accordion and enjoyed a little drink in a picturesque manner. Those who could afford it bought themselves a summer cottage. The plots were bought up, and the archipelago became depopulated.

Just as the worst of the frenzy was dying down and the residents of the archipelago began to think they might be able to relax, the killer blow came with Astrid Lindgren's book *Life on Seacrow Island*, and the subsequent TV series. Now it wasn't only the rich who had to have a summer cottage. Brokers bought up everything they could get hold of in order to build small houses which they could sell or rent out by the week or month. Everybody wanted to go to the archipelago, to have exactly the right knack for starting up an outboard motor, and to find a pet seal of their very own.

The young people of the archipelago got to know the summer visitors, and began to long for the nightclubs and cinemas of the capital. Houses and farms were left with no one to inherit them, and of course the brokers popped up again, buying everything in sight until the archipelago resembled a corpse that came to life for a couple of months in the summer, then sank back into its silent grave.

This was the gist of Holger's thesis, and he would usually end with some detailed fantasy concerning what he would like to do to

Evert and Astrid if they were still alive. These were terrible things involving both lead weights and petrol, and he would brook no contradictions.

The archipelago had been romanticised to death. That was Holger's considered opinion.

Anna-Greta

A wall of yellowing lilacs hid Anna-Greta's house from view. The only thing visible above the hedge was the metal roof of the tower, covered in verdigris. When Anders was a child he used to think it was a real tower, the kind you found in castles where knights lived, and he was frustrated because he could never find the way to it, and no one would show him.

Later he had realised that the pointed tower was purely decorative and the window on the gable was painted on. A hundred and fifty bygone years slumbered in that wind-battered wooden panel, and the impression of a haunted house lost in its own memories would have been complete, had it not been for the woman who opened the front door and came running down the garden path.

Anna-Greta was wearing jeans and a check shirt. On her feet she had rubber boots. Her long, white hair was woven into a plait that thudded against her back as she rushed up to Anders and threw her arms around him.

'Oh, Anders!' She hugged him, she shook him. 'It's so good to see you!'

She squeezed him so hard that for a moment Anders thought she was actually going to lift him off the ground, the way she used to do when he was little. He didn't dare respond with the same force—she was eighty-two, after all—so he stroked her back and said, 'Hello Gran.'

Anna-Greta suddenly let go and stared closely at his face for five seconds. Only then did she appear to notice Simon. She tilted her head to one side. Simon leaned over and kissed her cheek. Anna-Greta nodded as if to indicate that he had behaved correctly, and grabbed Anders' hand.

'Come on. The coffee's ready.'

She led Anders towards the house, and Simon lumbered after them. It wasn't that his gait had actually altered, but next to Anna-Greta most people looked as if they were lumbering, regardless of age.

It was as if she lived only on clear, salty air, and when the day came for her to pass away, she would probably do exactly that. Just take a step to one side. Dissolve into a north-westerly wind as it whirled around the lighthouse at North Point, then out across the sea.

The table was laid in the parlour: anchovy sandwiches with egg, delicate biscuits and cinnamon whirls. The hunger which Anders had refused to acknowledge suddenly caught up with him. Simon pretended to be offended, and said to Anders, 'I see, we're in the parlour because you're here. I have to sit in the kitchen. When I'm invited.'

Anna-Greta stopped and raised her eyebrows. 'Is that a complaint?'

'No, no,' said Simon. 'I'm just saying there seems to be some sort of preferential treatment going on here.'

'If you stayed away for almost three years, I'd probably set the table in the parlour for you as well when you came back.'

Simon scratched his chin. 'Well, perhaps I'd better do that, then.'

'In that case I'll walk straight into the sea and drown myself, as you well know. Sit down.'

Anders' father had once said that Simon and Anna-Greta were like an old comedy double act. They had their set routines, polished over the years; by this stage they knew them so well they were no longer routines, but rather a basis for improvisation. You recognised the theme, but the words were different every time.

Anna-Greta watched Anders as he gobbled two sandwiches. She pushed the plate towards him.

'I don't suppose you've got any food down there in the cottage.'

Anders paused with his hand half way to the plate.

'I'm sorry, I...'

Anna-Greta snorted.

'Nonsense. That's not what I meant. You help yourself. But we need to sort out some kind of arrangement.'

'Wood,' said Simon. 'Have you got any wood?'

The problem was discussed, and it was decided that Anders would take home a bag of provisions, that he and Simon would go shopping the following day, and that Anders' boat needed to be put in the water as soon as possible. He could help himself to wood if he ran short.

Anders excused himself and went out on to the porch for a smoke. He sat down on a stool, lit a cigarette and looked at Anna-Greta's plum tree, weighed down with overripe fruit. He thought about Holger and about Holger's wife, about the sea, which seemed to demand its dues at irregular intervals, about the anchor in the church-yard in Nåten, Maja.

It still seems strange...that there wasn't...that no one...

When he went back inside, the table had been cleared and the coffee pot topped up. Simon and Anna-Greta were sitting at the table leaning towards each other, their heads close together. Anders stood quietly, watching them.

That's what love looks like. It can happen. Two people can find one another, and then work together to sustain that amorphous, incomprehensible third party that has arisen between them. Love becomes an entity unto itself: the thing that determines how life is to be lived.

How does that happen?

Anders sat down on his chair, heavy and damp. Simon and Anna-Greta moved apart.

'It's nice to get a bit of fresh air, isn't it?' said Anna-Greta.

Anders nodded. Anna-Greta had never actually nagged him about smoking, but the barbs were many and varied.

'I was thinking about something,' said Anders. 'About Holger. The fact that he thought it was me.'

Anna-Greta pursed her lips. 'If you ask Holger, he'll tell you it's the Stockholmers' fault that there's no more cod.'

'Yes. But it wasn't that. It was more this business with…this business with Maja.'

Simon and Anna-Greta looked at him without moving a muscle. The atmosphere dropped like a stone, but Anders went on, 'It seems strange that…when I think about it now…that nobody suspected me. Or Cecilia. I mean, that's the obvious thing, isn't it? Two parents, one child. The child disappears without a trace. It's obvious the parents are guilty.'

Simon and Anna-Greta exchanged glances. Anna-Greta reached across the table and rubbed Anders' knuckles. 'You mustn't think like that.'

'That's not what I mean. I know, you know that's what happened. She disappeared. I still don't understand how that was possible. But why…'

Anders held up his hands as if he were trying to grab hold of a ball that wasn't there, something he just couldn't grasp. He saw it all again. The faces, the tone of voice, the questions and the condolences. And nowhere…nowhere…

'Why didn't, why *doesn't* one single person suspect me? Why does everybody seem to regard it as…something natural?'

Simon rested his head on one hand and frowned. He too seemed to have realised this was strange. Anna-Greta looked at Anders with an expression that was impossible to interpret. She said, 'I imagine they have some respect for other people's grief.'

'But what about Holger?' said Anders. 'His wife drowns and Simon told me that lots of people suspected him straight away. Despite the fact that it's sort of…natural, somehow. Drowning. It happens. But Maja…I mean, the police asked questions, of course. But nobody here. Nobody.'

Simon finished his coffee and put his cup down very gently, as if

83

he didn't want to break the silence. A gust of wind sent a flurry of aspen leaves whirling past the window.

'It *is* rather strange,' said Simon. 'When you put it like that.'

Anna-Greta passed the coffee pot to Anders, pressing him to have another cup. 'I expect it depends on who's involved,' she said. 'Everybody here has known you since you were little. And everybody knows you wouldn't do such a thing. Unlike Holger.'

Anders poured himself half a cup. He wasn't convinced, he still thought it was hard to understand. But he said, 'Yes. Perhaps.'

They talked about other things. About possible repairs at the Shack, what they would do if Anders' outboard motor proved unwilling to start, about village gossip. Anders had no desire to get up and go home. There was nothing waiting for him but a cold house.

When there was a lull in the conversation he leaned back in his chair, folded his hands over his stomach and looked at Simon and Anna-Greta.

'How did you two actually get together? How did you meet?'

The question provoked a simultaneous grin from Simon and Anna-Greta. They looked at each other, and Simon shook his head. 'It's a long story.'

'Is there anything that needs doing?' asked Anders. Neither Simon nor Anna-Greta could come up with anything urgent. 'So won't you tell me the story then?'

Anna-Greta looked out of the window. The wind was getting up. The sky was overcast and breakers had appeared on the grey water. A couple of raindrops hit the glass. She rubbed a hand over her forehead and asked, 'How much do you know about your grandfather?'

Love in the archipelago

The story of the story

On the island of Domarö there are two very special bottles of schnapps. One is down in Nathan Lindgren's old boathouse, and will no doubt remain there until his relatives finally get around to sorting through his belongings. The other is in the possession of Evert Karlsson.

Evert is almost ninety, and has kept that bottle for nearly sixty years now. No one knows what the cheap schnapps inside might taste like, and no one is going to find out either, not as long as Evert is alive. He has no intention of removing the cork. The bottle and its contents are much too good a story for that.

That's why Evert has kept it: just so that when some stranger comes along who hasn't heard the story before, he can take the bottle out of the cupboard and say, 'Have you heard about the time when Anna-Greta smuggled schnapps in on the customs boat? You haven't? Well, it was like this...'

And he tells the story as he strokes the bottle with his fingertips. It's the best story he knows and, even better, it's absolutely true. When he has finished he passes the bottle around, with strict instructions to hold it carefully and not to drop it.

People look at the clear liquid behind the glass, and nothing about it indicates that it came ashore under such remarkable circumstances. But this very liquid was part of the story that made Anna-Greta notorious throughout the entire archipelago. It is, as Evert says, the original schnapps.

Then he puts the bottle back in the cupboard, and there it stays, waiting for the next occasion when it will be brought out and the story will be told once more.

The smuggler king's daughter

Things didn't turn out the way Anna-Greta had expected at all. Erik seemed to have exhausted himself finishing the house and getting married. Once that was done he had no strength left over to set any new goals.

The summer went reasonably well, while the original flame of passion was still burning, but towards autumn Anna-Greta began to ask herself if Erik really had been in love with her. Perhaps it was just a project, like the house. Build house, install wife. Job done.

Hitler had invaded Poland in August, and there was feverish activity in the archipelago. The coastline was to be fortified, and the navy's destroyers and transport ships were shuttling between Nåten and the islands around Stora Korset, which was the last outpost facing the Åland Sea. Two gun emplacements and a number of defence posts were to be built, and several young men on Domarö were involved in the preparatory work: using explosives to make cable trenches, building walls and putting up fences. The Russian attitude to Finland had hardened, and there was a great deal of uncertainty.

Erik had used all his savings to build the house, and the newly-weds limped along on Anna-Greta's earnings as a seamstress, Erik's casual employment at the sawmill in Nåten and contributions from their parents. It grieved Erik to have to accept money from his father, and when it came to Anna-Greta's father...well, Erik came straight out with it one evening after Anna-Greta had come home with yet more money from him, 'That money comes from criminal activity, you know.'

Anna-Greta was not slow to respond. 'Better criminal activity than no activity at all.'

As the autumn progressed a chill grew between them, and when Erik's old schoolmate Björn joined the teams building defences on the outer islands, Erik went with him. Anna-Greta didn't hear a word from him for the first two weeks in October.

She went down to the jetty every time a boat came in, watched the soldiers streaming up to the shop or to their work on the building going on around the harbour, but no one knew anything about those who were working on the outermost islands. Instead she was harangued at length about the poor food, the terrible clothes, the misery in the barracks out on the islands.

After two weeks Erik came home. He did little more than change his clothes and hand over a little money, and then he was off again. Anna-Greta didn't even manage to tell him she was expecting a child, the opportunity didn't arise. But it was true. She was twelve to fourteen weeks gone, according to the midwife.

Anna-Greta stood with her hands resting on her stomach as she watched Erik climb into Björn's fishing boat. She waved with her whole arm, and got a raised hand in response. Erik was with the boys, and didn't want to embarrass himself. That was the last she saw of him.

Ten days later she received a letter. Erik had been killed in an accident while carrying out his invaluable work for the defence of his country. The body arrived the following day, and Anna-Greta couldn't bring herself to look at it. A block of stone had come away from its mortar and fallen on Erik's head as he was plastering the walls on the inside of the defence post.

'He's not exactly in peak condition, if you know what I mean,' said the lieutenant who accompanied the body.

There was a funeral in Nåten and many expressions of commiseration and half-promises of help and support, but there was no widow's pension from the army, because technically Erik had not been a member of the armed services.

Anna-Greta was nineteen years old, in the fourth month of her pregnancy and widowed. She lived in a draughty house in a place that was not her home, and she had no particular skills or expertise. It's hardly surprising that at first it was a bleak and difficult winter for her.

Torgny and Maja had become as fond of her as if she had been their own daughter, and they helped out as best they could. Her father, too, did his best. But Anna-Greta didn't want to live on handouts. She wanted to be independent, for own sake and for her child's.

On top of everything else, the winter was unusually cold. The army drove across the ice in all-terrain vehicles until the cold became so severe that the engines froze up and they went over to horses. The soldiers who were on leave had to walk across the ice from the islands out in the archipelago.

One Saturday morning as Anna-Greta sat by her kitchen window, watching yet another lemming-like procession of frozen young men approaching the shore, she had an idea. There was a demand. She would meet it.

Maja had several sacks of wool in the hayloft in the barn. It would never be used, and she was happy to pass it on to Anna-Greta, who carried the sacks down to the kitchen in the Shack, the only room she used because she wanted to save on wood. She set to work. In a week she had knitted eight pairs of gloves in felted wool, the warmest you could imagine.

On Saturday morning, she positioned herself down by the jetty in Nåten and waited for the soldiers. The thermometer had read minus twenty-two that morning, and the cold hung in the air like a silent scream. She jumped up and down on the spot while she waited for the silent horde approaching from out in the bay.

The men's faces were bright red and their bodies were like knots when they came ashore. She asked if their hands were cold. Only one of them managed a vaguely indecent comment in response, the others merely nodded silently.

She showed them her wares.

There was muttering among the group. The gloves certainly looked considerably more substantial than the pathetic pot-holders supplied by the army, but three kronor a pair? They were off into town to enjoy themselves, after all, the money was needed for other things. They would soon be sitting on a warm bus and thawing out as the memory of the cold melted away. Pleasure before usefulness, they agreed.

The ice was broken by the lieutenant who had accompanied Erik's body a few months earlier. He dug out his purse and place three one-krona coins in Anna-Greta's hand. Then he pulled on the gloves to see how they felt.

'Incredible,' he said after a while. 'It's as if they warm you up from the inside.' He turned to his men. 'We're on leave now and I'm not going to start issuing orders. But take my advice. Buy some gloves. You'll thank me later.'

Whether it was because they were used to obeying, or because he'd managed to convince them, it didn't matter. Anna-Greta sold all her gloves. Despite their initial resistance, the men seemed very pleased with themselves as they tramped off towards the bus stop.

The lieutenant lingered behind. He removed his right glove and extended his hand as if they were meeting for the first time. Anna-Greta took it.

'My name is Folke.'

'Anna-Greta. Still.'

Folke looked down into the empty basket and pinched his nose. 'Have you considered socks? Pullovers, maybe?'

'Is there a shortage of those?'

'Well, not exactly. We do have them, but perhaps they weren't made for a winter like this, if you know what I mean.'

'In that case, thank you for the tip.'

Folke put his glove back on and saluted. When he had gone a few steps towards the bus stop he turned around and said, 'I'm on leave again in three weeks, anyway. If there's a pullover for sale, I'm...an interested party.'

When Anna-Greta got back home, she tipped the coins out on to the table and counted them. Twenty-four kronor, earned in the very best way, through her own work and her own idea. When she tried to share the money with Maja, her mother-in-law wouldn't hear of it. However, she might be interested in coming in on the deal if demand grew too high.

And it did. By the very next Saturday the word had spread about Anna-Greta's gloves, and she didn't have enough stock to satisfy everyone who wanted to buy for themselves, or for comrades who were still out on the islands. Maja took over the gloves while Anna-Greta concentrated on socks. And a pullover, of course.

If someone's alert, it only takes a hint to sniff the possibility of love. And that's what happened. At least on Folke's part. Once he had his pullover, he wanted socks as well. But they must be striped, so she had to make a pair especially for him. And then he needed a hat, of course.

Anna-Greta was bright enough to understand what was going on. Folke was kind and decent, and she did search her heart for signs of love, but found not a trace. There was nothing she could do about it. She played along as well as she could, but veered away from his tentative invitations.

Spring came and her belly expanded. The demand for warm clothing ceased, and Anna-Greta had to look around for something else. One day in April, a month before her due date, her father hove to at the jetty in a fishing boat she hadn't seen before.

After patting her stomach and inquiring after her health, he explained why he was really there. He had become acquainted with a Russian sea captain, and there was the chance of a good deal if he could just sail out to the three-mile limit and collect a load.

'But it's a bit…difficult for me in these waters, as you're perhaps aware.'

Oh yes, Anna-Greta knew. If a customs boat caught so much as a glimpse of her father, he would be searched immediately.

'So I was thinking that maybe if you could go, that would reduce the risk significantly. And they don't know this boat.'

Anna-Greta weighed up the pros and cons. It wasn't the risk of getting caught that bothered her as much as the purely moral step involved in moving over to *criminal activity*. On the other hand, there were already people who looked at her sideways because of her father. She might as well fulfil their expectations.

'How much would I get?' she asked.

Her father glanced at her protruding stomach and made an expansive gesture.

'Let's say half of the profit. Seeing as it's you.'

'Which is?'

'Two thousand, more or less.'

'Done.'

The whole thing went without a hitch. Although the glory days of smuggling liquor were long gone, there was still the matter of rationing and housekeeping, and a thousand litres of Russian vodka could always find throats to slip down.

The transportation was taken care of in the old way. The cases were loaded into a torpedo that was towed behind the boat. If customs turned up, you simply cut the rope and the cargo sank, taking with it a little floating buoy and a bag of salt heavy enough to keep the buoy submerged. After a few days the salt would dissolve and the buoy rose to the surface. Then all you had to do was salvage the cargo.

Anna-Greta sat in the stern with the rudder in her hand, waving goodbye to the Russian captain. She turned her gaze to the prow, where her father was crouching, then lifted her eyes to the horizon. The child kicked in her stomach and a feeling of dizziness came over her. It felt a bit like fear, but when she thought about it she realised what it was: freedom.

She gazed out at the archipelago far away in the distance, where the soldiers were keeping watch in their defence posts and people were getting on with this and that in their cottages. All those people, sitting still and keeping watch over what was theirs. She tightened her grip on the rudder and lifted her face to the wind.

I am free. I can do anything.

The child was born in the middle of April, a healthy boy she named Johan. In the summer, Anna-Greta invested a thousand kronor of the money she had earned in a fishing boat of her own.

Ulla Billqvist was on the radio singing about the boys in blue, but the truth was the boys in blue were bored to death on their islands. The Russians hadn't so much as dipped a finger in Swedish territorial waters, and Sweden's defenders were sitting in their barracks playing cards, glowering at the gulls and being as bored as it is humanly possible to be.

Anna-Greta had spoken to quite a lot of people, and had identified a need. During the winter it had been warmth that was lacking, during the summer it was some kind of diversion. Anna-Greta set to work.

By various methods, some of them entirely legal, some slightly more shady, she bought herself a stock of things that can ease loneliness and dispel melancholy. Sweets, snuff, tobacco, magazines and easily digestible thrillers, along with a range of games and puzzles. She didn't dare take any alcohol, but she let the soldiers know that if they needed anything along those lines when they were on leave, it could be arranged.

Then she travelled around between the islands on regular days, selling her wares. Business was good. Anna-Greta was not vain, but she was aware of the effect she had on the men. Some of them probably bought from her just so that they could spend a short while in her company, having a bit of a joke and perhaps brushing against her hand by mistake.

She knew that, and to a certain extent she exploited it. But she declined all advances before they had even been formulated properly. She had her man, and his name was Johan. When she was out on her business trips he was with his grandparents, an arrangement that suited them all very well.

During the winter she went back to her knitting, and the following summer she was back out in her boat once again.

Anyway. What about those bottles of schnapps?

That didn't happen until after the war, and it was connected to Folke. He wouldn't give up. She sometimes bumped into him on her trips around the islands; he had been promoted to the rank of captain, and she always took the time to chat for a while, but never did anything to raise his hopes.

After the war, Folke left the army and went to work for the customs service. Within a couple of years he was the captain of one of the customs cruisers.

Presumably with the aim of impressing Anna-Greta, he moored the cruiser at her jetty one day and strode up to her house in full uniform: epaulettes, peaked cap, the lot. He asked if she would like to accompany him on a little trip, he had to carry out an official check.

Anna-Greta's father was visiting on that particular day, and there was an exchange of casual remarks with a caustic undertone between him and Folke. However, by that stage her father had given up his activities, and there was no real antagonism. Her father said he would be happy to look after Johan if Anna-Greta wanted to go out on a pleasure cruise with the enemy.

The cruiser raced out to the three-mile limit. Like most men, Folke was under the mistaken impression that travelling at a high speed can make a woman's heart melt, and he pushed the cruiser to the limit, standing there on the bridge and pretending to be unmoved. Anna-Greta thought it was quite entertaining to travel so fast, but nothing more.

The cargo boat just outside the limit was boarded with the usual polite exchanges. Anna-Greta thought it all looked somehow familiar. Everything became clear when the captain appeared. It was the same Russian captain who had sold vodka to her and her father several years earlier. He recognised her, too, but gave nothing away.

Anna-Greta had a little money with her, and when Folke and his men went below to check the interior of the boat, she whispered to the captain, 'Four cases.'

The captain looked at her with a mixture of terror and delight. 'But where?'

Anna-Greta pointed. Right at the back of the customs cruiser hung a covered lifeboat. 'There. Underneath the tarp.'

The captain took the money and gave the order to his crew. Then he went below to make sure Folke and the others stayed there until the goods had been stowed.

They found what they expected to find in the hold, but there wasn't much they could do about it as the boat was in international waters. They just wanted to check the amounts, and to see if there was any need for special vigilance.

Anna-Greta had never seen the Russian captain smile, but he was certainly smiling as he waved goodbye to Anna-Greta and the customs boat. In fact, he was grinning from ear to ear.

'He seems like quite a good bloke, in spite of everything,' said Folke.

'He does,' replied Anna-Greta.

When the cruiser hove to at Anna-Greta's jetty, she asked if she could perhaps invite the crew to her house for coffee and cake just to say thank you for the trip. They accepted with pleasure, and the men trooped up to the Shack.

While they were playing with Johan, Anna-Greta took her father to one side and said there were a couple of things that needed to be collected from the lifeboat. Perhaps he could put them in the boat-house for the time being. Her father's jaw dropped and a fire ignited in his eyes. He said nothing, he merely nodded and went out.

And then, of course, Anna-Greta was having some problems with the leaky woodshed at the front of the house. As her father disappeared around the corner, she took Folke and the others to the woodshed and listened to their advice on how she could reinforce the construction or how she might go about building a new one.

After ten minutes her father was back, at which point she thanked the men for all their help and invited them to enjoy the promised coffee.

When the cruiser was on its way and their visitors had been properly waved off, her father turned to Anna-Greta as she stood there holding Johan by the hand, and said, 'This is the best bloody thing ever.'

'Not one word.'

'No, no.'

Within a month the whole archipelago knew the story of how Anna-Greta had smuggled schnapps on the customs boat. Her father had probably tried to keep his mouth shut, but it just couldn't be done; he was far too proud of his daughter and of the great story in which he had played his small part.

Eventually the story must have reached Folke's ears as well, since he never came to call on Anna-Greta again. She told her father off for blabbing and thus destroying Folke's reputation, but what was done was done. Anna-Greta had never been one for regrets.

Anyway, the schnapps was decanted into bottles and one of them eventually ended up in Evert Karlsson's cupboard, where it stands to this day.

The magician

Life could have been perfect for Simon at the beginning of the 1950s. He was in his early thirties, the time when we reap, if we are lucky, what we have sown during our youth. And he was reaping a rich harvest. Success after success.

For a few years he and his wife Marita—under the name El

Simon & Simonita—had been among the most popular artists playing the summer shows in the big parks. For the last couple of summers they had even had to turn down some engagements to avoid double-bookings.

This spring, Simon had found out that they could look forward to the most desirable booking of all for the autumn: the variety show at Stockholm's Chinese Theatre, for two weeks in October. This would in turn give them the opportunity to ask for higher fees in the parks. Having performed at the Chinese Theatre was a mark of honour in the profession.

Their program wasn't actually anything special: a little mind-reading, some sleight of hand involving cards, a few tricks with cloths. An unusually quick substitution trunk, plus a version of sawing the lady in half, with the twist that Marita was divided into three sections rather than just two. An escapology feature. Nothing special.

But they did have a particular style on stage. Simon's measured, concentrated movements and patter set against Marita's light, whirling steps created a kind of dance that it was difficult to take your eyes off. In addition, Simon was elegant and Marita—well, Marita had glamour.

A weekly magazine had done an at-home-with feature on the couple, and the photographer had found it very difficult to stop taking pictures of Marita—posed beside the armchair, next to the gramophone; holding a lid and gazing ecstatically down into the saucepan.

And so everything should have been wonderful, but it wasn't. Simon was frankly unhappy and, as so often happens the same thing lay at the root of both his success and his unhappiness: Marita.

Simon had a tendency to brood. This could be very useful when it came to getting to the bottom of something, for example dissecting a conjuring trick so that he could work out how to improve it. Among other things, he was the first to saw the lady in half using a chainsaw. Most illusionists made a big thing of spinning the separated sections around on the stage. Simon had thought it through, and come to the conclusion that it wasn't the separate *parts* that were interesting, but the separation itself.

The huge handsaw that was normally used looked like a stage prop. But the raw physicality of a chainsaw, set against his own elegant appearance and Marita's feather-light frailty—that might possibly achieve the desired effect.

And indeed it was. At one performance a couple of people fainted when Simon started up the big chainsaw. Fortunately there was a reporter in the audience, and it proved to be excellent publicity. This was the result of Simon's brooding on the question of sawing the lady in half.

Marita was cut from a different cloth. When Simon met her in the mid-1940s, she had been a bright, energetic woman with ambitions to be a dancer, and she moved through the nightclubs of Stockholm like a wisp of smoke.

It was not until a year or so after they joined forces that Simon discovered her secret box. A shoebox containing some twenty Benzedrine inhalers. Simon assumed she was using it as an aid to slimming, and didn't mention the matter.

But he became vigilant, and soon he could see what she was doing. They might be having a drink, spirits or wine, and he would notice her fiddling with something in her handbag. Eventually one night he grabbed her hand, pulled it out of her bag and found…a strip of paper. He didn't understand.

By this stage Marita was quite drunk. She began to sneer at him in front of their companions at the table. How blind and stupid he was, and above all how boring. As Marita staggered off in the direction of the ladies' toilets, someone explained it to Simon: his wife was a drug user.

The strip of paper was what you found if you broke open an inhaler. It was impregnated with Benzedrine, a kind of amphetamine. All you had to do was roll up the strip of paper and swallow it: suddenly you had a spring in your step.

Simon left before Marita came back from the toilet. He went straight home and threw her destructive metal tubes down the rubbish chute. Marita went crazy when she found out what he'd done, but soon calmed down. Far too soon. Simon suspected she was confident she could replace the stash he had thrown away.

It took a few weeks for him to track down her supplier, a former boyfriend who had been a quartermaster in the army. He had stolen from the stores a huge quantity of inhalers meant to keep fatigue at bay during long watches. He had initiated Marita in the use of the drug and its effect on the central nervous system, and had carried on supplying her after their love affair ended.

Simon issued what threats he could muster. The police, a beating, public humiliation. He didn't know if it would have any effect, but he did his best.

The effect was that Marita's underhand ways took more dramatic forms. She could disappear for days on end, and refuse to say where she had been. She made it clear to Simon that he could sit and rot in their apartment if he wanted to, but she had a life to live.

She never missed a performance, though. Her disappearances always coincided with a gap between engagements. When it was time for her entrance she was there, sparkling as she always had, tripping lightly on to the stage. It was partly for this reason that Simon tried to keep their calendar as full as possible.

But he wasn't happy.

He needed Marita. She was his partner and the other half of his act—without her he would probably be no more than a competent conjuror. And she was his wife. He still loved her, in some ways. But he wasn't happy.

And so in the spring of 1953 Simon was at the peak of his career, leafing through their booking schedule with a feeling of unease in the pit of his stomach. The engagement at the Chinese Theatre lay ahead, and the summer was looking good. But the way things had turned out, there were three completely blank weeks in July. June and August were more or less full, but those weeks in July were bothering him.

He could see himself sitting there in the summer heat in Stockholm with a great lump of fear in his chest, while Marita was out enjoying herself God knows where or how. He didn't want that. He definitely didn't want that.

However, there was one possibility. Perhaps it was finally time to take action? He picked up the daily newspaper, *Dagens Nyheter*, and turned to the ads for accommodation. Under the heading 'Summer Cottages' he read:

'Well-maintained house on the island of Domarö in southern Roslagen. Sea frontage with own jetty. Hire boat available. 80 square metres. Large garden. Rented on an annual basis. Contact: Anna-Greta Ivarsson.'

Domarö.

Hopefully it really was an island, without a direct link to the mainland. If he could get Marita away from the destructive influence of Stockholm, then perhaps things would work out. And it wouldn't do any harm to have a place to get away to when life was moving too fast.

He made the call.

The woman who answered explained politely that no one else had expressed an interest, so all he had to do was come out and take a look. The rent was one thousand kronor per year, and that was non-negotiable. Would he like her to tell him how to get there?

'Yes please,' said Simon. 'But there was one other thing I was wondering about. Is it an island?'

'You're asking me if it's an island?'

'Yes, is there…is there water all around it?'

There was silence on the other end of the line for a few seconds. Then the woman cleared her throat and said, 'Yes, it is an island. With water all around it. Rather a lot of water, in fact.'

Simon closed his eyes as if he were in pain. 'I was just wondering.'

'Oh, we've just got a telephone link to the mainland, if that's what you were thinking?'

'No, it was just…so how do people get there?'

'There's a tender. From Nåten, which is on a bus route. Would you like more details?'

'Yes…please.'

Simon made a note of the numbers of buses to and from Norrtälje, and said that he would ring in advance and come over one day. When he hung up he was sweating profusely. He had made himself sound ridiculous and felt very uncomfortable. Her voice alone had been enough to make him realise he didn't want to look ridiculous in front of this woman. Anna-Greta.

Marita made no comment on his plans for the summer, but he had to go out and take a look at the place by himself. One day at the end of April, Simon followed Anna-Greta's instructions, and after two and a half hours travelling by bus and by boat, he was standing by the waiting room on the steamboat jetty on Domarö.

The woman who came to meet him was wearing a knitted hat, with two long, dark brown plaits emerging from underneath it. Her hand was small, her handshake firm.

'Welcome,' she said.

'Thank you.'

'Good journey?'

'Fine, thank you.'

Anna-Greta waved in the direction of the sea.

'There's…rather a lot of water here, as you can see.'

As Simon followed Anna-Greta up from the harbour, he tried to imagine it: that this would be *the place*. That this was the first of countless times he would walk up this path, see the things he could see now: the jetties, the boathouses, the gravel track, the diesel tank, the alarm bell. The smell of the sea and the particular quality of light in the sky.

He tried to see himself in two years, five years, ten. As an old man, walking along the same path. Could he imagine that?

Yes. I can imagine that.

When they reached the top of the path, Simon kept his fingers crossed that it would be *that* house. The white one with a little glass veranda looking out over a grassy slope down to the jetty. It didn't look much on a cloudy day like this with not a scrap of green in sight, but he could just picture how it would look in summer.

A boy of about thirteen was standing in the garden with his hands pushed deep in the pockets of a leather jacket. He was slim with short hair, and there was something mischievous in the look he gave Simon, weighing him up.

'Johan,' said Anna-Greta to the boy, 'could you fetch the key for Seaview Cottage, please?'

The boy shrugged his shoulders and ambled off towards a two-storey house a hundred metres away. Simon glanced around the plot, which also seemed to include a cottage on the other side of the inlet. Anna-Greta followed his eyes and said, 'The Shack. There's nobody living there at the moment.'

'Do you live here alone?'

'Well, there's me and Johan. Aren't you going to inspect the property?'

Simon did as he was told and took a random stroll around. Looked at the lid of the well, the lawn, the jetty. It was completely pointless. He had already decided. When Johan came back with the key and Simon saw inside the house, he was even more certain. When they got back outside he said, 'I'll take it.'

Papers were signed and Simon paid the deposit. Anna-Greta offered him a cup of coffee, as it would be an hour before the tender went back. Simon learned that Anna-Greta had inherited her house from her parents-in-law, who had both died a couple of years earlier. Johan answered his questions politely, but said no more than was necessary.

When it was time for Simon to think about leaving, Johan suddenly asked, 'What's your job?'

Anna-Greta said, 'Johan...'

'It's a natural thing to ask,' said Simon, 'if we're going to be neighbours. I'm a magician.'

Johan looked at him with a sceptical expression. 'What do you mean, a magician?'

'People pay to come and watch me do magic tricks.'

'*Really?*'

'Yes. Really. Well, the tricks aren't real, it's just—'

'I know that. But you're an illusionist, then?'

Simon smiled. Not many people outside magicians' circles would use that term. 'You're very well informed.'

Johan didn't answer. Instead he sat there nodding to himself for a couple of seconds, then he burst out, 'I thought you were just some boring bloke.'

Anna-Greta brought her hand down on the table. 'Johan! That's not the way to speak to a guest!'

Simon got to his feet. 'I am just some boring bloke. *As well.*' He held Johan's gaze for a few seconds, and something happened between them. Simon sensed that he had just made a friend. 'I'd better be on my way.'

At the beginning of July, Simon hired their usual driver to take him and Marita to Nåten with all their luggage. Marita loved the place, and Simon was able to relax. For five days. Perhaps the abstinence got too much for her, or possibly the isolation, but on the morning of the sixth day Marita declared that she had to go into Stockholm.

'But we've only just got here,' said Simon. 'Try to relax a little. Rest.'

'I have rested. It's wonderful here, and I'm going crazy. Do you know what I did last night? I sat out in the garden staring up at the sky and prayed to God that a plane might appear, so that at least *something* was happening. I can't handle it. I'll be back tomorrow.'

She didn't come back the following day, nor the day after that. When she turned up on the third day, she dragged herself up the hill from the steamboat jetty. She had dark circles under her eyes and she immediately fell into bed and went out like a light.

When Simon went through her overnight bag, he didn't find any

102

inhalers. He was just about to close the bag and thank providence for that small dispensation when he noticed the lining bulging oddly. He pushed his fingers inside and found a slender case containing a syringe and a small tin of white powder.

It was a glorious summer's day. There was a stillness everywhere; only the buzzing of the insects created any movement in the air at all. A pair of swans were teaching their young to look for food in the inlet. Simon sat in the lilac arbour beside the path as if he were in a trance, with a tin and a case in his hand. Yes, they fitted into his hand. Two innocent, trivial-looking objects that contained an army of devils. He didn't know what to do, couldn't summon up the energy to do anything.

When Anna-Greta walked by, there must have been something in his vacant gaze that made her stop.

'How are you?' she asked.

Simon was still sitting there with his hand open and outstretched, as if he had a present he wanted to give her. He had no strength left for lies.

'My wife is a drug addict,' he said.

Anna-Greta looked at the objects in his hand. 'What's that?'

'I don't know. Amphetamine, I think.'

Simon was on the verge of tears, but managed to pull himself together. If Anna-Greta did know anything about amphetamines, it wasn't appropriate to discuss it with her. Johan would sometimes come over for a chat, and Anna-Greta would hardly want her son to be spending time with drug addicts. Perhaps she might not even want to rent the house to him any longer.

Simon cleared his throat and said, 'But it's under control.'

Anna-Greta gazed at him incredulously. 'But how can it be?' When Simon didn't respond, she asked, 'So what are you going to do with that?'

'I don't know. I thought I might…bury it.'

'Don't do that. She'll just force you to tell her where you've hidden it. I've seen how alcoholics behave. I don't think there can be much difference. Throw it in the sea instead.'

Simon looked out towards the jetty, which seemed to be floating on the sparkling water. He didn't want to besmirch the place where he went down to swim every morning. 'Here?' he asked, as if seeking permission.

Anna-Greta also looked at the jetty and seemed to have the same thought. She shook her head.

'I was just going to go over to Nåten. If you come with me, you can…dump the rubbish on the way.'

Simone walked down to the jetty with her and stood there at something of a loss as she started up the engine with a practised hand, cast off and told him to climb aboard. Once they had set off he stole a glance at her as she sat by the tiller, gazing out to sea with her eyes narrowed against the sunlight.

She was no great beauty, her cheekbones were far too prominent and her eyes a little too deep-set for that. But she was arresting, and Simon caught himself following a chain of thought like the one he had followed when he came to Domarö for the first time.

Five years, ten years, a lifetime. Would I?
Yes.

He had seen enough of ephemeral beauty in the theatrical world to know that Anna-Greta's looks were the kind that lasted. One of those blessed individuals who actually grow more beautiful with the passing years.

Anna-Greta caught his eye and Simon blushed slightly, pushing the thought away. She had given no indication that she might have the slightest interest in him in that way, not with a gesture or a word. Besides which he was married, for God's sake. He had absolutely no right to be thinking like this.

Anna-Greta slowed the engine and nodded towards the water. Simon got to his feet unsteadily and held the case and the tin out over the side. 'It feels as if I ought to sing something.'

'Like what?'

'I don't know.'

He threw the objects into the sea and sat down again. Anna-Greta picked up speed. It felt as if they had just gone through some kind of ritual together, which was why he had got the idea about the song. He didn't know what kind of ritual it was, or what it meant. No song came into his mind. Just an emptiness and a sense of dread that grew and grew while they were in Nåten, developing into sheer terror by the time they moored at the jetty back home and said goodbye.

He was afraid of what was going to happen to Marita and he was afraid of Marita. Of what would happen now the mask was off and everything was out in the open.

Life with a junkie. The episodes are so tedious, and you've heard it all before. Let's just say that after this Marita made no effort to hide her addiction. She didn't spend many more days on Domarö that summer.

She held it together during the autumn, and her performances at the Chinese Theatre were stunning. Then things went downhill. Simon would go looking for her at addresses of ill-repute and would manage to get her into some kind of treatment for a short period. Then she would disappear again. She missed a couple of shows and was nowhere to be found, until Simon got a call from Copenhagen and went over there.

And so on, and so on.

He had called Anna-Greta and Johan to invite them to the Chinese Theatre. They came and were amazed. Then Johan rang and asked about other places where they could go to see illusionists, and when Simon called back it was Anna-Greta who answered.

After that they got into the habit of ringing each other once a week or so. Anna-Greta was completely self-sufficient, but she was also quite lonely. She let it be known, without going into detail, that she had been involved in certain activities which meant that certain people didn't want anything to do with her.

She enjoyed Simon's anecdotes from the theatrical world, and sympathised with his concerns for Marita. As spring moved into summer they both came to depend on these conversations, and became sulky and anxious if anything got in the way and led to the postponement of that week's call.

Via a hundred kilometres of copper cable they became friends, but neither of them touched on the topic of love with so much as a word. That wasn't the point; they were just two people with very different lives who could nevertheless meet on a level of mutual conversation. They understood each other, and they enjoyed each other's company. There was no possibility of anything else between them.

And Marita? What happened to her?

That was anybody's guess.

There was nothing to suggest that her drug use was increasing, and after a couple of lapses she was as reliable as before when it came to performances. But as soon as she had the opportunity, she disappeared. Simon heard from acquaintances that she was enjoying herself in various clubs at night, often with other men.

He had given up on her. When she asked for help he always gave it, but he no longer harboured any illusions of a normal home life with her, a woman who was too beautiful for her own good—or anyone else's. To avoid tempting fate, Simon put together a program that he could perform solo, and accepted a couple of bookings.

His attitude was stoical. As long as things didn't get any worse, he could cope. He had promised to love Marita for better or worse, and if he could no longer love her, he saw it as his duty at least to keep his promise when it came to the hard times.

One spring day Simon was walking along Strandvägen on his way down to the Chinese Theatre to discuss possible future bookings with the management. The leaves on the trees were just bursting into life, and all the happy little birds were chirruping away. Simon kept his eyes fixed on the ground, thinking about nothing.

Then a smell reached his nostrils. At first he couldn't even say what it was, but his chest expanded, he was suddenly able to breathe and tears came into his eyes. He looked up and saw that he had reached Norrmalmstorg. The smell was coming from the quayside at

Nybro, and it was the sea he could sense. That faint hint of salt that would grow stronger further away, further out. Out on Domarö.

He straightened up and filled his lungs with air. Not long to go. Despite financial pressures he had kept this summer free so that he could spend five, maybe six weeks on Domarö. He would have liked to stay longer, but Marita had expensive habits and he couldn't actually conjure up money, even if he made it look as if he could.

Perhaps I ought to do something out there? Try to arrange things so that I get a couple of bookings nearby?

He stopped on the edge of Berzelii Park and looked out towards Nybrokajen. That was when he got the idea.

Escape

Everyone had been waiting for it for almost a month now. At first it had been just a rumour, then posters had gone up. And then, the day before yesterday, it had even been mentioned on the radio. That magician who rented the cottage from Anna-Greta was going to perform his escapology number just by the Domarö steamboat jetty.

The time was set for twelve o'clock. Curious spectators began arriving from the mainland and from other islands as early as ten o'clock, to be sure of getting a good place and to sound out the terrain. You could see them walking around the jetty, staring down into the water to see if they could spot any special equipment to help him out, any secret arrangements.

At half-past eleven, a journalist and a photographer from *Norrtelje Tidning* arrived. By that time a couple of hundred people were crammed together on the steamboat jetty. The journalist explained to those who were interested that of course it was forbidden to advertise such risky enterprises in the newspaper, but writing about them was absolutely fine.

While they waited for the main attraction, it was a Stockholmer who rented a property on another island who drew the largest crowd of listeners. Many had heard of the famous Danish escapologist Bernardi, but the Stockholmer was the only one who had actually seen him appear, at the Brazil Jack Circus. The tense atmosphere was heightened as the Stockholmer told the story of how Bernardi had died on Bornholm during an escape attempt just like this one.

The crowd around the Stockholmer dispersed only when a police officer arrived. Although to be honest it wasn't a *real* policeman. It was Göran Holmberg. He had gone to the police training academy and worked in the field for a couple of years, that was true, but he was from the island after all. When he appeared dressed for the occasion in full uniform, complete with cap, he attracted teasing rather than genuine respect.

'Make way for the forces of the law', 'Arrest Karlsson, he's drunk and it's still only morning!' and similar comments were directed at Göran, who explained that it was Simon who had asked him to come along. For the effect, so to speak. He had also been asked to bring a pair of handcuffs with him, and these were passed around among all those who wanted to examine them. They were pulled and prodded, and it was established that, yes indeed, they were the genuine article.

A small number of people had seen Simon performing with his assistant in a show in the open-air venue Gröna Lund, but he hadn't performed an escapology number on that occasion. In any case, this whole event was a publicity stunt for the series of performances Simon was due to give at the local community theatre in Nåten during the summer. By twelve o'clock it looked as if he had undeniably succeeded. There were at least five hundred people gathered on and around the jetty as Simon came walking down from his cottage.

Which was a bit odd. A magician should make an entrance, after all, perhaps appear in a puff of smoke. But this was just that bloke who rented from Anna-Greta, strolling down from his cottage on the other side of the inlet. This diminished the mystique, but increased the level of anxiety. Would he be able to do it, this… summer visitor?

Room had been made for Johan and Anna-Greta right at the front when they came down to the jetty. After all, they were *involved*, in a sense. Someone nudged Anna-Greta.

'You might need to look for another tenant after this!'

Anna-Greta smiled. 'Well, we'll see.'

She wasn't in the habit of exposing her feelings for general consumption, and as she stood there on the edge of the jetty with her hands pushed deep into the pockets of her cardigan, her face gave away no hint of emotional turmoil.

But to tell the truth, even she was a little anxious. She knew that Marita had disappeared almost a week ago, and that Simon wasn't feeling well. And the water was cold. Nine degrees. She had checked it herself that morning.

It'll be fine, she told herself, gazing down into the dark water. *I'm sure he knows what he's doing...let's hope so, anyway.*

It wasn't easy to impress Anna-Greta. The number of people who had turned up didn't surprise her, people would gather for anything, as long as it was a novelty. When someone asked her how she thought Simon did it, she replied, 'I expect it's something to do with his joints.'

The person who had asked smiled indulgently: obviously Anna-Greta hadn't learned anything from Simon. But she had, in a roundabout way. When he walked around his garden without his shirt on, she had noticed that there was something strange about his frame: the bones stuck out at odd angles, as if the joints weren't quite in place.

She had come to the conclusion that his escapology had created that body, or that he had got into escapology because he was made that way. When she was young she had seen a contortionist at the circus, and he had looked very similar. Whatever it was that held the bones together was more flexible than in normal people.

From this she had concluded that some kind of manoeuvring lay behind the ability to free himself from chains and ropes. She didn't want to say any more: Simon's secrets were his own affair. Besides which, she didn't see how you could manoeuvre your way out of handcuffs. But there must be ways of doing that as well—at least, she hoped so.

As Simon approached the jetty dressed in his bathrobe, the crowd began to applaud. Anna-Greta joined in, glancing at Johan. He was clapping too, but his face was tense and his eyes were fixed on Simon, who was strolling along as if he were just on his way down to take a dip.

Anna-Greta knew that Johan was fond of Simon. Even the previous summer he would disappear for a couple of hours, then come home and show off some trick Simon had taught him. Simple things, according to Simon, but Anna-Greta certainly couldn't see how Johan did it when he smacked a salt-cellar straight through the table.

Anna-Greta stroked Johan's back and he nodded, without taking his eyes off Simon. It wasn't surprising that he was tense; Anna-Greta had read what it said on the poster:

CAN ANYONE ENDURE THIS???

To be fettered hand and foot
with chains and handcuffs?
To be sealed in a sack and
cast into the sea?
To cheat death as the sack
sinks to the bottom?

On Saturday July 15th **El Simon** will
attempt all this at the Domarö jetty.

WILL HE SURVIVE???

Johan was bright enough to realise that all this was for effect, but the very fact that the words 'drowning' and 'fettered' are on the same page as the name of someone you are fond of is quite enough to make you swallow a little harder. Anna-Greta had no particular feelings for Simon, he was pleasant company and a good tenant, nothing more.

And yet she still had to clench her fists in her pockets to stop herself chewing at her nails.

Simon went over to one of the boathouses, undid the latch and went inside. When he came out he was carrying a bundle, which he carried over to the spectators. There was a rattling noise as he threw the bundle on the ground and announced in a loud voice:

'Ladies and gentlemen! It's wonderful to see so many of you here. In front of me on the ground I have a set of chains, ropes and padlocks. I would like to invite two strong gentlemen from the audience to come up and use these items to bind and chain me to the best of their ability, until they are convinced that I cannot escape.'

Simon let his bathrobe fall to the ground. He was wearing only a pair of dark blue swimming trunks, and looked alarmingly thin and frail.

Ragnar Pettersson stepped forward, which was only to be expected. He was renowned for having single-handedly pulled out one of his cows that had got stuck in the bog down by the shore of the inlet. Nobody could work out how he had done it, but ever since then he had been generally regarded as a strongman.

He was followed by a man who worked at the shipyard in Nåten, but Anna-Greta didn't know his name. The short-sleeved shirt he was wearing looked as if it was a size too small. It strained over his muscles, and perhaps that was exactly the effect he was aiming for.

The two men got to work straight away, and something happened to their movements, their eyes. As soon as they had the chains and ropes in their hands, they ceased to regard Simon as a person. He was a nut to be cracked, a problem to be solved, nothing more or less. Beyond that there was nothing to be taken into account.

Anna-Greta gritted her teeth as the man from Nåten wound and pulled at the chains so hard that Simon's skin puckered and turned red. It looked as if it was painful, but Simon simply stood there with his eyes closed, his hands folded over his midriff. A couple of times his lips twitched when one of the men braced himself and gave the chains an extra tug before fastening the padlocks.

Finally they were satisfied. Both wiped the sweat from their foreheads and nodded to each other. There must have been thirty kilos of chains wound around Simon, secured in different places with four padlocks. They had hardly used the ropes, except in two places where they had brought them in as an afterthought, just to tighten the chains.

The men took a couple of steps back and contemplated their handiwork. They were quite satisfied, and you could see why. It looked utterly impossible to escape from the web of metal they had created.

Simon opened his eyes and Anna-Greta's stomach contracted. Around the fettered man was an empty circle perhaps twenty metres deep.

Alone.

Anna-Greta thought: *Alone.* Simon looked so horribly alone in that moment. Someone who had been ejected from the community, utterly disarmed. And now they were going to throw him in the sea. There was a powerful element of degradation about the whole thing: an individual allowing other people to do this to him. A second after Simon opened his eyes, it was as if he had caught a glimpse of that very thing. It was that expression that made Anna-Greta's stomach contract, before it disappeared and Simon looked from one man to the other and said, 'Are you satisfied? Are you convinced that I can't escape?'

Ragnar grabbed hold of one of the chains and pulled at it, then shrugged and said, 'Well, I certainly couldn't do it.'

Someone in the crowd shouted, 'You want to do that with your cows, Ragnar, then they won't go running off!'

People from Domarö laughed, the rest didn't get the joke. Simon asked the two men to carry him to the edge of the jetty, which they did. Anna-Greta and Johan moved back to make room, and Simon ended up only a metre or so away from them. Simon's eyes met Anna-Greta's, and a smile flitted across his lips. Anna-Greta tried to smile back, but couldn't quite manage it.

'And now,' said Simon, 'I would like to ask a third person to pull the sack up around me and secure the top.'

Before anyone had time to step forward, someone further back shouted, 'What about the handcuffs, then? What's happening with them?'

Suddenly Simon looked a little bit scared. He closed his eyes without speaking. Then he nodded to Göran, who stepped forward with the handcuffs and asked, 'Are you sure about this?'

'No,' said Simon. 'But I suppose I'll have to give it a try.'

Göran scratched the back of his neck and looked as if he couldn't quite decide what to do. Situations like this had presumably not formed part of his training at the police academy. In the end he fed the handcuffs through the chains and locked them around Simon's wrists.

By this stage Anna-Greta had folded her arms tightly across her chest to stop herself from chewing at her nails. She examined Simon's face, trying to gauge how much of this latest turn of events was merely theatre, part of the show, or if Simon really wasn't sure if he could do it. It was impossible to tell.

The photographer took some pictures of Simon as he stood there out on the edge of the jetty. A man Anna-Greta had never seen before—a Stockholmer, judging by his slender hands—stepped forward and declared himself willing to tie the sack. Simon turned to Johan and said, 'Would you like to check one last time?'

Johan pulled at the chains, and as he did so Anna-Greta saw Simon lean forward and whisper something to him. Then Johan took a step back and nodded. The Stockholmer pulled the sack up around Simon and tied the top with a piece of rope.

It looked horrible. The brown sack right on the edge. It was a point of darkness, of finality. People seemed to sense this; the banter and the jokes had died away, and there was absolute silence now.

'Throw me in,' said Simon's voice from inside the sack.

Five seconds passed. Then ten. Still there was silence, and no one volunteered. It wasn't irrevocable yet. They could open the sack, undo the chains. But once the sack was in the water, there wasn't much anyone could do. The sea was six metres deep off the jetty.

If Simon failed, the person who had pushed the sack into the water would be responsible. People looked at each other, but no one stepped forward. Simon was moving inside the sack, they could hear the chains squeaking slightly as the links rubbed against one another. A couple of cameras clicked. Still no one.

'Throw me in the sea.'

Presumably it would have been easier if Simon had said something ordinary and amusing, such as 'Am I supposed to stand here all day?' or 'The chains are starting to get rusty in here', but obviously he wasn't interested in relieving the dramatic tension.

And yet it seemed he might have to. After a minute, still no one had come forward. People were beginning to feel uncomfortable. Perhaps this was how it felt when Jesus told the person who was without sin to cast the first stone.

Suddenly the muscular man from Nåten cleared his throat, and without further ado he stepped forward and shoved the sack. It hit the water with a dull splash, and a collective gasp ran through the crowd. People pushed forward to look, and Anna-Greta had to fight to avoid being nudged into the water by the surge.

There wasn't much to see. A stream of bubbles rose from the sack as it sank, but after thirty seconds the last bubble had burst on the surface, and there was only the dark water to be seen. Those who had been hoping to see something of Simon's struggle were disappointed; it was impossible to see beyond a depth of three metres.

When one minute had passed, people began muttering to each other: did anyone know how long a person could actually hold their breath? Would it be possible to bring the man up if he didn't succeed? Did anyone have the keys to those padlocks?

Another minute passed, and now a large number of people were becoming anxious. Why hadn't anyone attached a safety line to the sack, why hadn't a time limit been set, after which they should try to rescue the man, why…?

The man who had pushed the sack into the water appeared to be the most anxious of all. He was staring down into the water, and the body that had been so confident in its strength and authority now seemed to have sunk in on itself; his movements were jerky, his eyes were flicking here and there, his hands constantly rubbing against each other.

Anna-Greta stood there motionless, hugging herself. Hard. All around her people were looking from their watches to the surface of the water, back and forth, but Anna-Greta had fixed her gaze on Gåvasten lighthouse, far away in the distance. She stared at the lighthouse and waited. Waited for the splash as Simon's body broke the surface, the sudden intake of breath.

But it didn't come.

When three minutes had passed, someone shouted out, 'But he's going to die!' A murmur of agreement was heard, but still no one did anything. Anna-Greta tore her gaze away from the lighthouse, and couldn't help herself from looking down at the surface of the water. It was black and empty. Nothing was moving.

Come on. Come on now, Simon.

She could see it right in front of her, she could see right through the water, past the limit of normal visibility, right down to the bottom where Simon lay battling among the mud and rusty bits of metal. She saw him escape, saw the sack open and saw him push away from the seabed, up towards the light.

But that wasn't what happened. What did actually happen took place inside Anna-Greta. Something that had been sunken and thrown away freed itself down there in the darkness, broke the chain she had wound around it and swam towards the surface. It rose up through her body and fastened in her throat in a lump. She wanted to cry.

I love this bloody man.

She started to tremble.

Love. Don't disappear.

Her eyes filled with tears when someone behind her shouted, 'Four minutes!' and she clamped her hands together, pressed them against her heart and cursed herself because it was already too late, it was going to happen again, it was going to…

Then she felt a hand on her arm. Her vision was blurred as she looked up and saw that the hand belonged to Johan. He winked and nodded. She didn't understand what he meant, how he could be so calm.

The man who had pushed Simon in pulled off his shirt and dived into the water. Anna-Greta squeezed Johan's hand as the crowd surged forward once again. The man broke the surface of the water. He shook his head, took a deep breath and dived once more.

Then they heard a voice from inland.

'Is it me you're looking for?'

There was a rustling noise as fabric rubbed against fabric and the whole crowd turned around as one. Over by the boathouse stood Simon. A pattern of red lines left by the chains criss-crossed his body. He walked over to Göran and gave him the locked handcuffs.

'I thought you might want these back.'

Simon pulled on his bathrobe, and someone next to Anna-Greta shouted to the man from Nåten, who had popped up again, 'Kalle, he's here! You can stop looking!'

'What the hell!' shouted Kalle from down in the water, and a collective paralysis was broken. First came laughter, and then the applause broke out. It echoed across the whole area like the beating wings of a flock of birds lifting from the surface of the water, and it seemed as if it would never end.

People came forward and patted Simon as if he were their greatest treasure, rescued at long last from the bottom of the sea. Kalle's attitude was somewhat less positive as he hauled himself up on to the jetty with his teeth chattering. Simon had obviously foreseen this situation, because he brought a bottle of decent schnapps out of the boathouse and offered Kalle a drink or two to help him thaw out, which he gratefully accepted. After quarter of an hour he was the most enthusiastic admirer of Simon's feat.

People stood around the boathouse where the two men were sitting side by side on the steps. They laughed at Kalle, who was tipsy from the schnapps and the rollercoaster of emotions he had gone through in such quick succession, as he flung his arms out in Simon's direction and shouted, 'This man was bloody well trussed up like... like I don't know what, and I did it myself! Maybe I'm sitting here with a ghost!' He grabbed hold of Simon's shoulder. 'How the hell did you do that?'

Simon said 'Boo!' and everyone laughed again.

Anna-Greta was still standing out on the jetty with Johan. A lifetime of trade had taught her the art of manipulating people's emotions, but it seemed as if she had met her match. Simon's humiliation as he stood there in chains on the jetty had been transferred to Kalle, when he jumped into the sea in a misguided attempt at heroism. Then Simon had skilfully restored the balance by drawing Kalle into the glow of his achievement. Now there was only joy.

Nice, thought Anna-Greta. *Polished.*

She was relieved, she was confused, she was angry. Mostly angry. She'd been conned. Simon had made her behave like a fool in front of all these people. Not that anyone appeared to have noticed, but she knew. She had lost control. Hypothetically speaking, she could have screamed. She hadn't, fortunately. But the barb was there, and she was annoyed.

'Wasn't that brilliant?' said Johan.

Anna-Greta nodded curtly and Johan ran a hand through his hair, looking over in Simon's direction. 'I think he's absolutely incredible.'

'Yes, but there are plenty of people who can do that sort of thing,' said Anna-Greta. When Johan looked reproachfully at her, she asked, 'Anyway, what did he say to you? Before?'

Johan smiled secretively and pulled a face. 'Oh...I don't really know.'

Anna-Greta slapped him gently on the shoulder. 'What did he say?'

'Why do you want to know?'

'I'm just wondering.'

Johan looked across at the boathouses, where Kalle had embarked on a new tirade, claiming that he would personally throw in the sea anyone who didn't go and see Simon's shows at the local community theatre. Johan shrugged his shoulders.

'He said I shouldn't worry. That he was going to keep out of the way for a couple of minutes for effect.'

'Why did he say that?'

Johan looked at Anna-Greta as if she were making fun of him.

'So that I wouldn't be worried, obviously.' He looked at Anna-Greta and added, 'Like you were.'

She didn't even bother to protest. Johan knew her, and his eyes were sharp. Instead she said, 'Anyway, I think I've had enough of this now. Are you coming home?'

Johan shook his head and looked down into the water. 'No, I want to stay for a while.'

Anna-Greta pulled her cardigan more tightly around her and left the jetty and the crowd. When she was halfway to her house she turned and looked down at the harbour. She couldn't recall ever having seen so many people down by the jetty, not even on Midsummer's Eve.

Johan wasn't there anymore, no doubt he had joined the circle of admirers.

Oh well, she thought. *I suppose it was good that he said what he did to Johan. It was considerate of him.*

She continued on up towards the house, and although she barely allowed herself to think the thought, she could feel it: *But he didn't say anything to me.*

That same evening Simon was sitting at the table in his garden with a glass of cognac. The last tender had arrived and there was still no word from Marita. A few youngsters were swimming down by the steamboat jetty.

His whole body was hurting; the worst pain was in his shoulder joints, which he had had to twist almost completely out of their sockets in order to free himself from the chains. It hadn't been a particularly difficult escape because very little rope had been used, but the chains had been unusually tightly pulled, and it had taken him almost a whole minute underwater to get out of them. If he hadn't had that extra minute before the sack was pushed in, he would have had to go straight up to the surface when he was done.

But he had had an extra minute, and he had used it to swim along the bottom to the furthest jetty and climb out, hidden by the boats. He had achieved the desired effect, and he thought the forthcoming shows would be well attended.

Simon raised the glass to his lips and grimaced as he felt a tightness across his chest. He couldn't carry on like this for much longer. It put too much of a strain on his body. He had once ended up with a broken rib when a man had been absolutely determined to chain him up as tightly as possible. After that occasion he had stopped offering a reward to anyone who could do it successfully. People were energetic enough as it was.

The lighthouse at Gåvasten flashed in the light summer's evening; the lamp was only a dot, casting no beams across the water.

I ought to be enjoying this.

The performance had been a great success, it was a beautiful evening, and the cognac was spreading its warmth through his stiff body. He ought to be enjoying it all.

But it was often like this. After a successful publicity stunt with all guns blazing, the emptiness afterwards was all the greater. Besides which, Marita had disappeared again, and Simon had already drunk one glass more than he usually did. He didn't want to go the same way as so many of his colleagues, tumbling down into a sea of booze, never to surface again. But on this particular evening he thought he'd earned it.

I suppose this is how it starts, thought Simon, refilling his glass.

He was less concerned about Marita in her capacity as his wife than in her capacity as his assistant. The shows in Nåten were due to begin in three days. If she didn't turn up he would have to scrap some of the best numbers: the mind-reading and the hat box. It would still be all right, but he really wanted to put on a good show in this particular venue.

Simon took a deep draught of his cognac and sighed. This wasn't the way he had expected his life to be. It worked, but that was about all. Happiness had got lost somewhere along the way. He allowed his gaze to rest on the water, which looked as soft as silk in the colours of the summer's evening. Far away a gull cried.

Oh yes, happiness exists. Just not right here.

Behind him he heard the slap of footsteps and a faint rattling noise. He turned in his chair with some difficulty and saw Johan pushing a wheelbarrow towards him through the grass. He was wearing only a pair of swimming trunks and a voluminous shirt covered in damp patches, and his hair was soaking wet.

'Johan?' said Simon. 'What have you got there?'

Johan grinned and pushed the wheelbarrow forward. It contained all the chains and padlocks Simon had left on the seabed. He tipped them out at Simon's feet.

'I thought it was a bit of a waste.'

Simon laughed. He would have liked to stroke Johan's hair, but for one thing he couldn't manage to get to his feet at this particular moment, and for another he wasn't sure if it was the right thing to do. Instead he simply nodded and said, 'It would have been. Thank you. Sit down if you like.'

Johan sat down on the other garden chair and let out a great puff of air.

'However did you manage?' asked Simon. 'They must have been heavy.'

'They were,' said Johan. 'I couldn't lift them, so I had to fasten them to a hook and drag them ashore, one by one.'

That was what Simon himself usually did, and what he had intended to do this time. However, he had no intention of telling Johan this, and he was grateful to be spared the job.

'Not bad,' said Simon.

'No,' said Johan, reaching into the breast pocket of his shirt.

'And then there's this. It was in the sack.'

He handed a thin, wedge-shaped piece of metal to Simon, giving him a conspiratorial look. Simon raised his eyebrows and pushed it into his own breast pocket.

Johan leaned back in his chair and said, 'I still don't understand how you do it.'

'Do you want to know?'

Johan sat bolt upright. 'Yes!'

Simon nodded. 'OK, go and fetch a bottle of Pommac from the fridge. My wallet is on the kitchen table; help yourself to five kronor for bringing back the chains. Then come back and I'll tell you.'

Johan shot out of his chair and raced inside. After thirty seconds he was back. Simon couldn't understand why he'd said that. The words had just flown out of his mouth. He never usually revealed his secrets. It must be the cognac, the atmosphere. And after all, Johan already knew the only part that really involved cheating.

So he told him. When he had finished the Pommac bottle was empty and the bay had darkened to a deep blue carpet, with the flashing light from Gåvasten lighthouse drawing thin scratches through it. A bat flitted around them, hunting for moths.

Johan let out a fizzy belch and said, 'I still think it sounds pretty dangerous.'

'Yes,' said Simon. 'But if you just…' He was struck by a thought, and raised a warning finger. 'You're not to go trying this yourself, Johan!'

'I won't.'

'Promise?' Simon extended his thumb towards Johan. 'Thumbs?'

Johan smiled and rubbed his thumb against Simon's. Then he inspected it as if to check if there might be a binding agreement somewhere in his thumbprint, and said, 'I think Mum's a little bit in love with you.'

'What makes you think that?'

Johan shrugged. 'I just do. She goes all peculiar.'

Simon emptied his brandy glass and refrained from pouring

himself a refill. That was enough, a pleasant warmth suffused his whole body. He held up the glass, looking at the light from Gåvasten as it was refracted through the remains of the liquid around the rim, and said, 'Well, there are lots of reasons why people go peculiar.'

'I suppose there are, but…this is a particular kind of peculiar.'

Simon narrowed his eyes at Johan. 'You seem very well-informed about this kind of thing.'

'I know my mum.'

They sat in silence for a while. The only sound was the flapping of the bat's wings as it darted here and there, swooping after something only it could perceive. When the engine of a boat started up down in the harbour, the atmosphere was broken and Simon said, 'Can you help me up? I'm still a bit stiff. It'll be better tomorrow.'

Johan stood up and held out his hand to help Simon out of his chair. They stood facing one another. For a couple of seconds a mutual approval flowed between them. Then Simon patted Johan on the shoulder and said, 'Thanks again for your help. See you tomorrow.'

Johan nodded, took the wheelbarrow and left. Simon watched him go. When he had disappeared into the darkness beneath the aspen trees, Simon snorted and said quietly to himself, 'A particular kind of peculiar…'

Then he shuffled into his house and closed the door behind him.

The uninvited guest

The next morning Simon made a few calls, trying unsuccessfully to track down Marita. Then he sat down in the lilac arbour with a pen and paper to work out an alternative program for the performances at the community theatre.

He couldn't settle to the task. His thoughts kept sliding away towards the most extreme issues. Why was he carrying on with this at all, what was the point of everything, how is a person supposed to live a life with no future, and should you even bother.

This was his mood when Anna-Greta called out a brief, 'Thanks for yesterday, it was very good', on her way down to the jetty. He asked her to come and sit down for a while. She perched on the edge of the chair opposite him, and seemed uneasy. Simon wondered if this unease was *a particular kind of peculiar*, but of course he had no way of asking.

They talked about this and that, safe topics, and Anna-Greta had just settled more comfortably on her chair when Simon realised they were being observed. Standing by the gate, watching them, was Marita. Simon felt as if he had been caught out somehow and was just about to leap out of his chair, but the anger got there before the guilt. He stayed put and stared at Marita without moving a muscle.

Marita was blinking slowly, her eyelids moving in slow motion, as if it took a conscious effort for her to open and close them. Her hair was unwashed and she had dark circles under her eyes. She was scratching her arm mechanically. 'Well, would you look at that,' she said. 'Isn't that sweet.'

Simon continued to stare at her. From the corner of his eye he could see that Anna-Greta was about to get up, and he gestured to her to stay where she was. In a low voice, Simon asked the question that had become something of a mantra in recent years, 'Where have you been?'

Marita waved her head around in a gesture that could mean just about anything, and therefore meant: *Here and there, but mostly out in space.*

Marita came and stood directly in front of Simon, looked down at him and said, 'I need money.'

'For what?'

She opened and closed her mouth; it sounded dry and sticky at the same time as she loosened her tongue from her palate.

'I'm going to Germany.'

'You can't. We've got work here.'

Marita's gaze slid between Anna-Greta and Simon. She seemed

to be having some difficulty in focusing. 'I'm going to Germany. You have to give me some money.'

'I haven't got any money, and you're not going to Germany. Go inside and go to bed.'

Marita shook her head slowly, and seemed to be stuck fast in the same movement, as if her head were a pendulum and she had to keep it moving so that time would not come to a standstill. Anna-Greta stood up.

'I'm going.'

The sound of her voice attracted Marita's attention. She pointed at Anna-Greta. 'Have you got any money?'

'No, I haven't got any money for you.'

Marita's lips curled upwards in an imitation of a smile. 'You're carrying on with my husband. That means you have to pay, you must realise that.'

Simon shot up out of his chair, grabbed hold of Marita's wrist and pulled her towards the house. 'Shut your mouth!'

The violent movement made Marita stumble, and Simon dragged her along behind him towards the steps. Marita allowed herself to be hauled across the lawn for a few metres, then she yelled, 'Help! Help!'

Simon looked up in order to convey some kind of message to Anna-Greta with his eyes, *I'm sorry* or *don't condemn me*, but before he had time to formulate his expression he saw a man step out from behind the lilac bushes. Someone who had been standing there waiting.

Marita twisted herself free of Simon's grip, and as she crawled towards the new arrival on all fours she said in a pathetic little voice, 'Rolf, he's hitting me.'

Rolf was so big that he looked as if he could easily pick Simon up and carry him in his arms. A pale, grubby linen suit concealed his muscles, but he seemed to have limited control over his body. He walked towards Simon: irregular, staggering steps, his arms dangling uselessly at his sides. The skin on his face was dark red, and his nose was flaking. The corners of his mouth pulled downwards in an unnatural way, as if he might have had a stroke.

Since Simon was part of the way down the hill, Rolf towered over him by twenty centimetres or more as he wagged his finger.

'You mustn't hit your wife. You must give her money.'

Marita curled up at Rolf's feet like something on the cover of a cheap novel. Simon's heart was racing as he folded his arms across his chest, looked up at the giant's eyes—which were bloodshot—and said, 'And what exactly has this got to do with you...*Rolf*?'

Rolf moved his cheeks upwards so that his eyes narrowed. This looked utterly bizarre with his drooping mouth, but Simon refrained from laughing. Rolf's pupils darted about for a few seconds, then he said, 'You don't like my name, is that right? You think it sounds silly.'

Simon shook his head. 'No, I think it's a wonderful name, I just don't understand what you're doing here.'

Rolf blinked a couple of times and looked down at the ground. His lips were moving as if he were analysing Simon's words carefully and considering his response. Marita was gazing up at Rolf as if he were an oracle. Simon looked around and noticed that Anna-Greta was no longer there.

Simon made a quick mental inventory of items in the vicinity that might be used as weapons. The closest was the spade leaning against the steps ten metres away. Rolf had finished thinking, and said slowly, 'So you're not intending to give her any money, then?'

'No.'

Rolf sighed. Then he placed a hand on Simon's arm as if he were about to share a confidence. Before Simon had time to react, Rolf grabbed hold of his right hand, wrapped his fist around the little finger and bent it backwards. The finger felt as if it might actually snap off, and Simon was forced to his knees. Marita was already down there, and she glowered at him in a way that made it clear he couldn't expect any help from that quarter. She looked...greedy.

She's been longing for this moment.

The finger was still being bent backwards, and Simon had no time to open his mouth to say he would give them money, or kill them or take them out for a boat trip, before Rolf jerked the finger and it broke. A spasm of pain shot up Simon's arm and came out of his mouth like a deep cough. For a fraction of a second all the things he would no longer be able to do with his hands went whirling by—

the cards, the cloths, the ropes, the torn-up newspapers

—before the dam broke and he screamed out loud. He saw his little finger hanging there like a pointless scrap of skin, filthy pain poisoning his blood as the tears filled his eyes. He screamed again, from despair more than pain. Marita sat quietly, watching him.

Then Rolf was on top of him. He sat on Simon's chest and forced his arm out to the side, pressing his hand against a rock. Out of his jacket pocket Rolf took a big clasp knife, which he managed to open using one arm and his teeth. He rested the tip of the blade on the rock just above Simon's useless little finger.

Once again, Rolf seemed to need time to formulate his next utterance. He looked at Simon's face, his hand. He looked as if he couldn't quite work out how things had ended up like this, and needed some thinking time before he could proceed.

Simon lay still, watching a little cloud drift by above Rolf's head. For a moment it looked as if Rolf had a halo. Then it tilted, freed itself from him and drifted on. A gull was calling out at sea, and for a couple of seconds Simon experienced absolute peace. Then Rolf spoke.

'You're a magician. So you need your fingers, right?'

Simon said nothing, didn't move. He listened to the waves lapping against the pebbles on the shoreline. It sounded…wholesome. He was terribly thirsty. Rolf had found the right train of thought, and went on, 'I'm going to cut off your little finger now. Then I'm going to get hold of…what's that one called? The ring finger. And I'm going to break it. Then I'm going to cut it off. And so on.'

Rolf nodded at his own statement, pleased that he had expressed himself so clearly. He summarised, 'And that will be the end of your magic. Unless…'

He looked at Simon and raised his eyebrows, encouraging Simon to fill in the rest. When Simon didn't oblige, Rolf sighed and shook his head. He turned to Marita, sitting curled up on the grass, following the course of events through half-closed eyes.

'You said this would be easy.'

Marita made that wavy movement with her head that could be interpreted in any number of ways. Rolf grimaced and said to Simon, 'Well, you've only yourself to blame. You leave me no choice.'

He turned his attention to Simon's hand on the rock. One cut and the finger would be gone.

'Stop that!'

Anna-Greta's shrill voice broke through the paradoxical calm that had reigned for a moment or two. Rolf turned his head, looking tired more than anything. Anna-Greta was coming towards him with a double-barrelled shotgun in her hands.

'Get away from him!' she yelled.

There was a long pause. Anna-Greta was standing a metre away from Rolf, pointing both barrels straight at him. Rolf had once again become enmeshed in a careful analysis of the course of events. His lips were moving and he was gazing out to sea. Then he stood up. The barrels of the gun were pointing right at his chest.

'Drop the knife,' said Anna-Greta.

Rolf shook his head. Then he very carefully folded up the knife and put it in his pocket. The gun barrels shook as Anna-Greta waved them in the direction of the steamboat jetty.

'Get out of here! Now!'

Only now did it occur to Simon that he was actually present. That he could take an active role in what was going on. His arm was numb and when he had pulled it towards him he had some difficulty in getting up. He had only got as far as a sitting position when the lawn started moving from side to side like the deck of a boat.

Rolf took a step towards Anna-Greta, and she moved backwards, raising and lowering the gun at the same time.

'Stop! I'll shoot you!'

'No,' said Rolf quite simply, and reached for the gun. Anna-Greta backed away still further and the battle was lost. When Rolf once again made a grab for the barrels, she moved them to one side instead of pressing the trigger. Rolf quickly stepped forward and slapped her across the side of the head with the flat of his hand. Anna-Greta fell sideways. The shotgun flew into the hazel bushes and Anna-Greta collapsed in a heap on the grass, whimpering as she pressed a hand to her ear.

As Simon attempted to get to his feet, he heard Marita's voice. 'Isn't he just incredible?'

Anna-Greta was lying a few metres away, with Rolf leaning over her. Simon's brain wasn't working properly, he couldn't decide whether to try and grab the spade or just hurl himself forwards.

Before had finished thinking it through, he heard a buzzing noise behind him, like some huge insect. There was a click and Rolf went down. Simon got to his feet and saw Johan standing by the lilac arbour with his air rifle in his hands. He was just lowering the gun, and was biting his lower lip.

Rolf got up. A dark spot had appeared on his temple, and a small amount of blood was oozing out. His eyes were crazy and he no longer hesitated, he didn't require any thinking time now. He took out his knife and opened it as he moved towards Johan.

Simon was right behind him, but instead of trying to stop him, he dived into the hazel bushes and grabbed the shotgun. Before he had even got hold of it properly he yelled, 'Stop, you bastard!' but Rolf took no notice.

Johan had dropped his air gun, which was useless after firing its single shot, and was running up towards the house. Rolf was after him, with the knife in his hand. With a grimace of pain Simon lifted the shotgun to his shoulder, just as Rolf disappeared behind the lilac hedge fifteen metres away.

Simon had never fired a shotgun before, but he knew that the whole point of them was that the shot covers a wide area. He aimed at the lilac hedge and pulled the trigger.

Then a number of things happened in less than a second. There was a deafening bang and the recoil hit Simon so hard that he fell backwards into the hazel bushes, but before he had even begun to fall a hole opened up in the lilac hedge and fragments of leaves flew up like a flock of frightened butterflies. The first hazel twigs were just scratching Simon's back through his shirt as Rolf began to roar.

Simon was still pressing the stock of the shotgun to his shoulder as the branches closed around him and he fell into shimmering greenery. Rolf carried on bellowing. The thicker branches further in stopped Simon falling any further, and he could feel blood on the skin of his back. He clutched the wooden stock and breathed; he stayed where he was and one thought went through his mind in time with his panting breath, in and out:

I hit him. I hit him. I hit him.

It was only a few seconds later, when he had disentangled himself from the branches and saw Anna-Greta sitting with her hands covering her mouth and Marita rocking back and forth that other thoughts began to force their way through:

If I've killed him, if I…

Rolf had stopped roaring. Simon swallowed, but without any saliva.

Thirsty. So bloody thirsty.

A drop of sweat trickled down into his eye, obscuring his vision. He wiped it away and rubbed his eyes. When he opened them again, Anna-Greta was standing next to him. She was squinting, and looked as if she were in pain. She pointed at the hand holding the butt of the gun and tried to say something, but no words came.

Simon looked at the shotgun. Only now did he discover that there were two triggers one behind the other, one for each barrel. He had only pressed the outer trigger. There was one cartridge left. Anna-Greta nodded and put her hand over her ear. She walked towards the lilac hedge and Simon followed her with the shotgun raised.

Rolf clearly wasn't dead, because he was moving. Quite a lot, in fact. He was hurling himself back and forth on the ground as if he were trying to shake off some invisible nightmare. His jacket was ripped and covered in blood from the left shoulder to halfway down his back on one side. Only some of the shot had hit him. If Simon had fired half a second later, Rolf would probably have been lying completely still right now.

Johan came back hesitantly, approaching the man on the ground as if he were an injured wild animal that might leap up and attack at any moment. Then he walked a long way around the thrashing body and fell into Anna-Greta's arms. She stroked his hair and they stood there in silence just hugging each other for a long time. Then Anna-Greta said, 'Take your bike and go and fetch Dr Holmström. And Göran.'

Johan nodded and ran off. After thirty seconds he rattled past along the track on his bike. Rolf had settled down and was just lying there clenching and unclenching one fist. Simon still had the shotgun pointing at him, with his index finger resting on the trigger. He felt sick.

This isn't me. This can't be happening to me.

After twenty minutes both the doctor and the police had arrived. Rolf's injuries were not life threatening, just extremely painful. Some fifteen shotgun pellets had penetrated the muscles and tissue in his left shoulder and upper arm around the shoulderblade. He was bandaged provisionally just to stop the bleeding, and the doctor rang for transport. Göran wrote a report that would need to be completed at the police station in Norrtälje. Simon's little finger was put in a splint.

True to form, Marita had vanished, and they later found out that she had managed to catch the tender before anyone started seriously looking for her. Rolf was transported to Norrtälje, and both Göran and Dr Holmström went home, after establishing that they would go to the police station together the following day.

Simon, Anna-Greta and Johan sat in silence in the lilac arbour. The torn leaves in the hedge were the only sign that darkness had abused their hospitality just a couple of hours ago. Just as the slight movement of a finger can release a devastating hail of shot, so an event that lasted no more than five minutes can send its repercussions through days and years to come. It is impossible to ignore the consequences, there is too much to say, and the result would be silence.

Johan was drinking Pommac, Simon was drinking beer and Anna-Greta was drinking nothing. They had all saved each other at different points in the complex web created by one simple act of violence; gratitude and embarrassment were mixed up together, and words were difficult.

Simon fiddled with his bandage and said quietly, 'I'm sorry. That you both got dragged into all this.'

'Don't be,' said Anna-Greta. 'It can't be helped.'

'No, but I'm still sorry. I apologise.'

When the initial shock had faded they began to talk hesitantly about what had happened. The conversation continued during the afternoon and later up at Anna-Greta and Johan's house, where they ate a simple dinner. Towards nine o'clock a different kind of silence took over, a fundamental exhaustion of speech. They just couldn't bear to listen to the sound of their own voices any longer, and Simon went back down to his cottage.

He sat down at the kitchen table with the crossword in order to distract his mind, and for once he cut it out, filled in his name and address and put it in an envelope. The summer evening was still lilac outside his window when he had finished, and he regretted turning down the invitation to sleep on the kitchen sofa up in the big house. The day's events were turning over and over in his mind. Until today the future had been dismal but predictable, he had been able to see himself plodding on through the years. Now he couldn't see anything anymore.

Just as the recoil from the gun had thrown him backwards, so he had been thrown outside himself at the moment he fired the shot. It wasn't the action itself that frightened him—that had been born of panic and necessity—but what had happened inside him.

He had seen Rolf's head explode as he pressed the trigger, in fact he had fully intended to blow Rolf's head to bits. When Anna-Greta had pointed to the gun afterwards and Simon had realised that there was one cartridge left, his immediate impulse had been to shoot Marita as well. To execute her. Blow her head off. Get rid of her.

He hadn't done any of those things. But he had thought it, and had experienced a wild desire to do it. Perhaps he would have, if there hadn't been any witnesses. He had been hurled into a different version of himself, someone who wanted to kill whatever stood in his way. It was not a pleasant thought, yet at the same time it was a very pleasant thought: he could be someone different from now on, if he wanted to be.

But who? Who am I? Who will I become?

His thoughts continued to go around and around after he had gone to bed. He was ashamed of himself. For what he had done and what he had not done, for what he thought and who he was. He tried to make himself think about the forthcoming performances in Nåten, how he was going to get through them with a broken finger, but the images were washed away and replaced by others.

After a few hours he fell into an uneasy sleep, which after a short while was disturbed by banging, thumping, knocking. Just knocking. He got up quickly and looked around the room. Somebody had been knocking. Somebody wanted to come in. There was still a hint of light in the sky, and he could see the silhouette of a head outside the bedroom window.

He breathed out and opened the window. Anna-Greta was standing outside with her hands clasped over her breast. She was wearing a white nightdress.

'Anna-Greta?'

'May I come in? For a while?'

Simon instinctively reached out to help her over the windowsill, but realised how stupidly he was behaving.

'I'll open the door,' he said.

Anna-Greta went around the side of the house and Simon opened the front door to let her in.

Driftwood

The dream about Elin

For a good two hours Simon and Anna-Greta had taken it in turns to tell their story. Anders' knees creaked as he got to his feet and stretched his arms up towards the ceiling. Outside the window the weather was neither worse nor better. Small raindrops caressed the pane, and the wind whispered among the trees without any great hurry. A walk seemed possible, and he needed some exercise.

Simon took the tray out into the kitchen and Anna-Greta brushed crumbs off the table. Anders looked at her wrinkled hands, imagining them holding the shotgun. 'What a story.'

'Yes,' said Anna-Greta. 'But it's only a story.'

'What do you mean?'

'Exactly what I say.' Anna-Greta straightened up with the crumbs in her hand. 'We can never know anything about what has happened in the past, because it has turned into stories. Even for those who are involved.'

'So…it didn't happen like that?'

Anna-Greta shrugged. 'I don't know. Not any more.'

Anders followed her into the kitchen where Simon was carefully stacking the best china in the dishwasher. Anna-Greta brushed the crumbs off her hands into the bin and got out the dishwasher powder. They moved around each other with a manifest ease. The dance of everyday life, worn smooth over the years. Anders looked at them in a kind of double exposure.

The smuggler king's daughter and the magician. Loading the dishwasher.

Whether their story was true or not, it had stirred things up in his mind. New associations must be made, new sequences of images must be put together. He felt a physical weariness as the synapses prepared the way for all these new connections.

'I'm going for a walk,' he said.

Anna-Greta gestured towards the fridge. 'Aren't you going to take some food with you?'

'Later. Thanks for the coffee. And the story.'

Anders stepped out on to the porch, lit a cigarette and strolled down the garden path. He passed the path to Simon's house and stopped, taking a deep drag.

My dad ran along here with his air gun. And without his air gun.

The gun was still around in a cupboard at the Shack, and he'd tried it once or twice when he was little. But the barrel was loose and the pressure was so poor that the pellet often got stuck in the bore. He'd wondered why his father kept it. Now he knew.

Leaves were rustling or falling all around him, and a light drizzle was dampening his hair as he carried on up towards the shop. The tender was just reversing away from the jetty after dropping off a small group of schoolchildren. A little girl of about seven came running along the track towards him, her school bag cheerfully thudding against her back. It was Maja—

not Maja

—who had come back at long last—

it isn't Maja.

—and he had to restrain himself from dropping to his knees and scooping her up in his arms.

134

Because it could have been Maja. Every child aged around seven or eight could have been Maja. The thought had ground him down into despair during the first six months after her disappearance. All the children who could have been Maja, but weren't. Thousands of eager, happy or sad faces, small bodies on the move, and not one of them was *the right one*. His little girl, and only his little girl, had been removed. No longer existed.

He had loved her so much. It should have been someone else who disappeared. Someone who wasn't loved. The girl ran past him and he turned, watched her rucksack with its picture of Bamse the Bear grow smaller as she headed for the southern part of the village.

It should have been you.

He had given up teacher training when Maja disappeared, and it was just as well. He would never be able to work with children, not when his feelings were so divided. His first impulse was to love and embrace them all, his second was to loathe them because they were still alive.

There were already a number of bags hanging on hooks on the wall of the shop, along with the odd new or old mailbox and a couple of buckets with lids, with the box numbers marked in ink. Anders made a mental note to put something there in a day or two, before the photos came back.

The steamboat jetty lay empty and the white geese were running across the sea without taking off, the wind was tearing at the plastic bags on the wall of the shop. There was an irregular squeaking noise. Anders listened hard to try and identify the sound. It was coming from the steps leading up to the shop, or behind them.

He went over and when he saw the source of the noise he couldn't understand why he suddenly felt so afraid. He took a step backwards, gasping for breath, the hair on his arms standing on end. The GB ice cream man was standing there.

The GB-man was a plastic figure mounted on springs on a block of cement, and the wind made him swing backwards and forwards, squeaking. He usually stood outside the shop, but had been put away for the season. Anders looked at his grinning face and his pulse rate shot up, his breathing ragged. He cupped his hands over his mouth and tried to take deep breaths.

It's only the GB-man. He isn't dangerous.

That's what he'd said. To Maja. It was Maja who had been afraid of the GB-man, not him.

It had started as a joke. Maja had been afraid of swans. Not the swans on the sea, which might have been natural. Even Anders had a certain respect for them. No, she was afraid that a swan would come in through the door or the window when she was in bed.

Since Maja was always pleased to see the GB-man—which meant there might be an ice cream in the offing—Anders tried to make a joke of the whole thing by saying, 'Swans aren't dangerous, they're nothing to be afraid of. They're no more dangerous than...the GB-man. And you're not lying here worrying that the GB-man might come in, are you?'

Maja continued to be afraid of swans, but she became even more afraid of the GB-man. It had never occurred to her before: the fact that the GB-man might be lying under her bed, or come creeping in through a chink in the door with that smile plastered on his face. Anders came to regret that he had ever mentioned it. After that night he always had to open her window to check that the GB-man wasn't standing outside. Maja's bed was very low, there wasn't really room for a lion under there. But there was room for the GB-man, since he was completely flat.

The GB-man was everywhere. He was in the sea when she wanted to go for a swim, he was hiding in the shadows. He was fear incarnate.

Now he was standing here squeaking behind the steps to the shop, and Anders was filled with a horror he couldn't pin down. He forced himself to stare the GB-man in the eye, despite the fact that he was so scared he just wanted to run away.

Home. Wine.

But presumably alcohol was to blame for the whole thing. His nerves were shot. Oversensitive. Could suddenly feel scared of just about anything. But he steeled himself. Wasn't going to go home and start drinking. Was going to stare at the GB-man until the bastard looked away or didn't seem dangerous any more.

The GB-man was swinging to and fro as if getting ready to pounce. Anders didn't take his eyes off him. They weighed each other up. A shudder ran down Anders' spine.

Someone is watching me.

He spun around and took a couple of steps so that he wouldn't be standing too close to the swinging plastic figure behind his back. The enemy came from all directions. Anders quickly glanced over the jetty, the boathouses, the gravelled area, the sea. A lone gull was struggling with the air currents, seemingly incapable of forcing its way down to the surface of the water. There was no sign of anyone.

But someone is watching me.

Someone had been watching him as he stood there shaking in front of the GB-man, someone was still watching him. The only thing missing was a pair of eyes, or more than one pair. But they were nowhere to be found.

Someone with no eyes is watching me.

With his heart pounding he left the shop and set off along the track to Kattudden. The feeling faded as he got further away. He could still hear the squeaking of the GB-man in the distance, but the sense of being watched had gone. Anders walked on quickly, passing the closed-down school, the mission house, which was as good as closed down, and the alarm bell in its white wooden tower.

After a few hundred metres his heart was still pounding, but by now it was because he was so unfit, not because he was afraid. He slowed down. Once he got in among the fir trees he stopped at the foot of the narrow path leading up to the rock, the erratic boulder. His hands were still shaking as he took out a cigarette, lit it, and took a deep, greedy drag.

What was that?

A strong sense of something unpleasant remained in his body, and he wished he had some wine with which to wash it away. The cigarette in his damp fingers tasted mouldy; he stubbed it out among the fir needles strewn across the track. He didn't feel well. Something was shifting inside his body, and not in a good way.

He took a step towards the path up to the rock, then changed his mind. He didn't want to go up there. The path belonged to him and Cecilia, and he and Cecilia no longer existed, so...

Memories. Bloody memories.

Everything on Domarö was steeped in memories. If not his memories, someone else's. If only it were possible to get rid of all the memories. The path wound its way into the forest like a whispered promise of something else. Another place or another time.

I need to get away from here.

Anders followed the route of the path with his finger, drifting into a wave, a farewell.

I need to be here. And I need to get away.

He could see it with perfect clarity. That was the whole problem, in all its impossible simplicity. As he set off towards Kattudden again, a solution came to him. A practical solution for conquering his constant fear and anxiety.

Anders continued through the forest and passed Holger's house, which lay there brooding in the darkness. He worked out the details of his plan for the future, and there was nothing left unaccounted for, nothing that couldn't be solved. When he emerged from the forest his planning was complete, and he was breathing more easily.

Kattudden was desolate at this time of year. The houses were not insulated against the winter weather, and in most cases they were intolerably small without the access to the great outdoors that you had in summer.

Anders had spent a large part of his summers at Kattudden. Almost all his friends had been the children of summer visitors, and it was in rooms or cottages here that he had drunk spirits for the first time, watched forbidden horror films and listened to Madonna. Among other things.

Now it was no more than a deserted holiday village in the autumn gloom, and a pretty ugly one at that. Most of the houses were section-built. Ready-made packages delivered from the mainland on Kalle Gripenberg's barge. Up with the walls, on with the roof, in with the windows and doors and then off to the cottage to have fun! The kind of houses that tend to age without dignity—although most of them were still better built than the Shack.

Anders strolled along the track down to the jetties, looking at the abandoned traces of summer, the covered garden furniture. In one garden he saw a half-finished game of Jenga just standing there, as if the owners had suddenly realised they had to set off for the city immediately, and had simply dropped what they were doing.

There was a light on in one of the houses closest to the jetties. Anders had been inside that house many times. Elin's house. It must be ten years since he had actually seen Elin, almost twenty since they had stopped hanging out together. Until a few years ago he had seen her frequently on television and in the press, as had half the population of Sweden. Since then, nothing.

The house was one of the better ones in the area, with its own well and its own jetty. Unlike most of the others it had been built on-site, and Anders remembered how the hollow sound present in all the other houses was missing from Elin's. The door he was knocking on now was quite solid, with a doorknocker and everything.

He waited. When nothing happened he knocked again. He heard footsteps inside, and a voice said, 'Who is it?'

It could hardly be Elin's voice, this one belonged to an older person, so Anders said, 'My name is Anders. I was looking for Elin. Elin Grönwall.'

It was only when he said her name out loud that he remembered. *Why* they had stopped hanging out. Why they had all stopped hanging out, why the summers and their childhood had ended.

Elin. Joel.

He had managed to forget. An impulse had made him knock on the door, but now he was grateful that Elin wasn't at home, that he didn't have to see her. He was just about to leave when the door opened. Anders attempted a smile, but it died away the moment he saw the person who opened the door.

If it hadn't been for the more recent magazine covers and the pictures on the gossip pages, he would never have recognised the woman who had been his friend long ago, and if he hadn't known her since she was a child, he would never have recognised the woman from the magazine covers.

What have they done to her?

He didn't know who 'they' were, but it was impossible to imagine that anyone would have done this to their appearance voluntarily. Anders managed to hitch up the corners of his mouth a fraction.

'Hi.'

'Hi.'

Even Elin's voice had changed. When she was seventeen she had adopted a babyish voice that had appealed to certain boys at the time, and which had later been ridiculed in the press. Now her voice sounded deeper and rougher. The voice of an older person, and that particular change was actually an improvement.

Anders couldn't say what he was thinking, so he said, 'I was just passing and I saw the light was on, and I thought…'

'Come in.'

The house smelled almost exactly the same as it had done when he was young. It didn't feel as if there was anyone else there. Anders had expected the person who had Elin under their thumb would be around.

'Can I get you anything?' she asked. 'Coffee? Wine?'

'Wine would be nice, thank you.'

Anders looked up as he answered, but immediately looked down again. It was difficult to look at her. He concentrated on undoing his shoelaces and Elin disappeared into the kitchen.

What has she done?

She had been pretty when she was young, she'd had her pick of the boys. In between *Big Brother* and the centrefolds, she had had surgery on her breasts and her lips, turning herself into a classic bimbo. One of those individuals who circulate between photo opportunities and parties and scandals. A night on the town followed by the full story; another relationship break-up followed by the full story. Slap the make-up on a bit thicker each time it all goes south.

It's easy to see how it takes its toll, how the person behind the mask slowly becomes hardened—the smile grows rigid, the skin grows stiff and numb—until all that remains is a shining, fossil-ised shell surrounding an empty space. How glamour loses out to gravity.

But this still didn't explain Elin's transformation. She hadn't just aged, she had *remodelled herself* into something far worse than anything time could create. In some way, for some reason she had made herself ugly.

The picture window in the kitchen looked out over Kattholmen, and despite the cloud both the tiles and stainless steel worktops were bathed in light from the sky and the sea. Everything was as clear as in a photograph. Anders sat down with his back to the window while Elin filled his glass with Gato Negro from a cask. They raised their glasses to each other and drank. Anders made an effort not to gulp.

'How are you?' he asked.

Elin ran her finger over the cat on the wine cask. 'We used to spend whole evenings sitting here, didn't we? When Mum and Dad were out.'

'Yes. And nights too. Later on.'

Elin nodded, still following the contours of the cat with her finger. As she wasn't looking at him, Anders plucked up the courage to study her face.

Her nose, which had been slender and straight, was now twice as big and flattened. Her chin, which had been firm, quite prominent and somewhat square, was now pointed and receding, so that it became part of her throat. Her high cheekbones and dimples had disappeared, and her lips…

Those lips that had pouted in so many close-ups, topless glamour shots and full-length shots, and which had been desirable even before the silicon implants, had now been compressed into two narrow lines that did no more than mark where her mouth began and ended, if that.

She had bags under her eyes that would have looked unnatural on a woman twenty years older, and the baffling thing was that in the clinical brightness of the kitchen Anders could see the marks of badly healed scars beneath her eyes. As if she had had surgery on the bags. As if they had been worse at some point.

He took a large gulp of his wine, almost half the glass, and when he realised what he was doing it was too late, he could hardly spit it out, so he swallowed it. Elin was looking at him, and he couldn't interpret her expression. It was impossible to read her, just as it would be impossible to read a book that had been torn to pieces.

Time for small talk.

Time for him to pick up the thread and chat about all the times they had sat here, everything they had done all those years ago, and he wouldn't mention her face or the boathouse on Kattholmen where everything had come to an end.

What did we actually do?

He searched for some amusing memory. Something they could laugh at, something that might dispel the strange atmosphere between them. He couldn't think of anything. All he could remember was that they used to drink tea, lots of tea, with honey, that sometimes they ran out of honey and…The words came tumbling out of his mouth, 'What have you done to your face?'

The groove between Elin's lips widened and the corners moved up towards her cheeks; it could be interpreted as a smile. 'It's not just my face.'

She walked into the middle of the kitchen floor and ran her hands over her body. Anders looked down, and Elin said, 'Look.'

He looked. The heavy breasts that had given the caption writers at *Slitz* an excuse to write *Bouncing beauties!* had shrunk and been flattened until they were hardly noticeable. Elin pulled up her sweatshirt.

Her stomach was hanging over the waistband of her jeans. The lips pretended to smile again.

'It was actually possible to use the breast implants and put them in here.' She grabbed hold of the bulge above her right hip and squeezed it. 'Then I had to have quite a lot cut away, of course. They were quite big to start with, beforehand.'

She pulled up the sweatshirt a little further, so that the lower part of her breasts was visible. Anders saw the badly healed scar, and looked down at the floor again. 'Why?'

She straightened her sweatshirt and sat down at the opposite side of the table again, took a sip of her wine and topped up his glass.

'I just wanted to.'

Her voice was breaking slightly. Someone with serious injuries or deformities might behave this way, showing them off as a challenge to the other person—to say something, to dare to question. But now her voice was breaking.

'I haven't finished yet.'

'What do you mean?'

'I haven't finished yet. I'm going to have more work done. More surgery.'

Anders searched her altered face, her eyes, for signs of insanity, but found none. He thought she ought to be radiating something other than sorrowful resignation. Some kind of fanaticism, at least.

'I don't understand.'

'Neither do I,' said Elin. 'But that's the way it is.'

'But what…what are you *aiming for*, so to speak?'

'I don't know. I just know I haven't finished.'

'But what doctor would agree to…'

Elin interrupted him. 'If you've got money, there's always someone. And I do have money.'

Anders turned and looked out of the window. The wind was blowing among the few random fir trees still standing upright on Kattholmen. A storm a few years earlier had brought down most of the trees, and the island became one huge game of pick-up sticks, almost impossible to find a way through. The boathouse might have been smashed to pieces. He hoped it had.

'Are you thinking about the same thing as me?' asked Elin.

'Probably.'

'Everything disappears. In the end.'

'Yes.'

They avoided the topic and started talking about things that had disappeared, what had become of old friends. Anders told her about Maja, making a huge effort not to fall down the shaft that always opened up beneath him when he relived the story by retelling it. He managed to balance on the brink.

The afternoon had drawn a veil of darker grey across the sea, and the wine cask was all but empty when Anders got to his feet, steadied himself on the table and announced he was going home. 'I live here now. I think.'

He had to concentrate hard in order to tie his shoelaces in the dark hallway. Elin stood watching him, her head on one side.

'Why did you come back?'

Anders closed his eyes so that he could manage the laces without being distracted by the way the room was moving. Why had he come back? He tried to find the right words, and eventually said, 'I wanted to be close to something that has some meaning.'

He hauled himself to his feet with the help of the door handle. The door opened and he almost fell out on to the porch, but straightened up and regained his balance. 'What about you?'

'I just wanted to get away. From all the eyes.'

Anders nodded tipsily and for a long time. Completely understandable. All the eyes. Away from all the eyes. He remembered something, something to do with eyes, but he couldn't quite get hold of it. He waved goodbye and closed the door behind him.

The afternoon was rapidly darkening into evening as Anders made his way towards the forest. The wind was picking up; a few particularly playful gusts made him wobble to one side. He was thinking about Elin.

I haven't finished yet. I'm going to have more work done.

He laughed. If you looked at it as a project it was odd, but not incomprehensible. You have to have projects, and destroying your own body is just one of many options. He certainly knew that, if nothing else. Throwing away your money by going under the knife and getting uglier every time, that was grandiose in its way, a real cultural commentary.

Or an atonement.

A big paper bag full of food stood outside his door. He sent grateful thanks across the inlet, hauled the bag into the kitchen and put everything away in the fridge and the larder. When he had finished he drank almost a litre of water to dilute his alcohol-laden blood, then he sat down at the kitchen table and started fiddling with the beads. He added a few blue ones at random around the edge of the tile.

The kitchen curtains were billowing out slightly in the draught from the ill-fitting window, and he lit a fire in the kitchen stove to drive out the dampness that had gathered since the morning. Then he went back to the beads.

Ten blue dots around the edge of big white pattern, like a little patch of sky behind a cloud. He added a few more.

Suspicions

They didn't make love so often these days, but when they did, they did it properly.

That first summer Simon and Anna-Greta hadn't been able to keep their hands off one another. Out of consideration for Johan it had been mostly the nights that had been at their disposal, but it did happen that lust would suddenly strike them like a boiling shoal of herring in the middle of the day as well. Then they would lock themselves in the boathouse and fall on each other on top of the nets, satisfying their hunger and paying for it with various abrasions.

They didn't do that any more. Just as well, really.

Weeks could go by before the circumstances were right. Since they didn't sleep in the same bed or even the same house, lovemaking wasn't something that just happened, unplanned, as an afterthought before they fell asleep. Nor had they got to the point where they could just come straight out with the question. They never would get there, because they both regarded sexuality as a mystery and a secret—not body parts seeking connection.

And so it was a matter of a web of unspoken questions and answers, small movements sounding out the terrain. A hand on an arm, a glance held for just a fraction too long, a smile hinting at mischief. It could go on for days, until they no longer knew who was asking and who was responding, but the certainty grew between them in silence: it was time.

Then they would go to the bedroom together, to Anna-Greta's bedroom as she had a bigger bed. They would light a candle and get undressed. Anna-Greta could still manage to get undressed standing up, but Simon had to sit on the edge of the bed to take off his underwear and socks.

It was increasingly rare that things went well from the start. Perhaps as some kind of preparation for death, Simon's spirit and flesh had begun to take their leave of each other. When Anna-Greta lay down beside him, it didn't matter how much his will wrapped itself around her beloved body, his lips caressing her hip. It just didn't work.

His failing erection was a problem that had been played down for many years, and nowadays it was an expected part of the proceedings. But it still bothered him; every time he thought: *Right—now. Just this once.* He had even thought about Viagra, if only so that, just once, he could surprise her with a really splendid hard-on right from the start, like a gift.

But for the time being, it just had to take as long as it took. They would caress each other, licking and nibbling. From time to time

Anna-Greta would suck tentatively, just to see if the erectile tissues had decided to wake up yet. If there was any sign of a response, she would carry on until he was ready, but usually it was like talking to the wall.

Simon had thought that this was the irony of old age: the only part of him that wasn't rigid and stiff was the part he wanted to be. The years of escapology had ruined his joints, and his skeleton felt like a beach monster, cobbled together from driftwood and rusty nails. He could feel, in fact he could almost hear, the creaking as he moved alongside Anna-Greta's more supple body.

It took longer every year, but gradually the miracle would begin to work. He would feel a warmth between his shoulder blades which slowly spread across his shoulder and down his back, until he could move his arms in a way that was never possible in his everyday life: gently. Anna-Greta smiled when his caresses became more flexible, his touch lighter.

He was at home in his body once again, and when Anna-Greta lowered her head over his midriff the response came like a tingle, and the dead rose. Even at that stage Simon was drifting in the pleasure that is the absence of pain, and he could easily have stopped there, satisfied with being soft and forgetful and close. But when Anna-Greta moved on top of him and guided him inside her, another slumbering feeling awoke. The preparations were over and his body was ready for action. He could release the *lust*.

When they had finally reached that point, their desire was perfectly matched. A burning sphere in the chest, sending red threads up into the head. He grabbed hold of her hips and they followed each other's movements or thrust against each other, doing whatever felt right, and only he and she existed in the whole world.

Once Simon got under way, he could go on for a long time. So they went on for a long time. It would have been stupid not to. Their bodies, weighed down by age, were never as light as they were then, and time and sorrows had never been of so little significance. They were swaying outside time and the years fell away; sometimes Simon

147

was even able to use his stiff fingers, and he took the opportunity to do so.

They no longer dared to change position, since Simon had broken a rib two years earlier throwing himself around. So they stayed where they were, moved in the same place and murmured quiet words of love until everything exploded and became one.

Anna-Greta was asleep. Simon lay next to her, watching her. Her lips were sunken because she had taken out her false teeth after making love. Even with the most supreme effort he could not claim that her mouth was beautiful without teeth, so he didn't look at her mouth.

Her eyelids were thin, almost transparent in the glow of the half-burnt candle, and under the skin he could see her eyeballs moving. Perhaps she was dreaming. The deep lines between her nose and mouth moved up a fraction, as if in her dream she had become aware of a smell she didn't like.

Who are you?

The wind was blowing hard outside the window, and the candle flickered. A shadow passed across Anna-Greta's face, and her expression altered for half a second, became something he had never seen before. Then she was back.

Who are you?

Fifty years together, and he knew everything about her. Except who she was. She had told him stories of the time before they met, he had been with her for almost two-thirds of her life and knew how she would react in virtually any situation. And yet he couldn't get away from that feeling: he didn't know who she was.

Perhaps it was something that everyone experienced, no matter how close they were, but he didn't really think so. This was something more. Something along the lines of…Spiritus. He had never told her what he had in the matchbox. So in some ways he was a stranger to her.

Why haven't I told her?

He didn't know. Something had told him not to. Presumably it was all connected.

Simon sighed deeply and rolled towards the edge of the bed, hauling himself up into a sitting position with some difficulty. If his body somehow shed thirty years when they were making love, it piled an extra thirty on again afterwards. Muscles and joints creaked and complained, and he felt ready for his coffin.

I don't suppose there will be many more times.

He managed to put on his socks, underpants and trousers. In recent years he had thought the same thing every time after they had made love. But when it was time, the machinery would no doubt rumble into life once again. For as long as it lasted.

He dug out his vest and shirt, blew out the candle and crept out of the room. With the help of the banister he made his way slowly and carefully down the stairs, one step at a time. The wind was whistling around the house, and the wood in the old place was complaining more loudly than his own body. The force of the wind had increased to a real storm, and he ought to go down and see to the boat.

And what if it's broken away from its mooring?

Nothing he could do about that. He couldn't cope with that kind of manoeuvre. But at least he would know what the situation was. He grabbed a sweater that was lying on a chair in the kitchen, pulled it over his head and opened the outside door.

The wind seized the door and he had to fight for a few seconds before he managed to close it without a crash. Then he wrapped his arms around his body and shuffled rather than walked down towards his house.

It was a magnificent storm, but it was difficult to enjoy it. The huge birch trees were swaying menacingly over the house, and if one of them came down in the wrong direction the damage would be extensive. As always when it was windy, Simon thought that he ought to cut them down, and as always when the wind subsided he would manage to forget about it, because it was too much work.

He turned his face to the sea and the north wind grabbed him with its full power. The lighthouse at Gåvasten flashed far away in the distance, and the sea…

...the sea...

Something came away inside him. Part of what he needed fell off.

...the sea...

He groped for support and got hold of a branch of the apple tree. A lingering apple was shaken free and fell to the ground with a barely audible thud.

...comes away...falls...

The branch gave way when he put too much weight on it, and he sank down on the grass. The branch slipped from his grasp and whipped across his cheek as it sprang back. He felt a stinging pain and fell on his back, his eyes wide open. The thing that had come away was floating around inside him and he felt ill. And weak. Weak.

The branches of the apple tree where whipping back and forth as if the tree wanted to erase the starry sky, and Simon lay there motion-less, staring. The stars twinkled through the remaining leaves and the strength trickled out of Simon's limbs.

I have no strength. I'm dying.

He lay there like that for a long time waiting for the lights to go out, and he had plenty of opportunity to think. But the stars continued to shine and the wind continued to roar. He tried to move his arm, and it obeyed. His hand closed around a fallen apple and he let it rest there for a while. The exhaustion was diminishing slightly, but he was still weak.

He got to his knees and then to his feet, stood there swaying like a poplar sapling in the wind. One hand felt peculiar, and when he looked he saw that he was still holding the apple. He dropped it. He set off for his house again, his feet dragging.

Something happened.

When he eventually reached his door he peered down at the jetty. It was difficult to see in the faint light from the lighthouse and the stars, but it looked as if the boat was exactly where it should be. The stone jetty was absorbing the worst of it. Not that he would have been able to do anything, particularly not now, but it was good that he still had a boat.

He got himself inside and switched on the light, sat down at the kitchen table breathing in weak bursts, trying to get used to the idea that he was still alive. He had been convinced that he was going to die; he had even managed to reconcile himself to that conviction. To collapse beneath Anna-Greta's apple tree and be swept away by the storm. It could have been worse, much worse.

But it didn't turn out that way.

A thought had taken root in his mind during his painfully slow trek home, a suspicion. He took the matchbox out of the kitchen drawer and opened it. Despite the fact that it was as he suspected, he couldn't help gasping out loud.

The larva was grey. The skin which had been so shiny and black had shrunk and dried, acquired an ash-grey colour. Simon shook the box carefully. The larva squirmed slightly and Simon breathed out. He gathered saliva and let it fall. The larva moved when the saliva landed on it, but not much. It was weak; it seemed to be fading away.

Like me.

The storm was rattling the window panes. Simon sat there staring down into the box, trying to understand. Was it he or Spiritus that came first? Did he influence the larva, or vice versa? Who was to blame—either of them?

Or some third party. Who influences both of us.

He looked out of the window and blinked. Gåvasten lighthouse blinked back.

Communication

Anders woke up because he was freezing cold. The storm was raging around the Shack and inside the house there was a light-to-moderate wind. The curtains were billowing, and cold air swept across his face. He got up with the blanket around his shoulders and went over to the window.

The sea was in turmoil, the waves hurling themselves forward furiously in the moonlight. Stray drops were actually reaching right up to the window, which was creaking ominously under the pressure of the storm. The old windows with their secondary double-glazing were a poor defence against the fury of nature. Plus a couple of windows were already cracked from before.

What will I do if something breaks?

He would just have to see what happened. He put the kitchen light on and drank a couple of glasses of water, lit a cigarette. The clock on the wall showed half-past two. The smoke from his cigarette whirled around in the draughts slicing through the house. He sat down at the table and tried to blow smoke rings, but without success.

Fifty or so blue beads and five white ones were pushed down in one corner of the bead tile. The white ones were in a little clump, surrounded by the blue ones. He rubbed his eyes and tried to remember when he had put them there. He had come home feeling quite tipsy, and had pushed in a few beads at random. After that he couldn't remember a thing until he lay down on the sofa and listened to the wind until he fell asleep.

The pattern formed by the blue and white beads was meaningless and not particularly attractive. He cleared his throat as the smoke formed a viscous lump there, and looked around for a knife or something similar with which he could ease the beads off. There was a pencil lying next to the tile and he picked it up before realising that it wouldn't do.

Then he caught sight of the letters.

The pencil had been lying on some letters, written directly on the surface of the table with so much pressure that they had made grooves in the old wood. Anders leaned forward and read. It said:

CARRY ME

He stared at the letters, ran his finger over the faint indentations they had made.

Carry mf?

It was as if his eyes were glued to the sprawling letters and he didn't dare to look either to the right or left. A shudder ran down his back.

There's someone here.

Someone was watching him. He tensed the muscles in his legs, swallowed hard and without warning he shot up from his chair with such speed that it fell over backwards. He looked quickly around the kitchen, in all the corners and shadows. There was no one there.

He looked out of the kitchen window, but although he cupped his hands around his eyes, the pine trees obscured the moonlight so that it was impossible to see if there was anyone out there. Anyone watching him.

He crossed his arms over his chest as if to keep his racing heart in its place. Someone had been in here and formed the letters. Presumably the same person who was watching him. He gave a start and ran over to the outside door. It wasn't locked. He opened it and saw the swing being hurled in the air, spinning around and slamming into the tree trunks. Nothing else.

He went back to the kitchen and sluiced his face with cold water, dried himself with a tea towel and tried to calm down. It didn't work. He was horribly afraid, without knowing what he was afraid of. An extra-powerful gust of wind made the house shake, and there was a creaking sound.

The next moment one of the windows in the living room shattered, and Anders screamed out loud. Glass came rattling in across the floor, and Anders kept screaming. The wind raced into the house, grabbed hold of anything that was light and loose, threw it around, whistled up the chimney, howled in every hollow and Anders howled along with it. His hair was flapping and damp air poured over him as he stood there screaming, his arms locked around his body. He didn't stop until his throat began to hurt.

His arms released their grip and he relaxed slightly, breathing slowly through his open mouth.

No one came. It's only the wind. The wind broke a window. Nothing else.

He closed the kitchen door. The wind retreated, withdrawing to the living room where Anders could hear it fighting with old newspapers and magazines. He sat down at the kitchen table and put his head in his hands. The letters were still there. The wind hadn't taken them.

CAꓤꓤY ME

He pressed his hands over his ears and closed his eyes tightly. Everything went dark red in front of his eyes, but he couldn't escape. The letters appeared in bright yellow, disappeared and were written once more on his retinas.

CAꓤꓤY ME

Suddenly he took his hands away, got up and looked around. No. The drawings weren't here. He reached the kitchen door in a couple of rapid strides, pulled it open and passed the living room without a thought for the wind that grabbed at the blanket he was wearing like a coat.

He went into the bedroom and closed the door behind him, dropped to his knees next to Maja's bed and groped around with his arm until he found what he was looking for. The plastic folder containing Maja's drawings. With shaking hands he managed to pull off the elastic band and spread the drawings out on the bed.

Most of them had no writing, and on those that did it said, 'To Mummy', 'To Daddy'.

But there was one…

He turned over the various drawings of trees, houses and flowers to check the back of each one, and at last he found it. On the back of a drawing of four sunflowers and something that could be either a horse or a dog, Maja had written:

TO GЯFAT GЯANDMA
AN NA GЯF TA

It had taken her ten minutes and two outbursts of rage before she was satisfied with what she had written. Earlier versions were angrily rubbed out. The drawing had been for Anna-Greta's birthday, and for some reason had never been handed over. It said, 'To Great Grandma Anna-Greta'.

The letter R was the wrong way round just as it was in the words on the table, but what made Anders press his hand against his mouth as the tears sprang to his eyes was a more unusual error: in both cases the bottom stroke of the letter E was missing.

Of course he had known all along what was written on the kitchen table. He had refused to accept it. The handwriting was exactly the same as on the drawing, and it said:

'Carry me'.

It was quarter-past three and Anders knew he wouldn't be able to sleep. The storm had abated somewhat and the sensible thing would be to try and sort out the mess in the living room, if possible board up the window somehow.

But he just didn't have the strength. He felt exhausted and wide-awake at the same time, his brain working feverishly. The only thing he could do was to sit at the kitchen table twisting his fingers around each other as he looked at the message from his daughter.

Carry me.

Where was he to carry her from? Where was he to collect her? Where was he to carry her to? How?

'Maja? Maja darling, if you can hear me…say something else. Explain. I don't understand what I have to do.'

There was no reply. The anxiety was wearing him away, he was about to dissolve into ghostly form. If she was a ghost. If she hadn't actually been here and…

But in that case why did she go away again?

He got up and walked around, unable to settle. He spotted some empty half-litre bottles of Imsdal, the water they had taken with them on outings sometimes. He still couldn't do anything, he was getting nowhere. He might as well put his plan into action.

From the larder he took the six one-litre cartons of Spanish wine he had brought with him to Domarö. He filled the four Imsdal bottles about one-third full. Then he topped up one of them with tap water and drank some of the mixture. It didn't taste good. More like flavoured tap water than diluted wine.

Right at the back of the larder he found two small packs of grape juice. He squeezed some into one of the bottles, on top of the wine. Then he added water. It didn't taste watery now, just like really weak wine. Four and half per cent alcohol maybe, about the same as beer.

He put the top back on and pulled up the cap so that he could suck at the liquid, then sucked down a good mouthful.

His plan to escape the constant urge to drink himself into a stupor was very simple: he would drink constantly, but he would drink less. Maintain a reasonable level of drunkenness from morning till night. He hoped that with this plan both the lacerating, tearing desire and the sharp edges of the world would be softened and made manageable.

He prepared the remaining four bottles in the same way. When he had finished he still had five cartons and a pack of grape juice left. He would use these to fill up the four bottles when they were empty.

Carry me.

He closed his eyes and tried to picture the scene. Maja coming into the kitchen, picking up the pencil, writing those letters and then… then…arranging some beads on the tile before leaving. She was still wearing the red snowsuit and it was soaking wet, she was dripping as she walked and her eye sockets were empty. Greedy fish had…

Stop it!

He opened his eyes and shook his head, took a drink from the bottle. The picture was still there. The small body, her round face, the soaking wet snowsuit…

He examined the floor to see if there was any trace of water. Nothing.

It's me who wrote it. It's me who put the beads on the tile.

That could be what had happened. In which case he was actually going mad. But it was just a memory lapse, surely? It was during that missing period that he…

No.

He had *thought* he'd had a memory lapse when he saw the beads, since he couldn't remember putting them there. Now, of course, there was another explanation.

Carry me.

He banged the table with his fists.

'Show yourself! Say something else! Don't do this!'

He couldn't believe he was quite this crazy. The only explanation was that somebody was playing a really sick joke on him, or…that it was exactly what it appeared to be. That Maja existed in the world, somehow, and was trying to communicate with him.

He placed his palms on the table. Breathed in and out a couple of times, calmly and deliberately.

Yes. All right, so be it. I'm making the decision. I choose to believe it.

He carried on nodding, had another drink of wine and lit a cigarette. He felt better now. Now that he had accepted the situation. He took a deep drag, held it in his lungs, leaned back in his chair and slowly let the smoke out. The storm had died down, so that the smoke reached the ceiling without dispersing.

I believe. You exist.

The circle of light cast by the lamp expanded and turned into a warm feeling that grew in his chest until it radiated a pure, clean happiness.

You exist!

He threw the cigarette in the bin, got up and spun round and round in the middle of the kitchen floor, his arms spread wide. He attempted a few clumsy dance steps, jumped up and down and whirled around until he felt dizzy, started coughing and had to sit down. The happiness was still there. It was crackling and gushing, it wanted to find a way out somehow.

Without thinking he pulled the telephone towards him and keyed in Cecilia's number. He could still remember it, because she had taken over her parents' apartment in Uppsala when they moved into a house. She had the same number as when they were teenagers, spending hours on the phone to each other and longing for their next meeting. If she was still living there.

The phone rang three times. Anders pressed the receiver firmly to his ear, looked at the clock and grimaced. It was just after four. It occurred to him belatedly that this might not be the best time to call. He took a swig from the bottle as the fifth tone rang out.

'Hello?'

It was Cecilia, and she sounded exactly as you might expect—as if she'd just woken up. Anders swallowed the wine in his mouth and said, 'Hi, it's me. Anders.'

There was silence for a few seconds, then Cecilia said, 'You're not to ring here when you're drunk. I've told you that.'

'I'm not drunk.'

'What are you, then?'

Anders thought it over. The answer was simple.

'Happy. I'm happy. And I thought I ought to…to ring and tell you. Why.'

Cecilia sighed, and Anders remembered. He had called her like this several times. After they had separated he had called her sometimes to say…what had he said? He'd been drunk and he couldn't remember. But he had never called and been happy. Well, he didn't think so anyway.

'I see,' said Cecilia. 'So why are you happy?'

It didn't sound as if she was genuinely interested, but he supposed he could understand that, so he took a deep breath and said, 'Maja has contacted me.'

He heard the rustle of bedclothes at the other end as Cecilia sat up. 'What are you talking about?'

Anders told her what had happened. He left out the detail about Elin and all the wine, just said he had fallen asleep and then woken up during the night, found the message on the kitchen table. As he was talking he ran his fingers over the letters on the table, over the beads.

When he had finished there was a long silence. Anders cleared his throat and said, 'What do you think?'

From the sounds at the other end he gathered that Cecilia was lying down again.

'Anders. I've met someone else.'

'Right. Yes.'

'So…there's not much I can do for you. Not anymore.'

'But…this isn't about that.'

'Then what is it about?'

'It's about…about…Cecilia, this really *is* what's happened. Honestly. It's true, what I told you.'

'What do you want me to do?'

What had been so simple suddenly became difficult. Anders looked around the table as if he were searching for a clue. His gaze landed once again on the seven spindly letters.

'I don't know. I just wanted…to tell you.'

'Anders. The time we had together…even though it ended the way it did…if you need help. If you really, *really* need help. Then I'll help you. But not otherwise. I can't. Do you understand?'

'Yes, I understand. But…but…'

The words got stuck just inside his lips. He heard what he'd said, how the conversation had gone. And he realised that she couldn't have said anything other than exactly what she had said.

What would I have said?

He thought about it. He would have fallen on the chance, been ready to believe just about anything. Wouldn't he? After all, he had resisted the miracle himself. But he still wouldn't have responded the way Cecilia did. He would have believed her, just so that he had an excuse to be with her. He felt a stabbing pain in his chest and he coughed.

Cecilia let him finish coughing before she said, 'Good night, Anders.'

'Wait! Just one thing. What could it mean?'

'What?'

'Carry me. What could it mean?'

Cecilia breathed out; it wasn't quite a sigh, because there was a little sound with it, a fragment of a whimper. She could have been on the point of saying something else, but what she actually said was, 'I don't know, Anders. I don't know. Good night.'

'Good night.' After a breath he added, 'Sorry,' but the line was dead and she didn't hear him. Anders put the phone down and rested his forehead on the table.

Someone else.

Only now did he realise how much he had hoped, in some corner of his pissed-up heart, that somehow, somewhere, they might…

Someone else. Had he been there, had he been listening? No. It hadn't felt as if there was another person there. Cecilia hadn't talked as if someone else was listening.

So they're not living together yet. Maybe…

He banged his head against the table. Hard. White pain surged through his skull. Tangled thoughts rose to the surface, were washed away.

Give up. Give up.

He raised his head and the pain was a liquid that altered the situation, was washed from his brow to the back of his head and stayed there. He looked around the kitchen with clear eyes and said, 'There's only you and me.'

The sea embraced the pebbles on the beach, relinquished and embraced them once again. Back and forth, back and forth. The same movement for all eternity. Take hold and let go, begin again.

He was tired now, he hadn't the strength to cope with anything else.

With his headache in place and quiet, he got up and walked through the living room, ignored the glass on the floor and the fire-lighter dust that had been blown around and crunched beneath his feet. He carried on to the bedroom. Without switching on the light or getting undressed, he slid into Maja's bed and pulled her blanket over him.

There now. Everything's all right now.

He looked at the double bed in the middle of the room, faintly illuminated by the moonlight shining through the window.

There's the double bed. I can go over there if I get frightened.

He closed his eyes and fell asleep in seconds.

A discovery by the shore

When someone knocked on his door at eight-thirty in the morning, Simon had been asleep for only a couple of hours. The wind and premonitions of evil had kept him awake until the first light of dawn broke through his bedroom window. By that time the wind had dropped and he had finally relaxed and given himself up to a light sleep. His body was stiff and heavy. He felt as if he was moving underwater as he got out of bed, pulled on his dressing gown and stumbled to the door.

Elof Lundberg looked as if he had woken up just as Simon was falling asleep. Wide-awake and bright eyed, his cap firmly in place. He looked Simon up and down and pulled a face.

'Are you still in bed?'

'No,' said Simon, twisting his head to relieve the stiffness in his neck. 'Not anymore.'

He glowered challengingly at Elof, encouraging him to spit out whatever it was he wanted. He wasn't in the mood for small talk. Not now. And not with Elof. Elof sensed the atmosphere and became truculent. His lower lip jutted out and he raised his eyebrows. 'I just wanted to tell you that your boat has come away from its mooring. If you're interested.'

Simon sighed. 'I am, yes. Thank you very much.'

Elof couldn't help making the most of this opportunity. He had come here with the best of intentions, and was met with a rebuff. He said, 'Of course, there are some people who prefer it that way. With just one rope. But the engine just keeps scraping all the time. And that might not be such a good thing.'

'No, it isn't. Thank you.'

Elof was standing there as if he was waiting for some kind of reward, but Simon knew that wasn't it. He just wanted to help out with the boat, then be invited in for coffee so that he could sit and chat about what could happen when boats broke free, and so on. About how things should be taken care of in the proper way, between neighbours.

But Simon wasn't in the mood, so when Elof had been standing there nodding for a while and Simon hadn't said the right thing, he rubbed his hands together and said, 'Right then. That's that then', and stomped off, every fibre of his body signalling that he had been treated most unfairly. Simon closed the door and lit a fire in the kitchen stove.

If the boat's been like that all night, it can stay like that for a while longer.

He and Elof had got on well until Maja disappeared. When Anders and Cecilia went back to the city, Simon had called on Elof to ask what he had meant when they were standing on the veranda: when he told Simon to ring Anders and tell him to come home.

'Why did you say that?' he had asked.

Elof had become extremely busy with the fry-up he was preparing, and hadn't even looked up from the chopping board when he replied, 'It just occurred to me, that's all.'

'What did you mean?'

Elof was dicing boiled potatoes with exaggerated care. He didn't want to look Simon in the eye.

'Nothing in particular. It just occurred to me that maybe it wasn't a good thing. For them to be out there.'

Simon sat down on a chair and stared at Elof until he had finished with the potatoes and had no choice but to meet Simon's gaze.

'Elof. Do you know something I don't know?'

Elof stood up and turned his back on Simon, started busying himself with the frying pan and butter. He shrugged his shoulders. 'Like what?'

In the end Simon had given up and gone home, leaving Elof with his potato and his chopped bacon. After that day the relationship between them had soured. Simon couldn't begin to guess what it was that Elof knew, but there was something, and he couldn't come to terms with the fact that Elof was refusing to tell him. It was Simon's grandchild they were dealing with here, after all. As good as his grandchild.

When he told Anna-Greta she had more or less taken Elof's part. Said it was probably just something that had come into his head, nothing worth bothering about. What else could it be?

Simon had let the matter rest. But he hadn't forgotten.

The fire in the kitchen stove refused to catch. After the storm during the night the wind had exhausted its strength. There was barely a breath of wind, and the chimney wasn't drawing well. Simon sprayed liquid firelighter on the little flame that was there, and the fire burst into life with a puff of surprise.

He gave an enormous yawn and pulled a chair up close. He had carelessly left the matchbox out on the kitchen table. When he opened it he could see that the larva seemed to have recovered slightly. The skin was no longer grey, but pale black, if such a shade existed. However, it was not shiny, not even after he had given it some saliva. It no longer looked as if it was dying, but it didn't look healthy either.

Spiritus had been in his possession for ten years now. He had given it saliva every day, and changed matchboxes when the old one grew too worn. And yet he had never done what he did now: he turned the box over and tipped the insect into his hand.

163

Something had happened during the night. After regarding Spiritus with a mixture of respect and disgust for all these years, his feelings had changed when he saw it looking pitiful, moribund. Sympathy was not the right word, it was more a kind of shared fate. They were subject to the same conditions.

The skin of the larva met his, and he bit his tongue gently. It is always slightly repulsive to hold an insect. The faint movement, the little life that exists independently of one's own.

But not in this case.

Nothing happened, and Simon relaxed. He sat with the larva on his open palm, and it was warm. Warmer than he was, since he was aware of it. Only a few degrees, but enough for him to perceive it as a warm spot on his hand.

Cautiously he closed his fingers around it and shut his eyes. Gently, gently the larva moved inside his loosely closed hand, and the tickling sensation on his skin ran up his arm, passed through his heart and continued up into his head, where it moved around like a weak electric current, making his scalp tingle.

Simon looked out of the window. The morning dew was shining on the grass and he felt as if he could see every single drop, could touch every single drop with his thoughts. In the trunks of the trees he could see the hidden vessels, the water being sucked up by the capillary action, out into the thin veins in the leaves. As if he were in a trance he walked to the outside door and out on to the porch, his hand still closed around the larva.

It was a shock.

All the water...all the water...

He saw all the water. The moisture in the earth and how it was constituted. The rainwater in the barrel, a living body wrapped around dead insects and old leaves. Through the lawn he saw the underground veins running through the bedrock. And he saw how everything, everything that lived and was green or yellow or red... how it consisted almost entirely of water.

He carried on down towards the jetty and he saw the sea.

Broken.

It was a wordless knowledge, not a clearly formulated thought: the sea was broken. There was something wrong with it. He walked out on to the jetty and he was walking over water. Broken water.

With an effort of will he managed to superimpose his own thoughts over the all-encompassing knowledge that had taken possession of him. The old cotton rope attached to the stern of the boat had broken, and the boat was pointing away from the jetty.

In the past he had needed to be in contact with the water for things to happen. Now he simply asked for a wave to give the boat a push so that it would drift towards the jetty. The wave came and the boat turned on its own axis until the stern bumped into a bollard.

He crouched down, but couldn't reach the stump of rope trailing behind the boat, so he asked the water to throw it to him. A movement from the seabed broke the surface and the rope was thrown up on to the jetty in a cascade of water. Simon was thoroughly soaked, and the end of the rope slipped back into the water before he managed to grab hold of it.

He wiped the water off his face and looked at the rope as it sank towards the bottom; he could see that it had soaked up water in its fibres, so instead he asked the water in the rope to come to him. Like a snake rising from a basket the rope obediently rose up from the surface and slipped into his outstretched hand. He made a simple knot with the short length of rope that was left, and the boat was safely moored once again.

He was frozen in his soaked dressing gown, and as he walked back to the house he asked the water in the fabric to get a little warmer, and the water obeyed. He didn't want to ask it to leave him, because it would probably look rather peculiar if anyone saw him. Walking up from the jetty in a cloud of steam.

The trembling from Spiritus was still running through his body as if his blood had begun to simmer, and he could still see all the water around him with overwhelming clarity. It was like a fever, and he was beginning to feel exhausted. It was overload: unsuitable for humans.

Once he was inside and had placed Spiritus in its box, he tried to complete his last thought.

Unsuitable for humans.

That was the way of it. He had something in his possession that was unsuitable for humans. Perhaps that was why he had kept it a secret: because he wasn't meant to have it. It belonged to someone else. Something else.

Eventually he got dressed and went outside. With Spiritus back in its box in his pocket, the perception of the water's presence had slipped back into its usual place: as a consciousness and a sense, nothing more. He sat down on the seat on the porch and tried to take in the beautiful autumn day without unnaturally heightened senses.

He couldn't quite do it. A pair of jays were rooting around among the bright red rowan berries and he saw only birds. The morning light was slanting across the maple leaves in a thousand nuances between red and yellow, but he saw only a tree. The clouds in the sky were clouds and the sky behind them a vast emptiness.

Everything was in its place, but with no mutual connection. He saw everything that his eyes saw, but the totality escaped him. From a quivering seismograph needle, he had become a rigid stick. He shook his head and patted his pocket.

You're dangerous, you are. I think a person could develop an addiction.

Liberated from his gift of second sight he gazed around his little kingdom on earth: the lawn, the garden, the jetty, the stony shore, the clump of reeds in the inlet. Everything was quiet and nondescript. But there was something in among the reeds. He narrowed his eyes against the glittering surface of the water, and stood up to see better.

It looked like a log. Perhaps a jetty somewhere had been broken up during the night, and strewn across the archipelago. If that was the case, there was probably more driftwood to be collected in the inlet. He straightened up with a groan and walked along the shoreline.

When he got closer he could see that it wasn't a log, unless of course someone had decided to dress a log in a skirt and cardigan.

It's a person. A woman.

The character of his footsteps changed. As he waded out into the water his gait was cautious, respectful. The thing he was approaching was a dead person, and he also thought he recognised the clothes.

Sigrid. Holger's wife.

The water was almost up to the tops of his boots when he was a metre away from the person he was now certain was Sigrid. She was floating on her stomach, but there was no doubt. The grey cardigan and the thick, brown skirt were the clothes she had always worn in the village and at sea, day in and day out.

Sigrid. He stopped. Her medium-length grey hair was floating outwards around her skull as if a big jellyfish was hovering over the back of her head. She was lying a couple of metres into the reeds, and had broken or bent a number of stems under her body on the way in. Simon didn't want to see what her face looked like. With the help of Spiritus he could easily have turned her over, even lifted her ashore, but it was pointless. She had definitely drowned. She had been lying motionless in the calm water all the time he had been moving towards her.

How long has she been lying here?

It must have happened during the night. She had been gone for almost a year, and now the movement of the sea had brought her up, dragged her towards the shore.

A year?

One of Sigrid's arms was stretched out, and he could see a white hand. Simon studied the fingers, and jumped when he thought he saw them move. But it was only the lapping of the water, the shifting sunlight. Nevertheless, he took a step back and rubbed his hand over his face.

Shouldn't she be...a skeleton by this time?

He didn't really know about these things, but he didn't think a person who had been lying in the water for almost a year should

167

still have their fingers intact. There are many hungry creatures in the depths.

Only now did he see himself, standing here with water almost up to his knees looking at a corpse. It was as if there was a bubble around them, an unpleasant spell that was difficult to break. He could remain standing here for a long time.

Göran.

That's what he had to do. He would wade back to the shore and contact Göran. That was it. Slowly he began to back away from the floating body. He didn't want to turn his back on it. Once he reached the shore he finally dared to turn around, and lumbered up to his house as quickly as possible. A couple of times he glanced back over his shoulder just to check.

That she isn't following me.

Fortunately Göran was at home and knew what had to be done. He telephoned the appropriate authorities and an hour later the lifeboat service had retrieved Sigrid's body and transported her over to Nåten. A young police officer asked Simon some questions about the details of his discovery. When he had finished he closed his notebook and asked, 'There's a husband, isn't there?'

'Yes,' replied Simon, glancing at Göran who was standing with his hands in his trouser pockets staring at the ground.

'Where does he live?'

Simon pointed towards Kattudden and was just about to give directions when Göran said, 'I can deal with that. I'll tell him.'

'Is that OK?'

Göran smiled. 'It's less awful. I think you might find Holger a bit…difficult to talk to.'

The police officer looked at his watch. He clearly had better things to do than talk to difficult people.

'Fine,' he said. 'But you ought to warn him that we might have some questions later. When she's been examined.'

'He's not going to run away.'

'What do you mean?'

'The same as you, I presume.'

They looked each other in the eye and nodded in a moment of professional accord.

The officer jerked his thumb in the direction of the inlet and said, 'I mean, she can't have been lying in the water for a year, can she?'

'No,' said Göran. 'Hardly.'

When the young man had gone back to the police launch, Göran and Simon remained on the jetty gazing out across the almost dead calm sea. Apart from the furrow ploughed by the police launch as it headed for the mainland, the water was a gigantic mirror, reflecting the sky and hiding its own secrets.

'Something is happening,' said Simon.

'What's happening?'

'Something to do with the sea. Something's happening to it.'

Out of the corner of his eye Simon saw Göran turn to look at him, but he kept on gazing out over the cold, bright blue surface.

'In what way?' asked Göran.

There were no words to formulate what Simon knew. The closest he could get was the perception that the sea was broken. He couldn't say that, so he said, 'It's changing. It's getting…worse.'

A very small event

Perhaps everything would have been different and this story would have followed a completely different course if a leaf had not fallen. The leaf in question was on the large maple tree that stood twenty or so metres inland from Simon's jetty. Only that morning Simon had glanced at that very leaf as he sat on his porch, liberated from the heightened sensory awareness evoked by Spiritus.

Since it was the middle of October, the maple had lost many of its leaves during the storm, and those that remained were only loosely

169

attached to their branches, in shifting shades of dying. However, it looked as if most of them would cling on for today. The afternoon was dead calm and only, very occasionally, the odd leaf drifted down to join the dry heaps already on the ground.

Who can really say how decisions are made, how emotions change, how ideas arise? We talk about inspiration; about a bolt of lightning from a clear sky, but perhaps everything is just as simple and just as infinitely complex as the processes that make a particular leaf fall at a particular moment. That point has been reached, that's all. It has to happen, and it does happen.

The leaf in question requires no more detailed description. It was an ordinary maple leaf in the autumn. As big as a coffee saucer, some black and dark red patches on a yellow and orange background. Very beautiful and absolutely unremarkable. The cellulose threads that had kept the stalk attached to a branch halfway up the tree had dried out, gravity gained the upper hand. The leaf came away and fell towards the ground.

After Göran had gone to talk to Holger, Simon stayed on the jetty for a long time, staring out across the water. He was searching for something that was impossible to see, the way it is impossible to see land in thick fog, but it was worse than that: he didn't even know what he was searching for.

He gave up and turned inland, intending to go inside and have a cup of coffee. As he left the jetty, his arms swinging and his gaze lost in contemplation, he saw a flickering movement. A second later he felt a caress on his hand. He stopped.

There was a maple leaf on the palm of his hand; it looked exactly as if it were stuck there. He raised his eyes and looked up at the crown of the tree. No more leaves fell. Just this one leaf had fallen, the leaf that he was holding in his hand through no effort of his own; it had drifted down and landed on his hand at the exact moment when he was passing the tree.

He lifted his hand and studied the veins on the leaf as if trying to decipher unfamiliar writing. There was nothing there, and the leaf had no message to give him. The wind was holding its breath, and everything was still.

Here I am.

A sudden and unexpected happiness rose up through his body. Simon looked around, close to tears. He experienced a bubbling gratitude for the fact that he existed at all. For the fact that he could walk under a tree in the autumn and a leaf could fall and land on his hand. It was like a message from the leaf, a reminder: *You exist. I fell and you were there. I am not lying on the ground. Therefore, you exist.*

No, the leaf was not lying on the ground and Simon wasn't lying dead beneath the apple tree or dead among the reeds. Their paths had crossed, and here they stood. Simon was perhaps a little oversensitive after everything that had happened, but it seemed to him like a miracle.

He no longer wanted to go home. He changed direction and headed up to Anna-Greta's house with the leaf in his hand, as some lines by Evert Taube played in his head.

Who has given you your sight, your senses? The ears that hear the waves come rushing, the voice you lift in song.

The autumn world was beautiful around him, and he walked with careful steps to avoid disturbing it. Gently he opened Anna-Greta's door and crept into the hallway, lingering in the feeling that the world was a holy place and every sensory perception a gift. He could smell the aroma of her house, he could hear her voice. Soon he would see her.

'No,' said Anna-Greta in the kitchen. 'I just think we have to talk about the whole thing. Something has changed, and we don't know what that means.'

Simon frowned. He didn't know who Anna-Greta was talking to or what she was talking about, and it made him feel as if he were eavesdropping. He was turning to close the door and thus announce his presence when Anna-Greta said, 'Sigrid is the only case I know, and I have no idea what it means.'

Simon hesitated, then grabbed the door handle. Just before the door slammed shut he heard Anna-Greta say, 'The day after tomorrow, then?'

The door closed behind him and Simon walked through the hallway, making sure he could be heard. He reached the kitchen just in time to hear Anna-Greta say, 'Fine. I'll see you then.' She put the phone down.

'Who was that?' asked Simon.

'Only Elof,' said Anna-Greta. 'Coffee?'

Simon turned the leaf between his fingers and tried to sound unconcerned as he asked, 'So what were you talking about?'

Anna-Greta got up, fetched the cups, brought the coffee pot over from the stove. Simon had asked his question so quietly that she might not have heard it. But he thought she had. He twisted the leaf and felt like a small child as he asked again, 'What were you talking about?'

Anna-Greta put down the coffee pot and snorted, as if the question amused her. 'Why do you ask?'

'I'm just curious, that's all.'

'Come and sit down. Would you like a biscuit?'

The joy that had been bubbling through Simon withdrew, leaving behind a dry riverbed in his stomach. Stones and thorny bushes. Something was wrong, and the worst thing was that he had experienced this before, on a couple of occasions. Anna-Greta had been away, and when he asked her where she had been, she avoided his questions until he gave up.

This time he had no intention of giving up. He sat down at the table and put a hand over his cup when Anna-Greta tried to pour him some coffee. When she raised her eyes to meet his, he said, 'Anna-Greta. I want to know what you and Elof were talking about.'

She tried a smile. When it found no response whatsoever in Simon's face, it died away. She looked at him and for a second something...dangerous crossed her expression. Simon waited. Anna-Greta shook her head. 'This and that. I don't understand why you're so interested.'

'I'm interested,' said Simon, 'because I didn't know that you and Elof had that kind of relationship.' Anna-Greta opened her mouth to give some kind of answer, but Simon carried on, 'I'm interested because I heard you talking about Sigrid. About the fact that something has changed.'

Anna-Greta abandoned the attempt to keep the conversation on an everyday level. She put down the coffee pot, sat up straight and folded her arms. 'You were listening.'

'I just happened to hear.'

'In that case,' said Anna-Greta, 'I think you should forget that you just happened to hear. And leave this alone.'

'Why?'

Anna-Greta sucked in her cheeks as if she had something sour in her mouth that she was just about to spit out. Then her whole posture softened and she sank down a fraction. She said, 'Because I'm asking you to.'

'But this is crazy. What is it that's so secret?'

That hint of danger, of something alien, appeared in Anna-Greta's eyes once again. She poured herself a cup of coffee, sat down at the table and said calmly and reasonably, 'Regardless of what you say. However disappointed you might be. I have no intention of discussing it. End of story.'

Nothing more was said. A minute later Simon was standing on Anna-Greta's porch. He still had the maple leaf in his hand. He looked at it and could hardly remember what he had thought was so special about it, what had made him come here. He threw it away and walked down towards his house.

'End of story,' he mumbled to himself. 'End of story.'

Old Acquaintances

Way back in the Bible
our nursery teachers
had made a note of our real origin:
floated ashore out of the shadows.

Anna Ståbi — Flux

About the sea

Land and sea.

We may think of them as opposites; as complements. But there is a difference in how we think of them: the sea, and the land.

If we are walking around in a forest, a meadow or a town, we see our surroundings as being made up of individual elements. There are this many different kinds of trees in varying sizes, those buildings, these streets. The meadow, the flowers, the bushes. Our gaze lingers on details, and if we are standing in a forest in the autumn, we become tongue-tied if we try to describe the richness around us. All this exists on land.

But the sea. The sea is something completely different. The sea is one.

We may note the shifting moods of the sea. What the sea looks like when the wind is blowing, how the sea plays with the light, how it rises and falls. But still it is always the sea we are talking about. We have given different parts of the sea different names for navigation and identification, but if we are standing before the sea, there is only one whole. The sea.

If we are taken so far out in a small boat that no land is visible in any direction, we may catch sight of the sea. It is not a pleasant experience. The sea is a god, an unseeing, unhearing deity that surrounds us and has all imaginable power over us, yet does not even know we exist. We mean less than a grain of sand on an elephant's back, and if the sea wants us, it will take us. That's just the way it is. The sea knows no limits, makes no concessions. It has given us everything and it can take everything away from us.

To other gods we send our prayer: Protect us from the sea.

Whispers in your ear

Two days after the storm, Anders was standing down in the wormwood meadow inspecting his boat. It was upside down on blocks, and it was a depressing sight. There were good reasons why he had got it for nothing five years ago.

Since there was no system for the disposal of worn-out plastic boats, they were either left lying around, or given away to someone in need. The last resort, if you were really determined to get rid of the wretched thing, was to tow the boat out into the bay, drill holes in it and let it sink. Anders' boat looked as if it might be ready for that final journey.

There were cracks all over the hull, and the engine mounting was split. The fibreglass around the rowlocks was so brittle that it would probably splinter if you attempted to row. Anders did actually have an engine, an old ten-horsepower Johnson up in the shed, but he wasn't sure if he'd be able to get it started.

The boat was really beyond repair, it was just a matter of having some kind of vessel, something to put in the water so he didn't have to borrow Simon's boat when he wanted to stock up on supplies.

He walked out on to the jetty, mainly to see if it was strong enough to bear his weight. Oh yes. Some of the planks were rotten and a log had come loose from the lower section, but the jetty would probably last for another couple of years at least.

A light breeze was blowing from the south-west, and he had to cup his hand around his lighter in order to light a cigarette. He blew smoke into the wind, pulled out the plastic bottle of diluted wine, took a couple of swigs and listened to the sighing of the wind in the reeds in the inlet. It was only eleven o'clock in the morning, but he was already pleasantly mellow, able to contemplate without a trace of anxiety the green reeds rippling in the breeze.

Without the wine he would probably have started imagining things. Sigrid's body had been found in the reeds a couple of days earlier. There was no end to what he might have been able to come up with to scare himself witless. Simon had told him it was as he suspected. Sigrid had been lying in the water for less than twenty-four hours when he found her. Where she had been lying before that, no one knew.

A couple of forensic technicians in waders had prodded around in the reeds. Anders had stood at the bedroom window watching them, but it hadn't looked as if they had found anything that might solve the mystery. They had left trampled reeds behind them and returned to the mainland.

After checking the piece of chipboard he had nailed over the broken window, Anders went inside, poured himself a cup of coffee and sat down at the kitchen table. The number of beads on the tile had now reached a good hundred. Apart from the very first ones, he hadn't put one single bead there himself. It happened at night, after he had gone to bed.

He was still waiting for a message, and the beads gave him nothing.

Apart from the white patch, only blue beads were used.

He could feel Maja's presence in the house more strongly with each passing day, but she refused to give him a clear indication. He was no longer afraid, but rather comforted by the certainty that something of his daughter lingered on in the world. He had her with him, he talked to her. The constant level of slight intoxication prevented him from gathering his thoughts, made him receptive.

There was a knock at the door. After three seconds it opened, and Anders could tell from the footsteps that it was Simon.

'Anyone home?'

'In the kitchen. Come in.'

Anders glanced around quickly to make sure he hadn't left any wine bottles out. All clear. Just a carton of grape juice, standing innocently on the worktop.

Simon walked into the kitchen and sat down without ceremony. 'Have you got any coffee?'

Anders got up, poured a cup and put it down in front of Simon, who was sitting contemplating the bead tile.

'New hobby?'

Anders made a dismissive gesture and caught his own cup, which wobbled but didn't tip over. Simon didn't notice. His gaze was turned inward, and it was obvious he had something on his mind. He sat there for a while running his finger over the surface of the table, drawing invisible shapes, then asked, 'Do you think you can know another person? Really know another person?'

Anders smiled. 'You ought to be the expert in that field.'

'I'm beginning to think I'm not.'

'What do you mean?'

'I mean you can never become another person. However much you might sometimes imagine you can. Have you ever been in the situation where you're so close to someone that sometimes…just for a moment…when you look at that person, you get the impression, just in passing, that…*that's me.* A kind of confusion, a vacuum where you don't know who is thinking the thought. If this other person is me.

And then you realise. That you were wrong. That I am me, after all. Has that happened to you?'

Anders had never heard Simon talk like this, and he wasn't sure he liked it. Simon was supposed to be uncomplicated and stable—Anders had enough existential uncertainty of his own. However, he said, 'Yes. I think so. I know what you mean, anyway. But why? Is it something to do with Gran?'

'Among other things. It's strange, isn't it? You can spend your whole life with another person. And yet you can't know. Not really. Because you can't become that person. Can you?'

Anders didn't understand what Simon was getting at. 'But I mean, this is obvious. We know all this.'

Simon tapped his index finger on the table. Quickly, crossly. 'That's the point. I don't think we do know it. We take ourselves as the starting point, and we imagine a whole lot of things. And just because we understand what the other person is saying, we think we know who she is. But we have no idea. No idea. Because we can't *be* that other person.'

When Simon had gone, Anders lay on Maja's bed for a long time, looking up at the ceiling where the cobwebs floated outwards like dirty lines. He had made up a new bottle, and at irregular intervals he sucked away at it. He thought about what Simon had said.

We can't become another person. But we think we can.

Wasn't that what had driven him to ring Cecilia? The fact that he had assumed she would understand, that she would be able to see what he could see, because they had been a part of each other for so many years. Become the same person, almost.

But there was no mystical connection. They separated, and no longer had anything to do with one another. If their affinity had been real, it would not have been so easy to break. They would have soldiered on and understood each other completely, all the way through the hell in which they found themselves.

Anders raised his bottle and made a circular movement with his hand, encompassing the room and the house, and said out loud, 'But I do understand you.'

Or did he?

He thought about all the times he had stood looking at Maja when she was a baby, sleeping in her cot. How amazed he had been at the rapid movements of her eyes beneath her eyelids when she was dreaming. How he had wished he could get inside her head, see what she could see, try to understand what it was that her young mind could possibly have to work through. What the world looked like to her, really.

No. We don't understand.

After Maja's disappearance he had carried her with him all the time. He had talked to her in his head, or out loud. As time passed, he had formed a clear picture of her. Since she was no longer alive, she couldn't change, and he had carried her like a doll, a frozen image to turn to.

'It's not like that any more,' he said out into the room. 'Now I'm wondering what you're doing. What it looks like where you are, what's happening to you. I'm pretty scared, and I wish I could see you again. That's what I wish most of all.' Tears welled up in his eyes, spilled over and ran down on to Maja's pillow. 'Just to see you again. Hold you in my arms. That's what I wish. That's what I wish.'

Anders snuffled the snot back up his nose, wiped his eyes, dried his tears. He sat up on the edge of the bed and drew his shoulders together, cowering like an anxious child afraid of a telling-off. He spotted the heap of Bamse the Bear comics under the bed, and picked up the top one. Issue number 2, 1993. He had bought a whole pile at a flea market so that Maja would have something to read, or rather look at, when they were on Domarö.

The cover showed Bamse and his friends Little Leap the rabbit and Shellman the tortoise on a boat, on their way to an island shrouded in mist. As usual Little Leap looked terribly worried. Anders lay down on his back on Maja's bed and started to read.

The story was about Captain Buster and some buried treasure, which turned out to be a trick. Anders carried on reading, smiling at the familiar dialogue he had read aloud to Maja so many times, in different interpretations:

'Wait, Bamse! I've got some thunder honey.'

'Puff…thank you, Little Leap…puff!'

'Oh no! He's dropped the pipe. Now they're in trouble.'

Anders moved on to the next story, which was about the vanity of Jansson the cat. From time to time he had a drink from his bottle of wine. When he finished the comic and was looking at the back cover, a picture of two children wearing Bamse hats that you could buy for only fifty-eight kronor, he caught sight of himself.

He was lying in Maja's bed with a Bamse comic in one hand and his bottle in the other. He laughed. Maja had stopped having milk and baby rice a long time ago, but at the age of six she still wanted her juice in a baby's bottle so that she could lie there sucking at it while she was looking at her Bamse comics or listening to tapes.

He realised what he was doing. As long as Maja's bed stood empty and her comics lay unread, there was an empty space where she had been. If he didn't want to erase her and throw away her things, then something had to fill that empty space, and he was using himself. Living her memories and doing what she had done meant that she hadn't disappeared. The things she had loved were still there.

'And in any case, you still exist. Somewhere.'

His legs were heavy as he climbed off the bed. In the hallway he pulled on the fluffy Helly Hansen top that Maja had called his bearskin, and went out to the woodpile.

If he was going to spend the winter living in the Shack, he was going to need wood, lots of wood. The small inheritance he had received after his father's death was almost gone, and he couldn't afford to run the oil-fired central heating any more than was absolutely necessary.

A pile of logs Holger had delivered that last winter still lay there, waiting to be dealt with. Anders went and fetched the chainsaw from the toolshed, topped it up with petrol and oil for the chain, said a little prayer and yanked at the starter cord. The saw didn't start, of course, nor had he expected it to.

When he had pulled the cord maybe thirty times, his right arm was beginning to feel numb and he was dripping with sweat. No sign of life from the saw. He got out his Phillips screwdriver and box spanner, unscrewed the spark plug and cleaned it. It could be something as simple as a rusty spark plug.

When he'd replaced the spark plug he lit a cigarette, took a swig of his wine and stared at the saw for a while; he patted it and tried to coax it along, persuade it that there was nothing wrong with the carburettor or some other part he couldn't fix. That the problem had been with the spark plug, and that was all sorted now.

'And I have to have wood, you see. If I'm going to stay here. If I haven't got any wood I'll have to move, and you'll end up out there in the shed rusting away for another winter.'

He took another swig of wine, thought things over and realised that there was a hole in his argument. The saw would be out in the shed even if he did get some wood.

'OK, how about this. If you start up now, you can spend the winter indoors in the warmth, just as you should have done in the past. My mistake. OK?'

With his heel he ground the cigarette stub into the carpet of old sawdust that covered the area.

I'm talking a lot. I'm talking to everything.

He picked up the saw, pulled out the choke, took a deep breath and yanked the cord. The motor coughed, one cylinder fired and Anders quickly pushed the choke back in, but the motor died. When he yanked again, it worked. The saw was obviously open to persuasion.

The chain was as good as new, and it was easy to slice the logs into manageable blocks. By the time the tank was empty, he had sawn up a good third of the logs.

His head was buzzing when he took off his ear protectors. During the half hour when he had stood bent over the logs with the saw, slicing and rolling, slicing and rolling, he had not thought about *anything*. No bad thoughts, no good thoughts, nothing. Just the roar of the saw and the tickling sensation of the sawdust spraying against his shins.

I could live like this.

He was sweaty and his mouth was dry, but instead of quenching his thirst with wine he went into the house and had a long drink of water. He felt better than he had for ages, he even felt as if he'd done something just a little bit worthwhile. It had been a long time since he felt like that.

Back outside he finished off the wine to celebrate, smoked a cigarette and fetched the axe. More than half the wood was fir, and it had been lying there drying for two years. He started on that. It was hard work, most of the blocks took several minutes to chop. In between he relaxed with a piece of birch or elm.

He had been working with the axe for about an hour, his arms were aching and he was just about ready to call it a day, when he felt it again. Someone was standing behind him, watching him. This time he wasn't afraid. With the head of the axe he pushed away the piece of birch that was lying on the chopping block, tightened his grip on the handle of the axe and spun around.

'Who are you?' he yelled. 'Come out! I know you're there!'

The yellow foliage of the poplars rustled and he squinted up at the quivering leaves as if they were metal slats on an advertising hoarding. At any moment a message would appear, or a face become visible. But nothing came. Only the continued perception of a dark threat. Someone weighing him up and sharpening a knife.

Suddenly he heard a flapping sound and a dark ball flew past his head. Instinctively he raised the axe to protect himself, but the ball carried on past his head, and soon afterwards he heard a thud from inside the toolshed.

A bird. It was a bird.

He lowered the axe. The bird was banging about inside the shed, a panic-stricken rustle of feathers, the scrabbling of claws. It was a small bird, he could tell that from the sound. Anders waited. The feeling of being watched had gone.

The bird?

No, it wasn't the bird that had been watching him. It was something bigger and darker. The bird had just happened to come along. Anders took a couple of steps towards the shed and peered in through the door. Even if it was a small creature, there is something about birds in enclosed spaces that encourages caution. The sudden, rapid movements, the beak and claws. They might be small, but they're also sharp.

It wasn't until he had summoned the courage to go right up to the open door that he spotted the bird. He was useless at identifying different species, it might have been a bullfinch. Or a great tit. It was sitting right at the back of the shed, on top of a plastic bottle on a shelf. It was clambering around like a circus artist, balancing on the bottle's narrow stopper.

Anders took a step into the shed. The bird shifted uneasily, its claws rasping on the plastic. The black eyes were shining, and Anders couldn't tell what it was looking at. He leaned closer and whispered, 'Maja? Is that you, Maja?'

The bird didn't react. Anders reached out his hand towards it. Slowly, a few centimetres at a time. When he was on the point of just brushing against the feathers, the bird jumped and flew out of the shed. Anders stood there with his hand outstretched, like someone who had tried to capture a mirage. He closed his fingers around the neck of the bottle instead.

He looked out of the door, but the bird had disappeared. For the lack of anything else to do, he examined the bottle in his hand. It was filled with a cloudy liquid that looked like neither fuel nor oil. He undid the stopper and a bitter odour came surging out. He had no idea what it could be. As he screwed the stopper back in he turned the bottle slightly and noticed a hand-written label.

He recognised the writing. The curly, unsteady letters belonged to his father. On a scrap of torn-off sticky tape he had written,

'WORMWOOD'. The bottle contained some kind of wormwood concentrate, perhaps to get rid of insects. Or roe deer.

Anders shook his head. Wormwood was poisonous, and this bottle must have been standing here when Maja was running around the place playing.

Typical lousy parent.

As a belated penance Anders screwed the stopper in firmly and placed the bottle on the shelf above the workbench, where Maja wouldn't be able to reach it. Then he went out and fetched the wheelbarrow. Before he could put the newly cut wood into the store, he would have to move the old, dry wood to the front.

Once again he found that the work gave him the peace of oblivion which he now realised was something worth striving for. After a good hour he had reorganised the wood store and was able to put the new wood inside. Twilight had begun to dim the brightness of the sky by the time he tipped the wheelbarrow up against the wall of the shed. He took off his gloves and rubbed his hands together as he contemplated the wood store, which was now looking much healthier.

A day's work. A good day's work.

He was famished after all his efforts, and cooked a meal consisting of a huge portion of macaroni with half a kilo of Falun sausage. When he had finished eating and smoked a cigarette, he sat for a long time looking out of the window. His whole body was aching, and he almost felt like a real person.

He considered taking a stroll over to Elin's to see if she fancied sharing a little undiluted wine, or rather a lot of wine, but he decided against it, partly because she had been away for two days and probably wasn't home, and partly because he didn't think he would need any wine in order to get to sleep tonight. For the first time in ages.

Meeting

Simon had had enough.

The discovery of Sigrid's body and what had followed had been the final straw. He could no longer close his eyes to what had been moving closer for fifty years. Enough was enough.

The story of his escape by the steamboat jetty had been polished over the years, bounced between him and Anna-Greta and worn smooth until it was now the jewel of a story they had told Anders only four days ago; he was merely the latest in a long line of listeners. A story of heroic deeds and awakening love.

Of course it was that kind of story as well, but something essential was missing. He had taken up that something with Anna-Greta, but she had refused to have anything to do with it, and it had been expunged from the official story. This bothered him.

But Simon remembered it very well. What had really happened.

It had been an unusually simple escape, to start with. Only chains had been used, and chains rarely posed a problem. While he was still standing in the sack he had got out of most of them, and had also picked the lock on the handcuffs.

When the push that sent him down into the water came at last, he had calculated that he would need a maximum of thirty seconds to free himself from the last of the chains and get out of the sack. Then all he had to do was swim over to the jetties and wait a minute or two, just for effect.

The sack hit the water and he sank. He had learned to close the airways in his nose so that he could even out the pressure without using his fingers. On his way down to the bottom he pressed twice, which made the eardrum push outwards in the right way and reduced the noise and the pain in his head. He closed his eyes to enable him to concentrate better as the cold water penetrated through the sack and began to make his limbs stiffen.

The greatest danger in spending a long time underwater was not the lack of oxygen. He had trained himself to be able to hold his breath for more than three minutes. No, the real danger was the cold. After only a minute the fingers would start to become incapable of precise movements. That was why he always tried to make sure the handcuffs were dealt with as quickly as possible.

This time that problem had already been resolved. When his body hit the bottom he had only a few simple twists left before he could rip open the sack with the sharpened picklock and swim towards his triumph.

It was then, just as he was easing the penultimate chain over his shoulder, that the water above him suddenly became heavier. Something laid itself on top of him. His first thought was that someone up on the jetty had thrown something into the water. Something large and heavy. He was being pushed down to the bottom, and had to make quite an effort to stop the air being forced out of his lungs.

He opened his eyes and saw only darkness. The cold that was working on his skin from the outside now had help from the cold fear on the inside. His heart began to beat faster, consuming the valuable oxygen he had left. He tried to understand what could possibly be lying on top of him, so that he would have a better chance of escaping from its grip. He couldn't come up with anything. It had no shape, no seams. The first feeling he had had was the closest he got: the water had become heavy.

Panic threatened. His eyes had now grown accustomed to the faint light that penetrated through the sacking and six metres of water. When a few bubbles of air escaped from his lips, he could see them as blurred reflections.

I don't want to die. Not like this.

With an enormous effort he managed to twist his body in the grip of the water so that the last chains fell off. He still had time. When he was training himself to hold his breath he had sometimes had Marita there to help, which had given him the courage to hang on as long as possible. He could tell when he was about to lose consciousness. He wasn't there yet.

But he couldn't escape from the weight. It was lying on top of him like a giant pestle, and the sack was a peppercorn in the bottom of the mortar.

He managed to rip open the sack with the picklock, and was rewarded with a glimmer of real daylight. He was lying on his back, pressed against the seabed, and way up above he could see the contours of the people on the jetty, the blue sky above them. Nobody had thrown anything, there was nothing on top of him. Except water. Six metres of impenetrable water.

The cold had now got a serious grip on him, and a feeling of calm was beginning to spread through his body. A calm that resembled warmth. He relaxed and stopped fighting. He had at least a minute left before it was over. Why should he spend that minute struggling and fighting? He had freed himself from the chains, the handcuffs and the rope, but he knew he wouldn't be able to free himself from the water. He had been defeated in the end.

Everything was beautiful.

Quiet and helpless, Simon lay there on the seabed. He lay there like the dead, and through the tear in the sacking he could see the sky and vague figures waiting for him. It was the angels calling him to them, and in a while he would be there. He was in darkness, but soon he would come into the light, and it was good.

He didn't know how long he lay like that. It might have been one minute or two, perhaps ten seconds, when the water suddenly released its pressure. As lightly as a veil the weight was withdrawn, and he was free.

With a calm which he would later find difficult to comprehend, he merely thought something along the lines of: *I see, we're doing it this way, then.* He got out of the sack and swam with even strokes over to the far jetty. Nothing grabbed at him, nothing wanted to get at him. There was no weight, only lightness. When he broke the surface of the water, hidden from view by the boats, he took a deep breath, and only then did everything go black. He grabbed at the rail of the nearest skiff and managed to stop himself from sinking. He breathed evenly and calmly, and the world began to come together once again.

From the steamboat jetty he could hear someone shouting, 'Three minutes!' and he couldn't believe they were referring to him. He had been gone much longer than that.

Simon hung on to the rail and tried to regain his grasp of reality. When the voice on the jetty yelled, 'Four minutes!' he had come to his senses. He recognised the faint smell of tar from the skiff, the taste of salt and old fear in his mouth, the piercing cold in his muscles.

I'm alive.

He swam towards the shore and after a couple of metres he was able to walk in the shallows, crouching down behind the boats. He carried on up on to the rocks, and the rest of the story matched the official version.

This was the first in a series of things he had allowed to pass over the years. A number of people had disappeared under dubious circumstances, he had found Spiritus, and Maja had vanished into thin air. He had allowed himself to be assured that everything was as it should be, because it was easier that way and because the alternative was impossible to put into words. It was just ridiculous to think there was some kind of silent conspiracy among those who lived on Domarö all the year round. And yet he had begun to wonder if that wasn't precisely the situation.

Simon pulled his old leather jacket on over his overalls and went out. There was a thread, and now he was going to tug at it to try and provoke a reaction. The thread was called Holger. The discovery of Sigrid's body had obviously shaken him, because there had been no sign of him, so perhaps he was off balance and susceptible to a chat.

It was four o'clock in the afternoon, and the sound of an axe chopping wood echoed across the inlet. Simon nodded to himself. Anders was obviously hard at work, and that was a good thing. The dull sound of a lump of wood being repeatedly thumped against the chopping block suggested that he had made a start on the dry fir.

Well, that will give him plenty to do.

The village was deserted in the soft afternoon light. The school children had gone home, and were probably having something to eat. Simon looked down towards the jetty and remembered that day long ago when he had stepped ashore for the first time. Astonishingly little had changed. The wooden boats around the jetty had become fibreglass boats, and some kind of transformer station stood there humming quietly at the end of the jetty, but otherwise everything looked just the same as it had done then.

The waiting room had been torn down and rebuilt. The boat-houses were listed as cultural heritage these days, and thus remained unchanged, the diesel tank was still there spoiling the track up to the village, and the sea buckthorn perhaps looked a little better, but was still in exactly the same place. These things had seen him step ashore, had seen him almost drown, and now they saw him walking through the deserted village kicking pebbles along in front of him as he went.

You know more than me. A lot more.

He was so absorbed by his own feet that he didn't notice there was a light on in the mission house until he was virtually on top of it. It was only in exceptional cases that the mission house was used at any time other than a Saturday morning, when a small flock of the older residents gathered to drink coffee and sing hymns to the accompaniment of a treadle organ.

The curtains were closed and the chandelier on the ceiling, the pride and joy of the mission house, was visible only as a pale blotch. Simon went up to the window and listened. He could hear voices, but not what was being said. He thought for a moment, then went around the side and opened the door.

The village council. I'm part of this village as well.

The sight that met his eyes as he walked in was in no way remarkable. A dozen individuals aged between sixty and eighty were sitting on chairs in a loose huddle beneath the votive nave. He knew or recognised every one of them. There was Elof Lundberg and his brother Johan. There was Margareta Bergwall and Karl-Erik something-or-other from the south of the village. There was Holger. And Anna-Greta. Among others.

The conversation stopped the second he opened the door. Every face turned towards him. They looked neither caught out nor embarrassed, but their expressions made it very clear that his intrusion was not welcome. He looked at Anna-Greta, and saw something different in her face. A hint of pain. Or a prayer.

Go away. Please.

Simon pretended not to notice anything; he just walked in and said cheerfully, 'So what are you all cooking up, then?'

Glances were exchanged, and the unspoken agreement seemed to be that Anna-Greta should be the one to respond. When a few uncomfortable seconds had passed without her saying a word, Johan Lundberg said, 'A Stockholmer wants to buy the mission house.'

Simon nodded thoughtfully. 'I see. And what are you thinking of doing?'

'We're wondering whether to sell.'

'Who is this Stockholmer? What's his name?'

When no reply was forthcoming, Simon went over to the group, pulled up a chair and sat down.

'Carry on. I think this is interesting as well.'

The silence was suffocating. A faint clicking sound came from the old wooden walls, and a petal drifted down from the wilting flowers on the altar. Anna-Greta scowled at him and said, 'Simon. You can't be here.'

'Why not?'

'Because...you just can't. Can't you accept that?'

'No.'

Karl-Erik stood up. He was the most well-preserved of those present, and a pair of still muscular arms protruded from his rolled-up shirt sleeves. 'Well, that's the way it is,' he said, 'and if you're not prepared to leave of your own free will, then I'll just have to carry you out.'

Simon stood up as well. He hadn't much to offer in comparison to Karl-Erik, but he looked him in the eye anyway and said, 'You're welcome to try.'

Karl-Erik raised his bushy eyebrows and took a step forward. 'If that's the way you want it...' Without any definite purpose in mind, Simon closed his hand around the matchbox in his pocket. Karl-Erik angrily shoved a couple of chairs out of his way, working himself into a rage.

Anna-Greta shouted 'Karl-Erik!' but it was no longer possible to stop him. He had a glint in his eye, and a task to see through. He stepped up to Simon and grabbed hold of his jacket with both hands. Simon lost his footing and hit Karl-Erik's chest with his head, but he didn't let go of the matchbox.

With his forehead pressed against his opponent's ribs, he asked the water in Karl-Erik's blood, the water in his tissues, to hurl itself upwards. The strength in Simon's request was not as great as when he had held Spiritus in his bare hand, but it was more than enough. Karl-Erik staggered, let go of Simon's jacket and put his hands up to his head. He reeled backwards a couple of steps, then leaned forward and threw up all over the antique rug.

Simon let go of the matchbox and folded his arms across his chest once more. 'Anyone else?'

Karl-Erik coughed and retched, threw a venomous look at Simon and retched a little more, then wiped his mouth and hissed, 'What the fuck do you...'

Simon sat down on his chair and said, 'I want to know what you're discussing.' He looked from one to the other. 'It's the sea, isn't it? What's happening to the sea.'

Elof Lundberg rubbed a hand over his bald head, which looked indecently naked without the obligatory cap, and asked, 'How much do you know?'

A couple of the others looked angrily at Elof, since his question implied an admission that there was something to know. Simon shook his head. 'Not much. But enough to know there's something wrong.'

Karl-Erik had pulled himself together and was on his way back to his seat. As he passed Simon he spat, 'And what exactly are you intending to do about it?'

Simon unzipped his jacket to indicate that he intended to stay. He looked at the group, which was tightly closed around an invisible centre, making no move to invite him into the circle. Anna-Greta wouldn't look in his direction, which he found hurtful. Despite his bad feeling, he hadn't wanted to believe it would be like this.

What are they so afraid of?

It couldn't be anything else. They sat there like some little sect, fearfully protecting their secret and their belief, terrified of any intrusion. What Simon couldn't understand was that Anna-Greta was part of this. If there was ever a person he had met in his life who didn't seem to be afraid of *anything*, it was her. But here she sat now, her eyes darting everywhere, focusing anywhere but on him.

'I'm not intending to do anything,' said Simon. 'What could I do? But I want to know.' He raised his voice. 'Holger!'

Holger, who had been deep in thought, jumped and looked up. Simon asked, 'What really happened to Sigrid?'

Perhaps Holger hadn't really picked up on any of the previous aggression towards Simon, because he answered sourly, as if Simon already knew, 'That's exactly what we're talking about.'

Simon was about to say something ironic about the fact that he thought they were talking about the mission house, but if he did that they could carry on attacking him and bickering until the cows came home, so instead he folded his arms and simply said, 'I'm not going anywhere. It's up to you how you deal with that.'

At last Anna-Greta was looking at him. Her gaze was direct and impossible to interpret. There was no love in it. No loathing or any other emotion either. She was a function looking at another function and trying to assess it. She looked at him for a long time, and Simon looked back. The sea lay between them. In the end she clamped her lips together, nodded briefly and said, 'Would you be kind enough to go out for a couple of minutes, at least? So that we can come to a decision.'

'About what?'

'About you.'

Simon considered the matter and decided this was a reasonable request. With exaggerated care he zipped up his jacket and went out. Just before the door closed he heard Karl-Erik say, 'Bloody summer visitors, they think...' then the door closed on the rest of his comment.

Simon walked a few metres away from the mission house and stood there contemplating the autumn. The thicket of dog roses next to the mission house wall was covered in rosehips, red and alive like insects. All the leaves were gradually turning yellow, and the rust-coloured roof tiles shone slightly with dampness. Odd chips of gravel sparkled on the path when a shaft of sunlight penetrated through the foliage.

The loveliest place on earth.

It wasn't the first time he had thought that. Particularly in the autumn, he had often been brought to a standstill in admiration of the beauty of Domarö. How could this be a depopulated community, why didn't everyone want to live here?

He walked a little way along the track, drinking in more of the autumn's miracles: the clear water in the rock pools, the wet tree trunks, the moss saturated with green dampness. The white-painted tower of the alarm bell, stretching up towards the sky. He wasn't thinking about anything other than what was before his eyes. He knew he could think about something else, about the change that was perhaps about to take place, but he refused. Maybe he was saying a kind of goodbye.

He had been ambling about in this way for perhaps five minutes when the mission house door opened. Anna-Greta came out and waved him over. He couldn't tell from her face what the decision was, and she turned away before he reached her.

When Simon walked back into the warmth he had no need to ask. An extra chair had been drawn into the circle, between Johan Lundberg and Märta Karlsson, who used to run the shop before her son took over. Simon didn't know if it was deliberate, but he had been placed opposite Anna-Greta.

He took off his jacket, hung it over the back of the chair and sat down with his elbows resting on his knees. Karl-Erik was two seats away to the left, sitting as if he were holding a barrel of nitro-glycerine on his lap. If he moved or slackened his grip, he would explode.

Anna-Greta looked around the group and licked her lips. She had obviously been nominated as chair. Or perhaps she always had taken that role.

'First of all,' she said, 'I want you to tell us how much you know. And how you know.'

Simon shook his head. 'So that you can work out what to tell me? No. It seems as if you've decided...' Simon glanced briefly at Karl-Erik. '...that I'm allowed to know. So tell me.'

Anna-Greta looked at him in that way again. But there was a difference. It took Simon a moment to work out what it was. Then he realised: she was embarrassed. All this was her fault, because she was the one who was Simon's partner. He was her responsibility.

Elof Lundberg slapped his hands down on his knees and said, 'We can't sit here all day. Tell him. Start with Gåvasten.'

So she did.

Gåvasten

It was a hazardous business, being a fisherman in the olden days, before meteorology. There were no forecasts to consult, nothing to tell you how much of its better nature the sea was planning to show; or whether it was intending to whip itself into winds that would smash both people and vessels to pieces.

And if things went very badly, if the fragile boats that had set out to gather in the nets ran into a strong wind, what chance was there for the crew to communicate the fact that they were in distress? The most they could hope for was that God would hear their cries, and his readiness to help was somewhat capricious.

But they did their best. When it seemed as if all hope had gone, when the crew were lined up along the gunwale to stop the waves crashing over the deck, they would sometimes make lists of the promised collections that would be taken up when they came ashore, if they ever came ashore. Sometimes God allowed himself to be persuaded, and the lists would be read out in church the following Sunday and the collection would be taken.

But it wasn't a reliable method. Many notes detailing extensive promises of contributions to the glory of God sank to the bottom with those who had made them. Incomprehensible, one might think. But Our Lord is no businessman.

Yes, life as a herring fisherman was a risky business in the olden days, but sometimes it could be very rewarding. Entire families moved to the outer islands during the summer, spending a few months laying, gathering in and checking their nets. The herring were salted in barrels and stored away, and later in the autumn they would be transported home and sold.

Sweden is built on salt herring. What did they use to feed the army, what did they give to the foreigners who came to build churches, and to other workers? Herring, that's what! And what kept those who lived on the coast alive during the dark winter months?

Exactly. Herring.

People were so afraid of upsetting this valuable fish that the official document of the harbour guild states, 'Any person who shows disrespect towards any fish, and calls it by an incorrect name in a spirit of contempt will pay a fine of 6 marks'.

The silver of the sea. It had to be brought up, and that involved risk. But people looked for opportunities to stack the deck, so to speak. To reduce the risks and be able to feel secure.

Anna-Greta's story took place many hundreds of years ago. The area that today comprises Nåten was still partly under water. Domarö with its surrounding archipelago made up the outermost islands. This was also the site of the rock that used to be called Gåfwasten even further back in time. This was the place where people were in the habit of leaving gifts for the sea, after, for example, a successful trip across to Åland and back.

Exactly how the next phase began is shrouded in darkness. It is possible that someone might have got stranded on Gåvasten and been swept away into the waves, or simply disappeared. At any rate, people noticed that after this event the catches improved significantly, and the sea remained obliging all summer long.

It made people think.

The following summer, an insolent young man who had no time for superstitious nonsense declared that he was willing to be left on Gåvasten. He was provided with sufficient food and drink for a week, and if nothing had happened during that time, someone would come and rescue him.

They left the young man on the bare rock, rowed back to the fishing grounds a nautical mile or so away, and carried on laying their nets as if nothing had happened. The very next day they had the record catch of the summer, and the herring continued to pour into their nets in the days that followed.

When they returned to Gåvasten after a week, the young man was gone. They inspected the leftover food and drink, and found that it was virtually untouched. He couldn't have spent many hours on Gåvasten before the sea took its tribute, and gave them herring in return.

And so the situation was clear. The problem was how to proceed in the future.

The catches were enormous that summer, and during the October market they were able to sell more than twice as much fish as in previous years. Come the winter, discussions were held, and this was the decision they made: since no one was willing to offer themselves as a gift to the sea, they would simply vote. Women and children were not allowed to participate, but nor were they at risk of being sacrificed. This was a matter for the men.

Now, it would be nice to be able to tell of the heroic resignation with which the chosen person received the verdict. Unfortunately this was not the case. The voting was carried out with no mercy, and simply turned into a vote as to who was least popular in the fishing community. It was usually some angry and unreasonable individual who was selected, and the dubious honour didn't make him any more amenable.

The victim would be hauled off to Gåvasten with something of a violent struggle, then his companions would row away as fast as they could with his curses echoing across the bay. Everybody kept their eyes down.

It came to be common practice simply to bind and fetter the victim before depositing him on Gåvasten. As the years passed, the custom was rationalised even further. No one really wanted to set foot on Gåvasten, and it turned out it was enough to chain up the victim and drop him in the sea. The desired effect was still achieved. The herring poured in, and the sea did not seek any further sacrifices.

By this stage people had settled permanently on Domarö. The pact with the sea made the population as rich as it is possible to be from fishing, and the houses were in no way inferior to those on the mainland. And yet it was not a happy island.

The annual sacrifice took its toll on the souls of the people. It wasn't many years before they stopped excluding women and children from the sacrificial duty. Since it was still only the men who voted, it was, shamefully, the women and children who ran the greatest risk of being selected.

It's unlikely that anyone was exactly happy at having to tie up a child, and then, as it sobbed and pleaded for its life, to throw it over the gunwale and watch it sink. But they did it. They did it, because that was the custom. And it ate away at the people.

No one was pleased when spring arrived, because spring was

merely a forerunner of the summer. The leaves burst into life late in the archipelago, and when the trees became flecked with green it was not long to the summer solstice, and the whole of Domarö lived in fear of that day, the day when the vote traditionally took place.

You might imagine that the risk of being voted out would make people amenable and less inclined to use harsh words, for fear of being regarded as difficult. You might certainly imagine that. However, that wasn't how it turned out.

Instead of friendliness, a climate of ingratiation flourished; instead of honesty, falseness blossomed. The kind words lost their way and turned into whispers and conspiracies, people gathered in clandestine groups and formed alliances. It had been bad enough when the vote was a matter of excluding the person who brought least joy to the group. That time was now past. Now they drowned the person who had failed in the game of intrigue.

There were heroic gestures, of course, born out of a kind of love. A mother or father took the place of their child, a brother allowed himself to be put in chains instead of his sister. But after a few years that love also disappeared. Someone whose life was spared one year could be the victim the following year. People sank into apathy, brought home their plentiful catch of herring and took no pleasure in anything.

At this time, Domarö was virtually isolated. The only contact with the outside world was in connection with selling the fish in autumn. However, as the years went by, rumours inevitably began to spread. The odd visitor reported on the oppressive atmosphere on the island, and the people from Domarö always kept themselves to themselves at the market. Spoke to no one unless it was a matter of business, never ventured a smile. And after all, people kept disappearing. That couldn't be concealed in the long term.

In 1675, a thorough investigation was finally carried out into the situation on Domarö. A delegation of aldermen, priests and members of the constabulary from Stockholm were conveyed to the island to see if the epidemic of heresy and devil worship that had taken root in the capital had also spread to the archipelago.

They found that indeed it had. Accustomed as they were to slandering each other and conspiring, the residents of Domarö were not slow to denounce others when they were under pressure. There was no end to the confessions that spilled out behind closed doors, but always about the neighbours. Always about the neighbours.

The members of the delegation found it impossible to untangle the skein of accusations and counter-accusations with which they were confronted, and they decided that as an interim measure they would have a number of men arrested—those who seemed to be the most compromised. These men were transported to Stockholm and held in custody.

Under questioning the men admitted that the sacrifices had been made with the aim of gaining material benefits, but they refused to admit there had been any kind of pact with the Evil One. After a couple of weeks of intense interrogation involving pincers and thumbscrews, most of them changed their minds. It seemed, when it came down to it, people had not only prayed to the Evil One but danced with him.

The torturers and the scribes between them finally managed to produce a comprehensive document that was completely in line with what the authorities had feared they might find. Domarö was a cauldron where the Devil's stinking juices were slowly stewing, and the island was a danger to the entire archipelago.

They were somewhat surprised when they returned to Domarö to call the rest of the population to account and found that nobody had fled. They interpreted this as obduracy and a stubborn belief that the powers of evil would stand by them. Therefore, they would be shown no mercy. Domarö was emptied of its people, and a long drawn-out investigation began.

After a whole year, the verdict was delivered. There was better evidence here than in many other trials going on at the time. This was not merely a question of a fleeting word that might have sullied the honour of God, or ambiguous confessions from children and servants—no, in this case human sacrifices had definitely taken place, and evil surrounded the accused like a cloud. They wanted to make an example of the people of Domarö.

All the men were sentenced to death, along with a number of women. For reasons that are unclear, some individuals were accorded the privilege of being beheaded first. Perhaps they had been particularly assiduous in denouncing others. The rest were burned alive.

The women who were left were sent to work in spinning work-houses, the children were distributed around different institutions. On Domarö the nets rotted on the drying racks, and the winter ice crushed the boats to matchwood. No one wanted anything to do with the island, and ideally they would have liked to erase it from the maritime charts if not from the surface of the earth.

To some extent their wishes were granted. The following summer, a few days after the solstice, a storm passed over the archipelago. Its effects were felt everywhere on the inhabited islands, large and small, but nowhere was the devastation greater than on Domarö.

As already stated, no one was keen to step ashore, but when the storm had abated and people dared to venture out in boats again, they could see from a considerable distance what had happened. The magnificent houses that the residents of Domarö had built and paid for with their evil trade were gone. Their boats were gone and the jetties off which the boats had been moored were gone.

Not that they had disappeared into thin air, oh no. The foundations of the houses were still there, and the wreckage of the houses they had supported was strewn across the rocks. The odd log from a jetty was still sticking up out of the water. But there was not one single building left.

It was impossible to interpret this in any other way than to assume that God had been offended by the sight of Domarö. The island had been like a needle in his eye, and now he had allowed the sea to draw its rake across it in order to free the archipelago of this abomination.

During the whole of that summer and far into the autumn the mainland and surrounding islands were tormented by driftwood from Domarö. Timber from houses and jetties drifted up on to other shores, and were received with the same delight as clothes handed down from someone who had died of the plague. Fire was the only cure, and at irregular intervals bonfires flared up on the rocks as they burned what was left of the settlement of Domarö, down to the very last splinter.

So ends the first chapter in the story of Domarö.

Call-out

Simon was feeling ill at ease. Anna-Greta had not told her story as if it were some shaggy dog story from the past, but as if she were relaying a sacred text. Her expression had been distant and her voice husky, thick with the seriousness of what was coming out of her mouth. Simon didn't recognise his Anna-Greta at all.

However, he couldn't just dismiss it as a folk tale which for some reason had become gospel. His own experience got in the way. What had happened to him by the steamboat jetty fifty years ago fitted perfectly with the story Anna-Greta had just told.

There was silence in the hall. Simon closed his eyes. The narrative had gone on for a long time; it must be dark outside by now. When he listened he could hear the sea far away. The wind was getting up. A tickling sensation ran down Simon's spine.

The sea. It hasn't finished with Domarö.

When he opened his eyes he discovered that everyone was sitting looking at him. These were not anxious, enquiring looks, there was no sense of *you do believe us, don't you?* Just a silent wait for what he might say. He decided to respond in the same vein; he cleared his throat and told them what had happened during his escape. When he had finished, Margareta Bergwall said, 'Yes, Anna-Greta told us about that.'

Johan Lundvall snorted and wagged a finger at Simon, 'So you *did* have a picklock after all. Just as I thought.'

So Anna-Greta had told the others his story, which she had simply dismissed when he told her.

'So this is historical fact?' Simon asked, turning to Anna-Greta.

'Yes. There are records from the interrogations. And from the interviews before…Satan entered the picture.'

'And you don't think it's him? Satan?'

A salutary wave of sniggers and giggles swept through the group. People smiled and shook their heads. Their reaction was answer enough.

To the right of Simon sat Tora Österberg, an elderly woman who was very active within the mission, and who lived in almost total isolation on the southern side of the island. She patted his knee and said, 'The Devil exists, you can be sure of that. But he has nothing to do with this.'

For once Gustav Jansson had kept quiet until now. In his heyday he had been the leading accordion player in the village, a legendary toper and an inveterate joker. Now he just couldn't stop himself. 'Maybe he's been to visit you, Tora?'

Tora's eyes narrowed. 'Yes, Gustav, he has, and he looked exactly like you. Although his nose wasn't quite as red.'

Gustav laughed and looked around, as if he actually had the nerve to be pleased about being compared with the Evil One. Simon realised that a normal human mechanism was coming into play. This was a closed group where everyone had a set role. Now they had a new audience, and immediately began to overplay their roles. Or perhaps they were just trying to get away from the subject under discussion.

'But why all this secrecy?' asked Simon. 'Why can't everyone who lives here know about this?'

The more relaxed atmosphere that had been about to join the company stopped dead in the doorway. The heaviness returned like a physical force, making shoulders droop and bodies slump on their chairs. Anna-Greta said, 'I think you've realised this is not something that belongs to the past. That it's something that's going on right now.'

'Yes, but—'

'We no longer give people to the sea, but it takes them anyway. Perhaps not one per year anymore, but it takes many. Summer or winter.'

The objection that had been bubbling inside Simon throughout Anna-Greta's narrative, making him so furious with the original population of Domarö, also applied to the group sitting here cowering in the mission house, and at last he could put it into words. 'But all you have to do is move! They could have done it, and you…we can do it. If the sea really is *taking* people in a way that isn't natural, if everyone is walking around in fear of becoming the next victim, why don't we just move, and leave this island?'

'Unfortunately it's not that simple.'

'Why not?'

Anna-Greta took a deep breath and was about to answer, when Karl-Erik straightened his back and said, 'Correct me if I'm wrong, but I thought we were meeting today to discuss this business of Sigrid and what it might mean, not to go over things we already know.' He looked at his watch. 'And I don't know about you, but I'd like to get home in time for the news, at least.'

Watches were examined, with some people expressing concern that it was so late; Simon was the target of some sideways glances, since it was his appearance that had led to the whole thing being so drawn out.

Simon couldn't believe it: they were sitting here discussing terrible forces, how they should be dealt with, and their own survival. And yet this paled in comparison with the risk of missing the news on TV. Then he realised it was only to him it looked that way. For them the threat had become a part of their everyday life, a depressing fact, not something that needed to be discussed. Like people in a war zone or a city under siege, they clung to the small elements of happiness that still exist in life. If the news can be regarded as a component of happiness.

Simon raised his hands to show that he was giving up, that he wasn't going to make any more demands on their time. For now.

Anna-Greta nodded to Elof. He looked bewildered, then realised that he was expected to carry on from where he had left off a couple of hours earlier.

'Right, well, as I said before...before we were interrupted...I can only think that this is a positive development.' Simon noticed that several of the others were shaking their heads, but Elof went on, 'It's never happened before, no one has ever...come back. I would say this is an indication that...it's getting weaker. Somehow.'

His lips moved but he couldn't work out how to proceed. Anna-Greta helped him out, 'And what do you think we should do about that?'

'Well...'

He didn't get any further before he was interrupted by a noise. At first Simon thought it was a distant foghorn, but then he remembered what it was. It had been heard that time when some idiot from Stockholm had set fire to some brushwood at the end of June, and almost set the whole of Kattudden alight.

Everyone was on their feet immediately.

'Fire!'

Jackets and coats were pulled on, and within a minute the room was empty. Only Simon and Anna-Greta remained. They looked at each other without speaking. Then Simon turned on his heel and went out.

After the light inside the hall, the autumn darkness was dense. The little megaphone in the alarm bell tower was sending out its pulsating tone, but there was no sign of a fire down towards the village. In any case, the wind was coming from the south-west. He should have been able to smell the smoke on the breeze if the fire was in that direction.

There was a fire service, but it was focused on the area around the harbour, the original settlement. A powerful pump next to the jetty was connected to a four-hundred-metre pipe, and in an emergency this could be used to hose sea water over most of the buildings in the central part of the village.

But the fire wasn't in the central part of the village. When Simon's eyes had grown accustomed to the darkness, he could see the outlines of the others from the meeting. They were heading for Kattudden. The low-lying clouds to the east were tinged with pink. When he had gone a few steps in that direction, Anna-Greta appeared by his side. She groped for his hand, and Simon pulled it away.

After about fifty metres they caught up with Tora Österberg. Her gumboots creaked slowly in the darkness as she moved along with the help of her wheeled walker. She was dangerously close to the edge of the track and the ditch. Anna-Greta grabbed her arm and stopped her from tipping over the edge.

'Go home, Tora,' said Anna-Greta. 'You're not needed here.'

'It's got nothing to do with being needed,' snapped Tora. 'I want to see what's going on.'

Simon took the opportunity to put some distance between himself and Anna-Greta. He strode out as fast as he could, and slowed down only when Tora's indignant voice was far behind him. He was so disappointed in Anna-Greta, and he just didn't know what to do.

The purely symbolic rent he had been paying for so many years had enabled him to put quite a bit of money away, and he could probably afford to buy a house. Perhaps he could buy the house he lived in from Anna-Greta?

He smiled bitterly. No. For one thing he wouldn't be able to pay what a house so near the shore was worth, for another he might not want to live close to Anna-Greta any longer, for another...for another it would be like paying back the rent he really owed.

Fuck her. Fuck the lot of them.

Suddenly the ground fell away beneath his feet and he tumbled over. The darkness in the forest, the darkness in his head had led him to the ditch. As he landed he grazed his hand on a rock. Tears of pain and fury welled up in his eyes and he screamed out loud, 'Fucking hell!'

Then he pulled himself together and checked himself over. Nothing was broken or damaged, and he didn't want Anna-Greta to see him like this. He crawled out of the ditch and got to his feet, pressing the cut on his hand against the edge of his shirt. He was about to set off again when he heard the sound of an engine approaching. It was coming from the forest, from the path leading down to the shore on the northern side of the island.

The sound was strained, hysterical, like a moped engine being revved much too hard. He peered into the forest and there it was, the headlight of a moped bouncing along the narrow track, its engine roaring.

Who the hell is that? It's virtually impossible to ride along there!

The only house in that direction was Holger's, and Holger didn't have a moped. Besides which, he would never have driven a moped with a cargo platform—because Simon could hear from the rattling noise that it was a platform moped—along the bumpy path.

The moped swung up on to the track ten metres ahead of him, and Simon was blinded by the powerful headlight. He had thought the moped would turn in the opposite direction, towards the fire, but instead it swerved to the right and came straight at him. He was about to step to one side, but remembered that he was already standing by the verge.

The dazzling light made it impossible for him to see anything at all. He just heard the roar as the moped zoomed past him, felt the faint thrust of air as the metal body passed by. The moped carried on at high speed along the track towards the village.

Anna-Greta, Tora!

He turned and saw the beam of light from the moped racing along the track. He could also see a vague silhouette of the person who was driving. He couldn't see who it was, just a figure bent over the handlebars with something on the platform, something roughly the same size as a child standing up.

Immediately afterwards he saw Anna-Greta and Tora caught in the beam. They had been sensible enough to step to one side, and the moped passed them with plenty of room to spare. Simon breathed out. He might be deeply disappointed in Anna-Greta, but he definitely didn't want to see her run over by some lunatic on a moped.

Who was it?

In his mind Simon went through the small number of young people living on the island, but couldn't come up with a single candidate. As far as he knew, they were all quiet kids who spent too much time playing computer games and longed for the day when they would be able to leave Domarö. At worst they might scrawl rude graffiti about Stockholmers on the steamboat jetty shelter.

Speculation was pointless right now, however. There was a fire to put out, and he was serving no purpose standing here debating with himself. But he felt dizzy and exhausted, and not at all in the mood for a rescue effort.

He had been involved last time. They had managed to link up a couple of garden hoses in order to spray water on the burning ground, but most of the water had been hauled up from the sea in buckets and passed from hand to hand along a human chain; and there had been more of them on that occasion.

When he emerged from the forest he could see that the finest house on the whole of Kattudden was burning, the Grönwall house. One of the first to be built when the summer tourist industry was in its infancy.

There wasn't much that could be done. The external walls were virtually gone, and through the yellow and red flames the beams and framework could be seen as darker lines. There was a loud crackling, and despite the fact that he was standing a good hundred metres away from the blaze, he could feel a faint breath of the fire's heat.

It was a pity about the beautiful house, of course, but at the same time it was fortunate that it was this particular house that was on fire. It was set in a large garden, and there didn't seem to be any real risk that the fire would spread to other properties, as long as they kept an eye on the sparks and burning fragments that might drift through the air.

The people delineated against the bright glow of the fire like matchstick men seemed to be of the same opinion. Nobody was doing anything, they were just standing at a safe distance or walking around checking that no new blaze was about to break out.

Simon really wanted to go home, but he realised that wouldn't look good. When he spotted Göran standing to one side talking on his mobile phone, he headed over to him. Göran said something into the phone, nodded a couple of times then snapped it shut. He caught sight of Simon and came to meet him.

'Hi there,' he said. 'The fire service are on the way, but it'll be mainly a matter of damping down, I think.'

They stood side by side for a while, contemplating the burning house without speaking. The heat now lay like a dry film over their faces, and a shower of sparks flew up as one of the roof beams collapsed.

'How did it start?' asked Simon.

'No idea. But it seems to have caught hold incredibly fast.' Göran jerked his thumb in the direction of one of the houses further up towards the forest. 'Lidberg, I think his name is. Lives up there. He said it just went *boom* and the whole place was on fire.'

'Was anyone there? Inside the house?'

'Not as far as I know. But I mean a fire doesn't start just like that for no reason.'

'The Grönwalls—they're only here in the summer, aren't they?'

'That's right. But I think the daughter stays here now and again.'

They took a few steps towards the fire, and Simon peered into the bright glow as if he expected to be able to see something in the flames. A person, something moving. Or a blackened skeleton. Another supporting post came down, bringing with it a couple of roof beams in a cloud of crackling flames. If there had been anything living in there, it certainly wasn't alive now.

The grass in the garden surrounding the house had dried out, and patches were beginning to burn. Simon, watching the fire moving towards the well, was overcome by the urge to do something

209

significant. He could call up the water from the well, order it to pour down on the fire and make the work of the fire service unnecessary. With Spiritus in his bare hand he might be able to do such things.

If it had been a matter of saving lives, he would probably have done it. But in the current situation it would just be a meaningless demonstration that would also give rise to unpleasant questions. He didn't want to touch Spiritus. He didn't know why, but there it was.

Who's that knocking on your door?

Anders didn't know if he was swimming up towards the surface, or deeper towards the bottom. He was trapped in a dreadful, shape-less nightmare of a kind he had never experienced before. Part of his consciousness was telling him it was only a dream, and without that small comfort he would probably have gone crazy.

He was under water, in total darkness. There wasn't the slightest hint of light anywhere, nothing that could tell him what was up and what was down. The only thing he knew was that he was under water, that it was dark, and that he was drowning.

His arms were flailing desperately, he was dying, and his eyes were wide open, to no avail. He waited for the calm resignation that is said to visit those who are drowning or freezing to death, but it didn't come. Instead there was only panic, and the certain knowledge that he had only seconds to live.

But the seconds passed; he kept drowning but was not allowed to die. If fear can be matter, then he was inside that matter. And it was growing more dense. His heart was racing and his head was about to explode. He wanted to scream, but he couldn't open his mouth.

Denser. Closer. Something came to him out of the darkness. An immense formless body had picked up his scent, and was getting closer. His head twisted from side to side, but there was nothing to see. Only darkness and the knowledge that something bigger than it is possible to imagine was getting closer.

There was a thumping and banging in his ears, and the thumping was a relief. A noise. Something real, something that had direction and permanency, something other than darkness. The thumping was very loud, something was banging and it wasn't inside him. The darkness dispersed and the abyss in which he had found himself was no deeper than his eyelids.

He opened his eyes, and the sound of the last blow on the door hung in the air like an echo. It took him a few seconds to realise that he was inside his own house, that he was alive. Then he got to his feet and ran towards the front door. He slipped on the kitchen floor and almost fell, but managed to grab hold of the lukewarm kitchen stove, and carried on into the hallway.

This time you're not going to get away.

He yanked open the door and yelled, hurled himself backward to avoid the thing that was standing on the porch. A grinning face loomed over him as he fell back on to the hall floor. Still in the grip of blind terror, he scrabbled a metre backwards, dragging the rag rug with him. Then the calmer voice of reason kicked in, plucking at the fear and beginning to unravel it.

It's only the GB-man. He can't do you any harm.

The plastic figure's violent swinging slowed down. Anders lay on the hall floor looking at it. His senses were returning, and he could hear two things: some kind of siren from down in the village, and the sound of a moped engine accelerating up the hill then fading into the distance. He could also hear a faint rattling, and Anders realised it was a platform moped.

The GB-man was still standing there staring at him, and Anders couldn't make himself get up. If he moved, it would leap on him. In order to break the spell, he looked away from the GB-man's hypnotic gaze and allowed his head to fall back and hit the floor. He stared up at the ceiling.

It's nothing to be afraid of. Stop it. It's…a plastic doll produced as a marketing tool. Stop it.

It made no difference. It was as if he were two people. Or like Donald Duck, with an angel on one shoulder and a devil on the other, each giving conflicting comments and advice. He couldn't get himself together.

'Go away you stupid ghost, you don't exist.'

What was that? Alfie Atkins, that's what. When he's going to go down into the cellar and he's scared of ghosts. That's what his daddy taught him to say. It had been one of Maja's favourite tapes. Anders raised his head. The GB-man was still standing there, and had completely stopped moving now.

'Go away you stupid ghost, you don't exist.'

The siren down in the village fell silent. He could no longer hear the moped's engine. Anders drew his legs under him and stood up. He pulled himself together and went over to the GB-man, gazing out into the darkness in vain. There was nothing to see.

Who put it there?

The same person who rode off on the moped, obviously. But who?

Despite the fact that the palms of his hands were saying *No* because they were terrified of touching it, Anders managed to make himself grab hold of the GB-man's sharp plastic edges and heave the thing down off the porch. The cement block on which it stood was unexpectedly heavy, and he only managed to drag it about a metre along the lawn before he had to let go. The GB-man swung back and forth a few times, then settled in its new spot. It was still staring at him.

Ought to smash it up.

He considered going to fetch the axe, but it was as dark over by the woodshed as it had been in his dream, and besides…*the GB-man might take his revenge.*

He tried moving the figure a quarter turn to the side, but that didn't help. It was looking at him out of the corner of its eye.

Who? Who knew?

The person who had placed the figure on his porch had done it to frighten him, and who could possibly know that he was scared of the

GB-man? Wrong. That he had *become* scared of the GB-man. Who?

The same person who's watching me.

The GB-man looked at him. Anders went and got a black plastic sack, which he pulled over the figure and tucked under the cement block. The sack rustled faintly in the wind, and to anyone else the figure probably looked even more unpleasant now. But it had stopped looking. He had shut off its eyes.

'I am not afraid.'

He said it out loud into the darkness. He said it again. Beneath the plastic the GB-man whispered: *You haven't even got the nerve to go and fetch the axe. But no, you're quite right. You're brave and strong. Always.*

Anders got angry. He went back into the hallway, pulled on his jacket, checked that there was still some wine left in the bottle in his pocket, grabbed the torch and went out again. He went and stood in front of the GB-man's indistinct outline beneath the sack, raised the bottle and said, 'Cheers, you ugly bastard'; he took a long drink, then switched on the torch and set off towards the track.

He wanted to check what the siren had been for. It had sounded a bit like an air-raid siren, but that was hardly likely to be the case.

As long as the Russians haven't come back.

The beam of the torch moved ahead of him along the path and he played with it, throwing it up the trees and down into the ditch, pretending it was an eager little animal investigating its surroundings. Snuffling through the bushes, running through the grass. An eager animal made of light, which no one could catch. To test himself, he switched off the torch.

The October darkness closed around him. He waited for the horror of the dream to seize him, but it didn't come. He listened to the sound of his own breathing. He wasn't under water. Nothing was chasing him. He tipped his head back and saw that the sky was full of stars.

'It's fine,' he said. 'There's no danger.'

He switched the torch back on and set off once more. He pulled out the bottle and had another drink to celebrate. His body was still a little dehydrated following the day's hard work, and his muscles were aching, so he took another swig. The bottle was almost empty.

The street lamps started by the ramblers' hostel. A light mist lay in the air and the glow of the lamps had taken hold, forming hovering enclosures of light around themselves. He switched off the torch and looked along the row of lights. It was reassuring. It led between people's houses and told him that nothing bad could happen, despite the autumn darkness and dampness.

The hostel lay in silence and darkness. He remembered when he was little he used to feel sorry for the people who had to live there. Those who didn't have a proper house. Even if the hostel was quite a stylish building, there were just so *many* of them who came to stay there. The ramblers. They would arrive by boat and stay for a day or two, then they would be off again, presumably to the next hostel.

But there's someone sitting there.

Anders switched on the torch and shone it on the hostel steps. There was indeed someone sitting there, the head drooping towards the knees. Anders swept the beam of the torch to either side to check if there was a moped nearby. There wasn't. But still he approached carefully.

'Hello? Are you all right?'

The woman raised her head, and at first Anders didn't recognise Elin. Her face had altered even more since he last saw her, it had become…older. She screwed her eyes up against the light and pulled back, as if she were afraid. Anders turned the torch on to his own face.

'It's me, Anders. What's happened?'

He directed the beam of the torch a metre to the right of Elin to avoid dazzling her, and saw that she had relaxed. He went over and sat down on the step below her, then switched off the torch.

Elin was hunched over, her arms tightly wrapped around her knees. He placed a hand on her shin, and she was trembling. 'What's the matter?'

Elin's hand seized his and held it tight. 'Anders. Henrik and Björn have burned down my house.'

'No,' he said. 'No, Elin. They're dead.'

Elin's head was moving slowly back and forth. 'I saw them. On that fucking platform moped. They burned down my house.'

Anders closed his mouth around the words he had been about to say.

The platform moped.

But then there were lots of platform mopeds on Domarö. Practically every other person had one. That didn't prove anything. On the other hand: the GB-man. Henrik and Björn's favourite hobby had been moving stuff around. Taking someone's water butt and putting it in a garden on the other side of the island, or sneaking into someone's woodshed, stealing the chainsaw and putting it in the neighbour's woodshed.

It all made sense. But there was a major problem with this line of reasoning.

'But they drowned. Fifteen years ago. Didn't they?'

Elin shook her head. 'They didn't drown. They disappeared.'

Hubba and Bubba

Every gang has them. The ones who don't fit in. Maybe at one stage they tried to belong properly, but after a while they realise it's never going to work and they begin to work on their outsider status, making it a badge of honour.

They. They can count themselves lucky if there are two of them. Usually it's just the one. They are not necessarily relentlessly victimised or bullied. Sometimes, yes; but often their role is to be the one against whom the gang measures itself, so to speak. The gang is a gang by *not* being the outsider.

These individuals are tolerated for that very reason. As a

yardstick, or as an audience. It's often a sad story. If a gang is a royal court, then this person is its fool— thrown a few crumbs of friendship or temptation occasionally so it will jingle its bells or say something stupid that can be brought up later. Over and over again.

Such is the role of the fool. It is disagreeable, but can work quite well as long as the quasi-outcast is aware of his limits. It is when he tries to overstep them that tragedy strikes and everything goes wrong.

So there were the two of them, Henrik and Björn.

Unlike the rest of the gang, they were the children of parents who lived on the island permanently. Björn's father was a carpenter who built jetties, and his mother worked in geriatric care. Henrik lived alone with his mother, and it wasn't clear what she actually did.

Usually the children belonging to the summer visitors and those belonging to the permanent residents were separate tribes who lived in separate camps, but in this case there was a go-between: Anders. His mother had been a summer visitor; she'd met his father and moved to Domarö when Anders was born. It lasted just about a year, and then his mother caught the boat back to the city and took her son with her.

Anders came out to visit his father in the holidays and sometimes at weekends, and thus ended up with a foot in each camp. He had his summer friends on Kattudden, but in the winter he sometimes played with Henrik and Björn, his only contemporaries in the village at the time.

They went sledging on the slope down to the steamboat jetty, played in abandoned barns and called each other 'dickhead'.

'Shall we do something, dickhead?'

'We could do, dickhead. Where's the other dickhead?'

After a few years Henrik and Björn moved closer to the summer gang via Anders and became part of it, to a certain extent. However, they refrained from calling each other dickhead when the rest of the gang could hear.

There was one summer, just one, when Henrik and Björn were fully fledged members of the gang. In 1983, when Henrik was thirteen and Björn was twelve, they were sought after and desirable in every situation. The reason for their popularity was purely mechanical: Henrik had acquired a platform moped.

Since there were no cars on Domarö, all the children were allowed to ride their bikes as much as they wanted as soon as they had mastered the art, and they would whiz back and forth between houses, along the forest tracks, between the harbour and Kattudden. In the summer of 1983 the bikes suddenly seemed rather childish; after all, there were cooler things out there.

Even though Henrik wasn't quite old enough, his father had given him the old but well-renovated three-wheel moped for the same reason that six-year-olds were allowed to ride their bikes wherever they liked: if there was an accident, it was because the child had run into something, not because they had been run over. And the moped didn't go fast. Thirty-five at the most, going downhill with the sun and the wind behind it.

However, the oldest members of the gang were thirteen and next to the often rusty just-for-the-country bikes, the moped was a Lamborghini. It was speed and it was cool and it was status, and since Henrik and Björn were inseparable, Björn got his share of the boom in Henrik's popularity.

That summer, and only that summer, Henrik manoeuvred skilfully between the desires, disappointments and petty intrigues that exist in every group. His newly won popularity made him bold, and suddenly he was doing everything right. He didn't give in to Joel's demands to be allowed to ride the moped when the whole group was together. He did, however, let Joel have a go when there were just the two of them, which gave Henrik points without the loss of status that would have resulted from allowing Joel to take over in front of everyone.

He also made sure he gave Elin a lift when he knew that some of the others could see, since the combination of his own moped and Elin was virtually unbeatable. The hormones were stirring, and Elin had acquired breasts. When Henrik pulled up in front of the shop with Elin on the platform, her breasts bouncing from the uneven track, he was king. That summer.

Otherwise he and Björn could often be seen riding along the tracks, down to the shore, through the forest. Since Anders was the only member of the gang apart from Henrik and Björn who lived in the old village, he often got a lift home after an evening at Martin's or Elin's.

'Jump on, dickhead.'

In the middle of August they all parted over a period of a few days. Henrik and Björn remained behind, while the rest of the gang disappeared to Stockholm and Uppsala. When Anders came out for a week during the Christmas holidays, the inlet down below his father's house had frozen, and he, Henrik and Björn amused themselves dragging each other around on skis behind the moped, or just generally slithering about.

The following summer, something had changed. When Henrik tried to impress by riding on two wheels along the entire length of the forest track, no one was particularly interested. Some had been riding mopeds in the city, slick models modified for better performance, and when it came down to it, a platform moped was actually quite…rural.

Henrik and Björn fell from grace, and they fell hard. Perhaps as a reaction to the artificial importance they had enjoyed the previous summer, they now started to attract a certain amount of ridicule. They had the wrong clothes and the wrong hairstyles, they talked funny and they knew nothing about music. It was during that summer someone came up with that business of H and B. Hubba and Bubba. Big bubbles, no troubles.

Both Martin and Joel had let their hair grow during the winter. Anders, somewhere in between as usual, had medium-length hair, as did Johan. Hubba and Bubba had very short hair, and the others decided it was so the fish scales wouldn't get stuck in it. Or the dung, come to that.

Both Malin and Elin teased their hair up like Madonna, lots of spray, and although Cecilia and Frida, who were a year younger, didn't go that far—or use that much make-up—they too had started to show an interest in how they looked.

Joel had a T-shirt with 'Frankie says RELAX' on it, and through his dad, who had been on a business trip to London, he had the single 'Two Tribes' before anyone else had even heard it on *Tracks*. Henrik and Björn didn't know who Frankie Goes to Hollywood were, but since Joel kept on referring to them as 'Frankie', they drew the wrong conclusion.

One evening at Elin's, Joel was going on and on about how incredibly cool the video to 'Two Tribes' was, with Reagan and that Russian guy, whatever his name was, punching each other until the blood flowed. Joel had spent a couple of days back home in the city; he'd been watching *Music Box*, and had all the latest info.

'Two Tribes' was thundering on the stereo in the background, and Björn was sitting there following the beat with his head. When there was a break in Joel's monologue, Björn said, 'He's pretty good, isn't he?'

Just as a tern catches a flash of silver in the water and dives, Joel snapped up Björn's comment. 'Who is?' he asked.

Björn nodded towards the stereo. 'Him.'

'Who do you mean, Holly Johnson?'

Björn realised he was on thin ice and glanced at Henrik, who was unable to provide any help. Then he said uncertainly, 'Frankie, of course.'

This reply would be quoted frequently in the future. Whenever anyone in the gang asked who someone was the reply would be, 'Frankie, of course.'

The episode was typical. A number of similar situations made it perfectly clear that even if Henrik and Björn were more or less OK, they were basically peasants and not worth bothering with.

When Martin climbed up into the alarm bell tower, it was a feat. When Henrik did the same thing a week or so later, nobody was interested, despite the fact that he climbed higher than Martin, so high that he could rap on the bell itself with his knuckles, and the tower ought really to have given way. What fools do has no importance.

Not that Anders got involved in the status of Henrik and Björn. That was the summer he and Cecilia went up to the rock one evening, and there were other things to think about. He also had *Music Box* at home in the city and read the music magazine *OK* from time to time, so he was able to keep up and avoid the worst of the hidden reefs; he was even able to venture an opinion sometimes, 'I just don't know what George Michael is *doing* with Andrew Ridgeley. They must be at it or something.' But he was mainly into Depêche Mode, and he was on his own there.

One evening before it was time to head home at the end of the summer, he and Cecilia had been alone in Anders' house, and he had actually done it: he played 'Somebody' to her. To his boundless relief she really liked it, and wanted to hear it again. Then they'd snogged. A bit.

When Anders came out for Christmas, Henrik and Björn had changed. There was six months between them, but even in their physical and psychological changes they seemed to stick together like Siamese twins. Both had grown, both had a fine crop of pimples, and they had left behind the innocent naivety that had characterised them up to now: they were quieter, more introverted.

But they still hung out together from time to time during the week; they rode the moped over to Kattholmen and played the odd fantasy game in the forest. There was no need to spell out that this was *not* to be mentioned to anyone else, it was self-evident. Through the same silent agreement they also stopped calling each other dickhead. Those days were gone.

Anders told them about his new discovery: The Smiths. He had been given a Walkman for Christmas, and it played *Hatful of Hollow* more or less continuously. Henrik had been given the guest cottage in the garden as his own room, and they sat there listening to 'Heaven Knows I'm Miserable Now' and 'Still Ill'. When Anders was due to go back to the city, Henrik asked if Anders could make him a tape.

Anders gave him the one he'd brought with him, because he could easily make a new one when he got home.

When the summer came it was clear that Henrik and Björn had found their thing. *Meat Is Murder* had come out a few months earlier; Anders thought it was OK, but nowhere near as good as *Hatful of Hollow*. Henrik and Björn had a different view. They knew every single line of every single song, and both had become vegetarians, possibly the first ever on Domarö.

It isn't necessary to go into any more detail about the music that was cool that summer, suffice to say that The Smiths were definitely *not* cool. If Henrik and Björn had enjoyed a higher status, then perhaps the whole gang might have joined in and embraced the notion of meat-eating as murder, but that was not the case. With hindsight, of course, it was Henrik and Björn who were the most hip and the most London, but what good did it do them at the time? None. They were farmers, head cases.

They tried to get Anders to become a member of their private sect, but Anders wasn't having any of it. For one thing it wasn't in his nature to get so obsessed about something to do with music, and for another there was now a kind of sickness surrounding Hubba and Bubba. If you spent time with them you risked being seen as infected. They were still tolerated when the whole group was together, but nobody wanted to be regarded as their friend.

If the gang had gathered on the shore to barbecue sausages and drink weak beer, Henrik and Björn wouldn't eat any sausages, because meat is murder. If 'Forever Young' by Alphaville was playing on Joel's ghetto blaster, they would sit grinning scornfully at the infantile lyrics in poor English, making comparisons with the greatest living poet of the day: Stephen Patrick Morrissey.

And so on. They cultivated their outsider status, and knew they had a friend in the pale young man from Manchester. Someone who knew what it was like to grow up in a place where nothing happens. A brother in exile.

That winter Anders paid only a short visit to Domarö, and he avoided Henrik and Björn. They called him in the spring when they were about to embark on their pilgrimage to Stockholm to buy *The Queen Is Dead*, and wondered if they could stay over, but Anders said he was going to dinner with Cecilia's mother. Which he was, but not until the following week.

By the summer when everything got blown apart, Henrik and Björn's interest had escalated to unhealthy proportions. They dressed like Morrissey, both had acquired rockabilly haircuts, and when it turned out that Björn's eyesight was so bad he needed glasses, he was absolutely delighted, because it gave him a reason to get mottled grey frames like the army-issue ones, and even more like…well, you get the picture.

Close study of Smiths' lyrics made them more proficient in English than anyone else on Domarö, and when Wilde, Keats and Yeats were mentioned in 'Cemetery Gates', they made a point of ordering their stories and poems in the original at the library in Norrtälje, then spent the dirty grey spring deciphering the books with the help of dictionaries.

They could have been happy.

They didn't try to fit in, because they knew it was impossible, and they regarded the others with ill-concealed contempt, tying leather cords around their wrists and listening to bands with a 'z' in the name. They peppered their conversation with oblique references to Smiths' songs, translated into Swedish, with particular emphasis on the riches of the poor.

But that line came from the song 'I Want the One I Can't Have', and therein lay the problem. It would have been OK to have Henrik and Björn as a couple of oddballs on the fringes of the gang, if only they had known their place. If only they hadn't reached out for what they couldn't have.

Summer 1986. Olof Palme was dead, and the blueberry bushes on the south side of Domarö were regarded with suspicion as they stood there sucking up water from rain clouds moving in from the east.

Sonny Crockett from *Miami Vice* was a style icon, and everything was pastel colours on the one hand, *Black Celebration* on the other. And Anders stuck with Depêche Mode, despite the fact that *Tracks* was playing 'A Question of Lust' to death.

Henrik and Björn dismissed more or less the whole lot as dickheads. The only thing that found favour in their eyes was *I, Claudius*, a fairly old production by the BBC. From England, from *London*. Björn could do an excellent imitation of the stammering emperor, but unfortunately this was as pearls before swine, since nobody apart from him and Henrik wanted to watch 'a load of old men wearing sheets and talking funny'.

Enough said. Some people remember how it was, and the rest will have to make do with these daubs—pastel splashes on a black background. Summer 1986. Mortal fear and white teeth, Armageddon and workouts. Enough said.

For the gang, that was the summer when they started to drink alcohol. It had started with the odd sneaky drink from their parents' supply the previous year, but in the summer of 1986 they started taking the ferry to Åland.

Martin was tall and well-built. He even had the start of a decent beard, which he made sure he cultivated a few days before they made a couple of trips in Joel's boat to transport the whole gang to Kapellskär, where they caught the ferry. Martin bought the booze in the duty-free shop, then they would slur their way around Mariehamn drinking as much as they dared.

Henrik and Björn weren't always included when the booze was doled out, and during the third trip that summer, at the beginning of August, they took the matter into their own hands. They were quieter than usual during the trip home, and only went into the duty-free shop to buy some sweets.

The reason for their secretive behaviour became clear when they had disembarked in Kapellskär, and were safe. They opened their jackets. In the waistband of their trousers and in their pockets they had stuffed twelve half-litre bottles of Bacardi. Everybody thought they were fucking crazy, and they were rewarded with pats on the back and places on the first run home in Joel's boat.

There was usually a litre or two of booze left over after a day in Mariehamn. Now they suddenly had a *stash*, and not only that, it was free. They decided the bottles should be hidden underneath the old boathouse on Kattholmen. Henrik and Björn were of course included in all these discussions—they were the heroes of the hour.

But by the following day it was all forgotten, and their incomprehensible comments and strange manner—a mixture of submissiveness and a maddening superciliousness—became the objects of the usual ridicule. But they were the ones who had nicked the bottles, there was no getting away from that fact.

And so when the time came for the final party of the summer, they were included from the start. Otherwise Henrik and Björn usually just turned up at parties without being invited, then sat on the sidelines making remarks that only they laughed at, while everybody else laughed at the gibes against Henrik and Björn.

But in that way they fulfilled their particular function. They consolidated the group and the language of the group by sitting outside and speaking a different language. Nobody would have admitted it or even realised it, but a good party needed Henrik and Björn sitting there like a couple of aliens in order to create the right atmosphere.

The evening had arrived. Sausages and charcoal, chips and drink were transported over to Kattholmen, and everyone was there. Joel and Martin, Elin and Malin, Anders and Cecilia. Frida's mother had said she couldn't go, but she was there anyway. Samuel who lived in Nåten and played in the same football team as Joel came in his own boat. Even Karolina, who spent only a couple of weeks on Domarö each year, was there. And Henrik and Björn. The suppliers for the evening.

The Bacardi was produced and mixed with Coke in plastic mugs, someone got a fire going outside the boathouse. Henrik and Björn had brought some kind of special meat-free sausages that were pale grey and looked like penises; they were informed of this fact, despite the Bacardi.

For once Anders was permitted to put Depêche Mode on the cassette player. 'A Question of Lust' had paved the way. But after the first couple of bottles, nobody wanted to listen to such gloomy music, and at the girls' insistence it had to be Wham! instead.

The fire died down and the party continued inside the boathouse. At first there had been nothing but a table, two chairs and a bunk bed for fishermen who were staying the night. A few wooden chairs and a rag rug had been added. It was a bit crowded with everybody in there, but Anders and Cecilia helped out by clambering up on to the musty horsehair mattress on the top bunk, where they lay kissing and cuddling.

They had had to put up with a good deal the previous summer after Malin had seen them kissing, but that was all in the past now. They were a couple and there wasn't much to say about it, even if it was a bit peculiar to be together for so *long*. They had slept together for the first time during the winter, and had carried on in spring, so there was none of that initial desperation as they lay on the horsehair mattress. They could take it easy now, resting on each other's lips and fingertips.

Down below them the atmosphere was even more over-excited. Somebody had produced a pack of cards, and they were about to play strip poker. Karolina immediately dropped out, barely raising even a dutiful protest. She was chubby and not particularly attractive. Unfortunately she had no way of getting home on her own, so she had to curl up on the bottom bunk and pretend, as far as possible, to be fine with the whole thing.

And so the fun lay with Elin and Malin, who were the best-looking girls. Frida was quite pretty, but she didn't have the kind of body you could talk or fantasise about. On the other hand, there was no way she was pulling out if the other girls were up for it.

When Elin and Malin gave each other a high five and said 'Go for it!', Anders saw how Frida's eyes darted from side to side, and her shoulders drooped slightly. But she gritted her teeth and straightened up. Perhaps she was hoping she might be able to play without losing. She would lose more by backing out.

Anders took a swig from the bottle of ready-mixed rum and Coke and buried his nose in the back of Cecilia's neck. He had a bad feeling about this, and was grateful for the fact that he and Cecilia were so far out of the reckoning that they'd been forgotten.

On the ghetto blaster Joey Tempest was singing about the final countdown, and Martin dealt the cards. He hesitated when he got to Henrik, who said he'd like to drop his trousers to the world, and Björn giggled. Nobody else understood what was funny, but they got their cards.

Martin carried on dealing, hands were won and hands were lost. As items of clothing were removed, they were thrown on a pile in the middle of the floor. After perhaps twenty minutes Anders must have fallen asleep, because the situation had changed completely when he raised his head again.

The door had just closed behind Joel, who had come back in. He was stark naked except for a scrap of torn fishing net which he had arranged so that it half covered his dangling penis.

Booing and laughter came from around the table. Joel threw his arms out wide and executed a couple of dance steps. He didn't seem unhappy with the situation. He went to the gym regularly and was making the most of the opportunity to show off what he had.

It was so hot in the boathouse that Anders' hair was sticky with sweat. The oxygen was being eaten up by all the candles and by the alcohol burning in their bodies. Another two half-litre bottles had been emptied and were lying next to the pile of clothes. They had drunk at least a litre more than they ever had before, and Samuel was just opening a new bottle.

Frida, who had done quite well and was still wearing her bra and pants, pointed at Joel and protested, 'Admit you've lost. That's just cheating.'

Joel went over to her and waggled his midriff in front of her face.

'What do you mean, I'm wearing something, aren't I? Go on, feel.'

Frida pushed him away and Joel almost fell backwards on top of Karolina, but grabbed hold of the bed frame and straightened up. He was very drunk, and sweat was pouring down his neck and back. He waved a hand over his fishnet pants and said, 'Last chance, OK? Last round. Then I'm…bust. OK?'

Despite the fact that Anders hadn't drunk all that much, his head was spinning, and it felt three times as heavy as it usually did.

They ought to open the door.

He opened his mouth to say so, but just didn't have the strength. He looked down at the table where the others were sitting. Joel was the one who had lost most, but Henrik, Björn and Elin weren't far behind. Henrik and Björn were down to their underpants, and even though Elin's lower half was concealed by the shadows under the table, Anders could see that she had sacrificed her pants before her bra.

He could hear from Cecilia's breathing that she was asleep. He placed a hand on her hip and tore his gaze away from the short strands of hair poking out from between Elin's crossed legs, trying to be faithful even in his thoughts.

The spirit was willing but the eyes were weak. He tried to focus on a couple of half-ripe pimples on Henrik's back, but his eyes refused to co-operate, sliding to the right and moving from the shadow between Elin's thighs to the sheen of sweat on the top of her breasts. The base of his penis was beginning to get hot, and he rolled over on to his back, staring up at the ceiling which was only half a metre from the tip of his nose.

I have to get out of here. Get some air.

The cards clicked as they were dealt out, the voices were slurred. He hoped Joel would lose so that it would be over, so that they could all go out into the fresh air and become human beings again.

It was Henrik who lost. Anders heard the sound of fabric against skin, and a rustle as the pile of clothes grew a little higher. Nobody seemed all that bothered. Henrik's nakedness was not something anyone wished to see, it was just a blip along the way. The cards were dealt again. Karolina sighed on the bottom bunk. This wasn't quite how she'd imagined the evening.

The sweat prickled in Anders' eyes, and he felt unpleasantly itchy beneath his clothes. He wished it had just been him and Cecilia here. He would have woken her and asked her if she wanted to go for a swim in the moonlight. In the current situation all he could do was lie there staring up at the ceiling, which was increasingly beginning to resemble the lid of a coffin. Which, judging by the warmth, had just been slid into the oven.

'What the fuck!' he heard Elin shout from down below. 'But I've got three pairs as well!'

'Yes, but look...' said Martin, who seemed to be finding it difficult to express himself. 'Look...you can see Frida's got...her top card is higher than yours. So that means hers is higher. It's higher.'

A murmur of agreement was heard; Elin tried a couple of lame protests, but then a reverent silence fell. There was a faint metallic click, and a piece of clothing landed on the pile. A chair was pushed back and Joel said, 'Where are you going, you're supposed to sit here now and...'

'Fuck that,' said Elin. 'I can do the same as you.'

There was the sound of naked feet crossing the wooden floor, several of the boys whistled and Anders carried on staring up at the ceiling. Then his eyes took control again and he glanced at the door just in time to see Elin disappearing outside.

Someone turned up the music and A-Ha's 'Take On Me' blasted through the room, dispelling the darkness a little and lightening the air. Or perhaps it was just that the door opening had let in a little oxygen.

Everyone at the table sang along with the chorus. Cecilia woke up and turned sleepily towards Anders. He stroked her cheek and skin stuck to skin. Cecilia blinked and rubbed her eyes. 'God, it's hot in here.'

Anders put his arms around her. 'Shall we go outside?'

She pressed herself against him and said, 'In a minute.' Over her shoulder Anders saw Henrik get up from the table and walk over to the door. Then Cecilia's lips found his and he sank down into the soft, sticky warmth.

They kissed until 'Take On Me' faded away in a shimmer of harmonies and drum machines. There was a moment's silence, then they heard a scream. It came from outside, and it was Elin who was screaming. Like an adrenaline shock to a heart that has stopped, a jolt ran through the room. Skin stuck to skin was torn apart, chairs scraped as they were pushed back or fell over to the opening bars of 'I Should Be So Lucky'.

Joel and Martin were first out through the door, and the others who had been sitting around the table followed, with Björn bringing up the rear. Cecilia climbed down from the top bunk and Anders followed her, but almost fell over Karolina, who was getting up with a groan, like an old woman.

Kylie Minogue was singing about the lack of complication in her imagination, but was drowned out by Elin's hysterical screams outside the boathouse.

'You disgusting bastard...fucking disgusting...'

Anders got outside just in time to see Joel place a hand on Elin's shoulder. She had tied a fishing net around herself and was hitting out at Henrik, who was trying to protect his face. The full moon over the water gave their bodies a white glow.

'What's the matter, what's the matter?' asked Joel.

Elin was still hitting out at Henrik, who was moving backwards towards the shoreline as she yelled, 'This disgusting bastard tried to rape me, he came at me with his disgusting fucking cock and tried... tried to rape me!'

Henrik held up his hands as if to show that he was unarmed and said, 'I didn't, I just...' but even if the crime could not be proved, the weapon was clearly visible. It was sticking out from Henrik's body, angled upwards, and it refused to go down even though Henrik's eyes were bright with fear.

Joel took a couple of steps towards Henrik and punched him in the stomach. The air went out of Henrik with a puff and he bent double. Joel grabbed the back of his neck and dragged him towards the glowing embers of the fire, yelling, 'You just don't do that, get it? I'm going to make sure you get it, I'm going to make sure you understand...'

It's hard to imagine a more serious test of Henrik and Björn's friendship, but Björn passed with flying colours. As Joel dragged Henrik, coughing and waving helplessly, towards the embers, Björn ran forward and grabbed him, slowing him down.

'Pack it in, you mad bastard, let him go!'

With his free hand Joel hit out at Björn, who had grabbed hold of his shoulders. When he couldn't manage to shake him off, he shouted to Martin, 'For fuck's sake, come and give me a hand!'

Martin rushed forward and used his considerably greater weight to pull Björn away and force him down on to the ground on his stomach. Henrik was still coughing after the vicious blow to his stomach, gasping for breath between coughs. Joel hit him on the head and shook him as he hissed, 'You want to fuck, do you? In that case I think you ought to fuck somebody who *wants* to be fucked, you bastard.'

He hurled Henrik down on top of Björn. Martin stood on Björn's hands so that he couldn't move.

'There you go, now you can fuck,' screamed Joel; he stood astride Henrik's body, grabbed his hips and pulled backwards, then pushed down again. Henrik tried to wriggle free, but Joel got hold of a stone the size of an egg, and using its extra weight he slammed his fist into the back of Henrik's head.

'Enjoying yourself, are you? Maybe you haven't got it all the way in yet...'

Henrik lay helpless on top of Björn, who was now weeping, and Joel groped around his pale backside to direct him the right way.

'Pack it in Joel, pack it in for fuck's sake!'

Anders let go of Cecilia and went over to the naked bodies,

twisted around each other. He said it again. 'Joel, pack it in! That's enough!'

When he was a step away, Joel turned his face to him. Saliva was dribbling from the corners of his mouth. His eyes were inhuman and expressed only one simple emotion: *Touch me and I'll kill you.* Joel raised the hand holding the stone ready to strike, and Anders backed down. The nausea rose from his stomach he stepped back. And turned away.

The others stood as if paralysed, following the drama with eyes wide open. Only Elin's face betrayed anything other than incredulous horror. She was smiling. A stiff smile curled her lips, and her eyes were...avid. Behind him Anders could hear Joel struggling with Henrik, unable to achieve the result he desired. Perhaps the humiliation had finally forced the guilty erection to subside.

Björn was weeping in despair, howling like a whipped animal. Joel panted and swore, but finally gave up. He turned away from the bodies on the ground and spat. As he walked past the remains of the fire he kicked a few glowing embers over Henrik's back with his bare foot.

Henrik jerked and rolled off Björn. Joel went into the boathouse, and after a few seconds he was back with a bottle of Bacardi. His eyes were still hazy, flickering with excitement, and Anders noticed that the fight and the punishment had given him a hard-on. The scrap of fishing net was draped over his cock as if it had been hung out to dry.

He walked up to Elin, grabbed her hand and said, 'You and I are going to have a little chat.'

Elin went with him. The half-finished fishing net sarong trailed after her like a bridal veil as they went around the corner of the boathouse and disappeared into the forest.

There was silence now. Martin had stepped off Björn's hands a long time ago, and now looked guilty as he stood there gazing down at the huddled, weeping boy. He glanced around as if he hoped someone might tell him why he had done it. Everyone was avoiding each other's eyes.

Cecilia went into the boathouse and dug out Henrik and Björn's clothes. By that stage they could hear noises from the forest, where Joel was either taking or being given his reward. From the sounds Elin was making, it sounded as though it was more a case of the latter. Samuel went inside and turned up the music.

The tape had gone back to the beginning, and Henrik and Björn were slowly pulling on their clothes to the sound of the fanfare from 'The Final Countdown'. Anders would never be able to hear that song again without a flush of guilt.

He saw Björn's face, wet with tears, his slender, trembling hands pulling on the ugly underpants, he remembered the snow fortresses they had built together and the chocolate Björn's mother had given them, the children's programs they had watched and the things they had laughed at. He wished he had picked up a bigger stone and thrown it at Joel's head.

But he hadn't, and now Björn was weeping even more violently as he discovered that his Morrissey-glasses were snapped in the middle.

Anders went over to him, crouched down and said, 'Are you OK?'

Björn's hand shot out and hit him on the forehead. Not hard, but enough to make the point. He didn't want anyone to look at him or speak to him. After a couple of minutes Henrik and Björn were dressed and set off along the shoreline, past the boats.

Later on Anders found out they had swum across to Kattudden.

The final week of that summer passed in a state not unlike a hangover. Once the real hangover after the party in the boathouse had gone, everyone still talked more quietly than usual, laughed less often, and went around with a gnawing little pain. Except for Joel and Elin.

They had finally found each other seriously, and wanted to show off that fact. They crashed about paying no heed to anyone else, and gathered people together mainly so that they could have an audience as they groped each other. This might possibly have been their way of dealing with their feelings of guilt, but nobody took it that way. It was hard work, mostly. A couple of times Joel gave Elin a slap as a kind of joke, and it is possible that his later career as an abuser of women started that very summer.

Nothing was heard of Henrik and Björn, nor did anyone seek them out. Their exclusion from the gang was something that had been coming for several years, and now it was a fact. It hadn't really been a banishment as such, it was more that the gang had spat them out. It was a shame, but there was nothing to be done about it.

The day before Anders was due to go back to the city, he went over to Henrik's cottage anyway. As he approached the door he could hear the music from inside, 'There Is a Light That Never Goes Out'. He knocked.

The music was turned off and Henrik opened the door. He looked just the same as always, except that he had more pimples than before. Anders could see a pile of chocolate biscuit wrappers on the floor inside. Henrik made no move to let him in.

'Hi,' said Anders. 'I just…I'm going home tomorrow, so I…I just thought I'd say goodbye.'

A bitter smile distorted Henrik's mouth. When Anders didn't say or do anything else, the smile disappeared, and for a couple of seconds Henrik's face was naked.

'I didn't do it,' he said. 'Just so you know. I didn't do it. I just… it was nothing. I brushed against her. And she started screaming.' Henrik fixed his naked gaze on Anders' eyes. 'Do you believe me?'

Anders nodded. 'Yes.'

'Good.' Henrik's face closed down again, that smile came back. He said, 'In the days when you were hopelessly poor, I just liked you more.'

Anders realised this was a quote, but couldn't place it, so he simply said, 'Mm.'

'Bye then,' said Henrik, and closed the door.

The following summer the gang had begun to break up from the inside. Someone had gone on an InterRail trip, some had got summer jobs. Henrik and Björn could be seen riding around on the moped, and Anders was the only one who acknowledged them with a nod, but they never stopped to talk.

Strange things had begun to happen in the village. Things disappeared and turned up somewhere else. The notice board outside the shop was pulled down, and one morning a summer visitor who was going for a swim made a horrible discovery. From the lower branch of the pine tree next to the changing room a swan was dangling, hanged by the neck with a steel wire.

Another summer visitor who had three rabbits in a large hutch came out one morning and found them all dead. The only living thing inside the hutch was a neighbour's famously bad-tempered bulldog. There was nothing to indicate that the dog had dug its way in. It had been taken off its leash and placed inside the hutch.

Suspicion soon fell on Henrik and Björn. They rode around the village generally behaving oddly and negatively. Viciously, you could even say. They were taken to task here and there, but simply denied everything. Since nothing could be proved, nothing could be done. But people started to lock up their possessions and their animals.

The winter came, and The Smiths split up. When Anders was out on Domarö in the week between Christmas and New Year, he saw that Henrik and Björn were going around dressed in mourning, but he didn't meet them or speak to them.

The following summer he and Cecilia went interrailing for a month, and for the rest of the time Anders worked in a supermarket warehouse. During his winter week that year he didn't see Henrik and Björn. However, he learned via his father that they had made themselves completely impossible. They didn't talk to anyone and although they had had a few sessions with the youth psychology team, the vandalism and the nasty little events continued, if on a smaller scale.

When Anders rang his father in February, he heard that Henrik and Björn had drowned. They had set off across the ice on the moped and had fallen through. Neither of them had been wearing a lifejacket, and it had probably happened very quickly.

The village could breathe a sigh of relief. The final expulsion of Hubba and Bubba had taken place. Their parents left the island soon after, and disappeared from the general consciousness. It's always very sad when young people die, but...

It was finally over.

Nobody loves us

If you exist

In the light of the lamp above the kitchen table, it was easier to see what had happened to Elin, what she had done to herself now. The stitches were still there, and parts of her face were swollen with healing scar tissue, but it was still possible to see what the latest operation aimed to achieve.

Two deep grooves lined with livid scars ran from the outer edge of her nostrils down to the corners of her mouth. Beneath her eyes, which were now deep-set, were angry red patches criss-crossed by a number of thin lines that continued out towards her temples. She had had her wrinkles emphasised. The operations she underwent had the opposite aim of normal plastic surgery. She was making herself older, cruder, uglier.

She had declined the offer of coffee, as she had some difficulty using her mouth, and had wine in a tumbler instead. Anders couldn't find a straw, so he cut off a piece of thin rubber tubing and gave her that. She sucked down half the glass in one go, and Anders looked at her.

Pitiful.

The mention of Henrik and Björn had reminded him even more

powerfully of what Elin had done, who she had been. Now she sat here eighteen years later with trembling hands, her face in bits, sucking wine through a rubber tube.

Perhaps there is a kind of justice in the world, after all.

Since it was difficult to look at her for any length of time, his gaze wandered across the table, and he noticed that the number of beads on the tile had increased considerably. Another patch of white beads had been added, and a good sixth of the surface was now covered in beads.

Elin sucked up the last of the wine with a loud slurping noise. It was impossible to read her emotions from her face. Anders was on the point of asking about Henrik and Björn, but Elin got there first. Since her lips weren't working properly, all the consonants were weak and her tone was monotonous.

'I have this dream,' she said. 'A recurring dream. I don't sleep very well, because I have this dream all the time. I haven't slept properly for several weeks.'

She poured herself more wine, and Anders fetched himself a glass to keep her company. Once again Elin sucked down half the glass, coughed, and went on:

'There's a man lying in a boat. A skiff, an old skiff. He's lying in the bottom of the boat with his head up by the side, and he's dead. His eyes are open. And around him…there's a net in the boat as well, with fish in it. And some of the fish are loose, jumping around. Floundering and jumping. And the fish in the net are moving too. There are lots of fish, and they're alive. But the man is lying there dead. Do you understand? The fish are alive, even though they're in the boat, but he's dead.'

Elin sucked up more wine and grimaced with pain. Perhaps one of her cuts was pulling.

'That image is there, all the time. And I think I ought to get used to it, but every time it comes…I'm just as frightened every time, in the dream. I approach the boat and I see that man lying there dead among the fish and then it's as if I fall apart, I'm so frightened.'

The last drop of wine was sucked into Elin's mouth. It went down the wrong way and she started coughing. She coughed and coughed, pausing only to whimper with pain, then coughed again until Anders was afraid she was going to throw up. But eventually the coughing subsided and Elin sat there panting for a while, gasping for air. Tears poured down the gashes in her cheeks.

Anders wasn't particularly interested in Elin's dreams. He took a swig of wine and closed his eyes, saw before him the unclear image of Henrik and Björn's bodies in the moonlight, the ugly smile that had played around Elin's full lips.

It doesn't go away. Nothing goes away.

He opened his eyes and looked at Elin, who was hunched over, staring at the floor.

'You said they disappeared. That they didn't drown, Henrik and Björn. What did you mean?'

'They didn't find them.'

'But they went through a hole in the ice.'

Elin shook her head. 'That's not what I heard.'

'So what did you hear?'

Elin now had the same expression in her eyes as when they arrived at the Shack twenty minutes earlier, when she caught sight of the GB-man wrapped in the plastic sack. She had wanted to run away, but Anders had stopped her. The same expression now. Like an animal surrounded on all sides, with nowhere to run. The only solution was to implode, to disappear into herself.

'It was them, Anders. They had that fucking plastic man on the platform and they were...no older, do you understand? They were just like they were when...when all that happened. They haven't got any older.'

Anders leaned back in his chair. 'What did actually happen? Back then?'

Elin clamped her lips together, blew out her cheeks and looked at him with a pleading expression that might once have worked, but now just looked revolting. She wound the rubber tube around her index finger, let her shoulders drop and said, 'Joel's in prison, did you know that?' Anders didn't reply, and she went on, 'It was some woman…he nearly beat her to death. I don't know why. I don't suppose she'd done anything.'

She snivelled and pulled the tube tighter around her finger. The top of the finger turned dark red like the skin on her face, and she said to the surface of the table, 'I don't know. I don't know anything. I suppose I was evil. Can a person be evil?'

Anders shrugged his shoulders, took a deep breath and exhaled. A fraction of the weight that had been lying in his stomach lifted. He got up and fetched a new carton of wine. 'Would you like some more?'

She nodded and unwound the tube. They drank, or sucked, respectively, in silence. After a while Anders asked, 'What did you hear? About them?'

A trickle of wine ran from the corner of Elin's mouth, and she carefully wiped it away, then said, 'Just that they rode out on to the ice on their moped. And then they were gone.'

'You mean they didn't fall through the ice?'

'No.'

'No hole, no…it hadn't cracked, they…?'

'No. They just disappeared.'

Anders pressed his fist against his lips so hard that there was a taste of metal in his mouth, then he got up and staggered around the kitchen. Elin followed him with her eyes, sucked up some more wine and asked, 'What's the matter?'

Anders shook his head to indicate that he didn't want to talk, grabbed his cigarette packet and frantically smoked a cigarette as he paced back and forth, out into the hallway, into the living room.

What can I do? What shall I do?

There was no guarantee that the same thing that had happened to Henrik and Björn had happened to Maja. Perhaps they just…took off. Went somewhere else and started a new life.

And now they've come back without having aged?

Anders stopped by the window in the living room and looked towards Gåvasten's flashing lighthouse far away in the distance. Tears welled up in his eyes.

Without having aged…

He saw Maja's little hands reaching for the baby's bottle with her juice in it, her thin fingers curling around the edges of a Bamse comic as she lay on her back in her bed, reading. Her feet sticking out from under the covers. Six years old.

Anders stared out into the vast darkness with its single, flashing point of light. The wine had gone to his head and the light was swaying, sliding across the sea, and he could see Maja in her red snow-suit. She was glowing in the darkness, and she was walking across the water. The little body, the soft skin, the muscles tucked into her warm suit. A patch of red that was moving closer, but which dissolved when he tried to focus his gaze on it.

He whispered, 'Where are you? Where are you?'

No reply. Just the lapping of the sea against the rocks and the single constantly repeated message from Gåvasten, the message of every lighthouse: *Here I am, here I am. Be careful, be careful.*

Anders stood by the window staring out into the darkness until the draught through the frame made him shiver, and he went back into the kitchen.

Elin was lying across the table, her head resting on her arms. He shook her shoulder and she looked up in confusion. 'You'd better go to bed.' He gestured towards the bedroom. 'Take the big bed.'

Elin disappeared into the bedroom and Anders stayed at the kitchen table, drank more wine and smoked several cigarettes. He stared at the words scratched into the surface of the table.

Carry me.

Anders nodded drunkenly and clasped his hands as if in prayer, whispering, 'I will. I will. But where will I find you? Where are you?'

Perhaps half an hour had passed when Elin came out of the bedroom with the quilt wrapped around her. Her fingers scrabbled nervously at the fabric of the cover. Anders closed one eye so that he could see her more clearly. She looked as wretched as it is physically possible to look.

'Can't you come to bed as well?' she asked. 'I'm so bloody scared.'

Anders went into the bedroom with her and lay down beside her on top of the quilt. One hand came creeping out and found his.

What does it matter? What does it fucking matter?

He took her hand and squeezed it as if to say that everything was OK, that there was nothing to worry about. When he tried to let go, her grip tightened and he didn't pull away. The beam of the lighthouse at North Point swept through the room, flashing across the wall opposite and making the profile of Elin's flattened nose stand out. He lay there looking at it, and when the beam had swept past perhaps ten times, he asked again, 'Why are you doing this? Having all this surgery?'

'I have to.'

Anders blinked and realised he was feeling sleepy. His thoughts were far from lucid, but the suspicion of a theory came into his head, and he asked, 'Is it…a punishment?'

Elin was silent for a long time, and he thought she wasn't going to answer. The lighthouse beam had swept past many times before she finally said, 'I suppose it is,' let go of his hand and rolled over on to her side.

Anders lay there thinking about crime and punishment, the balance that is perhaps built into the world and into the souls of men. He didn't come up with anything, and his reasoning had begun to dissolve into disjointed images when he came to his senses, and heard from Elin's breathing that she was asleep. He got up, undressed and climbed into Maja's bed.

Sleep refused to come. He had probably nodded off for a few minutes in the big bed, and now he was wide-awake. He counted the flashes of the lighthouse and had reached two hundred and twenty; he was just considering switching on the bedside light and reading a Bamse comic when he saw Elin getting out of bed.

He thought she was going to the toilet. But there was something wrong with her movements. She walked towards his bed without seeing him. In only her bra and pants her body was shapeless, swollen, and when the light illuminated her face he was suddenly scared, and cowered as if expecting a blow.

The monster is coming for me.

But she passed him, oblivious, and the fear died away. Elin opened the door with the movements of a sleepwalker and went out of the room. Anders hesitated for a few seconds, then got up, pulled on his shirt and followed her.

She went through the kitchen and into the hallway, but instead of turning off towards the toilet, she carried on towards the front door. When she started fiddling with the catch to open the door, he went up to her.

'Elin, what are you doing?' he said to her back, without getting any reaction. 'You can't go outside like that.'

The lock clicked and she pushed down the handle. He grabbed her shoulder. 'Where are you going?' She stiffened in his grip and answered without turning around, 'Home. I'm going home.'

When the door opened and cold air swept in over his bare feet, he gripped her shoulder more firmly and turned her to face him. 'You can't. You have no house to go to.' He grabbed her other shoulder too and shook her. Her expression was absent.

'Listen,' he said. 'You're not going anywhere.'

Elin looked vacantly at him. Her lips were moving jerkily, as if she were saying *what, what, what, what*, without being able to produce any sound. Then she shook her head slowly and repeated, 'I'm not going anywhere.'

'No. Come on.'

He drew her back into the hallway, closed and locked the door. She allowed herself to be led back to bed, where she fell asleep immediately. Anders had no key to the bedroom door, so he jammed a chair under the handle and hoped he would hear if she tried to get out again.

What if she does? It's not my responsibility.

He slid into Maja's bed again and noticed to his surprise that his body had now decided he could sleep, if he wanted to. He did want to. He closed his eyes and soon slipped down into rest on a gently sloping plane. His last thought before he fell asleep was: *As if I didn't have enough.*

After the fire

Only blackened beams and grey sludge remained after the fire service had done their work. Hundreds of cubic metres of sea water had been pumped over and around the burning house, and despite the fact that odd curls of smoke were still rising from the devastation, there was no risk that the fire would catch hold again; the whole area was too wet.

Many people had gone home, but Simon was still standing in the sour-smelling ashes, contemplating the ruins and meditating on the transience of all things.

You have a house. Then you don't have a house.

Just one little match or a spark in the wrong place. That's all it took for everything you had walked around in for so many years, everything you had made beautiful and kept secure, to go up in smoke. A careless word or a glimpse of something you shouldn't have seen, and the web of life you had taken for granted was ripped up and scattered in pieces before your eyes.

The rug is pulled from under your feet.

You really can see it: the oblong rag rug you are walking on, but what's that figure down there at the end? Is it a devil or an angel? Or just a little old man in a grey suit, a tiresome individual who has been waiting for his chance? At any rate, he's holding the end of the rug in his hands. And he is patient, very patient. He can wait.

But if you lose your balance, if for some reason you are found wanting, then he gives the rug a quick tug. It's pure magic as your feet leave the ground and for a brief moment you hover, horizontal, the tips of your toes in line with your nose. Then the ground comes up to meet you with a crash and it hurts.

Simon pushed his hands deep in his trouser pockets and walked over to the remains of the house. There was a squelching sound from underfoot, and the smell of ash was suffocating. He had no particular relationship with the house that had burnt down, had never even been inside it. And yet it was as if it meant something.

He had had a confusing day and perhaps he was feeling over-sensitive, but he had definitely had enough of looking at things that happened on Domarö as isolated incidents with no internal connection, he'd been deceived—

Yes. Deceived.

—for long enough. The sooty sludge beneath his feet squelched and slurped around his feet as he waded through. The firemen had said that the way the fire had started definitely sounded suspicious, but it wasn't their job to investigate. The police would take over when it was daylight.

Despite the risk that he might be destroying important clues, Simon carried on ploughing through the mess until it thinned out and stopped a couple of metres before he reached the well. That was where he'd been heading, although he hadn't been aware of it.

It was an old well. A circular wall a metre high, made of stones cemented together, with the well itself covered by a wooden lid. The older construction with its winding mechanism, chain and bucket was still there for decoration. A thick plastic hose emerged from a hole in the lid, and presumably had been attached to a pump inside the house. Now the hose was burnt off a few metres from the well.

Simon moved the lid slightly and looked down into the darkness.

What am I doing?

He didn't know. Just as he didn't know why he'd come here at all. There was just something…drawing him. He closed one hand around the matchbox and waited.

Nothing. It's nothing.

He felt something, but he couldn't put his finger on what it was. It was just a feeling, a breath of something vanished, the ripples on the water after a fish has surfaced, but the fish itself is already far away.

But still he unhooked the bucket and used the chain to lower it into the well. After perhaps five metres it reached the surface down below. When he hauled it up it was half full of clear water. He cupped his hands and drank a mouthful, first cleaning the cut on his hand which had already begun to heal.

Salt.

It wasn't unusual for a certain amount of salt to find its way into wells so close to the sea. If they'd asked him he wouldn't have advised them to dig just here, but there was nothing to be done about that now. He hung the bucket back in its place. The feeling grew neither stronger nor weaker, it was simply there like a faint aroma, and he didn't know what it was.

He took a step back and looked at the well.

What a pity.

What a pity that such a fine old well would no longer have a house to belong to. He turned to look at the devastation once again and caught sight of a person standing where he had been standing a little while ago. The starlight was not bright enough to see who it was, so he raised an arm in greeting. The greeting was returned.

When he got closer he could see that it was Anna-Greta, standing waiting for him. His body stiffened, he replaced his apologetic expression with one of rebuff, and squelched with the greatest possible dignity the last few metres through the ash porridge.

Anna-Greta looked amused. 'What are you doing?'

'Nothing. I was just thirsty, that's all.'

Anna-Greta pointed to the public tap at the crossroads a dozen metres away. 'Wouldn't it have been easier to…?'

'Never thought about it,' said Simon, walking past her. He carried on towards home as quickly as he could, but Anna-Greta's legs were considerably more sprightly and she had no difficulty in catching up with him. She appeared by his side and switched on her torch to light the way for them both.

'Are you angry?' she asked.

'No. Disappointed, mostly.'

'Why?'

'Why do you think?'

They reached the track between the fir trees and Simon was forced to slow down. His heart didn't want to run away from Anna-Greta. His *physical* heart, for heaven's sake. He didn't know where he was with the other one. But it was certainly an insight worth acquiring at death's door: he couldn't run away from Anna-Greta even if he wanted to. She was simply too fast.

A hundred metres inside the forest he stopped to catch his breath. Anna-Greta stood calmly beside him, shining her torch along the track. There was no one else around.

'Let me put it this way,' said Anna-Greta. 'It was for your own good that I didn't tell you anything.'

Simon snorted. 'How long have we been together? Almost fifty years? How could you…Are there more things you haven't told me?'

'Yes.'

The admission should have surprised him, but Simon knew Anna-Greta. She told it like it was, even if it was inappropriate. That was precisely what made all this so difficult to swallow: the idea that perhaps he hadn't known her at all, not really.

'Well, let me tell you something,' said Simon. 'I was married once, and do you know what Marita said about the fact that she was on drugs? That she hadn't told me about it *for my own good*. So you could probably say I'm allergic to that particular argument.'

'It's not the same thing.'

'But I think it is, you see. And I find it incredibly difficult to accept it. I'm not sure I want to be with you anymore, Anna-Greta. I don't think I do.'

Simon had been bending over, his hands resting on his thighs. He pushed himself upright and set off into the darkness. Anna-Greta's torch was not following him. He had a lump in his stomach and wasn't looking where he was going, but at least it had been said. Now he must take the consequences, whatever that involved. He couldn't live with someone who lied like that.

The forest was pitch dark and he had to go carefully to avoid falling in the ditch again. The circle of light from the torch was still fixed on his retina, and he stopped and waited for it to disappear. He looked back along the track and saw that the real torch was lying on the ground, illuminating Anna-Greta's legs; she was lying next to it.

Simon opened his mouth to shout something, but nothing suitable emerged.

That's not fair. That's not a clean fight.

He clamped his jaws together. He had made the situation perfectly clear, explained how he felt. And then she did this. It was disgraceful, it was…Simon peered at the figure on the ground and wrung his hands.

Surely something hasn't really happened to her?

Anna-Greta was in good health, and was hardly likely to have a heart attack or a brain haemorrhage just because she'd been rejected. Or was she? Simon looked along the track in the direction of the old village. What if that moped came back? She couldn't just lie there like that.

Why is she lying there like that?

With the taste of lead in his mouth, Simon hurried back to Anna-Greta, guided by the glow of her torch. When he was a couple of metres away from her he could see that she was alive, because her body was shaking. She was weeping. Simon went and stood next to her.

'Anna-Greta, stop it. We're not teenagers. Don't do this.'

Anna-Greta sobbed and curled herself into a tighter ball. Simon could feel his own eyes burning, the tears welling up, and he angrily dashed them away.

Not fair.

He couldn't bear to see her like this, this obstinate, strong woman he had loved for so long, couldn't bear to see her lying on the forest track like a helpless, snivelling bundle. He had never imagined that something he said would provoke such a reaction. He had a lump in his throat, the tears were flowing, and he didn't bother wiping them away.

'Come on,' he said. 'Come on, Anna-Greta. Up you get.'

Between sobs Anna-Greta said, 'You're not. To say. That. You're not. To say. That you. Don't want. To be. With me.'

'No,' said Simon. 'I won't. Now come on.'

He reached out his hand to help her up, but she didn't see it. Simon didn't think he could manage to bend down and lift her up; there was a risk they'd both end up on the ground.

He had never been involved in anything like this. Not with Anna-Greta. She could be terrible if they had a quarrel, then cry for a while when it was over, but he had never seen her in utter despair like this. On the other hand he had never said, even hinted, that he wanted them to split up.

He waved his hand in front of her face. 'Come on. I'll help you.'

Anna-Greta snivelled up snot, her breathing slowed a little and she relaxed. Her breaths were slow but panting, and she lay quiet for a while. Then she asked, 'Do you want to be with me?'

Simon closed his eyes and rubbed them. This whole performance was just ridiculous. They were adults, more than adults. To think that everything could come full circle and end up with the simplest and most basic of questions, the one that should have been resolved decades ago.

But it hasn't been resolved, has it. Perhaps it never will be.

'Yes,' he said. 'Yes, I do. But now you need to get up. You're going to be ill if you lie there like that.'

She took his hand but didn't get up, she simply let her hand rest in his, caressing his palm with the tips of her fingers. 'Sure?'

Simon smiled and shook his head. For a couple of seconds he walked through the labyrinth of rooms in his heart, and was unable to find anywhere the feeling that had told him he wanted to leave her, never wanted to see her again. It was gone, as if it had never existed.

Nothing to be done. It's over.

'I'm sure,' he said, and helped her to her feet. Anna-Greta crept into his arms and they stood and held each other for so long that by the time they let go, the light of the torch had begun to fade from white to yellow. It was over.

For this time, thought Simon. They took each other's hands and found their way home by the fading glow of the torch. Both were exhausted by the unfamiliar storms of emotion, and their hearts were aching with the unaccustomed exercise. They held hands and that was conversation enough, but once they had emerged from the forest, Simon said, 'I want to know.'

Anna-Greta squeezed his hand.

'I'll tell you.'

When they were back in Anna-Greta's house they flopped on the sofa for a while, regaining their strength. It was as if they were shy, and found it difficult to look each other in the eye. Every time it happened they smiled hesitantly at one another.

Like teenagers, thought Simon. *Teenagers on Mum and Dad's sofa.*

Perhaps teenagers didn't behave like that nowadays, but to keep the analogy consistent Simon went into the kitchen and fetched a bottle of wine. To lighten the atmosphere. Loosen tongues and…make things happen.

Not like that, *though, no thank you. That would just be…*

He paused with the corkscrew halfway to the cork. Was it three days ago he and Anna-Greta last made love? It felt like much longer. But the fact they were behaving like teenagers didn't mean their bodies were singing from the same sheet.

The cork was stuck. Simon pulled as hard as he could, and realised that wasn't actually all that hard.

As I said…

He took the bottle in to Anna-Greta, who sat up, pushed the bottle firmly between her thighs and managed to extract the cork. As if to excuse Simon, she said, 'It was stuck pretty firmly.'

Simon sank down on to the sofa. 'Mm.'

Anna-Greta poured and they both took a sip, rolled the wine around their mouths and swallowed. The unaccustomed taste remained on his tongue, and Simon sighed with pleasure. He didn't often drink wine these days. He gave Anna-Greta a challenging look; she put down her glass and rested her hands on her knee.

'Where shall I start?'

'Start with the question I asked you. Why didn't people move away, why don't people move away? And what did you mean when you said you didn't tell me for my own good? Why has no one—'

Anna-Greta raised her hand to stop him. She picked up her glass again, took a tiny sip, then ran her finger round the rim.

'In a way it's the same question,' she said. 'If I tell you this, you won't be able to move away from here either.' She glanced out at the dark sea. 'Although it's probably already happened. You probably can't leave.'

Simon tilted his head on one side. 'Like I said. I have no intention of going anywhere. You don't need to scare me into staying.'

Anna-Greta gave a wan smile. 'It comes looking for us. If we try to leave this island, there is a considerable risk that it will come looking for us.'

'"It"', Simon interrupted. 'What do you mean by "it"?'

'The sea. It comes looking for us and it takes us. Wherever we are.'

Simon shook his head dubiously. 'But you go to Norrtälje, you go to Stockholm sometimes. We go over to Finland on the ferry, you and I. It's all been fine, up to now.'

'Mm. But you've suggested going further afield now and again. To Majorca, places like that. And I've said no, because…then it might think I'm trying to get away.'

Anna-Greta licked her index finger, ran it around the rim of the glass and produced a sound. A lonely, wailing sound rose from the glass and spread through the room like the voice of a ghost. A perfect note, so pure and clear that it seemed to strengthen itself by using the air as a sound-box. Simon placed his hand on Anna-Greta's finger to silence it.

'But this sounds crazy,' he said. 'You mean the sea goes ashore and finds you? That just doesn't happen.'

'It doesn't need to,' said Anna-Greta. 'It exists everywhere. It's connected to everything. The sea. The water. It doesn't need to go anywhere. It already exists everywhere.'

Simon took a bigger swig of wine. He thought back to the experience he had had the previous day. When he held Spiritus in his hand and saw how the water ran through everything, how everything basically consisted of water. Now he widened the perspective in his mind, and saw all the seas connected by rivers, creeks, streams. The veins of water running through the bedrock, the bogs and the pools. Water, water, everywhere.

It's right so far, but…

'I'm just wondering what you mean by "take". How does it "take" you?'

'We drown. In the most unreasonable places. In a little creek. In a puddle. In a handbasin.' Simon frowned and was about to ask the logical follow-up question, but Anna-Greta pre-empted him, 'No. I have no idea how it happens. Nobody has. But those who…belong to Domarö and try to get away…they are found drowned, sooner or later. Usually. Those who stay, survive. Usually.'

Simon placed his hand on top of Anna-Greta's, which was still resting on the rim of her glass. 'But this just sounds completely—'

'It doesn't matter what it sounds like. That's the way it is. We know that. And now you know it too. To use a word that has fallen out of use, we are damned. And we live with it.'

Simon folded his arms over his chest and flopped back against the sofa. It was a lot to take in at once, to put it mildly. The answers he had been given led to even more questions, and he didn't feel as if he could cope with much more tonight. The small amount of wine he had drunk was enough to make him sleepy, since he wasn't used to it.

He closed his eyes and tried to see everything in front of him. The fishermen who had made their pact with the sea, how it had continued and propagated itself over the years, continued and spread like the sea itself, seeping into every crack.

Seeping into...

He smacked his lips as he thought about the water he had drunk from the well at the burnt-down house. The faint taste of salt, the sea that had found its way in. The taste was gone now, replaced by the biting sweetness of the wine. Without opening his eyes, Simon asked, 'Do I belong to Domarö as well now? Am I also...damned?'

'Presumably. But only you can know that.'

'How do I know?'

'You just know.'

Simon nodded slowly and took a sounding in the very depths of himself, let the plumbline sink down through the darkness, the unspoken, the things he knew without being able to put them into words, and found that he reached the bottom sooner than expected. The knowledge was there, but he had not had the tools to find it. He belonged to the sea. He also belonged to the sea. Perhaps he had done so for a long time.

'Something has happened,' said Anna-Greta. 'That's what we met to talk about today. This business with Sigrid. As far as we know, no one has ever...come back.'

'But she was dead.'

'Yes, but even so. It's never happened before.'

'So what does it mean?'

Anna-Greta stroked his knee. 'Well, that's what we were discussing. When we were interrupted.'

Simon yawned. He tried to put into words one of the many questions writhing around in his head like indolent serpents, but before he managed it Anna-Greta said, 'There's something I want to ask you as well.'

'Oh yes?'

Simon yawned again, he just couldn't help it. He waved his hand in front of his mouth to indicate that he would have taken away this yawn if he could, but it just wasn't possible.

Anna-Greta tucked her legs up on the sofa and wrapped her arms around them. Simon sat there blinking, amazed at her suppleness and agility as she built her own little fortress around her like this. It must be fifteen years since he'd been able to do that, if then.

She leaned her chin on her knees and looked intently at him. Then she asked, 'Will you marry me?'

Despite his best efforts Simon was overcome by yet another enormous yawn which broke his eye contact with Anna-Greta. He held up his hands as if to say *No more, no more,* and said, *'That.* Is the limit when it comes to what I can cope with during the course of one day. We can talk about *that* tomorrow.'

What are you looking at?

Anders woke to an unfamiliar aroma, unfamiliar sounds. The aroma was coffee, the sounds were someone moving around in the kitchen, opening drawers and cupboards. He lay in bed for a while and pretended that everything was normal. That the person who had made the coffee and was busy in the kitchen was someone he loved and wanted to be with. That it was another beautiful morning in a good life.

He folded his hands over his stomach and looked out of the window. A cloudy sky with patches of blue, a lovely and probably quite cold day in the middle of October. The smell of coffee was tempting, and he heard the clink of china from the kitchen.

Cecilia is making breakfast. Maja is sitting at the kitchen table, busy with something. I am lying here, ready and rested in...Maja's bed...

The fantasy was fraying at the edges. The dirt in his body after yet another evening's drinking and smoking made its presence felt. He looked at his fingers. They were slightly yellow, black beneath the cuticles, and they stank of tobacco. His mouth felt sticky and he leaned over the edge of the bed, found a plastic bottle a third full of diluted wine. He picked it up and drank, hair of the dog.

OK. Back to reality.

The excitement of the previous evening had faded. What Elin had told him about Henrik and Björn's disappearance had seemed feverishly promising at the time, but in the cold light of morning he could see that this wasn't necessarily the case. The two events were separate. There wasn't necessarily any connection, and even if there was, what could he do? Nothing.

He heaved himself out of bed. The floor was cold beneath his bare feet, and he pulled on cold socks and a cold T-shirt. The headache began to pound at his temples. He dragged on his jeans and went into the kitchen.

Elin was just putting bread and cheese on the table. She looked up and said 'Good morning'. In the bright morning light from the kitchen window she looked fucking awful. He grunted in reply and got a new carton of wine out of the larder, opened it and took a couple of big gulps. Elin was watching him. He didn't care. The headache was getting worse and he screwed up his eyes, massaged his temples.

'You've got a pretty big problem with alcohol, haven't you?' she said simply.

Anders grinned as a quip he'd heard from a stand-up comic shot out of his mouth, 'I'm a drunk and you're ugly. I can stop drinking.'

Silence fell, and that was the way Anders wanted it. He poured himself a cup of coffee and looked at the clock. It was after eleven. He had slept longer than usual. Despite Elin's escape attempt during the night, perhaps her presence had given the room some kind of security that had enabled him to sleep.

He took a couple more swigs of coffee and glanced at her. The headache was easing slightly and his conscience pricked as he saw her sitting there breaking a cheese sandwich into tiny pieces so that she could get it into her mouth. He wanted to say something, but while there are plenty of nasty, smart-arse remarks, the kind that can put something right are harder to come by.

He finished off his coffee and was about to pour her a cup when it occurred to him that she probably wouldn't be able to drink something that hot. She'd made it for him. He put the cup on the draining board and said, 'Thanks for the coffee. That was kind of you.'

Elin nodded and took a cautious sip of juice from her glass. The wounds must have healed a little, since she didn't need to use a straw. What she had done to her face was incomprehensible. She was thirty-six, like him, but was starting to look like a sixty-year-old who'd had a difficult life.

'I'm going to check the post,' said Anders.

He hurried out of the kitchen and pulled on his Helly Hansen top, fleeing the agonising desolation that lay like a fog around Elin.

Down below the porch stood the GB-man, wrapped in the plastic sack. He couldn't understand why it had frightened him so much. He picked it up and carried it over to the woodpile, where he kicked it and made it fall over.

'Not so fucking tough now, are you?' he said to the prone figure, which had nothing to say in its defence.

The air was clear and cold, the demons of the night were dispersing. He looked with satisfaction at the well-filled wood store, pushed his hands into his pockets and set off towards the village. It was as if he had two different states. One which was comparatively clear and lucid and could chop wood, think sensible thoughts, and was on the way up. And then there was the other, the night side, which was in the process of getting lost in a labyrinthine darkness of fear and speculation, and was on the way down.

At least it's a fight, he thought. *In the city there was nothing but apathy.*

That's how he chose to see it at the moment, at any rate, as he approached the shop with his work-worn hands in his pockets. When the rays of the sun broke through the cloud cover at irregular intervals and made the sea sparkle, when he was in the light of the new day. When the night came no doubt everything would look very different.

He opened the old mailbox he had been given by Simon, expecting to find nothing as usual, but today there was a yellow envelope in the box. The films. The pictures had been developed.

He weighed the envelope in his hand. It was thinner and lighter than usual, because he had only taken a few pictures before his photography stopped for good. But they were in there. The last pictures. He picked at the flap of the envelope and looked around. Not a soul in sight. He ripped it open.

He didn't want to go home because Elin was there, he wanted to be in peace with this moment. He sat down on the steps of the shop and pulled the smaller folder out of the envelope, weighing that in his hand as well. How many pictures were there? Ten? Eleven? He couldn't remember. He took a deep breath and carefully fished out the little bundle of photographs.

My darling...

First of all a couple of bad pictures of the Shack, and then there they were, on the way up to the lighthouse. Maja in her red suit, ploughing ahead through the snow, Cecilia right behind her, straight-backed despite the difficult terrain underfoot. There they were in front of the lighthouse, side by side with rosy cheeks. Cecilia's hand on Maja's shoulder, Maja pulling away, off somewhere else as usual.

More photographs of the two of them in front of the lighthouse, the two people he had cared about most in all the world, both gone. Different degrees of zoom, the hands in different positions. Pictures from a distance, head and shoulders, close-ups. Maja up by the reflector.

A lump formed in Anders' throat, and he found it difficult to breathe. How could they be gone? How could they have ceased to exist for him, when he was sitting here holding them in his hands? How could that be?

The tears began to fall; a screw was boring its way through his chest. He lowered the pictures and let it happen. He wrapped his arms around himself and thought: *If there was a way...*

If there was a way, a machine, a method of releasing people from photographs. Of capturing those frozen moments and thawing them out, making them real and bringing them back into the world. He

257

nodded to himself as the tears continued to flow and the screw was twisted around and around.

'It ought to be possible,' he mumbled. 'It ought to be possible…'

He sat like that until the pain began to subside and the tears had dried. Then he looked at the photographs one by one, running his finger over the two-dimensional faces that would never be his again.

That's funny…

He flicked back and forth through the pile. Maja wasn't looking into the camera in one single picture. Cecilia was gazing obediently into the lens every time, in one she had even managed a beaming smile. But Maja…

Her eyes were looking away, and in a couple of pictures it wasn't only her eyes. Her whole face was turned to the left. To the east.

Anders studied the pictures more closely and could see that in every picture her eyes seemed to be fixed on a particular point. Even when she was directly facing the camera, in the close-up for example, her pupils were drawn to the left.

He lowered the bundle of photographs and stared straight ahead, open-mouthed. He remembered. Up in the lighthouse. How she had pointed and…

Daddy, what's that?

What do you mean?

There. On the ice.

Far away in the distance Gåvasten was no more than a diffuse elevation in the grey-blue sea. With his index fingers and thumbs Anders made a small diamond-shaped hole, and looked through it to sharpen his focus. The contours of Gåvasten became slightly clearer, but he couldn't see anything in particular.

What was it she saw?

He got up from the steps, pushed the photographs in his pocket, and strode purposefully home. He had a job to do.

Anders walked around the upturned boat, looking at it from a more pragmatic point of view. Yes, it looked scruffy, but could it serve its purpose: to stay afloat, and to carry an engine that would get him to Gåvasten?

The weakest element from a practical point of view was the mounting for the engine. The metal plate in the stern had virtually fallen to bits with rust, and if you tried to attach an engine to it, it would probably fall into the sea. Anders studied the construction. With a couple of bolts through the whole thing, the metal plate could be reinforced with a piece of wood. It wasn't a complicated job, but the boat would have to be turned over so that he could get at it.

He went up to the house and asked Elin to help. It was hard work, but eventually they managed to tip the boat up so that it was balanced, and Anders was able to go round to the other side to take the weight and break the fall as it landed the right way up.

Elin looked at the cracked seat, the splits around the rowlocks and the fringes of fibreglass along the broken gunwale. 'Are you intending to go out in this?'

'If the engine works, yes. What are you going to do?'

'About what?'

'About everything. Your life. What are you going to do?'

Elin tore off a couple of wormwood leaves and crushed them between her fingers, sniffed at them and pulled a face. Anders glimpsed a movement behind her, and saw that Simon was heading towards them. When Elin caught sight of him she whispered, 'Don't tell him it's me. If he asks. I can't…'

She had no time to say any more before Simon reached them. 'So,' he said, nodding towards the boat. 'Are you off to sea?'

'Yes.'

Simon turned to Elin and gave a start. He stood there frowning for a couple of seconds, staring at her face. Then he held out his hand.

'Hello. Simon.'

He continued to stare at Elin's face as if he were trying to remember something. Anders couldn't understand his reaction. OK, Elin looked ghastly, but Simon's behaviour was downright rude, and not like him at all. If you bumped into a person whose face

259

was scarred from severe burns, for example, you didn't stand there gawping at them like that.

Simon seemed to realise this himself; he let go of Elin's hand, smoothed away his stunned expression and asked, 'So, are you…'

Elin didn't stop to listen to the question, but excused herself and went back up to the house. Simon watched her go. Then he turned to Anders. 'Is she a friend of yours?'

'Yes. Or…it's a long story.'

Simon nodded and waited for Anders to continue. When he didn't oblige, Simon contemplated the boat instead and said, 'This doesn't look too good.'

'No, but I think she'll float.'

'And what about the engine?'

'Don't know. I haven't tried it.'

'You're welcome to borrow my boat if you need it, you know that.'

'I want something of my own. But thanks.'

Simon clasped his hands together and walked around the boat, saying 'Hmm' to himself at regular intervals. He stopped beside Anders and rubbed his hands over his cheeks. It was obvious he had something to say. He cleared his throat, but it wouldn't come out. He tried again, and this time things went better.

'There was something I wanted to ask you.'

'Ask away.'

Simon took a deep breath. 'If Anna-Greta and I were to…if we were to get married. What would you think about that?'

Simon looked deeply worried. Something burst out of Anders' chest and for a fraction of a second he didn't know what it was, he was so unused to the feeling, but it was a laugh. 'You're going to get *married*? Now?'

'Well, we're thinking about it, yes.'

'What about all that business of not knowing another person?'

'I think we'd better regard that as…somewhat exaggerated.'

Anders looked up at Anna-Greta's house as if he expected to see her standing up there, anxiously eavesdropping. He didn't get it. 'Why are you asking *me* about this? What do *you* want?'

Simon scratched his head and looked embarrassed. 'Well, I want to, of course, but I mean it's also a question of…I mean, I'd inherit everything, if she were to die before me. Which doesn't seem particularly likely, but…'

Anders placed his hand on Simon's shoulder. 'I'm sure we can get something in writing. Something that says I can keep the Shack. If it comes to that. I'm not bothered about anything else.'

'That's OK with you? Are you sure?'

'Simon, it's more than OK. It's the first piece of good news I've heard in a long, long time, and…' Anders took a step forward and gave Simon a hug. 'Congratulations. It's about time, to say the least.'

When Simon had gone, Anders stood with his hands in his pockets for a long time, staring at the boat without thinking about the boat. For once his internal organs felt warm and easy to carry. He wanted to hang on to that feeling.

When he went up to the timber store after a while, he discovered that he could take the feeling with him. It stayed with him while he cut a piece of treated wood, lingered as he drilled holes in it and fixed it to the stern.

Will there be a wedding?

He hadn't asked Simon if they were planning a proper wedding in the church at Nåten, or if they were planning to have it at home, or just a civil ceremony. They probably hadn't thought about it themselves either, since nothing was decided yet.

Who proposed to whom?

He just couldn't picture it, how it had happened or what had led to it. But it was fun to think about it. The feeling remained with him.

It was only when he had nailed a plank between two trees, hauled the engine on to it and connected a pressure tank that the usual gloom began to take over once again. The engine wasn't co-operating. He pumped up the petrol, pulled out the choke and yanked at the starter until his arm started to go numb. Nothing.

Why does everything have to fucking play up? Why can't anything work?

He lifted off the cover and saw that he'd flooded the engine, the petrol had run out of the carburettor and gathered in a puddle underneath the fuel filter. He did all the things he could think of, checked all the connections and cleaned the spark plug. It was starting to get dark by the time he put the cover back on and yanked at the starter until he was sweaty, with no success.

He resisted a powerful urge to lift the engine off the plank, carry it down to the jetty and throw it in the sea. Instead he took the cover off once again, sprayed the whole engine with WD-40 with an air of resignation, put the cover back on and left it.

Major and minor questions

As Simon approached Anna-Greta's house with the evening drawing in, he saw that she had lit candles in the kitchen. His stomach contracted, and he suddenly felt nervous. He felt he was on her wavelength to a certain extent, having put his best pullover on under his jacket, but he perceived a ceremonial air that he wasn't quite sure he could rise to.

When he looked back at his life it seemed to him that he had lived it without making any actual *decisions*. Things had turned out the way they had turned out, and he had just gone along with it all. His alliance with Spiritus was perhaps an exception, but that had been dictated by necessity. He couldn't have done anything else.

Or could he?

Perhaps it was just that he had never been faced with such a clear question before, such a definite choice as this proposal. He had probably made decisions and choices, but it had happened quietly, so to speak. No bells and whistles, no candles, no sinking feeling in his stomach.

The business of children, for example. He and Anna-Greta had been unable to have children, and presumably he was the weak link. They had never consciously tried to have children. If their love had resulted in a child they would no doubt have accepted it with joy, but when it didn't happen, they left the matter alone. They didn't have any tests and they never discussed adoption.

It just didn't turn out that way.

That expression contained the essence of an attitude to life that was embraced by many people on Domarö, and that Simon also shared. A kind of fatalism. The meeting in the mission house had shown him where the roots of this fatalism lay. Things happened, and that was just the way it all turned out. Or they didn't happen, and things just didn't turn out. Nothing to be done about it.

But now he was on his way to the prettily illuminated house to answer a question that wasn't just going to turn out one way or the other by itself. It was Yes or No that mattered here, and his best pullover was chafing slightly at the neck. He wished he had brought a present, a flower, or something to hold in his hands at least.

With his customary combination of city behaviour and village behaviour he knocked on the door first and then opened it. He hung his jacket in the hallway, ran a finger inside the neckline of his pullover and went into the kitchen.

He stopped by the stove. The ceremonial air he had sensed was definitely there. The candelabra had been brought out, there was a clean white cloth on the table, and a bottle of wine was waiting. Anna-Greta was wearing her blue dress with the high neck and the Chinese embroidery. Simon hadn't seen it for ten years, at least, which was why he stopped dead.

There she was, the woman he…

the woman he…

the woman.

Her. The other one. *You.* And wasn't she beautiful, wasn't she elegant. She certainly was. The candles made the silk of the dress shimmer, and the glow spread to her face, which seemed to lose its age altogether rather than looking twenty years younger. It was just her, Anna-Greta, through all the years and all the different ways she had looked. Just Anna-Greta.

Simon swallowed and didn't know what to do with his hands. There should have been something in them, something to hand over, some kind of gesture to be made. Instead he waved vaguely in the direction of the table, the room, Anna-Greta, and said, 'This is…lovely.'

Anna-Greta shrugged, said, 'Sometimes you just have to make a bit of an effort,' and a little of the communion-like atmosphere eased. Simon sat down on the opposite side of the table and reached out his empty hand, palm upwards. Anna-Greta took it.

'Yes,' he said. 'Of course.'

Anna-Greta leaned forward. 'Of course what?'

'Of course I want to marry you. Of course I do.'

Anna-Greta smiled and shut her eyes. With her eyelids closed she nodded silently. Simon swallowed around the lump in his throat and squeezed her hand.

This is how it is, he thought. *This is how it's going to be.*

With his free hand he dug in his trouser pocket and took out the matchbox, placing it on the table between them.

'Anna-Greta?' he said. 'There's something I have to tell you.'

Bloody tourists go home

Anders and Elin dedicated the evening to a lot of wine and a little chat. Elin lit a fire in the living room and stayed in there, Anders sat in the kitchen staring at the bead tile, trying to find a pattern. Nothing occurred to him. The silence that had been acceptable when he was alone in the house was suffocating with Elin there.

From one of the kitchen cupboards he dug out his father's old cassette player and a plastic bag of tapes. They were well used and grubby, and had been played many times. They were mostly compilations from a program of top twenty hits, Alf Robertsson and Lasse Lönndahl. He had come to terms with the idea of listening to Alf Robertsson's growling voice for a while when he found a tape that was so worn that the label was almost illegible. It didn't matter, he recognised it and knew what it said, 'Kalle Sändare Makes a Call'.

The cassette player had no lead. He searched through the drawers frantically, with growing anticipation. He had listened to this particular tape with his father many times. As a child he had thought Kalle's mischievous phone calls were very funny, and he was looking forward to finding out what he thought of them now.

He found the lead and pushed it in, inserted the cassette and pressed Play. He heard the faint beep indicating that the conversation was starting, and turned up the volume; the tape was so old and worn that the sound itself seemed to have been eroded.

'Ah, good afternoon, my name is Måstersson and I'm an engineer...'

Anders sat with his ear pressed close to the machine, listening as Kalle pretended to be interested in buying some Svea brand beehives, asking detailed questions about his prospective purchase. The innocent victim on the other end willingly answered his questions, which became more and more insane.

Anders laughed out loud when Kalle asked if the beehives had reflector aggregates like those in boat tanks, and laughed even more when he started talking about the buried beehives he'd seen in Germany. Towards the end, when he told a completely pointless story about a little dinghy that had been stuck in the ice over the winter, 'and then, when the spring came...the boat just floated up!' Anders found himself so helpless with laughter that he missed a bit and had to rewind the tape.

When the conversation was over, Anders pressed the Stop button. He had a pain in his stomach and tears in his eyes. But it was a good pain, and they were good tears. He wiped them away and poured himself another glass of wine. Just as he was about to restart the tape to listen to the next call, Elin came into the kitchen.

'What are you listening to?'

'Kalle Sändare. Don't you think he's brilliant?'

'Not really.'

Anders got annoyed, and had to restrain himself from making a nasty comment. Elin yawned and said, 'I'm going to bed.'

'You do that.' She lingered for a moment, and Anders added, 'I'm staying here for a while. You carry on.'

Elin went off to the bedroom and Anders was alone in the kitchen with Kalle Sändare. He drank a toast to the cassette player, lit a cigarette and kept listening. Kalle was looking for a job as a drummer in a dance band, investigated tree-felling opportunities and was interested in buying an electric guitar. There were no more belly laughs, but Anders giggled almost non-stop.

When the tape ended there was silence in the kitchen, and he felt more abandoned than ever. Kalle's gentle, friendly voice had kept him company. Anders took out the tape, twisting it over and over between his fingers. It was recorded in 1965.

This is culture.

The humour consisted almost exclusively of linguistic twists and turns, and was *nice* through and through. There was nothing harsh or cynical in Kalle's treatment of his unsuspecting victims, he was just a funny little old man, an eccentric part of Swedish life.

Anders thought about the comedy programs he had seen on television in recent years, and started to cry. Because Kalle Sändare wasn't around any more, and because everything was so terrible nowadays. After he had cried for a while he stood up, rinsed his face in cold water and tried to pull himself together.

Stop it. You can't carry on like this.

He dried his face on a tea towel and felt somehow purged inside. Laughter and tears had followed on from one another, and at last he was tired enough to be able to sleep. A good evening, in spite of everything. On his way to the bedroom he ran a finger over the tape.

Elin must have been able to hear Kalle Sändare as well; the

bedroom door was ajar, and the tape had clearly acted as a lullaby. She was fast asleep, breathing deeply, and Anders was grateful he didn't have to talk. He undressed and got into Maja's bed, then lay for a while looking at the bundle in the big bed that was Elin.

What am I going to do with her?

There wasn't much he could do. She had to reach her own decision. He would tell her that she could stay on for a few days if necessary, but after that she would need to find a different solution. He didn't want anyone else living here, he wanted to be alone with his ghosts. And Kalle Sändare.

Anders smiled. There had been another tape, where had that gone? 'The Tales and Adventures of El Zou-Zou the Magician'. There was some story about a monkey who went in and out through the handles of a paper bag and fetched out different tools…

With the monkey by his side he tumbled into dreams.

He was woken by a cold draught and sat up blinking, trying to see the clock on the floor next to the bed. Half-past twelve. He had been asleep for maybe an hour.

One night. Can I please be allowed to sleep for one *whole night?*

The bedroom door was wide open, and the big bed was empty. Anders flopped back on his pillow and listened. There wasn't a sound inside the house, but the outdoor noises sounded much too clearly, as if the outside door was open. He had forgotten to barricade the bedroom door, and now he had to deal with the consequences.

Yawning, he pulled on his clothes and went into the kitchen. The outside door was indeed open to the night, and the house was bitterly cold. The thermometer outside the kitchen window was showing four degrees. Elin's clothes had been neatly folded on the bedroom chair, so she must have gone out in her bra and pants.

Gone home.

That was where she had been heading the previous night, and that was presumably where she had gone now. Right across the island, perhaps two kilometres to Kattudden.

Anders rubbed his face angrily with the palms of his hands.

Shit! Shit shit shit!

There was nothing else he could do. He found a warm sweater and a jacket, shoved Elin's clothes into a carrier bag, pulled on a woolly hat and set off. If he was lucky she hadn't been gone long, and he would catch up with her along the road.

His head was buzzing with the intoxication that had been on its way towards a hangover, but had been stopped in its tracks. The dancing beam of the torch moving along the track made him feel slightly unwell. When he got to the point where the track divided, he had a stroke of genius and turned off for Simon's house.

Simon's bike was propped up against the birch tree by the track. It wasn't locked. It was an old army bike and not really worth stealing, even for the most desperate thief. Besides which, Simon had said he couldn't use it any longer, and anyone who needed it was welcome to take it.

Anders took it. He noticed something unusual: Simon's house was in darkness, but there was a light on in Anna-Greta's. Then he remembered.

They're probably sitting up making plans.

The thought cheered him up, and the chilly night air had cleared his head. He hung the bag of clothes on the handlebars, got on the bike and pedalled off, using the torch to light his way, since the lamp on the front of the bike had been broken since time immemorial. There was a chance that someone else might have stopped Elin, but it wasn't great. It was only in summer that people on Domarö were moving about at night.

He passed the shop and the mission house without seeing any sign of the sleepwalker. By the time he got on to the track through the forest, he was puffing and sweating. There was a sour, smoky taste in his mouth, and as he swept the torch over the gloomy trees, despondency came over him once again and a line from 'Heaven Knows I'm Miserable Now' popped up in his head.

The Smiths. It was many years since a line from one of their songs had come unbidden into his mind, and it made him follow a chain of thought back through the years as he pedalled through the forest. He came out into the opening leading towards Kattudden, continued for fifty metres or so, then caught sight of something that made him brake so sharply that the tyres skidded through the gravel.

He tried to correct the bike, but couldn't keep it upright. It slid sideways and he went down with a clatter and a ping from the bell. His right knee scraped along the gravel then the speed took him and rolled him over a couple of times before he was eventually stopped by a fence. He pulled himself up into a sitting position and tried to make sense of what his eyes were seeing.

Henrik's platform moped was parked under a lamppost. In the garden next door, Elin was walking with two other people. The sound of Anders crashing his bike made them turn around. It was Henrik and Björn. They both looked roughly the same age as when Anders had last seen them, eighteen years earlier.

This isn't real. This isn't happening.

Henrik and Björn were contemplating him calmly as he sat there like a dazed animal, caught in the glow of the lamp. Elin carried on along the side of the house. It wasn't a house Anders was familiar with. Just one of many summer cottages. Elin was carrying something heavy. It was hard to see what it was, because the light didn't reach that far.

The taste of blood seeped into Anders' mouth and he looked around for the torch. It was by his feet, and it was still shining. He pointed it at Henrik, who gave a start as the bright light hit him. Then he smiled.

'Unfortunately it's not that simple, Anders.'

Something in Henrik's hand reflected the light and dazzled Anders before the reflection vanished. A knife. The blade was so long it almost reached the ground as Henrik held the handle between his index and middle finger, letting the sharp edge swing to and fro. If it hadn't been for the shape of the blade, it could have been a machete.

Anders got to his feet. His trousers were ripped over his right knee, which was throbbing with pain. There was no point in questioning the evidence of his own eyes. Henrik and Björn were standing there. They looked the same as they had done all those years ago, Henrik's voice was the same. Anders spat out a gob of saliva mixed with blood and asked, 'What are you doing?'

Henrik looked at Björn and Björn said, 'Burning down the discotheque.'

Henrik gave him the thumbs-up sign. Anders shone the torch towards the house. Elin really was wearing only her underclothes, and the narrow band of her bra glowed white against her back. She was carrying a can of petrol in her hands, and was just throwing the last of the petrol over the corner of the house.

Why...

The thoughts whirled around in Anders' head, tinged with red and with no sense of order. The only thing he could manage to get out was that one simple question, '...why?'

Henrik pursed his lips and frowned, as if Anders' lack of knowledge annoyed him. He said, 'I think you know.'

'No.'

'Oh, come on.'

'I don't understand what you mean.'

Henrik waved the knife around and said to Björn, 'Now I'm fucking disappointed. Aren't you disappointed?'

The corners of Björn's mouth turned down. 'Truly disappointed.'

They were playing some kind of game, and Anders didn't want to join in. The fact that they were standing there in front of him, alive and talking and playing their game, was just too much to take in, so Anders clung to the reason he had come here. 'What's Elin got to do with all this?'

Björn shook his head. 'You really don't understand anything, do you? Mind or body? Which rules the other? I dunno.'

Henrik waved the knife in Elin's direction and said, 'Come on, old woman.'

Elin went and stood between them. She was moving like a

sleepwalker, just as she had done the previous night, and her eyes were empty. The cold had made her skin deathly pale, and it was difficult to tell where the skin ended and the fabric began. As Anders looked around for the bag containing Elin's clothes, Henrik ran his hands over her breasts and stomach and said, 'Have you earned it, baby? I don't think so. Not yet.'

The carrier bag was lying by the fence a couple of metres away from where Anders had landed after the crash. Whether Henrik and Björn were ghosts or crazy or both, this couldn't go on. Elin would freeze to death.

Anders pulled her sweater out of the bag and went over to the group. Despite the impossibility of Henrik and Björn's presence, and despite the knife in Henrik's hand, Anders was not afraid. In the same way as a school reunion tends to cast everyone in their former roles once again, he regarded Henrik and Björn as nothing more than the slightly ridiculous boys they had been in the old days; he had no respect for them. He held out the sweater to Elin. 'Here. Put this on.'

Elin didn't move, and her gaze was turned in on herself. When Anders rolled the sweater up to put it on her, Henrik took a step forward and placed himself in the way. He looked Anders in the eye and said, 'What's changed? Nothing, I just love you less. Slightly less than I did, anyway.'

As he uttered the last word he swept his hand in an arc over Anders' legs. It felt as if he had been lashed with a whip, and when he looked down he saw that his jeans had been slashed across both thighs; there were two cuts the width of a hand in the fabric. For a second he could also see the pink flesh in the cuts. Then came the blood. It filled the gashes and dark stains spread over the fabric.

Before Anders had time to think the thought: *I've been cut*, his chin was hit by the metal knob on the end of the knife's handle. Everything went black and he staggered backwards for a couple of steps before he fell over and hit his shoulder on the platform of the moped. The adrenaline was running riot in his body, and he started shaking.

Henrik pointed the knife at him and mused, 'What do you think the knife wants?' He grinned and made a slitting motion.

Björn laughed as though he had heard an unusually funny joke. Without taking his eyes off Anders, Henrik extended the palm of his hand. Björn gave him five and said, 'That was good.'

Anders had drawn up his knees and warm blood was pouring down his thighs, tickling its way over his groin and gathering under his bottom. His head was reverberating with a sound like the lingering echo of a church bell, and he was too weak to get to his feet. Henrik continued lecturing him.

'Elin here,' said Henrik, placing an arm around her shoulders, 'she was a great girl, wasn't she? Looked after herself. If anyone came too close, she started screaming. Times have certainly changed.'

Incapable of doing anything more than lifting one arm in an impotent attempt to put an end to all this, Anders leaned against the moped and watched as Henrik grabbed the blade of the knife and pushed the metal knob on the handle inside Elin's pants. He glanced at Anders, nodded, then pushed the whole of the handle inside Elin's vagina.

She didn't make a sound. The blade was sticking out of her pants like a metal penis. When Anders looked up at her face, he saw that she was smiling. A big, ugly smile. His stomach turned over and sour vomit spurted out between his lips, all over the gravel beside him.

He wiped his mouth and took a deep breath. Through his burning throat he managed just one harsh word, 'Elin!'

Elin's eyelids flickered and she looked at him. Her eyes came back to life, and when she looked down below her belly she screamed. Henrik snorted, grabbed the blade and pulled out the handle. Björn grabbed her from behind, locking her arms as Henrik caressed her skin with the blade. He turned to Anders.

'You still haven't answered the question,' he said.

A tiny amount of strength was beginning to return to Anders' body. Soon he would be able to stand up, and he thought: *A weapon, where can I find a weapon?* as he said, 'What question?'

'The one about the disco,' said Björn, adopting a pedagogical tone, as if he were addressing a particularly stupid pupil, 'Why are we burning down the disco?'

'I don't know.'

The fence post. The one that came loose.

Elin was screaming wordlessly and writhing in Björn's grip. Henrik put his arm around her neck with his hand over her mouth, then turned to Anders again, nodded briefly and slashed her stomach.

A muffled scream escaped from beneath Henrik's firmly clamped hand and Elin's legs kicked out as she tried to free herself, while a trickle of blood spread horizontally along a crease in her stomach. Anders staggered to his feet and Henrik pointed the knife at him.

'Calm down,' he said. 'Chill. That was worth a clue.'

Anders wasn't sure his body would obey him if he tried to rush over to the fence, so he stayed where he was and tried to gather his strength as Björn said, 'For the same reason as we're hanging the disc jockey.'

Henrik nodded and loosened his grip on Elin's mouth, dug his hand inside her bra and grabbed one nipple, pulled it out and rested the blade of the knife against it. Elin was now dangling helplessly in Björn's grasp, too frightened even to scream.

'Last chance,' said Henrik. 'Why are we going to hang the DJ and burn the disco?' He made a couple of sawing movements with the knife a centimetre above Elin's stretched, pink flesh, and said, 'Come on Anders, you *know* this.'

There was no possibility that he could reach the fence post before Henrik let the knife fall. Anders pressed his wrists against his temples. *Hang the DJ, burn the discotheque.*

Something clicked. He switched the words around and then blurted out the name of the song that was so relevant to his present condition.

'Panic!' he cried. 'Panic!'

Henrik stiffened. Then he let go of Elin's nipple and lowered the knife. He made a gesture not unlike applause. 'There you go! That wasn't so difficult, was it?'

Anders ignored the question. 'Why are you doing this?'

Henrik considered for a couple of seconds. Then he shook his head and turned to Björn, who was still holding on to Elin. Björn said, 'Mmm...because...we are human and we need love just like anyone?'

'No,' said Henrik. 'Try again.'

Björn frowned. Then he brightened up. 'We're clinging because we know it's over, but we don't know where else to go.'

Henrik nodded. 'Close enough,' he said. 'And so true.'

The cuts in Anders' thighs were not as deep as he had first thought. They had stopped bleeding, but his trousers were soaked and the cold was starting to get to his legs. 'Can we stop this game now?' he said. 'Let Elin go.'

Henrik looked surprised.

'That's not possible. We're going to drown her.'

Elin started screaming again as Henrik and Björn used their combined strength to drag her towards the water, her bare feet scoring a track in the gravel. Anders stumbled over to the fence and tugged at the loose post until it came out.

When he turned around Elin had been dragged twenty metres down towards the sea, forty metres to go. He let the adrenaline take over, desensitising him to his physical problems. He ran to catch up with them. When he was a couple of metres away, he yelled, 'Let her go!'

Henrik turned, and Anders hit out at his head with the metre-long post. Henrik's arm came up in defence, and the post struck his elbow. The sensation of two hard objects meeting should have carried on into Anders' hands, but that wasn't what happened. When the wooden post hit Henrik's body it felt more like hitting a big sponge full of water. Henrik's arm curved around the post and a shower of water hit Anders in the face.

Henrik tore the post out of his hands and hurled it to the ground. 'I don't think it's time for you to die. Yet. So pack it in.'

Anders stood there with his arms dangling by his sides as they continued to drag Elin towards the water. Then he turned and ran up towards their moped as he fumbled in his pocket. *Let me have, let me have...*

Yes. In his pocket he found both cigarettes and matches. He ran over to the moped, unscrewed the petrol cap and yelled to the group, who were now very close to the shore, 'Listen! Let her go, or else...' He lit a match and held it over the hole.

They stopped. Anders shook the box of matches and discovered it was half-full. He had no plan, couldn't work out what to do next. He had been forced to find a way to stop them, and so far it had succeeded. But what next? He could stand here striking matches until the box was empty, but then what?

In any case, they must be able to see through him. He had no desire to be blown up along with their moped for Elin's sake. He looked at the match, which had almost burned down.

Besides which...

Besides which it wouldn't work, he now remembered. He couldn't think who it was or in what context, but somebody had once dropped a lighted match into a petrol tank to impress the others. It had simply gone out. Petrol needs air in order to burn. It might even have been Henrik, that summer when they were kings with their new moped.

Maybe it had been, because they were unimpressed by his threat and were still dragging Elin, who was now screaming at the top of her voice, down towards the shore.

Air...

Anders grabbed the edge of the platform and tipped the moped over. It rolled and came to rest on the handlebars as the petrol gurgled out of the tank. He looked up and saw that they were now down by the shoreline with Elin. There was no more time for threats. He moved back a couple of metres, just as far as the petrol had trickled down through the gravel, struck a fresh match and threw it, jumping backwards at the same time.

The flames shot up from the ground like a blue and yellow wall, and Anders screamed, 'Listen!' as loud as he could. Through the fire, which was now licking at the wooden planks of the platform, he saw

Henrik and Björn let go of Elin and come racing up towards him.

He had done what he could and given Elin a chance to escape, now it was up to her. He ran to the bike and the denim was ripped agonisingly from his legs as he threw himself on to the saddle and pedalled towards the forest as hard and as fast as he possibly could. He didn't even turn around to see if they were following him.

The enemy of the water

Anders' legs pedalled as if they had been disconnected from his body and were being controlled by another will. The darkness around him was dense, but he didn't give a thought to the fact that he could end up in the ditch at any moment, and perhaps that was why it didn't happen. Instinct kept him on the right track, and he managed to drive himself on right through the forest without falling off.

For the last part of the journey he was guided by the faint lights from the village, and at that point he wobbled for the first time and almost went over. He managed to brake and get one foot on the ground before the bike tipped sideways. He looked back at the forest path. They didn't seem to be following him.

He set off again and pedalled through the village, feeling slightly protected by the pale street lamps. Only when he had passed the hostel did he allow his thoughts to come belching out. A cloud of horrible, incomprehensible pictures filled his head, and suddenly he felt as if he had a temperature of forty degrees. His body lost all stability and he just wanted to let himself fall. Down on to the track, down into the darkness. To rest.

However, he managed to whip himself on to the point where the track split in two, and headed off to the left. The slight slope down towards Anna-Greta's house meant that he could simply roll along, his legs dangling. As he wobbled on to the drive leading to the house, he saw that there was still a light in the kitchen window.

He dropped the bike on the grass and dragged himself to the door, his legs heavy. He was sweating and shivering, managed to miss the handle once before he grabbed it and pulled open the door.

Simon and Anna-Greta were sitting at the kitchen table, bent over a whole lot of photographs spread all over the surface. When Simon saw Anders his face lit up for a moment, then his expression changed to one of horror.

'Anders, whatever have you done?'

Anders leaned against the stove and waved in the direction of Kattudden, but no sound emerged from his lips. Simon and Anna-Greta reached him and he let his body fall into their arms, let himself sink down on to the rag rug. When he was lying on his back and had taken a couple of breaths he said; 'Just need to...have a little rest.'

He stayed where he was while the kitchen lamp was lit, while Simon and Anna-Greta fetched water and placed a pillow under his head. By this stage the shivering had stopped and he might possibly have been able to get up, but he stayed where he was and let them take care of him, just because it was so utterly blissful to leave everything to someone else for a while.

They took off his trousers and washed the cuts on his legs, dressed them with compresses and gauze bandages. Simon gave him two painkillers and some more water. After a couple of minutes of drifting blissfully in the care of others, Anders hauled himself up on to a kitchen chair. He tried to gather his thoughts and looked at the photographs, spread out across the table.

They were old photographs, very old. They showed houses and farms, people working, close-ups. Many of them were yellow with age, and the people in them wore that expression of grim concentration that is so common in old pictures, as if the very act of being photographed demanded a special effort.

Directly in front of him lay a close-up that made him give a start. It was taken outdoors, and printed on something that looked like matt card. Across the picture ran a couple of flames of patchy yellow, as if someone had splashed urine over it. The picture showed a woman of about sixty, staring angrily into the camera.

'Yes,' said Simon. 'I thought I recognised her.'

On the table in front of him Anders found another picture of the same woman, this time taken from further away. She was standing in front of a scrubby little house on a headland.

'Who is she?' asked Anders.

Anna-Greta came to stand behind him, and pointed. 'Her name was Elsa Persson, and she was a cousin of Holger's father. She used to live in that house. On Kattudden. Until Holger's father sold the lot. She was evicted and the house was torn down. Then the summer visitors came.'

'It was your great-grandfather who took the pictures,' said Simon. 'Torgny. He took photographs of all the houses on the island, according to Anna-Greta. I like to sit and look at them from time to time. That's why I recognised her.'

The stubby chin, the flat nose, the deep-set eyes and the thin lips. The woman in the photograph was the image of Elin as she looked now. Or rather, Elin was a somewhat clumsily executed image of the woman in the photo. All the details weren't there yet, but just as it's obvious that a cheap plastic mask of George Bush is meant to represent him and no one else, it was obvious that...

...that this is the woman Elin is meant to look like.

Anders pointed to the house behind the woman. He recognised the location, the position of the island of Kattholmen in the background, but still he asked, 'This house. It was where her house, Elin's house is now, wasn't it?' He corrected himself. 'Where Elin's house was. Until the other night.'

Simon nodded. Anders sat with his mouth open, staring at the photographs. Then he said, 'Let me guess. She drowned herself?'

Anna-Greta picked up the photograph of Elin looking furious and sighed. 'This all happened before my time, but...Torgny said she threatened to drown herself if they took her cottage away from her. Then they took her cottage away from her. And then she disappeared.'

If you can imagine that all the impressions that have poured into Anders since he came back to Domarö have been collected in a kind of container, then this last drop of information was the one that made the container overflow.

The words just came flooding out of his mouth. He told them everything. From the first sense of Maja's presence to the growing conviction that she was in the house. The bead picture slowly growing, the photographs he had had developed and the letters scratched on the kitchen table. From the first blows on the door in the middle of the night and the feeling that he was being watched to tonight's encounter with Henrik and Björn. It all finally came pouring out.

Simon and Anna-Greta listened attentively, without any interruptions for questions. When Anders had finished, Anna-Greta pulled out a kitchen chair and climbed on it so that she could reach the top cupboard. She took out a bottle and placed it on the table. Simon didn't seem to know what it was either, as he was looking enquiringly at Anna-Greta.

Whatever was in the bottle looked like some kind of infusion. Twigs and leaves filled the entire space, surrounded by a liquid that half filled the bottle. Anna-Greta fetched a shot glass and filled it with the cloudy liquid.

'What's that?' asked Anders.

'Wormwood,' said Anna-Greta. 'It's supposed to protect you.'

'From what?'

'From things that come out of the sea.'

Anders looked from Simon to Anna-Greta. 'So does this mean that...you believe me?'

'I do now,' said Simon, pointing to the glass. 'Although I didn't know about this.'

Anders sniffed the contents. It was alcohol, which was fine up to a point. But the aroma carried on the alcoholic fumes was oily and bitter, with a hint of putrefaction. 'Isn't wormwood poisonous?'

'Well yes,' said Anna-Greta. 'But not in small quantities.'

Of course he didn't think his grandmother was trying to poison him, but he had never smelt anything closer to the essence of poison than the one that was rising from the glass in his hand.

Wormwood...

A whole series of associations ran through his mind as he raised the glass to his lips.

The wormwood meadow by the shore...the plastic bottle in the woodshed that the bird was sitting on...and the name of the star was Wormwood...Chernobyl...and the rivers shall be poisoned...wormwood, enemy of the water...

What decided the matter was the fact that he was desperately in need of a drink. He knocked back the contents of the glass.

The taste was horribly bitter and his tongue curled up in protest. It felt as if the alcohol had gone straight to his brain, and everything was spinning around as he put down the empty glass. His tongue felt as if it were paralysed, and he managed to slur, 'Didn't taste very nice.'

The heat coursed through his veins and reached the very tips of his fingers, then turned around and raced through his body once again. With lips that were still curling from the vile taste, he asked, 'Can I have another?'

Anna-Greta refilled his glass, then put the top back on the bottle and replaced it in the cupboard. Anders emptied the glass, and since his palate was already numb from the first shock, it didn't taste half as bad this time. When he put down the glass and smacked his lips, he even got a hint of an aftertaste that was...good.

He got to his feet, using the table for support. 'Could I borrow a pair of trousers? I have to go down to the Shack to check if Elin's there, otherwise...I don't know what we're going to do.'

Simon went to check in the 'hidey-hole', the little storeroom where clothes and belongings from past generations were kept. Anders was left alone in the kitchen with Anna-Greta. He looked longingly at the empty shot glass, but by putting the bottle away Anna-Greta had made her point.

'Protection from the sea,' said Anders. 'What does that mean?'

'We'll talk about it another time.'

'When?'

Anna-Greta didn't answer. Anders examined the photograph of Elsa. She looked angry; angry and disappointed. If the people in the other pictures looked as if it were hard work being photographed, Elsa looked as if she regarded it as an insult. Her furious gaze reached him through seventy years, making him feel distinctly uncomfortable.

'Was she always alone?' asked Anders. 'Elsa?'

'No, she had a husband who was quite a bit older. Anton, I think his name was. He had heart problems, and...he had a heart attack and died.'

'When he was out fishing?'

'Yes. How did you know that?'

'And she was the one who found him in the boat. Some of the fish were still alive, but he was dead.'

'I don't know about that, but she was the one who found him, that's definitely true. Who told you all this?'

'Elin.'

Simon came into the kitchen with a pair of flimsy trousers that looked as if they might have had something to do with the army. He gave them to Anders along with a belt, and said, 'I don't know if these will do, but they're all I could find.'

Anders pulled on the trousers, which were much too big, and fastened the belt around his waist. The wide legs felt good, because they weren't tight over his cuts. Simon stood looking at him, his arms folded.

'Are you really going out again? Is that a good idea? Shall I come with you?'

Anders smiled. 'I don't think there's much you can do, and besides...' he nodded at the kitchen cupboard '...I'm protected now, aren't I?'

'I don't know about that, and I don't think Anna-Greta does either, not really.'

'That's true,' said Anna-Greta. 'It's only hearsay.'

'I'll go down and check,' said Anders. 'I'll call you. Whether she's there or not. Then we can decide what to do.'

He borrowed a torch, hoisted up the trousers and grimaced as his wounds pulled. On his way to the outside door he stopped and turned around. He had suddenly realised something. He had been carrying the knowledge with him for quite some time, but it wasn't until that moment it became obvious and possible to say out loud.

'Ghosts,' he said. 'There are ghosts.'

He nodded to Simon and Anna-Greta and went out into the darkness.

Before he switched on the torch he gazed at the sky. Wasn't that a tinge of orange in the thin clouds over Kattudden? Yes, it was, and he couldn't have cared less. However, he turned, went back into the kitchen and said indifferently, 'I think there's a fire over by Kattudden again.'

If Simon and Anna-Greta wanted to do something about it, they were welcome. He just couldn't. It had been a long night, and it was almost three o'clock. He wanted Elin to be fast asleep in bed when he got home, as if everything that had happened to her had happened in her sleep, and could be forgotten.

As he approached the Shack he veered off to the toolshed and picked up an axe. It might well be as useless as the fence post he'd used but it felt good in his hand, and perhaps a sharp weapon would work better.

The fire alarm up in the village went off just as he pushed down the handle of the outside door. The door was locked. He thought about it. No, he hadn't locked it when he went out. And there was no light in the kitchen window. It had been on when he left.

'Elin!' he shouted through the closed door. 'Elin, are you there?'

The door was old and in poor condition; many winters of patient work had made it settle in the frame. He pushed the blade of the axe into the broad gap above the lock and prised the door open with a cracking sound. He stepped into the hallway and said tentatively, 'Elin? Elin, it's only me.'

He took off his shoes and locked the door, which was now even more warped, behind him. Despite an exhaustion that felt much too big to be accommodated in his skinny body, fear kicked the adrenaline into action once again as he crept through the hallway, clutching the shaft of the axe.

No more now, he thought. *No more.*

The beam of the torch made the perfectly ordinary kitchen furniture look ominous, creating shadows with unpleasant shapes.

'Elin,' he whispered. 'Elin, are you there?'

The kitchen floor creaked beneath his feet and he stopped, listened. The fire alarm could be heard less clearly indoors, but still covered all the small noises that might indicate the presence of another person.

He went on into the living room. A little warmth was still emanating from the Roslagen stove, and he swept the beam of the torch around him without noticing anything strange, apart from the fact that the bedroom door was closed. He licked his lips. His tongue was still stiff from the wormwood, and the taste seemed to have penetrated so deep into the flesh of his palate that it would never be possible to wash it away.

When he pushed down the handle, the door was barricaded from the inside. But it had been done badly, and the chair that had been placed behind the door fell over when he pushed.

Elin was sitting in the bed, leaning against the bedpost. She had wrapped the quilt around her so that only her head was sticking up. The sheet at the foot of the bed was streaked with blood and covered in lumps of mud.

'Elin?'

Her eyes were staring at him in terror. He didn't dare go into the room or switch on the light, because he didn't know how she would react. He became aware of the axe in his hand, and put it down next to the door. He shone the torch around the room, listened to the fire alarm. He looked at Elin, and a shudder ran through his body.

She's dead. They've killed her and put her here.

'Elin?' he whispered. 'Elin, it's Anders. Can you hear me?'

She nodded. A faint, faint nod. He made a gesture, *just hang on*, and turned away. Behind him he heard Elin say, 'Don't leave me.'

'I'm just going to make a phone call. I'll be right back.'

He went into the kitchen, switched on the light and rang Anna-Greta's number; he told her Elin was back, and they would deal with everything when they'd had a couple of hours' sleep. When Anna-Greta had hung up, Anders stood with the receiver in his hand, staring at the grubby tape on the table.

The music you play, would you say it was…just between ourselves… cheerful music?

He wanted to ring somewhere and ask for help. He wanted to ring Kalle Sändare. Sit at the kitchen table with the phone pressed to his ear listening to Kalle's gentle Gothenburg accent, like balm to the soul, talking about little things and laughing from time to time.

How can the world be like this? How can what happened tonight exist at the same time as Kalle Sändare exists?

He put the phone down and felt a strange pain in his chest. It wasn't Kalle Sändare he missed, but his father. Kalle was just a simpler and more manageable substitute. Because they had had so much fun together with Kalle, Kalle had come to mean Dad, but without the difficult associations.

It was really his father he wanted to talk to. The sense of loss that he had refused to recognise came crawling up through his chest, reaching for his heart with its long claws. He pushed it back and went into the bedroom.

Elin was sitting just as he had left her. Cautiously he sat down beside her on the edge of the bed. 'Shall I put the light on?'

Elin shook her head. The light from the kitchen was enough for him to be able to see her face. In the half-light it was even more like Elsa's. Elin had had quite a prominent chin. It was gone now, running on from her throat just like Elsa's.

How did they do it? They must have…smashed her legs.

His eyes moved to the signs of blood and mud at the foot of the bed. 'We need to…get you bandaged up.'

Elin pulled the quilt more tightly around her. 'No. I don't want to.'

Anders didn't have the strength to insist. It was as if he had an anchor chain around his neck. His head kept trying to droop, and all he wanted was to go to bed. From time to time flashes of white shot through his eyes, and he didn't know if it was just tiredness, or if the wormwood really had poisoned his exhausted body.

'There's something wrong with me,' whispered Elin. 'I'm insane, I ought to kill myself.'

Anders sat there with his elbows on his knees, staring at the wardrobe. He didn't know what was best: to tell or not to tell. In the end he sought refuge in one simple sentence: *It's better to know.* He'd heard it in the context of illness, and didn't know if it was appropriate here, but he hadn't the energy to work it out.

'Elin,' he said. 'Somebody is making you do all this. All these operations. The things you do at night. Your dreams. They're not yours.'

In the silence that followed Anders noticed that the fire alarm had stopped, he didn't know how long ago. He could hear Elin breathing. The sound of his own poisoned blood in his ears.

'Whose are they then?' she asked.

'Someone else's. Another woman. She's inside you.'

'How come?'

'I don't know. But she lived at Kattudden before your house was built. She wants revenge, and she's using you.' Anders hesitated, then added, 'She looked exactly the way you do now. She's the one who's made you...recreate her through all this surgery.'

If Anders had had the energy to be surprised, he would have been surprised by what happened next. Elin exhaled, a long, deep sigh, and her body slumped, relaxed. She nodded slowly and said, 'I knew it. Deep down.'

Anders put his head in his hands and closed his eyes. The white flashes flared up and disappeared.

It's better to know. It's better...

He must have fallen asleep for a few seconds, because he only woke up when he was about to fall over sideways. Elin said quietly, 'Go to bed.'

Anders stood up, took one step and collapsed on Maja's bed. He laid his head on the pillow, scrabbled for the quilt and managed to pull it over him. As he was falling asleep he heard Elin say, 'Thank you. For coming after me. For helping me.'

He parted his lips to answer, but before the words had time to emerge he was asleep again.

A child was screaming. A single long, wailing note.

Screaming is the wrong word, wailing is the wrong word. Child is the wrong word. It was the monotone sound of pure fear that a human being can produce when it is trapped in a corner, and the thing it is most afraid of in all the world is approaching inexorably. The tongue is not used, the lips are not used, it is only air being forced out of the lungs and resonating through a closed-up throat. A single note, the primeval note that quivers through the breastbone as death approaches.

Anders woke up and saw everything through a fog. The room was still dark, and the sound was coming from the big bed. It was so horrible that he was terrified as well. He curled up inside himself, pulled the quilt more tightly around him. The sound continued to pour out of Elin. Something was frightening her out of her wits.

He heard steps on the porch, then someone was banging on the door. Three hard, sharp blows. Elin's long drawn-out scream became a little louder and penetrated Anders' body like a vibration, transmitted itself to him and made him start shaking.

Something sensible within him stared at the axe propped up by the door, told him he ought to dash over and grab it, but blind fear anchored his body to the bed.

It's the GB-man. The GB-man is coming.

The outside door was smashed open and Anders pulled the quilt over his head. His teeth were chattering and he pulled his feet up, not one tiny part of him must be visible outside the quilt.

The axe! Get the axe!

Heavy steps moved through the hallway, but he was incapable of movement. Through a tiny gap in his cocoon he looked at the axe and his will reached out for it, but his body refused. Elin's song of horror went up another notch and Anders' buttocks suddenly felt warm as he shat himself.

Steps through the living room and then Henrik's voice, 'Hellooo? Anyone home?'

Do something! Do something!

He closed his eyes and put his hands over his ears. Silence fell. The footsteps stopped as well. There was the stench of excrement under the quilt. Despite the fact that he didn't want to, he opened his eyes again and peeped out through the gap.

Henrik and Björn were standing in the room. Henrik had his knife in his hand, Björn was holding a bucket, a white plastic bucket full of water.

I'm dreaming. This isn't real. If it were real I'd do something.

Like a child Anders pinched his arm hard so that he would wake up, but Henrik and Björn were still standing there. They were facing the big bed, from which Elin's note of terror continued to pour out into the room.

Anders stayed put as they dragged Elin out of the bed and said, 'Sorry, darling, this can't go on any longer. You know what they say about pretty girls, don't you? They make graves.'

He bit his knuckles as they dragged her into the middle of the floor and forced her head down into the plastic bucket. Björn grasped her legs while Henrik held the back of her neck in an iron grip, pushing her head further down into the bucket so that the water surged over the sides. Her legs jerked, but Björn held her ankles firmly, pressing them against the floor.

A muffled scream could be heard from the bucket and bubbles rose up, making the water splash on to the floor. Elin's body suddenly arched, then slumped and lay still. Henrik wound her hair around his hand and yanked her head up out of the bucket. He looked at her face and said regretfully, 'Fifteen minutes…I don't think I would have said no,' at which point he let go. Elin's face hit the floor with a wet crunch.

As if on a given signal they turned towards the little bed. Anders curled up into a tighter ball and gnawed the skin off his knuckles. 'Please,' he whimpered. 'Please. Don't hurt me. I'm so little.'

Henrik walked over to him and ripped off the quilt. 'Little children, how they suffer.' He raised his eyebrows as if he were pleased with himself, and clicked his fingers. 'That's just perfect, isn't it?'

He grabbed hold of Anders' shoulder, but withdrew his hand as if he'd had a shock. An expression of revulsion distorted his face.

'What's the matter?' asked Björn. 'He's shat himself, has he?'

Henrik contemplated Anders as he lay there with the only weapon he had left: his pleading eyes. Henrik gazed into them as if he were searching for something. Björn came over to the bed and put the bucket down. There was something in it, something that was making the small amount of water that was left move around. Something invisible.

Björn looked at Henrik and said, 'Is he hidden?'

Henrik nodded and squatted down by the bed. Anders exhaled in a trembling, panting breath, and Henrik looked as if he was about to throw up when the smell hit his face. Without speaking to Anders, he said, 'So how did you find out?'

'What shall we do?' asked Björn.

'Nothing we can do,' said Henrik. 'Just at the moment.'

He glanced down into the bucket and seemed happy with what he saw. Something was whirling around down there, splashing about. Henrik stood up, towering over Anders. He leaned down and whispered in his ear, 'You can't be here either, little Maja. We'll take you too, in time.'

Björn picked up the bucket and they left the room. Anders heard their footsteps moving through the living room and the hallway. Then the outside door closed. He lay there motionless, staring at Elin's lifeless body on the floor, the strands of her wet hair radiating out from her head like black sunbeams.

His fear of the GB-man. The way he'd recited words from Alfie Atkins, the fact that he had started making bead pictures, that all he wanted to do was lie in her bed reading about Bamse. I'm so little.

He finally understood what it meant: *Carry me.*

2

Possessed

As long as the little boat can sail
As long as the heart can beat
As long as the sun sparkles
On the blue billows

EVERT TAUBE — AS LONG AS THE LITTLE BOAT CAN SAIL

Bodies in the water

Beware of the sea, beware of the sea
The sea is so big, the sea is so big…

Taking care of business

The dawn came creeping behind the eastern islands and a glimpse
of the sun was just appearing between the windblown pine trees
on Botskär. Anders was standing right on the end of Simon's jetty,
squinting into the approaching light. Despite his scarf and padded
jacket he was frozen, and couldn't stop his body from shaking. He
jumped as Simon dropped a chain in the boat behind his back.
He tried to find a point of warmth inside himself, tried to find Maja.
There was nothing there, and he felt like the sloughed-off skin of a
human being. He turned around.

The chain lay in a heap in the prow of Simon's boat. In the stern
lay Elin. He couldn't remember why they had decided to wrap her
in two black plastic sacks with parcel tape wound around them. He
wished they hadn't done that, would have preferred her empty, staring
eyes to the person-shaped package on the deck. It looked horrible, and
he didn't want to go anywhere near it. 'Are we really going to do this?'

'Yes,' said Simon. 'I think it's the only thing we can do.'

With half-dried excrement smeared over his legs, Anders had crept to the telephone and called Simon. Simon had come, placed a tea towel over Elin's face and helped Anders to wash himself. Then they had sat opposite each other at the kitchen table, staring out of the window until a lone pink cloud drifted across the sky, a starting flag for the new day.

There were two possible courses of action.

Nobody would believe that two dead teenagers had turned up and drowned Elin in a bucket. On the other hand, as far as everybody was concerned, there had been no sign of Elin since the fire.

Therefore, one possibility was to come up with a different story: a story that would be closely scrutinised under interrogation, since this was a murder. Would Anders be able to stick to a made-up story when the police started questioning him? Probably not.

Which left the other possibility. To get rid of Elin and pretend it had never happened.

After Simon had argued back and forth for some time, mostly with himself, they agreed that this was the lesser of two evils.

Anders took the torch and went out to the shed to fetch a couple of plastic sacks. Once inside he stopped, and his knees gave way. He had a bowling ball stuck in the middle of his chest. A black, shining sphere of guilt. He had done nothing when they were murdering Elin, he had just stayed in his bed and watched.

'It's not my fault,' he whispered.

Say it once, twice, a thousand times. Eventually you might believe it.

He was finding it difficult to breathe, because the bowling ball was in the way, pressing on his lungs. Stiffly he swept the torch over the walls of the shed, and caught sight of the plastic bottle.

Wormwood...

He unscrewed the top, raised the bottle to his mouth and took two swigs. If there was a thought in his head it was *burn away.* What was to be burned away he had no idea. Maybe it was the ball, maybe it was he himself. The liquid coursed down his throat and he waited for the fire, but the fire did not come.

This wormwood was not dissolved in alcohol but in something else, and the substance running down into Anders' stomach had a thick, slippery consistency. Like oil. Only when he had finished swallowing did the taste come. It didn't explode on his palate as it had at Anna-Greta's, but came creeping along and squeezed his tongue, his palate, his throat, his chest.

Anders sank down into a crouching position as the upper part of his body was turned inside out. He lost all feeling in his fingers, and his breathing stopped.

Cramp. Cramp in my lungs. I'm going to die.

Poison. Not the instantaneous shock of a toxin that compels the body to spit it out immediately, but the treacherous effect of something that slips down and takes root, spreads through the bloodstream and kills.

Anders pressed his hands to his temples and his brain crackled with discharging electricity. He took a deep breath, and discovered that he could do it. His lungs were not paralysed, he had actually been holding his breath. The air he inhaled brought his tastebuds to life, and he was wormwood. It tasted so vile that it wasn't a taste at all, it was a state of being. He grabbed hold of the workbench and pulled himself to his feet.

I am wormwood.

The ball in his chest was gone. The revolting taste had encased it, and it had shrunk and disappeared. He blinked and blinked again, trying to focus his gaze. He fixed on a piece of rope with a frayed end. He shone the torch on it and he could see every single fibre. There were fifty-seven threads.

Fifty-seven. The same age as Dad was when he died. The same number of screws and plugs as there were in the cupboard Cecilia and I bought from IKEA for the bedroom. The same number of centimetres as Maja's height when she was two months old. The same...

The outlines of everything perceived by the eye of the torch were blurred, yet at the same time all too clear. He wasn't seeing the objects, he was seeing what they *were*. He reached out for the roll of plastic sacks and knew there were eight sacks left on the roll and together they would hold one thousand six hundred litres.

One thousand six hundred litres of things. Leaves, twigs, toys, tins of paint, tools, gramophones, pairs of glasses, pine cones, microwave ovens. One thousand six hundred litres of things…

As he picked up the roll he found a still point inside his head, a rock in the river where he could stand and think clearly as everything flowed past and around him.

Take the bags. Go to the house.

That was what he did. As the world continued to come adrift, dissolve and pour through him, he stood on the rock and watched his hands helping Simon to dress Elin's body in plastic for this final journey. Then the perception grew weaker and he began to shiver.

Anders crouched down in the prow, as far away from the plastic bundle as possible. Simon had to sit with his feet pushed underneath Elin's thighs in order to fit in the driving seat.

How can he do this.

Simon's lips were clamped together and his forehead was furrowed, as if he were concentrating hard the whole time. But he was doing it. Anders realised he ought to be grateful, but he had no room for any such emotions. The world had frayed like the rope in the shed.

Simon started the engine and they set off from Domarö, rounded North Point and set their course for the bay between Kattholmen and Ledinge. There was a light breeze, and Anders fixed his gaze on the horizon as the rising sun warmed his cheek.

A dozen or so metres ahead of the boat a gull took off from the surface of the water and soared away with a scream. Anders followed it with his eyes, saw it cross the disc of the sun and disappear in the direction of Gåvasten.

Daddy…

How many early mornings had Anders lain in the prow of his

father's boat as the sun rose, on their way to the fishing grounds to lift their nets? Forty? Fifty?

Daddy...

He hadn't thought properly about his father for a long time. With the fleeing gull and the rising sun, it all came back. Including that time.

That time...

Fishing for herring

The summer Anders turned twelve he was saving up for a radio-controlled boat. He had seen it in the toy shop in Norrtälje, and had been seduced by the fantastic picture on the box. The white hull racing across the water, the blue go-faster stripes along the side. It cost three hundred and fifty kronor, and it would be his before the summer was over.

It wasn't impossible. He and his father would lay their net twice a week, then Anders would sell the fish outside the shop. Six kronor a kilo, and he got half. So the boat represented one hundred and seventeen kilos of herring, he had worked out. With one krona left over.

He was no Uncle Scrooge, saving every krona he earned, but he had managed to put away one hundred and ninety kronor. Every catch brought between thirty and forty kilos, but by the time it got towards the end of June and the herring were beginning to move further out to sea, each catch was slightly smaller. He still needed to sell fifty kilos of fish, and they were unlikely to put the net out more than twice before the end of the season.

So that was the first thing Anders thought about when he woke up that morning: *fifty kilos.*

He got out of bed and dug his fishing clothes out of the bottom drawer. The smell alone would have given his mother palpitations. Both his jeans and pullover were covered in old scales and dried roe, and had approximately the same aroma as the dried pieces of fish you give to dogs.

Finally he put on his cap. It was a cap with a logo from the shipyard in Nåten where his father worked, and it too was so full of scales and solidified herring gunge that a dog could probably have eaten it just as it was.

Anders liked his outfit. When he put it on he was no longer Anders-nobody-in-particular, he was Anders the fisher boy. This was not something he could share with his friends from the city, and he made sure he changed his clothes before he sat down outside the shop. But in the mornings when they were all still sleeping, he was just his father's son, the fisher boy, and he liked that.

It was a fine morning. Anders and his father sat opposite each other at the kitchen table with a cup of hot chocolate and a cup of coffee respectively, looking out towards the bay, which was dead calm. The reflector in Gåvasten lighthouse was bouncing back the first rays of the sun. The odd cloud drifted across the sky like swansdown on a puddle.

They each ate a sandwich and finished their drinks. Then they put on their lifejackets and went down to the boat. Dad cranked up the compression ignition engine, and it started first time. At the beginning of the summer Anders had asked to have a go, and had been frightened by the recoil in the crank handle when the engine didn't fire. He left it to Dad after that.

Fine weather. The engine started straight away. Good omens. Fifty kilos.

He knew they wouldn't get fifty kilos *today*, that had only happened to him once, last summer, and that had been right at the beginning of June. But thirty. Thirty would do. From now on he was going to save every single krona.

They rounded North Point and came out into the sunlit stretch of Ledinge Bay, where a slight breeze was blowing from the east. The low-lying sun had just freed itself from the tops of the pine trees on Ryssholmen, and was celebrating by spreading its light across the rippling surface of the sea. Anders sat by the gunwale, trailing his fingers in the water. It was already warm enough to swim, varying between seventeen and nineteen degrees depending on the wind.

He moved into the prow and lay down full length on the wood warmed by the sun, gazing towards the spot where they had laid their net, in the narrow inlet between Ledinge and the Ledinge skerry. When he screwed up his eyes he thought he could make out the flag marking the location of the net.

The gentle chugging of the engine was making him sleepy, so he rubbed his eyes and thought about the radio-controlled boat. How far could it go before it lost contact with the remote control? Fifty metres? A hundred? How fast did it go? *Probably faster than Dad's boat at any rate,* he thought as they glided towards the inlet.

Anders was still lost in boy-racer fantasies when his father slowed the engine. The chugging changed to a knocking sound, with longer and longer intervals between strokes. The flag was getting closer. Anders started moving just as his father shouted, 'Action stations, captain!' and put the engine in neutral.

Anders jumped down and edged towards the helm as his father moved towards the prow. They crossed on either side of the engine. They had done this before. His father smiled and said, 'Take it slowly and carefully now'. Anders pulled a face that said *Have I done this before, or what?* and sat down at the helm.

His father got hold of the flag, hauled it in and grabbed the rope. Anders edged the boat gently into reverse, until it was completely motionless. As his father began to haul in the net, he edged forward so that the boat was following the line of the net. This was the time he loved best during their morning trips. When he was the one in charge. He could race the engine, slam the boat into reverse and turn the rudder if he so wished—but did he?

Of course not.

Slowly and carefully he adjusted the steering and the speed to make it as easy as possible for his father to lift the net. Anders was good at this. He was the captain.

He leaned over the rail and looked down into the dark water. It was usually possible to glimpse enough of the shining silver on its way to the surface to get some idea of how big the catch was likely to be. Anders looked down and frowned.

What's that? Can it be…

What he could see moving upwards was not the scattered, metallic shimmer of this many or that many herring, no, it looked more as if they had caught one single, gigantic herring in the net this morning, a compact mass being pulled slowly towards the boat.

His father had stopped hauling the net and was now standing motionless in the prow, staring down into the water. Anders peered down and he could now see that the apparently solid body did in fact consist of individual herring. It was a record catch beyond all expectation. His heart began to beat faster.

There's fifty kilos there, at least. Maybe more. Will I be able to sell that much?

He waited for the catch to get closer to the surface so that he would be able to see better, but nothing happened. His father was still standing in the prow, the rope dangling from his hands.

'What's the matter?' asked Anders. 'It's a massive catch!'

His father turned to face him with an expression Anders didn't understand. He looked…frightened. Frightened and worried. Anders shook his head.

'Aren't you going to bring them up, then?'

'I think…maybe we shouldn't.'

'But why? I mean, it's a record! There's loads of them!'

His father let go of the rope with one hand and pointed at the surface. 'Feel the water.'

Anders did as he said and dipped his hand in the water. He yanked it back quickly. The water was ice cold. He blinked and cautiously slipped his hand in once again. It nipped at the tips of his fingers, and the water was so cold it was on the point of freezing.

How can it be like that?

He looked enquiringly at his father, who was staring down into the water as if he were searching for something. Anders looked around. There was nothing to indicate that winter was suddenly on the way. The only explanation was an unusually cold and strong current. Wasn't it?

'Why is it like that?'

His father sighed deeply. The rope began to slip out of his hands. 'Dad!'

The rope stopped. 'Yes?'

'We have to land this catch, don't we?'

His father turned his head towards the broad strip of sunlight and said quietly, 'Why?'

The question confused Anders and frightened him a little. He babbled, 'Because…because there's such a lot and you know that boat I'm saving up for, this is…and…it won't do any good if we leave it, will it?'

His father turned to Anders once again, nodded slowly and said, 'No, I don't suppose it will. You're probably right.'

He started hauling on the net again, the muscles in his jaw working as if he were chewing on something he was never going to be able to swallow. Anders didn't know what had happened, what he'd said, but he was relieved it had worked. The catch would be brought in.

Apart from the problem that Anders didn't understand, it was very difficult for his father to lift such an enormous catch. Anders moved the boat as helpfully as he could, but the net his father was hauling into the prow was not a net full of individual fish, but rather a thick cable of silver enclosed in mesh.

When the whole of the net was in the boat and the anchor had been raised, his father went over to the engine without a word and put his hands on the cylinder head gasket.

'What are you doing?' asked Anders. If his father's behaviour during the later part of their trip had been strange, this was yet another new thing.

His father gave a wan smile. 'Warming my hands.'

Anders nodded. Of course. That was understandable, at least. The water was cold—his hands had got cold. He left the helm and went to have a look at the catch. He was no expert, but surely this was a good bit more than fifty kilos? Seventy? Eighty? When he looked at the massive pile of fish ensnared in the net, he noticed something else unusual.

Herring did not have the endurance of perch or flounder, which could live for a long time after being pulled out of the sea, but they would normally move about and twitch in the net for a good while after the boat had set off for home. But not this time.

The herring were lying completely motionless, with not a twitch to be seen. Anders crouched down and felt at a fish that had fallen out of the net. The little body was stiff, almost frozen, and the eyes were milky white. He held it out to his father, who was still standing with his hands resting on the engine. 'Why are they like this?'

'I don't know.'

'But...I mean...what's happened?'

'I don't know.'

'But how can the herring just—'

'I don't know, I said!'

It was very rare for his father to raise his voice. As he did so now a hot stabbing sensation went through Anders, making his cheeks flush bright red, and he closed his mouth on any further questions. He didn't know what he'd said that was so wrong, but it was something, and he was upset. Because he had destroyed the great atmosphere between them without knowing how.

The herring had softened in the warmth of his hand. He dropped it on the deck and crept into the prow, squinting into the sun with a heavy feeling in his stomach. The big catch was no fun any more. As far as he was concerned, they could chuck the whole bloody lot back in the sea.

He rested his cheek against the wood and lay still. *Strange...*

He lay still for a while, listening. Then he raised his head and gazed out across the bay.

Why hadn't he noticed until now? There wasn't a single gull in sight. Normally they would have been screaming and fighting over the fish that had fallen out of the net as it was being hauled up, flapping wings or white, dipping bodies waiting for Anders to throw them scraps or herring that were too small to sell.

But now: Not a sound. Not one bird.

Anders was still considering this when he felt his father's hand on his foot.

'Listen, I'm sorry I…shouted like that. I didn't mean it.'

'OK.'

Anders stayed where he was, lying on his stomach, and waited for more. When nothing was forthcoming, he said, 'Dad?'

'Yes?'

'Why aren't there any gulls?'

A brief pause, then his father sighed and said without anger, 'Don't start again, Anders.'

'OK. But it's odd, isn't it?'

'Yes.'

His father patted Anders on the calf, then went to start the engine. After a few minutes Anders sat up and gazed out over the sea. Not one gull anywhere in sight. And no other birds either. The sea was deserted. The only movement was the bow wave around the boat, the only sound the even chugging of the engine.

During the trip home, Anders fantasised that he and his father were the only survivors of a disaster that had wiped out all life on earth. What would their lives be like from now on?

Other creatures had evidently survived the disaster, since Simon's cat Dante was waiting for them on the jetty. Anders grabbed the stern rope and jumped up by the outermost capstan. As the cat wound around his legs, he carefully tied the half hitch he had learned the previous summer.

When the boat was safely moored he stroked Dante's head, climbed down into the prow and threw a couple of herring on to

303

the jetty. He was curious to see how the cat would react. At first everything seemed just the same as usual. Perhaps because his pride demanded it, Dante always pretended that he had caught the prey himself. He crouched down, crept towards the lifeless fish as if the utmost vigilance was essential to ensure that his food would not escape.

Then he leapt forward and sank both paws into one of the herring, holding it firmly with his claws extended. When he was absolutely certain the fish was not going to get away, he would sink his teeth into it. What happened next looked so funny that Anders laughed out loud.

Dante stopped with his teeth on the way to the herring, then raised his head and sneezed twice. He looked at Anders as if to ask: *Is this some kind of joke?*, and poked at the herring with his paw, rolling it around the jetty a couple of times.

His father was sitting on his haunches, watching the cat's movements with tense interest. When Dante felt he had spent enough time rolling the fish around, he settled down and sank his teeth into the herring, and this time they could hear the crunch of breaking bones. The cat polished off the herring in a minute, then picked the other one up in his mouth and left the jetty with his tail pointing straight up in the air.

His father stood up and rubbed his hands together. 'We'd better make a start, then.' Before Anders had time to set off ashore to fetch the necessary equipment, his father glanced down into the boat and added, 'You know, that's quite a catch.'

Oh, so now you've noticed, have you? thought Anders, but all he said was, 'How much do you think there is?'

His father pursed his lips. 'About ninety kilos. That'll keep us busy for a while.'

Ninety...two hundred and seventy kronor. But I won't be able to sell that much. If I drop the price...

Anders went ashore and fetched the rinsing net and the boxes. Meanwhile his father swung out the beam, hoisted up the net and started to shake it. The herring flew out of the net into the bottom of the boat. A few landed in the water, but still there wasn't a single gull there to snap them up. However, a couple of crows had arrived at the bottom of the jetty. They stood there moving their feet up and down, unsure how to behave now they didn't have to compete with the gulls.

Anders jumped into the boat with the rinsing net and threw a couple of herring to the crows. They swallowed them whole, croaked excitedly, and after a couple of minutes three more crows had arrived.

The herring whirled around Anders' head and it was all he could do to pour them into the rinsing net, sluice them in the sea and tip them into the boxes. It was more difficult than usual because the herring were still stiff, and kept slipping out of his hands. When he looked up from his work after filling one box, he saw a couple of gulls bobbing on the water just off the jetty.

When he bent down to his task again he heard the sound of flapping, and a splash next to the boat. The gulls had started to help themselves to the fish that had sunk to the bottom, and everything was back to normal.

It took his father a good hour to shake out all the fish, and then they worked together rinsing them and tipping them into boxes. When they had finished they each sat down on a capstan and contemplated the pile of five full twenty-kilo boxes on the jetty.

Anders took off his cap and scratched his sweaty scalp. 'Are we going to be able to sell this much?'

His father pulled a face. 'I doubt it. I'll have to take a box with me to work, and…well, I suppose we can smoke whatever's left over.'

Anders nodded gloomily, but inside he was jubilant. Although selling herring could be a bit slow, buckling was snapped up in no time on those rare occasions when his father decided to fire up the smoker. The tourists went mad for buckling, and his father's considered opinion was that they regarded it as *quaint*.

Anders took the wheelbarrow and went down to the steamboat jetty to fetch some ice from the store that was run by the village committee since the fishing industry had come to an end. When he got back, his father had carried the boxes ashore and hung the net up to dry. They packed the boxes with ice and placed a thick tarpaulin over the whole lot.

Anders went down to the shore and rubbed his hands with sand to get rid of the fish scales, then he squatted down on a rock for a while and warmed his face in the sun, which had now climbed high above the pine trees on North Point.

When they got home, Anders went to bed to sleep for a couple of hours more. To him, this was the best part of their fishing days. Lying there in the fiery yellow light pressing against the blind as his hands thawed out under the covers, sleepily listening to the cries of the gulls from the sea. If he didn't fall asleep straight away he would lie there for a while, satisfied with a job well done, picking individual scales off his hands. Then he would drop off as the summer day came to life around him.

Weight

But we're not there yet...

Anders had been so far away in his memories that he didn't realise why the engine had been cut, why the boat was slowing down when they were only halfway to the inlet. The net wasn't here, right in the middle of the bay.

Then he noticed that the deck he was lying on was made of fibre-glass, and that he was so big there wasn't really room for him. He was a grown man, his father was dead and everything that had happened later that day had nothing to do with the task in hand.

Although it does. Everything is connected to everything else here. I'm the only one who doesn't see it.

The engine died and silence fell. Simon was sitting in the prow looking around. There wasn't a boat in sight, no eyes that might spy on them. Anders stepped back into the present, although he wished he could have stayed in the past. The black sacks at Simon's feet were real, and demanded an act of which he would never have believed himself capable.

It's all my fault. I have to…contribute.

He gathered up the chain and hauled it forward, letting it coil down on top of the black bundle. Simon smiled sadly. 'Do you know where that chain comes from?'

'Is it the one you used when you…?'

'Mmm. It's been in the sea before.' Simon nodded to himself, and neither of them spoke for a while. Simon stroked the plastic covering Elin's head.

'She's dead. Nothing we do now will make any difference. To her. She drowned. Somebody drowned her. And now she's going into the sea. There's nothing strange about that. It isn't wrong. We just have to do it. Because we need to go on living.' Simon looked Anders in the eye. 'Don't you agree?'

Anders nodded mechanically. That wasn't really the problem. The problem was actually starting to touch the dead body, feeling muscles and bones through the black plastic without knowing for certain… that she was really dead.

'What's the plastic for?' asked Anders.

'I don't know,' said Simon. 'I thought…it would be better.'

'It isn't.'

'No.'

Anders understood the thought behind it, the idea of hiding what they were doing from themselves. And yet it was a relief when they pulled off the sacks and had Elin's corpse at their feet. Her skin had lost all its lustre, and the colour had faded from her wide-open eyes. It was a horrible sight, and yet it was better.

As Simon bent down and grabbed hold of the chain, he caught sight of the scars on her face and body, glowing white in the morning light. 'What are these? Scars?'

'I'll tell you all about it,' said Anders. 'But not now.'

They worked together to lift the body, turn it, wrap the chain around and secure it with a couple of locking pawls. However tightly they pulled the chain, there was no response from Elin's skin, no reddening or swelling. Her eyes stared up at the sky without blinking, and Simon was caught in her empty gaze.

'Who was she?' he asked.

That was the question that needed to be asked, the final question. Unfortunately, Anders didn't know the answer.

'I don't know,' he said. 'I think she was someone who...was looking for approval. Someone who tried, in a lot of...roundabout ways...to get the whole world to think she was wonderful. But...'

The memory of Elin's smile when Henrik and Björn were being humiliated by the boathouse flashed through his mind, and Anders lowered his head.

'In that case, we will remember someone who wanted to be wonderful,' said Simon, taking hold of the chain around her thighs and stomach.

They heaved Elin over the rail. Her legs hooked over the edge and she hung there for a few seconds with her head and upper body in the water. Then Simon gently lifted her feet. The body came free and slipped into the water with a faint splash.

Anders leaned over and watched her sink. A few air bubbles escaped from her mouth and rose to the surface like transparent beads. Her hair floated outwards and hid her face as she was dragged down into the depths. After a few seconds she had sunk so far that she was nothing more than a blurred, pale patch in the great darkness. Anders kept on staring until he was no longer sure he could see her, until she was replaced by the shifting pattern of the light on the surface of the water.

The black water. He was so dreadfully tired, he could sleep for a year. He leaned his head against the rail, closed his eyes and whispered, 'I'm so tired, Simon. I just can't cope any more.'

His head was expanding and shrinking, his brain was a lung. Expanding and contracting quickly, panting. His consciousness was gasping for air as if it was drowning, the lung close to bursting point.

There was a creaking sound as Simon got up and came to sit beside him, eased him away from the rail and placed his head on his knee. Anders curled up and put his arms around Simon's waist, resting his head on Simon's thighs. Simon's cold hand caressed his hair.

'There now, little Anders,' said Simon. 'Everything will be all right. Everything's fine. It'll all work out, Anders.'

Simon's hand went on gently stroking his hair, and it was like oxygen. He stopped panting inside, the panic subsided and he relaxed. He might have fallen asleep for a few seconds. If he did fall asleep, the worst was over when he woke up. Simon's hand was resting on the back of his head.

'Simon,' said Anders, without raising his head.

'Yes?'

'Do you remember saying…that we can never become another person, do you remember that? That however close we get, we can never become the other person.'

'Yes, I did say that. But it seems as if I was wrong.'

'It isn't just Elin. It's me as well. I'm turning into Maja.'

'What do you mean?'

There was in fact a word for what was happening to him. It wasn't the right word, it had the wrong kind of associations. Demons and devils. And yet it was the only word there was.

'I'm possessed. I'm turning into someone else. I'm turning into Maja.'

Anders pulled himself up into a sitting position and moved over to sit opposite Simon. Then he told the story again, in the light of his new insight. How he could sometimes hear her voice inside his head, his fear of the GB-man, the Bamse comics, her bed, the writing on the table and the bead tile.

Simon didn't ask any questions, didn't raise any objections. He simply listened and said 'Hmm' from time to time, and it was as if the strong hand that had been squeezing Anders' mind more and more tightly loosened its grip a little more.

'So I think…I know,' said Anders eventually, 'that she's doing all this through me. She's the one who's making a picture with the beads and reading about Bamse, but she's using my fingers and my eyes to do it and I don't know…I don't understand what I ought to do.'

The sun had now risen so high that it had some heat. During his long narrative Anders had started to sweat in his warm clothes. He took off his hat and dipped his hand in the water, scooped up a handful and bathed his eyes. Simon was gazing towards Nåten, where the first tender of the morning was just setting off from the jetty. He asked, 'So what does she want?'

'You…believe me?'

Simon wagged his head from side to side, 'Let me put it like this: it isn't the strangest thing I've heard. Recently.'

'What do you mean?'

Simon sighed. 'I think we'll leave that for now.' When he noticed that Anders was frowning, he added, 'I need to talk to Anna-Greta. Is it OK if I tell her what you've told me?'

'Yes, I suppose so, but…'

'Speaking of Anna-Greta, I think we'd better head for home. She's probably getting worried by now.'

Anders nodded and gazed over the rail. Elin was lying on the seabed by now, perhaps fifty metres beneath them. He imagined the fish nudging at the new arrival, the eels crawling up from the mud as they caught the smell of food…

He cut off the thought before it started wallowing in physical details.

'Simon?' he asked. 'Did we do the right thing?'

'Yes. I think so. And if we did the wrong thing…' Simon looked down at the surface of the water, '…there's not much we can do about it now.'

Anders got up and went to the prow, curled up on the seat as well as he could as Simon started the engine and turned the boat, heading for home. For a long time Anders sat there trying to keep his eyes fixed on the spot where they had let Elin go. There should have been something there. A buoy or a flag, some kind of memorial. Something to mark the fact that there was a person down there. But there was only the constant shifting of the water, and Elin belonged to those who have disappeared into the sea.

They parted in silence at Simon's jetty, and Anders dragged himself back to the Shack. If someone had leapt out of the bushes and pointed a shotgun at him, he would have been incapable of reacting. He would simply have shuffled on, perhaps looking forward to the burning sensation in his back.

He looked at his feet, and they were moving without his co-operation or input. He was being drawn. Just as an animal hunted beyond endurance, with no strength left, still creeps towards its lair out of instinct or a blind sense of self-preservation, so he kept on moving homeward, homeward.

He walked in, pulled off his clothes, lay down on Maja's bed and pulled the covers over him. Then he lay there staring at the window, too tired to close his eyelids. He was lying in the same place and the light was roughly the same as on those mornings when he had gone back to bed after going fishing with his father.

He thought he was the same person, the same child. That time moved in circles, and soon it would be time for him to get up and load the wheelbarrow, set off for the shop.

That was a fine catch this morning...

Perhaps he fell asleep with his eyes open.

Pulling power

He had written the sign himself, 'FRESH HERRING 6KR A KILO', because his father was dyslexic and besides, his handwriting was atrocious. The sign stood beside him on the bench outside the shop as he sat there waiting for the morning's first customers.

It was nine o'clock and the shop had just opened. Two people who had gone inside had said they wanted to buy some herring once they had done the rest of their shopping.

This seemed promising. Despite the enormous catch Anders hadn't lowered the price, mainly because he hadn't had time to alter the sign. He had slept for an unusually long time, right up until quarter to nine. It had been a rush to get a box loaded on to the wheelbarrow and push it up to the shop before they opened.

The first customer came out, an elderly lady Anders had seen every summer for as long as he could remember, although he didn't know her name or where she lived. She would always say hello when they met, and Anders would return the greeting without any idea who he was saying hello to.

The lady came over and said, 'I'll have one kilo, please.'

Anders had a stroke of genius. 'We're having a sale today,' he said. 'Two kilos for ten kronor.'

The lady raised her eyebrows and bent over the herring, as if to check whether there was something wrong with them. 'How come?'

Anders realised the best thing would be to tell the truth. 'We caught a huge amount, and we need to get rid of it.'

'But what am I going to do with all that extra?'

'Pickle it. Freeze it. There might not be any more herring this summer. This could be the last.'

The lady laughed and Anders steeled himself for what might come next: the ruffling of his hair. That was the kind of thing you just had to put up with. But the lady just laughed and said, 'What a businessman! OK then, I'll take two kilos. Since there's a sale on.'

Anders slipped a plastic bag over his hand and counted forty-two herring into another bag, added a couple extra to be on the safe side, tied a knot in the top and handed it over, and accepted the payment just as the second customer emerged from the shop. A middle-aged man who was probably a yachtsman, judging by his outfit.

The lady held up her well-filled bag and said to him, 'There's a sale on.'

The jocular way she said it made Anders suspect that *sale* might not be the right word. That suggested you were selling off something that had been left over, which wasn't appropriate in the context of fresh herring. He decided to say *special offer* from now on.

It wasn't the success he had hoped for when he got the idea, but roughly every fourth customer could be tempted to take an extra kilo. Perhaps more to help him out than because they wanted to snap up a bargain. Anders didn't think two kronor here or there meant a great deal to most adults.

However, there were more customers than usual, and Anders went back to fetch another box in time for the eleven o'clock boat, since the first box was more or less empty. There was a bit of a rush with the eleven o'clock boat, and he only just had enough fish. A small queue formed in front of the box; Anders stopped adding a couple of extra fish, and put only eighteen or nineteen in a bag if the customer was someone he didn't recognise, who was only over for the day.

By twelve o'clock he was ready for the third box. The boat was moored by the jetty and his father, who was on holiday from work, was back from the shipyard where he had obviously got rid of the fourth box.

It was looking more than promising. Even if sales slowed down now, it wasn't out of the question that Anders would manage to sell the contents of the third box as well. Despite the special offer this would mean that he was home and dry, that the radio-controlled boat would soon be surging through the waters of the inlet.

Buoyed up by this thought he carted the third box off to the shop and found a customer waiting by the sign. When he managed to sell two kilos once again, Anders decided to celebrate with an ice cream. He went into the shop and bought a Pear Split, then sat back down at his post.

He blew into the paper to loosen it from the ice cream, read the funny story on the collectable card, then sucked on the ice cream while counting the boats out in the bay. He could see his own radio-controlled boat storming past the lot of them, its engine roaring.

He had just got to the best part of the Pear Split, where the ice shell was beginning to melt on his tongue and its sweeter flavour blended with the vanilla ice cream inside, when a man came walking along the track from Kattudden.

The man's eyes looked strange. As if he were drunk. Anders' father sometimes had the same purposeful walk when he'd had too much to drink, as if nothing existed but the goal before his eyes, as if life were merely a question of getting the body to the place it had to be.

Anders recognised him. He was the son of someone his grandmother knew—perhaps he used to live on the mainland and now he'd moved back to the island, Anders couldn't remember. He was a bad-tempered individual. He had once shouted at Anders because his wheelbarrow was in the way outside the shop, and since then Anders had never asked him if he wanted to buy any herring.

He was wearing blue jeans and a checked shirt, like most of the permanent residents. He had wooden clogs on his feet and was marching determinedly towards the jetty.

Marching, yes. That was the word. The man was moving in a way that brooked no interference. If anything got in his way, he would ignore it or walk straight through it rather than give way. Perfectly consistent, bearing in mind how angry he had been when Anders got in his way.

When the man got near the jetty he turned off towards the thicket of sea buckthorn on the right. Anders was so fascinated by his behaviour that he forgot about his ice cream, and the sticky, melting stuff trickled down the stick and over his fingers.

The man disappeared from view behind the sea buckthorn, and Anders took the opportunity to lick the sticky sweetness off his fingers. Then he spotted the man again. He had reached the shoreline, and was on his way out into the water. He hadn't even taken off his clogs.

Only now did Anders start to feel there was something unpleasant about the whole thing. The man slipped on the wet stones and fell, but immediately got up and carried on walking. Anders looked around, searching for some adult who could explain the situation to him, or simply indicate with a calm glance that everything was as it should be.

There were no adults in the vicinity. Nor anybody else, for that matter. Only Anders and the man who was now up to his waist in the water, forging ahead with heavier and heavier strides, heading straight for Gåvasten as if there were a secret track leading out there, a track you could only use if you had the right attitude.

When the water reached the man's chest, he started swimming. Anders stood up, not knowing what he ought to do. He sucked on the lolly, took a couple of bites and saw the man's head slowly moving further and further away from the steamboat jetty. He didn't seem to be an accomplished swimmer, he was splashing about and making strange movements.

Perhaps it's because he's wearing clothes.

When he'd finished the ice cream and the man was showing no sign of turning back, Anders threw the stick in the bin and went into the shop.

There was nobody in there either, thanks to the midday lull. Anders found Ove, the owner, in the fridge behind the dairy cupboard, filling up the milk.

'So how's business?' asked Ove without looking up from his work.

'Good, thanks,' said Anders.

'Same here. Plenty of people about today.'

'Yes.' Anders began to feel unsure of himself. He had never spoken to Ove like this before, and he was a frightening figure, with his huge stomach and gigantic eyebrows. Anders rubbed one arm and said, 'There's a man swimming out there.'

Ove put the last carton of milk on the shelf and straightened up. 'I'm not surprised. It's hot today.'

'Mm. But he's still got his clothes on and…' Anders didn't know how to describe the feeling of foreboding that had come over him as the man walked down to the jetty, '…and there was something kind of strange about him.'

'Strange in what way?'

'Well...the fact that he didn't take off his clothes. He just walked out into the water...and he was walking in an odd way too.'

'So where is he now, then?'

'Still swimming.'

Ove closed the door on the milk, wiped his hands on his apron and said, 'We'd better take a look, then.'

When Anders got outside the shop a couple of steps behind Ove, he saw that it was as he feared. The man was no longer anywhere in sight.

'Where is he, then?' asked Ove.

Anders felt a faint blush creeping over his cheeks. 'He was there just now.'

Ove looked at him suspiciously, as if he were trying to come up with a reasonable explanation as to why Anders would have made this up. Evidently he couldn't come up with anything, since he walked quickly down to the jetty with Anders following in his wake.

There was no sign of anyone when they got down to the jetty either, and Ove shook his head.

'Well, young Anders. There doesn't seem to be anyone here.'

Anders gazed out across the water and spotted a couple of ducks bobbing on the surface ten metres off the jetty. But they weren't ducks. They were two clogs. He pointed them out to Ove, and then the circus got under way.

Ove rang and people came. They went out in boats and the coastguard was called out from Nåten. Anders had to describe the man who had walked out into the water, and everyone agreed it must be Torgny Ek, the son of Kristoffer and Astrid Ek who lived just a few houses past the shop.

Curious tourists from Kattudden and the ramblers' hostel came to see what all the fuss was about. Soon everyone knew the story of what the poor little boy—Anders—had witnessed, and how could they best show their goodwill towards the unfortunate child? By buying his herring, of course.

To tell the truth, Anders didn't feel particularly badly affected or upset by what had happened, but realised it was best to adopt a serious expression as the herring flowed out of his hands and the money flowed into his pockets. He even had the sense to avoid mentioning the special offer, which would obviously be inappropriate.

By the time the box was empty there were still a lot of people standing around the harbour waiting to see what the divers might find, and Anders pushed the wheelbarrow towards home for the third time that day. As he approached the Shack he saw a column of smoke rising up into the sky.

His father was crouching by the smoker, pushing juniper branches into the fire. The last box of herring was by his side, but he hadn't started threading the fish yet. He looked surprised when he caught sight of Anders.

'Back already?'

'Yes,' said Anders, tilting the wheelbarrow to show him the empty box. 'All gone.'

His father got to his feet and looked. First at the box, then at Anders. 'You've sold...sixty kilos?'

'Yup.'

'How come?'

Anders told him about Torgny Ek. How he had come walking along, how he had swum out to sea. All the people who had gathered in the harbour. His voice became more and more tentative as the story went on, since he noticed that his father was very upset by the whole thing, for some reason. He was sitting on the bench by the smoker, staring at the ground.

'And then the coastguard arrived...' Anders' voice died away and silence fell. There was only the crackling of burning juniper branches from inside the smoker. 'Three hundred and twenty kronor. That's how much I've taken. It's a bit less because I did a special offer.'

His father nodded heavily. 'Well done.'

Anders picked up a metal skewer and threaded a couple of herring on to it. His father made a slow, dismissive gesture. 'You can leave that. I don't think we'll do any smoking today.'

'Why not?'

'Well, you've...sold such a lot.'

The heavy feeling in his stomach came back, and Anders was drawn down towards the ground. He lowered the skewer he'd started. 'But...it's always good to have buckling.'

His father slowly got to his feet, and said, 'I'm just not in the mood.' He made an effort and drew the corners of his mouth up into a kind of smile. 'It's really good that you've sold such a lot. Now you can afford that boat. Take it easy for a while.'

Without saying any more he went towards the house, his shoulders drooping. Anders waggled the skewer in his hand. The two herring hung there, threaded through the eyes. The eyes themselves were dangling from their heads, attached by thin membranes. Anders pushed the herring right to the end of the skewer, drew back his arm, flicked his wrist. The herring flew off in a wide arch, landing in the sawdust by the woodpile.

That's that, then.

He washed his hands in the rainwater barrel and went back up towards the shop. He didn't know what had happened, but there had been something wrong with this catch from the start.

Except for one thing.

He felt at the bundle of notes in his right-hand pocket, the clump of coins in his left. He might have a funny feeling in his stomach, and maybe the day could have been better in many ways. But there was no denying one thing: he had made plenty of money.

Find the one you love

As long as just one of her young remains, the female scoter appears to be quite contented, and behaves normally. But it often happens that the entire brood is wiped out during their very first hour of life. When this happens, it can be clearly seen that she is overcome by neurosis. She spins around on the spot where the young disappeared, returns to the same spot and searches for them, day after day, and she searches for them along the route she followed with them—as if their scent were still there on the surface of the water.

STEN RINALDO—TO THE OUTER ARCHIPELAGO

Instead of Las Vegas

Simon was woken by a tickling sensation on his upper lip. The next moment two lips were pressed against his forehead, and he opened his eyes. Anna-Greta drew back, and the strand of hair that had been tickling him was gone.

She was sitting on the edge of his bed with her hand on his hip. 'Good morning,' she said. Simon nodded in response, and Anna-Greta lowered her voice, as if someone might hear.

'How did it go? This morning?'

When Simon came ashore he had simply told Anna-Greta that he was too tired to talk about what had happened, then he had gone straight home and fallen asleep immediately.

He still didn't want to talk about the morning's outing, so he just said it had gone as well as it could, and asked what time it was.

'Half-past eleven,' replied Anna-Greta. 'I didn't know whether to wake you, but…I have a suggestion. You might not like it. In which case, feel free to refuse.'

'What kind of suggestion?'

Simon thought he'd probably had enough surprises to last for some considerable time. Anna-Greta's posture, the way she was picking at her cuticles, suggested she was about to ask a difficult question. Simon sighed and flopped back on the pillow; he was about to say that the answer to all suggestions at this particular moment was *No*, when Anna-Greta asked, 'Do you still want to marry me?'

The *no* would have to wait a while. Simon gave the opposite answer, but added, 'Why do you ask?'

'Do you want to marry me *now*?'

Simon blinked and looked around the room as if to check whether there was a priest hiding somewhere. There didn't appear to be. He didn't understand the question.

'*Now*? What do you mean by *now*?'

'As soon as possible.'

'Is it…urgent?'

Anna-Greta rested her chin on one hand. There was sorrow in the look she gave Simon, her eyes fixed on his for a while until she said, 'Perhaps it is. You never know. And I want to be married to you if… if anything happens.'

'What do you mean?'

Anna-Greta traced the lifeline on her palm with her index finger, not looking at Simon as she replied, 'You know I'm not particularly religious. But still. There's something in all that. I want us to be…' She took a deep breath and expanded her chest, as if she had to make an effort to get the big words out, '...to be married in the sight of God. If anything should happen.' She looked at Simon apologetically. 'So there.'

'OK,' said Simon. 'I understand. What's the suggestion, then?'

Anna-Greta had made a number of calls that morning. In order to marry, it was necessary to have proof that there was no impediment to the marriage. That had to be obtained from the national registration office in Norrtälje. It would normally take a week or two to receive the papers, but it was possible to obtain them more quickly if it was urgent. The same day, in fact.

'I said we'd booked the church for tomorrow,' said Anna-Greta. 'But that we'd forgotten this one detail.' She glanced out of the window. 'We'll just make it if we catch the one o'clock boat.'

Simon had forgotten that he was going to say No, and started to take off his pyjama jacket. When he was halfway he stopped and let the jacket fall back down over his head. 'And have you? Booked the church?'

Anna-Greta laughed. 'No. I didn't know if you'd think this was a good idea.'

She moved up so that Simon had room to get out of bed. He took off the jacket and stood up, using the bedpost for support. 'I'm not so sure about good, but I understand the reasoning. Would it be possible to have a cup of coffee before...the wedding trip?'

Anna-Greta went into the kitchen to make the coffee. Simon leaned against the bedpost. He wobbled as the morning's events hurled themselves at him from behind. He suddenly felt dizzy, and sat down on the bed again. With hands that felt unreal he took off his pyjama trousers and pulled on his underpants and socks. Then he came to a full stop. He held his hands up in front of his eyes.

These fingers of mine.

His entire life's work had been built on what he could do—or what he used to be able to do—with these fingers. Thousands of hours in front of the mirror, polishing the tiniest movement to make it look natural, even though it was hiding something else. He had trained his fingers to obedience, and had had them under control.

Earlier that morning those same fingers had wound his old chain around a dead person, those same hands had tipped a pair of feet over the rail and let a young woman disappear into the depths. To escape awkward questions. To avoid problems. These things his trained fingers had done.

The thought wouldn't go away. As he got up from the bed and opened the wardrobe door, he was looking at his hands the whole time as if they were prostheses, alien things that had been screwed on to the ends of his arms while he was asleep.

He took out a pair of trousers, a shirt and a jacket. His best clothes. He put them on. Perhaps the disruption to his normal daily routine had done something to his head, but it really did seem as if his fingers were behaving as if they had a will of their own, and it was only with some difficulty that he could get them to do as he wished. Fasten his buttons, buckle his belt.

He stopped dead as he was fastening the top button of his shirt.

Is this what it feels like? To be possessed?

He looked at himself in the mirror on the wardrobe door. Not that he knew how it was supposed to feel, but he didn't think that was what was going on here. It was more like the English expression: he was *beside himself.* One person carrying out the actions, another looking on, side by side.

He pushed back his long grey hair, pulled on his jacket and looked at himself in the mirror again.

Here I am.

He tried to recall the feeling that had come over him when a maple leaf had crossed his path. Without success. But still he made a slight bow to the mirror, said thank you for the divided life that had been given to him, in spite of everything.

Clap, clap.

Anna-Greta was leaning against the doorframe watching him, and she brought her palms together a couple more times. 'Very elegant. Coffee's ready.'

Simon followed her into the kitchen. Once he had drunk the first cup of coffee, his thoughts began to clear. He looked out of the window and his eye caught the spot on the grass where Marita had sat that time. When he had stood in front of her with a shotgun, considering whether to execute her.

On that occasion too he had felt as if he had been thrown outside himself, standing beside himself and looking on.

It's all just excuses, he thought, pouring himself another cup. We talk about being out of our mind, that we weren't ourselves, that we lost control. Different ways of saying the same thing. But we are always ourselves. There are no imaginary friends carrying out actions in our name.

Except…except…

'What are you thinking about?' asked Anna-Greta.

Simon told her what Anders had said to him in the boat. That Maja had entered into him and was influencing him, guiding his hands at night. That he was possessed, just as Elin had been.

When he had finished, Anna-Greta sat quietly for a while, looking over towards the Shack. Eventually she said, 'Poor little soul.'

Simon didn't know if she was referring to Anders or Maja, and it didn't really matter which it was. Everything suddenly seemed utterly impossible, and Anna-Greta's simple compassion merely intensified the feeling.

'Do you really believe that's what's happening?' he asked. 'That the souls of the dead come up from the sea and…and…'

'There's no guarantee they're dead. We know nothing. Nothing. Not for certain.'

'But what can we do?'

Anna-Greta reached across the table and placed her hand on top of his. 'What we can do right now,' she said, 'is to take the one o'clock boat over to Norrtälje and sign some papers so that we can get married.'

Simon glanced at the clock. It was twenty to one, and they would have to leave right away if they were going to get there in time. He picked up the matchbox from the windowsill and said, 'Yes. This is our day. Let's do it. Could you just…wait outside for me for a minute?'

Anna-Greta raised her eyebrows enquiringly, and Simon showed her the box. 'I have to…'

'Go on, then.'

'I'd prefer to be on my own.'

'Why?'

Simon looked at the white silhouette of the little boy on the box. *Why?* He could have come up with reasons, but instead he told the truth, 'Because it's embarrassing. It would be like…having an audience when you go to the toilet. Can you understand that?'

Anna-Greta shook her head and smiled. 'If we're going to grow even older together, there's a good chance that one of us will have to wipe the other's backside before it's all over. Go on, do what you have to do.'

Simon hesitated. He hadn't realised how suffused with shame his relationship with Spiritus was, and he felt dirty as he pushed open the box. He glanced at Anna-Greta and saw that she was kindly looking out of the window.

The insect really didn't look healthy. It's skin, once black and shiny, was dull and parchment-like. It was beginning to look more and more like the dead specimen he had seen in the great magician's display case. Simon cleared his throat and gathered up spit.

The clock was ticking. Time was passing. The boat was getting closer.

Let go.

The bubble of spit emerged, fell and spread across the dry skin. The insect moved, absorbed the liquid and came to life a little. Simon looked up. Anna-Greta was watching him.

'Shall we go?' she asked, pointing at his chin. Simon wiped away a string of saliva, stood up and put the box in his pocket. When they got outside, Anna-Greta took his hand and said, 'That wasn't too bad, was it?'

'No,' said Simon, and meant it.

They were going to get married. So it was probably time to embrace the words from the letter to the Corinthians, the words that form part of the promise of love, 'When I became a man I put away childish things.'

Let go.

He followed Anna-Greta up on to the track, and the morning stiffness in his limbs began to ease. He looked out to sea and saw that the tender had covered half the distance between Nåten and Domarö. They hurried along, and Simon was worn out by the time they reached the jetty.

Anna-Greta stood in front of him and pushed back his hair, brushing a few loose strands from his shoulders.

'Will I do?' he asked.

'You'll do. In fact, you'll more than do. Do you know which word suits you?'

'No.'

'It's a beautiful word. You're mysterious.'

The tender slowed down as it approached the jetty. Simon was just about to say something about glass houses and throwing stones when the angry roar of an engine came up behind them. Just as the prow of the boat touched the jetty and Roger came forward to throw the mooring rope, Johan Lundberg arrived beside them on his platform moped and pulled up.

'Here you are,' he said. 'Good.'

However, his expression did not suggest that things were good— quite the opposite, in fact.

He ignored Simon and turned to Anna-Greta.

'You have to come. Karl-Erik has lost it completely. You have to talk to him. He'll listen to you.'

'What do you mean, lost it?' asked Anna-Greta.

'We're busy clearing up around the house that burned down and he...you have to come. He's out of his mind.'

Roger came up to them with the mooring rope in his hand.

'Are you coming? I have to go now.'

Anna-Greta nodded and turned to Johan. 'Unfortunately I'm busy today. We'll be back at six.'

Johan's jaw dropped, as if Anna-Greta's response had just revealed one of the great mysteries of the universe to him. Before he had time to come up with any objections, Simon and Anna-Greta stepped on board. Roger followed them and climbed up to the cockpit. The boat reversed away from the jetty.

Johan stood there gazing after them with the expression of a foundling left to rely on the kindness of strangers. If Simon had needed any proof that Anna-Greta was the unofficial leader of the village, he had it now.

As the boat began to swing around to head for Nåten, Johan raised his hand feebly in farewell, straddled his moped, kicked it into life and set off back towards the village.

Anna-Greta and Simon stood leaning against the rail as they swung away from Domarö, towards the mainland. The bay was busy, dotted white with gulls taking off one by one or in groups, flying around in circles then coming in to land once again.

'What do you think all that was about?' asked Simon.

Anna-Greta was gazing out to sea. 'I don't know,' she said. 'And I don't want to know, either. Have you seen how many gulls there are? I don't think I've ever seen so many.'

The boat carved its way through a throng of white bodies that paddled or flew away at a leisurely pace. It really was unusual to see so many.

Wedding guests, thought Simon. *And here come the happy couple.*

He put his arm around Anna-Greta and let his thoughts turn to the mainland.

Duel

This time there was no room for doubt: it was arson. As they worked to put out the fire, the smell of petrol had been noticeable, and when the worst was over they had also found the can. Someone had set the fire in the Wahlgrens' summer cottage, and it was a small step to assume it was the same person who had set fire to the Grönwalls' place.

For a while during the night it had looked as though things might go very badly. The fire had taken hold in the conifers in the Wahlgrens' garden, and sparks and burning fragments were being carried inland. Before the fire service arrived, a panic-stricken decision had been taken to fell a number of trees that might otherwise have led the fire up into the forest. It had been a dry autumn, and if the fire caught in the tops of the fir trees, it could be a disaster. The flames would spread through the forest all the way down to the old village, not stopping until they reached the sea.

Three men worked with chainsaws to fell some forty fir and pine trees that ran along a spur from the forest, an arm that was just dying to grab hold of the fire. It was the kind of feat about which songs are sung. But such songs are no longer sung, and at best Karl-Erik, Lasse and Mats had a small mention in the local newspaper to look forward to.

The report should, however, mention that they had to work fast, that the trees could not be felled in the direction of the fire, and that they also had to make sure the trees did not fall on to any of the cottages in the area, which meant they had to fell every single tree with precision, and of course all this was done in darkness, with little more than the light of the street lamp and the fire itself to help them.

Who would have taken on such a task, and who succeeded?

Why, Karl-Erik, Lasse and Mats!

OK, so they nearly knocked down the Carlgrens' outhouse, and those people from Örebro might have lost a few panes of glass from their greenhouse, but by and large nobody could have done a better job and the three musketeers, wielding chainsaws instead of rapiers, were the heroes of the night. Since the fire was under control, they could go home and sleep as long as they pleased. They had done their part, and more besides.

That was how they were greeted when they turned up the following day to chop up the felled trees, 'Here come the three musketeers again!'

But Mats was the only one who grinned and tossed out a reply. Lasse's expression was grim, and Karl-Erik looked furious, to put it mildly. It was as if the memory of the previous night's co-operation had been blown away. What happened next could only be described as incomprehensible, an event not unlike that business in Söderviken with Gustavsson and the swan.

Gustavsson used to feed a swan. It came back to him year after year, accepting pieces of bread from him and providing him with a little company. As soon as you met Gustavsson he would start talking about that swan, how beautiful and clever it was, what a good friend it had become.

And then one day Gustavsson took his shotgun down to the bay and shot the swan, fired a blast at its neck so that the head flew off. Afterwards he had been inconsolable, unable to come up with any explanation for his behaviour, except that he had got it into his head that he was going to shoot the swan.

However, this incident with Karl-Erik was more extensive in that it went on for longer than the time it took to load a shotgun, take aim and fire. And it wasn't only Karl-Erik—Lasse was seized by the same irrational behaviour.

The morning's work of removing branches and chopping up the trees proceeded more or less as normal, although Mats did say later that there was something slightly odd about Karl-Erik and Lasse. They had each kept themselves to themselves, working in silence. When they took a break to have a drink of water and eat their sandwiches, they sat a long way from each other.

After their break all three of them put on their ear protectors, started up their saws and set to work again. Mats was working his way through the root of one of the thicker fir trees. Progress was slow, and the saw got very hot. Therefore, when he had finished he switched off the saw, took off his ear protectors and began to sharpen the chain.

Lasse's saw was also switched off, and so Mats was able to hear the sound of sawing from elsewhere, up towards the village and quite a distance from the newly felled trees they were busy clearing. He stood up and looked for the source of the noise. When he found it he dropped his saw and ran.

At the time when Holger's father sold Kattudden to the agent from Stockholm, a couple of families from the village had managed to secure a promise that they could at least divide up and purchase a small area, so that not everything would pass into the ownership of strangers. They had been allocated a few small parcels of land furthest away from the sea, up towards the forest.

The Bergwall family, to which Lasse belonged, was one of them. His mother, Margareta Bergwall, now owned the two summer cottages that lay up on the hill to the west, perhaps three hundred metres from the shore, but with something of a sea view. The cottages were rented out to summer visitors, but Lasse's brother Robert was planning to renovate one of them and move back home.

Between the two properties stood the largest birch tree on Kattudden: a real giant some twenty metres tall. A grown man could just about get his arms around it. And it was this birch that Karl-Erik was busy cutting down.

When Mats saw what he was up to, he dropped his saw as well and hurried towards Karl-Erik. The birch was between the two proper-ties, but leaned slightly towards Lasse's mother's house, and judging from the way Karl-Erik was making the face cut, he intended to use the tree's natural lean to ensure that it would land right on top of Lasse's future inheritance.

'Karl-Erik!' yelled Mats as soon as he was within earshot. 'Karl-Erik, what are you doing!'

But Karl-Erik was wearing his ear protectors, and couldn't hear a thing. He was just cutting the final part of the wedge, and kicked it out so that a wide, deep cut at the base of the tree gaped towards Lasse's house like a hungry mouth. He examined his work, seemed satisfied and went around the other side of the tree to start making the felling cut. It was no more than a minute's work, and then the tree would fall.

Mats reached Karl-Erik just as the sawdust began to whirl up from the tree, grabbed his shoulder and shook him. Karl-Erik looked up and Mats took a step backwards. The eyes that were looking at him were neither angry nor confused. They were as empty and ice-cold as the sea in November. It is a testament to Mats's courage that he still, when Karl-Erik revved up the saw again, pulled off his ear protectors and screamed, 'Are you crazy! Stop it! You can't chop this tree down! Stop!'

Karl-Erik jabbed at him with the saw and Mats was forced to step back again. He ran his hands over his sweaty face and thought: *He's gone completely mad. How am I going to stop him?*

There was no time to think about that, because Lasse had realised what was happening and came running, with his own saw in his hands. When Karl-Erik once again inserted the blade of his saw into the felling cut he had started, Lasse came rushing towards him, and Mats saw that his eyes were also empty. They were staring straight at Karl-Erik, but showed no emotion whatsoever.

Only now did Mats begin to feel afraid.

Karl-Erik's saw roared behind him, and the sawdust was tickling his calves; Lasse was racing towards him with his saw held high and the motor running at full speed. It's no surprise that Mats did what anyone else would have done under the circumstances. He took a couple of steps to one side and yelled to the people who were clearing up down on the site of the fire, 'Help! Up here! They're going to kill one another! Help!'

When Mats screamed, Karl-Erik looked up and saw the approaching threat at the last minute. He pulled the saw out of the cut and jumped back as Lasse rushed forward, swinging the saw at him. The howling chain missed Karl-Erik by a fraction, and the force of his own action made Lasse fall down headfirst, with the saw in his hands and chain oil splashing over his face.

Mats saw Karl-Erik push the speed to maximum and lower the saw over Lasse's back; he just had time to think: *He's going to do it!* before a reflex took over and hurled him towards Karl-Erik. The blade cut through the braces of Lasse's overalls, reaching his skin, and Lasse would have been chopped in half like a rotten log if Mats hadn't tackled Karl-Erik at that very moment, making him stagger sideways so that he couldn't complete the incision.

Lasse got to his feet and his trousers fell around his ankles as the blood started to gush from the wound on his back. He raised his saw and bared his teeth. For a couple of seconds the two men stood face to face, their chainsaws screaming and their empty gazes locked together.

Mats could see that people were on their way up from the shore, but the closest still had at least a hundred metres to go, and he turned to the combatants and screamed like a despairing child, 'Stop it, stop it, stop it!' as the tears scalded his eyes.

It had no effect whatsoever. Lasse took a clumsy step forward, sweeping at Karl-Erik's arm with his saw, but Karl-Erik managed to lift his saw and parry the blow. Sparks flew as the howling chains made contact.

Karl-Erik responded with a low sweep towards Lasse's unprotected legs, but despite the fact that his trousers were in a heap around his feet, Lasse managed to jump backwards towards the birch so that the whirring blades missed his shins and merely tore up earth and grass.

Once again there was a brief lull as the two men measured each other and revved their chainsaws.

Mats looked around on the ground for something to throw, but as he spotted a stone the size of a fist, he realised it was pointless. If he managed to knock one of them down, the other one would kill the man who was down. He heard shouts behind him, and all he could do was hope that the others would get there in time.

A hint of emotion was now visible on Karl-Erik's face. The corners of his mouth curled upwards in a nasty smile. He swung the saw backwards and took a step forward, while at the same time letting go with his left hand, so that he was holding the machine with his right hand on the throttle as he swung it in an arc towards Lasse's head.

Mats let out a gasp, and it was all too late. But at the very last second Lasse managed to raise his blade in his defence, and the chains met a few centimetres from his ear. Sparks flew, then there was a dry snapping noise and Lasse fell back.

Later it was established that the chain on Lasse's saw had broken and whipped him across the forehead. All they could see at the time was Lasse's head jerking backwards as the saw flew out of his hand. With a heavy thud he hit the birch tree and slipped to one side.

Whatever Karl-Erik's intentions might have been, he didn't manage to carry them out. Göran got there first, closely followed by Johan Lundberg. Together with Mats they managed to wrestle Karl-Erik to the ground and get the saw off him.

But in another way it was too late. When they turned their attention to Lasse they saw that he was lying flat on the ground with a wound in his forehead, and that he was alive. But the birch tree…the birch tree into which he had thudded, its trunk now spattered with his blood—the birch tree had started to fall.

It had started to fall and it couldn't be stopped. The tree was too big. Mats and the others could only stand watching open-mouthed as the enormous tree majestically and with studied slowness keeled over, tipped and fell.

The notch had been perfectly placed for its intended purpose, and the thick trunk went through the roof of the glass veranda first of all, shattering a number of panes, before smashing the chimney and snapping the roof beams. With a clatter of broken tiles, the entire roof of the little cottage folded and fell in. The trunk got halfway to the floor before its crown bounced in a cloud of splinters and brick dust, and lay still.

By this time several people had arrived and were taking care of Lasse, who was bleeding profusely from the wound on his head and the cut on his back. The falling tree had so completely occupied everyone's attention that they had forgotten about Karl-Erik for a while. He had a good deal to answer for, but when they turned around he was no longer there.

However, he wasn't far away. As if nothing had happened he had got up, picked up his saw and was now on his way towards one of the neighbouring gardens, heading straight for a couple of tall pine trees with a swing between them.

This time there was no negotiation. Mats, Göran and Johan caught up with him, wrenched the saw out of his hands and grabbed him before he could cause any more devastation. Karl-Erik struggled, but whether he was crazy or not it was three against one, and they managed to hold him.

While Mats and Göran held on to his arms, Johan stood in front of him and tried to catch his eye. It was impossible. The eyes were there and they were looking into his, but it was impossible to make any kind of contact.

'Karl-Erik?' Johan asked anyway. 'What's got into you? What the hell are you doing?'

During the whole of the terrible duel Karl-Erik hadn't made a sound, and they didn't expect him to answer now either. But they still had to try to talk to him as if he were a sensible person who had a reason for his actions. And they got an answer.

Tentatively, as if he were unused to his mouth and in a voice that sounded like Karl-Erik but yet not like Karl-Erik, he said, 'Those houses. Have got to go.'

'What do you mean?' asked Johan. 'They're not our houses. It's not up to us to decide.'

This objection made no impression on Karl-Erik. With stiff, grimacing lips he said, 'Those houses have got to go.'

He twisted and turned in their grasp, but Mats and Göran managed to hold him. Elof Lundberg came over to them, glanced at Karl-Erik and asked, 'What's the matter with him?'

'He's lost the plot completely,' said Johan. 'If you can help out here I'll go and fetch Anna-Greta. He'll listen to her.'

So that was why Johan Lundberg got on his moped and rode off to the old village to ask Anna-Greta for help, then found himself standing on the jetty like an orphaned child, watching her and Simon disappearing towards the mainland in a cloud of gulls.

At something of a loss he climbed back on his moped and set off back to Kattudden to do what could be done.

That magician, he thought as he rode along, *is someone we could do without.*

In Norrtälje

At half-past three Simon and Anna-Greta were sitting in a pizzeria in Norrtälje, each with a capricciosa in front of them which they cut into small, easily chewed pieces, washed down with lukewarm Fanta. Simon had the required certificate in his inside pocket and two smooth gold rings in his outer pocket. Anna-Greta had asked to use the telephone in the national registration office and had rung Geir, the priest in Nåten, and booked the church for Sunday, in two days' time, after High Mass. They were ready.

There was something...youthful about the haste with which they had gone about things. Perhaps it was that same feeling of rejuvenation that had led them to celebrate their speedily executed preparations with a pizza. Neither of them had eaten pizza since the days when it was a novelty, and they chose a capricciosa purely because they vaguely recognised the name.

When Anna-Greta had eaten about half of hers, she pushed the plate away and said, 'It was tasty at first, but it seems to be growing.'

Simon had exactly the same feeling. His stomach felt as if he had shovelled down half a litre of flour with a teaspoon. It was bubbling and swelling, and he stopped while he still had a delicious taste in his mouth.

Anna-Greta looked out of the window as Simon poked at the remains of what was probably the last pizza he would eat in this life. If you contemplated it when you weren't hungry, it didn't even look like human food.

'Simon,' said Anna-Greta. 'You have to be careful.'

Simon, who was still meditating on the suitability of pizza as food, replied, 'You mean about what I eat?'

Anna-Greta shook her head. 'If I'd known you were intending to do what you did this morning, I would never have let you go.'

'Do we have to talk about this?'

Their errands at the registration office and the goldsmith's had distracted Simon's thoughts from the horror of the morning, and he wanted to remain in this blissful state of forgetfulness for as long as possible. Anna-Greta turned her palms upward to indicate that she had no intention of continuing along this line, took a deep breath and said, 'A long time ago. When I used to travel around selling things. During the war. I was involved in something…something I haven't told you about.'

Simon didn't need to ask. Things had changed. He was now one of those in the know, someone who could be told. He leaned back as far as he could on the straight-backed chair as Anna-Greta went on.

'I was allowed to travel with the soldiers sometimes because I was…popular. I don't think they were really supposed to have civilians on board, but after all I knew the archipelago and so…' Anna-Greta looked up and frowned. 'What are you grinning at?'

Simon waved a hand. 'Nothing, nothing. I'll just say one thing. *Belle of the boat.*'

'I was not a belle of the boat! I knew every single…'

'Yes, yes. But I'm sure there were plenty of others who knew the archipelago even better. They just weren't as pretty as you.'

Anna-Greta gasped for breath, but stopped herself and looked suspiciously at Simon. 'Are you *jealous*?' she asked. 'Are you sitting here sixty years on feeling *jealous*?'

Simon thought about it. 'Now you come to mention it, yes.'

Anna-Greta looked at Simon, then shook her head at the absurdity of it all.

'They were thinking about laying mines. Out towards Ledinge. Since the major shipping lane to Stockholm runs along there. And I went along on one of those...reconnaissance trips where they were diving to check out the conditions on the seabed. They had just started using modern diving equipment with tanks on their backs. But because visibility in the water was poor and they still weren't sure about these new things, they used a safety line, attached to the diver.'

Anna-Greta nodded to herself and pointed vaguely in the air as if she'd just thought of something. 'That was probably why I went along, I think. Because I wanted to see the diving.'

Simon had a very witty comment on the tip of his tongue, but he kept it to himself and Anna-Greta went on:

'So down he went, this diver, and the line ran from a pulley on deck. There was something hypnotic about it. I mean, you couldn't see the diver, you just had this pulley to look at, and it made a clicking sound as it turned, paying out the line as he went down. And then... it stopped. The line stopped moving, as if he'd reached the bottom. But that couldn't be right, because only about seven or eight metres of the line had been paid out, and it was at least thirty metres deep there. The line just didn't move for a good while, and I thought he must have found a new reef, that he was standing there speculating about what it should be called, if it should be given a name. And then...'

Anna-Greta flicked her hand so that it made a small circular movement.

'...and then the line started moving again. But more quickly than before. Much more quickly. Ten metres, fifteen, twenty, twenty-five. And the pulley was no longer clicking, it was...clattering. Then the speed increased until it was just a continuous hum. Thirty, forty, fifty

336

metres. In just a few seconds. As if he were falling through the air rather than sinking through water. There was nothing we could do. Somebody tried to grab hold of the line, and burned the palms of their hands. Then it ran right to the end, another thirty metres, came off the pulley and disappeared into the water. At the same speed.'

Anna-Greta drank some of her Fanta and cleared her throat.

'That's what happened. And that's why I want you to be careful.' She put down her glass and added, 'They had to come up with some kind of explanation, of course. So they decided he'd somehow got himself attached to a submarine. Stupid but true. He was never found. But perhaps you suspected that already.'

Simon looked at her as she sat there wiping her mouth with her serviette. She didn't give the impression that she had just described something incomprehensible; it was more as if she had just been *forced* to explain this business of electricity so that you wouldn't poke your fingers in the socket.

'I am careful,' said Simon. 'I think.'

They went for a walk through Norrtälje and discussed to what extent they would change their current living arrangements after they were married. Well, it wasn't so much a discussion—they *joked* about it. In fact they were both in agreement from the start that they wanted to carry on as before.

There was no question of a honeymoon, but they decided to take a trip on the ferry to Finland and back. Some fine dining and a few symbolic dance steps, God (and their hips) willing.

At five o'clock they caught the bus back to Nåten, and at quarter to six they were on board the tender once again. Simon looked out over the dark sea and thought that it had changed. He no longer saw the surface, he saw the *depths*. He had studied the maritime charts, he had talked to people and he knew that the bay was between twenty and sixty metres deep outside Nåten. To the north and east there were deep trenches of a hundred metres or more.

The depths.

The colossal extent of it, the immense amount of water just between Domarö and Nåten, just lying there biding its time in its darkness, showing only its shining, harmless surface.

In his mind's eye Simon could see the ferry to Finland they would travel on before long. *Silja Symphony*. Hundreds of cabins and a long shopping mall down the centre. Ten storeys; at least one hundred and fifty metres from prow to stern.

He looked down at the sea, foaming up around the bow and thought: *It could sink here and it would be gone. There would be no sign of it at all. It would be lying down there.*

A shudder ran down his spine and he put his arm around Anna-Greta's shoulders as they approached Domarö.

A welcome committee was standing on the jetty. It consisted of the same people who had been in the mission house, apart from Tora Österberg and Holger, who were missing. And Karl-Erik.

Tora hadn't felt strong enough to come, and Holger was sitting with Göran, keeping an eye on Karl-Erik. 'So that he doesn't come up with something else,' as Johan Lundberg put it.

Lasse had been taken to the hospital in Norrtälje and had his wounds stitched, but had refused to stay one minute longer than necessary. When he was delivered back home his wife Lina had been just as unreasonable. She was normally the kindest, most helpful person you could imagine, but she had spat and hissed at Lasse's companions, transformed beyond recognition. She had let her husband in, but that was it. She hadn't even offered them coffee.

All this was relayed to Anna-Greta. Simon was deliberately ignored, and despite the fact that Anna-Greta took his hand to keep him within the circle, the group managed to close around her and exclude him. After a couple of minutes he had had enough. He squeezed Anna-Greta's hand and whispered to her that he was going to see how Anders was getting on.

He felt a pang of guilt when he turned around after a few steps and saw her standing on the jetty surrounded by dark figures, like a flock of crows. Although perhaps it wasn't guilt, he thought as he continued on towards the Shack. Perhaps it was jealousy.

She's not yours. She's mine. Mine!

The Shack was dark and silent, but when Simon went into the kitchen he could see light seeping out from beneath the bedroom door. He opened it gently and discovered Anders, fast asleep in Maja's bed with his arms around Bamse the Bear. Simon stood looking at him quietly for a while, then went out and closed the door silently behind him.

In the kitchen he switched on the light, found a pen and some paper and wrote a note about the wedding. As he was just about to leave he caught sight of the bead tile. He studied it carefully. Then he added something to the note and left the house.

Anna-Greta was already home. There hadn't been all that much to discuss, really. The only course of action on which they could agree had already been put in place: to keep Lasse and Karl-Erik under supervision and see how things developed. She pulled off her best boots and massaged her feet, which were feeling the effects of all that walking in Norrtälje. 'I'm sorry the others were like that,' she said. 'I'm sure they'll get used to the situation in time.'

'I doubt it,' said Simon, sitting down. 'Did you tell them? About Elin?'

'How could I possibly do that?'

'No. Of course not.'

Anna-Greta put her feet up on Simon's knee and he kneaded them absently. His hands were back in place, a natural part of his body.

Magic. Mysterious.

The whole thing was like a magic trick. An effect that could be seen on the surface, which seemed fantastic, but behind it all lay a mechanism that was basically very simple, if only you understood it. Perhaps. Perhaps not. Simon wished he could put his former talent to work on this particular effect and find the hidden compartment, the secret mechanism. Perhaps it was all as simple as an invisible thread or a false base, if you could just see it. But he couldn't see it.

'There is one thing I don't understand,' said Anna-Greta, wiggling her toes and making them creak slightly. 'Elin. Anders. Karl-Erik. Lasse. Lina. Why those people in particular? Why *them*?'

'There are a lot of things I don't understand. And that's one of them. Where are the strings?'

Hide and seek

When Anders managed to get hold of the alarm clock and decipher the position of the hands through eyes gritty with sleep, he couldn't believe what he was seeing. It was twenty to seven. Judging from the light outside it was morning, not evening. Which meant he hadn't slept more than quarter of an hour, despite the fact that he had been bone weary.

He rolled on to his back and pressed the clock to his chest. Strangely enough, he felt rested in a way that he hadn't felt for a very long time. His body was soft and his brain was empty, relaxed. It felt as if he'd slept…

Hang on a minute…

There was one other possibility. That he had slept for an entire day. That it was Saturday now. He closed his eyes, but they had already come to life and certainly didn't want to be closed again. He had finished sleeping. There was no other explanation: he must have slept for fifteen minutes plus twenty-four hours.

Or forty-eight. Or seventy-two. Or…

He was desperate for a pee, his bladder felt like a huge tumour. But he still didn't get up. It was so indescribably wonderful to lie there in bed feeling warm and *rested*. He hadn't had one single peaceful night since he came to Domarö. Now he felt as if he had recouped everything in one fell swoop. He drew up his knees and turned to the wall, where he found an old friend.

Bamse.

The big Bamse bear had been Maja's favourite when they were on Domarö. She hadn't wanted to take it back home to the city with her, no, Bamse belonged on Domarö and had to stay here and wait for her until the next time she came over.

Anders stroked the blue felt hat, the wide-open eyes, the buttons on his overalls.

'Hello, Bamse.'

He felt so *calm.* Yesterday or the day before his thoughts would probably have started whirling around in his head by now, scrabbling for an explanation of the fact that Bamse was lying next to him, even though he had been right under the bed when Anders fell asleep.

But not now. No problem. Bamse was here. Nice.

Besides, he now knew how things worked. He was the one who had dug out Bamse, or rather his body had done so. Maja had wanted Bamse next to her while she was sleeping, and had used Anders to get what she wanted.

'Morning, sweetheart.'

He listened inside himself for a reply, but none came. That was OK too. He thought he ought to be able to feel something, to be able to find a place inside himself that was Maja, but he had no intention of going into that right now. Things were OK as they were, with Bamse and everything. She was there.

He smiled. 'Do you remember this?' He cleared his throat and silently sang Maja's version of the Bamse song:

'Hey there Bamse, strongest bear of all
But oh, how he loves to fight!
Thunder honey, Grandma's thunder honey
That's what he eats when it's time to start a fight.'

She had really loved to play with songs and expressions, with language. Above all she liked making things...well, worse. It would often start with a mispronunciation, which she would then develop. A favourite had been to exchange the word 'Christmas' for 'Christmess'. They gave each other Christmess presents, brought in the Christmess tree and before Christmas they sat making different kinds of Christmess puzzles. Then Father Christmess came.

Pain shot through Anders' midriff and he frowned. He remembered how she had sat there gabbling a list of different things that were 'messy'. Christmess music and the Christmessy atmosphere. The verse she had added to 'I Saw Mommy Kissing Santa Claus', which involved Daddy coming in and killing Santa Claus. Father Christmess.

I can't go on like this.

Anders rolled over quickly and slipped out of bed, half-crouching as he ran to the toilet where he achieved what was probably a world record in pissing for the longest time. His body felt purified, capable, ready for anything. He flushed the toilet and Elin came into his mind. Her hair floating outwards around her head as she sank down...

No!

He rinsed his face with cold water and slaked his thirst. He wouldn't think about that. Ever. It was over, it was gone, it belonged in the past. It was as if he had been given the gift of a new body and a new brain this morning. He had no intention of using them to wade around in the sludgy mess of things that couldn't be altered. He'd done enough of that.

He was famished, and stood by the fridge wolfing down three pieces of crispbread smothered in cheese spread while the water trickled through the coffee machine. He chewed and chewed, hearing the crunch inside his head as he gazed out of the window and noticed that the bay was full of gulls. He was not afraid.

I am not afraid.

He munched the last of the crispbread and studied the movements of the gulls as they drifted with the currents, taking off and blinking as they were caught by the light of the low-lying sun, then drifting back down towards the surface again.

I am not afraid.

He had been walking around more or less in a state of horror and fear for so long that it had become part of his nature. Now it was gone. There was only the bay, the blue sky, the gulls and his own body, unafraid, seeing everything in the autumn light.

It was wonderful.

He turned away from the window and caught sight of the bead tile. His eyes opened wide and he went across to it, ran his hand over the smooth surface, which was now larger than the knobbly area. Beads had been added, many beads had been added—

I have added the beads.

—while he was asleep. Lots and lots of blue beads had been added, and the large white patch in the middle was finished, surrounded by blue, and had been joined by a smaller white patch diagonally up to the left.

As he stood contemplating the incomprehensible picture an idea began to take shape, but before he managed to catch it he spotted the note.

Anna-Greta and I are getting married in Nåten on Sunday at two o'clock. We would very much like you to be there. Simon.

Under the signature was a postscript, and when Anders read it he slapped his forehead and shouted, 'Idiot! It's so obvious!' He studied the bead tile again and couldn't understand why he hadn't seen it straight away.

P.S. Isn't it a maritime chart?

The blue was the sea, the white patch in the middle was Domarö, and the smaller white patch was Gåvasten. It was clumsily executed and light and dark were transposed in comparison to a normal maritime chart, but he was still annoyed that he hadn't spotted it long ago, as soon as the contours of Domarö began to form.

It was a revelation, along the lines of: *at last the pieces fell into place, the penny dropped, the veil was swept aside.* The discovery made Anders feel quite intoxicated, and he clapped his hands in pure delight, but stopped in the middle of a clap. He stared at the beads.

It's a maritime chart. Right. So?

What he had in front of him was a rudimentary chart showing

Domarö, Kattholmen and Gåvasten, with Ledinge gradually emerging.

So?

It looked just like an ordinary chart, but executed less skilfully. An ordinary chart that he already had on the bookshelf. What was he supposed to do with this one? What could it tell him that he didn't already know?

'Why are you doing this? Why have you made this…messy chart?'

He was suddenly furious, and was seized by a powerful urge to throw the whole fucking thing away, had even reached out for the tile with both hands before he managed to stop himself. He looked at his hands, got hold of one hand with the other and shook it.

One of his own plays on words popped into his head. It hadn't gone down very well with Maja, but he'd thought it was funny. Swapping the word 'hand' for 'hound' in different expressions. Holding someone by the hound. Give me your hound, I am your right hound. And then there was his favourite. He looked at his hands and said it out loud, 'One hound doesn't know what the other is doing.'

That's it.

He sat down heavily on a kitchen chair. The sudden rage had not been his, it was Maja who could be so unreasonably angry over little things. Like her socks the day she disappeared. She had just got angry with the chart, through him. Just as she had been so happy when she saw that it *was* a chart showing the sea and the islands.

No. Yes.

He leaned over the bead tile again. If she was the one who had made the chart, then she couldn't be delighted at the discovery that it *was* a chart. And besides…how on earth could Maja build a maritime chart with beads? He had probably shown her the chart at some point when they were out in the boat, but there was no possibility that she would be able to make an…image of it.

He was the only one who could do that. Therefore, he was the one who had made the chart without knowing, and she was the one who had…

344

He put his head in his hands.

One hound doesn't know what the other is doing.

If she wanted to communicate with him, why do it in this complex, time-consuming way? Why not just write or say what needed to be said?

Because one hound doesn't know what the other is doing.

And besides...

Anders took a deep breath and held it, listened inside himself and outside. There was nothing there. Nobody was watching him, nobody was after him. For the moment. But they did exist.

You can't be here either, little Maja. We'll take you too, in time.

It was a question of being careful. If you showed yourself too much, they would spot you. That was what had happened to Elin. Perhaps. So you had to be careful. Take a little bit at a time and avoid discovery.

Maja had been good at hide and seek. Almost too good. She could stay hidden for a long, long time if she found a good hiding place. She wouldn't even come out when they gave up and shouted to her. They always had to find her.

That last summer they had played hide and seek outside, and it was the same as always. She could be extremely impatient in other contexts, but when it came to games, her patience was endless. She would remain hidden far away until the person who was supposed to find her dropped their guard and set off in the opposite direction. Then she would come running out. She could wait for as long as it took.

Anders poured himself a cup of coffee and drank it slowly and methodically, visualising the hot, slightly poisonous liquid running through his body, once again cleansing the channels. His brain was beginning to feel clogged up again, and he didn't want that to happen.

He looked at the sea, the sky, the gulls, and concentrated on the warmth in his throat, his chest, his stomach.

It worked, to some extent, and with reasonably clear eyes he looked at the bead tile again. *If* it was as he thought, if Maja was playing some kind of hide and seek where the important thing was to avoid discovery, then there should still be some kind of clue.

He went and fetched the real chart, compared it with the bead tile. The distances and proportions were accurate, by and large. The shape of the islands was too square, but more or less correct. There was no noticeable deviation that stood out from the original.

He put down the chart and rubbed his eyes. When he looked again he spotted something that *didn't* stand out, quite the opposite.

There's something missing here…

He bent over the tile and studied the patch of white beads representing Gåvasten. At the top there was a narrow corridor where no beads had been fixed, a band of emptiness.

What does that mean? Does it mean anything?

He got the photographs out of the kitchen drawer and spread them out on the table. He concentrated on Maja's face, Maja's eyes. Yes, it was just as he had thought. Her attention was drawn to something over in the east, by that empty band.

Daddy, what's that?

Anders looked out of the window. Beyond the carpet of gulls covering the bay he could just see the tiny white lighthouse. No more than a glint in the morning light, a dot on the sky.

Ten minutes later he had pulled on his outdoor clothes, fetched his tools and mounted the outboard engine on the plank of wood. The temperature had fallen by several degrees and was now close to zero, but after yanking on the starter cord several times he was quite warm.

He checked everything that could be checked, sprayed lubricant on all the moving parts and starter fluid into the air filter, took out the spark plugs and dried them even though they were already dry, put them back, pumped up the petrol and slapped the engine with the palm of his hand.

'Now start, you bastard.'

He yanked the cord five times without the engine making the slightest effort to start, not even a cough from the carburettor.

He yelled, 'What the fuck's the matter with you, you evil fucking bastard!' and pulled on the cord as hard as he could. He put his entire body weight behind it, and when the cord ripped off in his hand he fell backwards and hit the bottom of his back on the hard ground.

A red mist descended in front of his eyes and he leapt to his feet, lifted the engine off the plank and staggered down to the jetty, where he pushed from the shoulder and hurled it as far out into the water as he could.

A few gulls bobbing close to the jetty panicked and flapped away as the engine hit the water and sank from view. Anders was panting with the exertion; he bent over, his hands resting on his knees, and whispered, 'That'll teach you. You weren't expecting that, were you?'

The gulls settled back on the surface, watching him with their black eyes.

When he came to his senses he realised that what he had just done wasn't particularly clever. It could have been a simple fault, and there were people in the village who knew about these things. At the same time he had a sudden urge to run away and hide. He had done something wrong, and now he needed to go and sit in a dark place where nobody would be able to find him.

The woodshed flashed through his mind. If he crept in beside a pile of wood and pulled a sack over his head, nobody would be able to see him.

Quick! Before somebody comes!

He turned and was halfway along the jetty, taking short, creeping steps before he pulled himself up. He shook his head and wrapped his arms around his body.

What am I doing?

He knew what he was doing: he didn't know what he was doing. One hound didn't know. They were circling around each other, sniffing at each other's tails. He hugged himself, said in a gentle, reassuring voice, 'It's OK. Everything's fine. I'm not cross. Nobody's cross.'

Sure?

'Yes, yes. Quite sure. The engine was stupid.'

Don't say that about the engine. It'll be upset.

It wasn't Maja's voice he was hearing, it was just his own thoughts, but they were being...guided. He was being led into patterns, ideas that were not his. He pressed his wrists against his temples.

This is driving me mad. That's the sort of thing people say, but this...this really is driving me mad.

He straightened up and took a couple of deep breaths. He was in control, he was Anders. He heard the faint soughing of the wind in his ears, the lapping of the waves and voices from over on the steamboat jetty. Agitated voices and the sound of children screaming. For a moment he thought it was something to do with him, but it was too far away. There were a lot of people standing on the jetty and there was some kind of quarrel, but he couldn't tell what it was about.

It's nothing to do with me.

He pulled himself together and walked away from the sea. Simon had said he could borrow his boat whenever he wanted, and that was precisely what he intended to do.

The confusion left him; with every step he took towards Simon's jetty, more and more of the morning's decisiveness and clarity returned. He knew what he had to do, he had a direction.

Now all he had to do was follow it.

Horrid children

Seven children in years 1 to 6 lived on Domarö. Seven children who stood on the steamboat jetty at quarter to eight every morning, waiting for the tender to the mainland, to Nåten and school. Adults and high-school children travelled earlier in order to get to their school in Rådmanby or to their jobs in Norrtälje.

Despite the fact that the children's ages ranged from Mårten and Emma in Year 1 to Arvid in Year 6, there was a sense of community in the group. The smaller ones were taught the routine by the older ones, and they travelled together, waited together and made sure everything happened as it should.

Up to a point this sense of community extended into life at school as well. If a younger Domarö child was teased or bullied in the playground, it could easily happen that one of the older children from the group would step in and put a stop to it. Perhaps it was for the honour of Domarö, perhaps it was so that they could look each other in the eye, perhaps it was due to a spontaneous empathy, acquired during those mornings in the rain and cold, or brilliant sunshine.

At any rate, they were a group, and they knew it. There were seven of them, and they were from Domarö.

On this particular morning, several of the children were preoccupied with the large number of gulls gathered in the bay. The temperature had fallen by several degrees during the night, and the birds looked frozen as they sat there drifting along with the currents, shaking themselves from time to time as if to try and keep warm.

The children were more warmly dressed. Mårten and Emma wrapped up in snowsuits, Maria in Year 5 wearing an enormous hat and scarf, Johan and Elin in Year 3 somewhat more modestly but still warmly clad.

Arvid was inside the shelter, shivering. He had inherited a leather jacket from his grandfather and it was his most treasured possession, but it didn't provide much warmth on a day like today. His grandfather had worked for the coastguard and was immune to both the cold and the heat. He pulled nets out of holes in the ice with his bare hands and extinguished his cigarettes between his thumb and forefinger. He had been Arvid's idol, but he had died of cancer a few months earlier. Arvid had taken over his jacket and had discovered that it was much too big and provided little warmth. But it was Grandfather's and—if the truth were told—it also looked pretty good.

That made six children. There was no sign of the seventh yet. Sofia Bergwall, the daughter of Lasse and Lina. She was late this morning.

Maria gazed up towards the road. Despite the fact that Sofia was a year younger, she was Maria's best friend, and they had been together since they went to day care together. Waiting for the boat was boring when Sofia wasn't here. Maria turned towards the sea, and saw the tender approaching just beyond the carpet of gulls. It would be a few minutes before it hove to, but Sofia was always there in plenty of time. Maria chewed on her lip and spotted Sofia, walking up from the shop.

Maria waved, but her best friend didn't seem to notice her. There was something stiff and odd about the way she was walking; she was dressed in thin clothes and seemed preoccupied by some difficult problem. Maria knew what had happened to her father, Lasse, the previous day, and thought it probably had something to do with that.

Sofia didn't even say hello when she reached the jetty, she simply went and stood at the far end and stared at the gulls, which had begun to take off in disorganised flocks as the boat came closer.

'Soffi, what is it?' Maria placed a hand on her friend's shoulder, but Sofia merely snorted and turned away. Maria inspected her clothes and shook her head. It didn't make any sense. Sofia's mother always made sure Sofia was suitably dressed, but today she had no hat, no gloves, and only a thin anorak that wouldn't provide much protection from the wind.

There was an ache in Maria's chest. Ever since she was very small she had been a sensitive soul, who felt pain when someone else had a problem. Therefore she took off her scarf and began to wind it around Sofia's neck.

'You must be frozen, I mean it's—'

The words 'really cold' froze on her lips as Sofia turned around. The expression in her eyes was so horrible that Maria whimpered and let go of the scarf.

'Don't touch me!' snapped Sofia, and Maria held up her hands to defend herself or to indicate that she had no intention of doing anything else, but before she had time to say a word, Sofia grabbed hold of her jacket.

Arvid was studying the graffiti in the shelter. He heard Maria scream and didn't take any notice, assuming the girls were just being silly. But then the tone of the scream altered, and shortly afterwards he heard a splash.

Arvid looked out of the shelter just in time to see Sofia running over to Mårten and Emma. She grabbed their snowsuits by the chest and pulled them towards her. Emma managed to twist herself free, which gave Sofia two hands to hold on to Mårten. The little boy screamed at the top of his voice as Sofia dragged him towards the edge of the jetty and threw him over. The scream continued as he went over the edge, then stopped abruptly.

The tender was perhaps fifty metres from the jetty and the gulls rose into the air, hauled up into the sky like a flapping, screaming curtain.

The whole thing was so far beyond rhyme and reason that it took a few seconds before Arvid's brain was able to accept that they were not playing tag or some other game, that Sofia really had thrown little Mårten down into the ice-cold water.

And where's Maria?

Sofia bared her teeth and rushed towards the other children, who fled from the jetty with terrified squeals. It was like What's the Time, Mr Wolf?—but this wolf really was dangerous, and tiptoeing gingerly forward wasn't going to help.

As Arvid ran over to the edge of the jetty he could see that the tender was still too far out for Roger to be able to help. He looked down into the water and saw Mårten's pale blue snowsuit just below the surface.

He hesitated. He shouldn't be the one doing this sort of thing. He was only thirteen and the temperature of the water was close to freezing and there must be some adult who—

Grandfather. Grandfather would—

He didn't get any further before his hands took the initiative, unzipping the leather jacket and dragging it off. The pale blue of Mårten's snowsuit grew darker as he sank, and there was no one but

Arvid who could save him.

He had just managed to get the jacket off and was about to take a deep breath when a hard shove from behind sent him over the edge. He half turned and saw Sofia staring at him with madness in her eyes before he fell two metres and hit the water.

The cold knocked all the air out of him and his lungs contracted, preventing him from taking in more. He could see the sharp prow of the tender perhaps ten metres away. It was heading straight for him, and he could hear the engines roaring as Roger slammed it into reverse.

Purely by exerting his muscles Arvid managed to take in a tiny amount of air, held his breath, put his face in the water and swam downwards. His nose, mouth and eyes froze instantly, but right now there was only one thing on his mind, and that was to reach the blue shape directly below him.

He swam another stroke and the roaring of the engines filled his head as he felt his feet leave the surface. There was an immense pressure in his ears and he tried unsuccessfully to kick off his heavy boots, but he took another stroke, the last one before he ran out of air, stuck out his arm and managed to grab hold of the fabric on Mårten's back.

Incredibly, he had the presence of mind to swerve to one side before he swam to the surface. He flapped his free arm, pushed as hard as he could with his legs and forced Mårten up out of the water as if he were lifting a trophy before following on himself, gasping for air.

Their heads broke the surface just a metre from the metal hull of the tender. He could no longer hear anything, it was as if he were wearing earplugs made of ice. Above his head, the sky was swarming with silent gulls.

Mårten's snowsuit was full of water and would have dragged them both down, but Arvid managed to grab hold of one of the tractor tyres fixed to the edge of the jetty, then pulled himself along and switched his grip to the next tyre. When he reached the corner of the jetty he heard someone shouting to him from far away, but took no notice. He kept Mårten's head above the water and made his way towards the shore.

He edged around the corner and became vaguely aware of another figure crawling ashore a few metres away.

Maria...good...good...

His hands were no longer prepared to obey him. When he tried to get a grip on the last tractor tyre his fingers were frozen stiff, and slipped on the hard rubber surface.

Someone reached down from the jetty with a boat hook, but he couldn't manage to close his fingers around the pole. He thought he was going to sink, but the hook caught the neck of his pullover and he was pulled towards the shore with his burden.

After a couple of metres he noticed that his legs were moving oddly, and realised they were dragging along the bottom. The hook was detached from his pullover and water splashed in his face as Roger jumped in and hauled him ashore. He noticed that Maria was already lying there, staring at him with wide-open eyes and a face as white as paper.

Somebody was tugging at him.

'Arvid, Arvid. Let go. You need to let go.'

Roger was pulling at his left arm, the arm that was holding Mårten. Arvid tried to let go, but couldn't; the arm was locked. The only place where there was any warmth left was inside his mouth, and he managed to part his lips and say, 'I can't.'

He looked at Mårten and saw something wonderful. His mouth was moving, and he coughed up a little water over Arvid's face. He was alive. With gentle force Roger managed to move Arvid's arm and release Mårten.

While Roger worked to get Mårten's snowsuit off and wrap him in his own fleece, Ulla and Lennart Qvist, who had been aboard the tender, came to look after Maria and Arvid.

There was the sound of screaming from up on the jetty, and when Arvid managed to get to his feet with some support, he could see that two adults were holding on to Sofia, who was flinging herself from side to side, howling like an animal and trying to bite them. The gulls were circling above the scene like an excited audience at a boxing match, flapping around them, screaming and urging them on.

Mårten wept in Roger's arms as he was carried home, and Maria was also sobbing, her lips blue with cold, as Ulla led her along by the hand. Arvid took off his pullover and Lennart wrapped him in a big overcoat, patting him on the shoulder.

'Well done, Arvid. Well done.'

Arvid's jaws were trembling so much he could hardly speak. He nodded stiffly towards the crazed gulls and Sofia, who was being dragged along swearing and kicking. 'Why. Is it. Like this?'

'Nobody knows,' said Lennart. 'Nobody knows. Let's get you home.'

On shaking legs Arvid allowed himself to be led around the sea buckthorn thicket and up towards the village. When he saw that his path was going to cross Sofia's, he stopped.

'Could you do me a favour?'

'Of course,' said Lennart. 'Anything.'

'Could you get my jacket?'

While Lennart went back for the jacket, Arvid stood there with the overcoat tightly wrapped around him, watching as Sofia was bundled towards her home. The gulls pursued them, circling above their heads as if they had spotted their prey and were just waiting for the right moment to swoop.

When Lennart came back Arvid returned his coat, pulled the leather jacket over his bare skin and said he would be fine now. Then he staggered homeward, with water squelching in his boots.

When he reached the shop he stopped and looked along the track where Mårten was being carried home to his mum and dad, still wailing loudly, but alive. Arvid pulled his jacket closer and thought about how he felt.

It was strange, somehow.

For the first time it felt as if the jacket was warming him. And it was no longer too big. It fitted. Perfectly.

Back to Gåvasten

The cold nipped at Anders' cheeks and brought tears to his eyes. He had wrapped up as warmly as he could and was wearing a lifejacket under his padded jacket, but the headwind found its way into every nook and cranny and by the time he was halfway to Gåvasten, he was frozen through.

At first he had thought there was something odd about his eyes, that he was seeing dots, but from this distance he could see that the dots swarming across the sky around Gåvasten were actually birds. It was impossible to tell what kind they were, but it looked as if they were different sizes, and therefore different species.

Simon's twenty-horsepower engine hummed monotonously and the fibreglass hull slapped against the waves. Anders' face was so stiff with the cold that he no longer felt it when a few drops flew up and hit his cheeks or chin. He kept his eyes fixed on Gåvasten and his left hand clenched around the throttle, turned up to maximum. He was an arrow fired from Domarö, heading straight for his target: the lighthouse.

And yet he couldn't prevent something from seeping in and eating away at his deep-frozen resolve. An unpleasant, jelly-like quivering was growing in his chest the closer he got to the lighthouse and the teeming birds. A feeling as familiar as an obnoxious relative: fear. Good old fear, causing the arrow to veer off-course and slow down.

The resonance of the engine deepened as he cut the speed and allowed the boat to chug along for the last hundred metres. The birds around the lighthouse really were a mixture of species. The wildly flapping wings of golden-eyes, the heavy bodies of the eider ducks and the elegance of the gulls, soaring along on the air currents. There were even a number of swans bobbing on the sea off the lighthouse.

What are they doing?

Many of the birds were up in the air circling around the light-house, but even more were gathered on the surface of the water. Their behaviour didn't appear to have any purpose, other than to show a united front, to say: *Here we are.*

And yet it was unpleasant. Anders hadn't see *The Birds*, but he could well imagine what it would be like if such a large number of birds decided to attack. They were showing no inclination to do so at the moment, but perhaps when he stepped ashore?

When the boat slipped in among the first group of birds, they paddled quickly out of the way glaring at him aggressively, he thought. He decided to use the only weapon, or at least protection, to which he had access.

He let go of the throttle and allowed the engine to idle as he picked up the plastic bottle, took a deep breath then took a couple of swigs of the wormwood concentrate.

The nausea seared his mouth, his throat, his stomach, and the flames shot up into his head, licking around his brain. He fought back the urge to vomit, put the top back on and grasped the throttle. The birds swam away, leaving him a feather-free route up to the rock.

He hesitated for a few seconds before setting foot ashore. Then he climbed out of the boat and looked around. The birds were still whirling around in the air and it seemed to him that their screams were becoming more intense. But they weren't attacking. He pulled up the boat as far as he could and fastened the mooring rope to a rock.

And so he was standing on Gåvasten once again.

The first and last time he had been here before, the rocks had been covered in snow. Now he could see that they had been polished by the sea, and that veins of pink and white ran through the grey rock, forming a pattern beneath the spatter of guano. He stood motionless, his arms dangling by his sides and his mouth open, as the pattern freed itself from its foundation and drifted together, forming itself into…an alphabet.

A language.

The lines running vertically and horizontally, the separate dots and curlicues were all characters, parts of a system of writing that was so complex his brain was unable to encompass it; he could only establish that it existed.

Like a baby who has picked up a bible and tosses it aside when it proves impossible to chew, Anders tore his gaze away from the writing on the rock and carried on up towards the eastern side of the island. It was not his language, it meant nothing to him.

He didn't know how to look because he didn't know what he was looking for, but his consciousness was sounding out the area as if it were a knot that must be untied. He needed to find the point where there was a little slack, where he could get his finger in and start to work it.

He couldn't find any such point. The world was impenetrably solid and filled with messages he was unable to interpret.

The formation of the rock was like a broken flight of steps leading down into the sea, the individual free-standing blocks of stone and the lines of gravel in the crevices formed new characters that wanted to say something. When he looked up it was to the disorienting sight of the flocks of birds creating figures against the sky, figures that continuously dissolved and reformed into new beings.

Everything is talking to me. And I don't understand what it's saying.

Anders crouched down and dipped his hands in a puddle of crystal clear rainwater, rubbed his face and eyes, closed his eyes for a while.

When he opened them a little of the visionary impression had left him, and he was able to walk up to the lighthouse, screwing up his eyes as he went. The door was unlocked, as it had been on the previous occasion. One thing he was grateful for: the hallucinatory effect of the wormwood blocked almost all his memories. In fact, what it actually did was to place him so powerfully in the *here and now* that it was painful. But it was still better than the alternative.

He opened the door and was welcomed by the little collection box and the request for money. He rummaged in his pockets but didn't find any, and walked past. He stopped and giggled.

Perhaps the birds will attack now.

No. As he walked up the stairs he could hear them outside, still screaming and clucking to one another. Did they understand each other's language, the different species? Probably not, but in that case how did they know they were supposed to gather like this?

Everything is talking. Everything is listening.

He stroked the outside wall with his right hand as he climbed upwards. He passed the circular room and carried on up the stairs to the reflector.

The room looked just as he remembered it, nothing had changed. The big windows and the gleaming mirrors on the reflector bounced the daylight around so that the room seemed brighter than outdoors. He went and stood in the spot where Maja had asked him *What's that?* and looked out across the sea, waiting to see what he might feel.

At first there was nothing.

His eyes were unusually sensitive to the light, and despite the fact that the sky was covered in clouds, he was forced to squint in order to be able to see out across the slightly foaming water. He looked down at the sharp edges of the rocks, the congregating birds, and felt the poisonous liquid running through his body like a fluorescent green thread.

Nothing.

Then it came. Faintly at first, like the perception of another person's breathing in a darkened room. Then stronger. A knowledge that was hard to describe. Anders gasped and stumbled, leaned against the glass case surrounding the reflector.

The depths.

The depths. How deep...

He was standing on nothing. The depths were everything.

It is said that only ten per cent of an iceberg protrudes above the surface of the water. What Anders perceived throughout his entire body in one cold, burning moment was similar, only much bigger, more intense: what was sticking up, what he was standing on wasn't even *one* per cent. It was almost nothing. A strand of cotton over an abyss.

His legs gave way and he sank down, falling backwards until his head hit the wooden floor.

We are so small. Just poor little people with our flashing lights.

He had foolishly thought that the *lighthouse* had something to do with it all. Its ghostly eye flashing across the sea at night had misled him. But what is a lighthouse? A human invention of wood and stone. A building with a lamp inside it, nothing more. The light can be extinguished and the building can decay, but the depths...

The depths remain.

The insight slipped out of him like a wave retreating from the shore, and he lay on the floor with only the dry knowledge left. The rivulets of poison were diluted in his blood, and he breathed deeply, out and in, out and in.

He rolled over on to his side and glanced over the graffiti on the whitewashed interior walls of the lighthouse.

FRIDA WAS HERE 21/06/98

J M

When in trouble, when in doubt
Run in circles, scream and shout

NÅTEN BOYS = IDIOTS

One sentence was written in bigger, clearer letters than most of the rest. Anders thought he remembered seeing it the last time he was here, but he hadn't attached any importance to it. Now he did.

Printed beneath the date 28/01/89 it said:

STRANGE WAYS, HERE WE COME.

Henrik and Björn had disappeared some time around that date.

Strangeways, Here We Come was the title of The Smiths' last album.

They had sat here and written, almost carved that final message on the wall with a ballpoint pen and then...set off. Along the strange ways.

They knew. They knew what they were doing.

Anders got to his feet and raced down the stairs.

'I'm going to get you, you bastards! I know where you're hiding and I'm coming to get you! Somehow, I swear to God, I'm going to get her back!'

Anders was standing on the eastern rocks screaming to the sea and the wind, screaming along with the birds that drifted past his face like a gigantic curtain that his arms were too short, his knowledge too limited, to be able to peep through. But he would do it. Somehow he would do it.

He went on screaming and threatening the sea until his throat was swollen and his rage had subsided.

When he came to his senses again he saw that the birds had moved closer. Almost all the golden-eyes, ducks and swans had gathered on the surface of the water off the eastern side of Gåvasten. They were there in front of him, bobbing on the waves. Thousands of birds packed so tightly together that it looked as if it would be possible to walk a hundred metres out to sea on their backs. The gulls had stopped circling around the island and were now flapping directly in front of him in a single white cloud that seemed to rise from the sea and drift towards the spot where he was standing.

At any moment an audible or inaudible command would reach them and he would drown in a swarm of hacking, tearing beaks.

They understand. I have to get away from here.

Slowly, one step at a time, he walked backwards towards the boat, never taking his eyes off the birds. If they showed the least sign of attack there was a chance he could make it into the lighthouse before they tore him apart—just as long as he made sure to keep watching them.

The lichen made the rocks slippery as soap on this side and he lost his footing once. But still he kept his eyes on the birds and although he banged his hip sharply, he managed to stop himself from falling.

The flock of gulls had moved closer; they were circling above the rocks on the eastern side as he undid the mooring rope without looking at his hands, and shoved the boat out into the water with his back. The agitated screams of the gulls shredded through the air and filled his head, making it impossible to think rationally. The only thing he could see in his mind's eye was: *Get the boat out. Get away from here.*

The boat moved smoothly away from the rocks and he walked backwards in the water, pushing off from the seabed with one foot as he climbed aboard. The boat glided a few metres away from the island. There was no longer any chance of making it to the lighthouse. He didn't dare turn his back on the gulls to start the engine, so he grabbed an oar and paddled backwards like a gondolier, one side at a time.

When he was about a hundred metres from Gåvasten, the birds began to calm down. The flock of gulls broke up and spread out into a thinner cloud that encompassed the whole island. Anders dropped the oar, sat down and let out a long, quivering breath. He put his head in his hands and caught sight of the plastic bottle, rolling around on the deck.

He had forgotten about it, forgotten that its contents could have protected his retreat from the menacing birds. Perhaps it had done so anyway. He looked at the bottle, which did a half roll as a wave lifted the boat. The label with his father's childish handwriting came into view: WORMWOOD.

He understood. At last he understood what had happened to his father. That day and all the other days.

Wormwood

He really ought to go home and put the cash in his money box, but Anders wanted to hang out for a while enjoying the feeling of being *rich*. His pockets full of money. Like the boy with the golden trousers, he could simply peel off a note with a rustling sound, and another, and another.

He went up to the shop with no other plan in mind: just to saunter around as the richest boy on Domarö for the time being.

The boats were still out searching for Torgny Ek, but the crowd on the jetty had thinned out. Anders hesitated. If he went down to the jetty there would be a load of adults asking him questions, and he didn't know if he wanted that.

'Hi.'

Cecilia pulled up beside him on her bike. Anders raised a hand in greeting. When the hand was in the vicinity of his nose, he realised it smelled of fish. He shoved both hands in his back pockets and adopted a relaxed attitude.

'What are you doing?' asked Cecilia.

'Nothing special.'

'What's going on down on the jetty?'

Anders took a deep breath and asked, as if in passing, 'Would you like an ice cream?'

Cecilia looked at him as if he were joking, and smiled uncertainly.

'I haven't got any money.'

'I have.'

'Are you paying, then?'

'Yes.'

Anders knew perfectly well that it was a strange question to ask, a strange thing to do. But none of the others were around, and his pockets were full of money. He just had to ask her.

She pushed her bike up to the shop and he walked alongside her, still with his hands in his back pockets. She had put her hair up in two medium-length plaits, she had freckles on her nose and he was struck by an urge to touch her plaits. They looked so…soft.

Fortunately his hands were deep in his back pockets, which prevented him from giving in to that particular impulse.

Cecilia propped her bike against the wall and asked, 'So did you sell a lot of herring, then?'

'Yes, this morning. Loads.'

'I usually sell Christmas magazines.'

'Is that worth doing?'

'It's OK.'

Anders started to relax properly. This was the first summer he had really considered the fact that he was different from his friends, who were only summer visitors. That there might be something embarrassing about the fact that he sat outside the shop selling herring and ended up with his hands smelling of fish. That he was…a bit of a hick. But it turned out that Cecilia sold things too. Although presumably Christmas magazines didn't smell.

They went into the shop and studied the contents of the freezer.

'So what can I have?' asked Cecilia.

'Whatever you like.'

'Whatever I like?' She looked at him suspiciously. 'A Giant Cornet?'

'Yes.'

'*Two* Giant Cornets?'

'Yes.'

'*Three* Giant Cornets?'

Anders shrugged his shoulders and Cecilia opened the lid. 'What are you having?'

'A Giant Cornet.'

She picked up two Giant Cornets and when Anders leaned over to pick up another, Cecilia slapped him on the shoulder, said 'I was only joking, idiot!' and handed him one of the ice creams she was holding.

At the till Anders pulled a ten kronor note out of his pocket without managing to create that special rustle you always heard when the boy with the golden trousers took out his cash.

They sat down on the bench outside the shop to eat their ice creams. Anders told her what had happened that morning, and Cecilia was seriously impressed that he had seen a person *drown himself for real.*

While they were eating their ice creams, while Anders was telling his story, while they sat looking out over the water afterwards, a little prayer was running through Anders' head: *don't let anybody come along, don't let anybody come along.* He wondered if Cecilia was thinking the same thing, or if this sort of thing was perfectly normal for girls.

OK, it wasn't particularly embarrassing to be sitting here with Cecilia eating ice creams that he had paid for, but nor did he want the moment, the atmosphere to be broken. Even though he felt uncertain and didn't really know how he ought to behave, he was having such a *fantastic* time. It was just the *best*, sitting here with Cecilia.

When they had finished their ice creams and looked at the sea for a while, Anders' suspicion that girls were more used to this sort of thing was confirmed when Cecilia stood up, wiped her hands on her shorts and said, 'Shall we go back to yours?'

All he could do was nod. Cecilia picked up her bike and pointed to the parcel rack. 'Hop on. I'll give you a lift.' He sat astride the parcel rack and Cecilia kicked off and rolled the bike down the hill from the shop.

There was nothing else to do. It was completely natural. At first he tried to keep his balance by hanging on to the back of the parcel rack, but the track was uneven and he wobbled and nearly made the bike fall over. So he placed his hands on her hips.

He could feel the warmth of her skin on his palms, the sun was shining in the sky and the wind was caressing his forehead. They coasted through the village and he held on to her. The few minutes it took to coast and pedal to his house were the happiest he had experienced in his life, so far. They were…perfect.

Cecilia parked her bike by the woodshed and nodded in the direction of the smoker, which was still giving off a faint aroma.

'We were going to do some smoking, but we didn't get round to it.'

'Were you going to smoke buckling?'

'Mm.'

Anders didn't bother to correct her. Buckling was smoked herring. To say 'smoked buckling' was like saying 'a curved bend' or 'a cold ice cream', but this was probably the sort of thing a hick would know, and not something to show off about.

When Cecilia was with him he saw it so clearly: his garden didn't look like theirs. In his garden there was a woodpile and smoke and old rubbish his father had saved because 'it might come in handy'. No beautifully mown lawns or fruit bushes in neat rows. No badminton court and no hammock. He didn't usually notice. But now he noticed.

Cecilia walked towards the house and Anders thought that at least his *room* looked like the others' rooms, fortunately.

What are we going to do in my room? What are girls interested in?

He had loads of comics. He didn't know whether Cecilia read comics. He had books. Maybe they could *bake* something? He could bake sticky buns and scones. Did she like baking?

He didn't get any further in his pondering, because Cecilia had stopped and was looking down at something on the ground. He hurried over to her and when he saw what she was looking at, his lungs sank down to his thighs.

Beside the spindly gooseberry bush next to the house, his father was lying on his stomach with his arms by his side, face down on the ground. Cecilia was on her way over to him, but Anders grabbed her shoulder.

'No,' he said. 'Come on. Let's go.'

Cecilia pulled herself free. 'Don't be silly, we can't leave him like that. He could suffocate.'

Anders had never seen his father so drunk that he lay down and went to sleep like this in the middle of the day, but the drinking itself was nothing new to him. Sometimes when he got home in the evening his father would be sitting there with glassy eyes, talking rubbish, and at those times Anders tried to stay out of the house as much as possible. Right now he was so embarrassed he didn't know where to put himself.

Cecilia crouched down beside his sleeping father and shook his shoulder. 'Hey,' she said. 'Hello.' She turned to Anders. 'What's his name?'

'Johan. Look, just leave him. He's drunk.'

'Johan,' said Cecilia, shaking him more roughly. 'Johan, you can't lie here.'

Johan's body twitched and a deep cough rumbled up through his chest. Cecilia drew back as Johan raised his head and rolled over on to his side. He had been lying on a half-full plastic bottle that had been squashed out of shape by the weight of his body.

He caught sight of Cecilia and his eyes were made of dirty glass, a thread of saliva dangled from the corner of his mouth down to the grass. He smacked his lips, cleared his throat and slurred, 'Love one another.'

The humiliation crushed Anders into the ground and splashed his cheeks with red. His father's hand was groping for Cecilia's foot as if he wanted to get hold of it. When he couldn't reach he looked up at her and said, 'Just be careful of the sea.'

The shame of it all exploded into blind rage and Anders ran over to his father, aimed a kick. However, a faint glimmer of sense made him change the direction of the kick at the last moment, so that instead of his father's head he caught the plastic bottle, which bounced away across the overgrown lawn.

It wasn't enough. His father attempted a foolish smile, and Anders was about to hurl himself at him to beat the rage out of his body and into his father's when Cecilia grabbed his arm and pulled him away.

'Stop it! Stop it! There's no point.'

'I hate you!' Anders yelled at his father. 'I really hate you!'

Then he fled. He had no words to say to Cecilia, nothing that could excuse or explain. He was shit, with a shit father, and worse than that, he was a hick who was shit. *None* of the others had parents who did this sort of thing. They drank wine, they were fun. They didn't lie there dribbling outside their cottages in broad daylight. That's what the fathers of useless country kids did.

He ran across the rocks down to the boathouses in the harbour, he just wanted to get away, away, away. He would pick up a great big rock and jump in the sea, he would obliterate himself, he would no longer exist.

He passed the boathouses and ran out on to one of the small jetties where brightly-coloured leisure boats were moored, he ran all the way to the end and stopped, looking down at the sparkling water. Then he sat down, right on the edge of the jetty.

I'm going to kill him.

He'd been sitting there for a long time, weighing up different ways of killing his father, when he heard footsteps behind him on the jetty. He thought about jumping in the water, but stayed where he was. Then he heard Cecilia's voice.

'Anders?'

He shook his head. He didn't want to talk, he wasn't here, he wasn't Anders. There was a faint rustle of fabric from Cecilia's shorts as she sat down behind him on the jetty. He didn't want her to console him or to say something nice, something to smooth over the situation. He wouldn't believe it anyway. He wanted her to go away and leave him alone.

They sat like that for a while. Then Cecilia said, 'My mother's the same.'

Anders shook his head again.

'She is,' said Cecilia. 'Well, not *quite* as bad. But almost.' When Anders didn't say anything, she went on, 'She drinks a lot and then… she does the stupidest things. She chucked my cat off the balcony.'

Anders half turned around. 'Did it die?'

'No. We live on the first floor. But it was scared after that. Of practically everything.'

They sat in silence. Anders pictured the cat being hurled off the balcony on the first floor. So Cecilia lived in an apartment. He turned so that he could see her out of the corner of his eye. She was sitting cross-legged on the jetty, resting her chin on her hands. He asked, 'Do you just live with your mum?'

'Yes. When she's like that I usually go over to my grandmother's. She's great. She lets me sleep over and stuff.'

Anders had seen Cecilia's mother a couple of times, and she hadn't been drunk then. But when he thought about it now, she did have that look. Something strained about the face, something wet in the eyes. Maybe she had been drunk, but he hadn't been able to see it as clearly as in his own father.

They went on talking, and after a while the conversation moved

367

on to other topics. It turned out that Cecilia enjoyed baking as well, and that she read books too, mostly by Maria Gripe. Anders had read only one story by her, but Cecilia told him about some of her other books, and they sounded good.

With hindsight Anders could see that that day had mostly brought good things. It wasn't until the following summer that he and Cecilia had kissed each other and become a couple up on the big rock.

But it all started on that day.

Homeward bound

The engine started first time and Anders roared away from Gåvasten. The speed made him feel safe, he didn't think a gull could manage fifteen knots. When he had travelled a few hundred metres he looked back. The gulls had reverted to circling around the lighthouse.

He picked up the plastic bottle and waggled it back and forth in his free hand. The liquid was cloudy, opaque. The same painful clarity of vision that had affected him when he drank the poison had been in his father's eyes as he looked at Anders and Cecilia that day.

Love one another. Just be careful of the sea.

That was probably the story of Anders' life since that day, in brief. But why had his father drunk the poison in the first place? After all, it wasn't the sea that got him in the end.

Or was it?

Anders was twenty-two years old when it happened. By that time his father had taken early retirement, because he had 'lapses'. He would turn up to work at the shipyard feeling groggy, then he wouldn't turn up at all for a couple of days, then he'd come back, work normally for a week, then disappear again. It couldn't go on, and they managed to work out an early-retirement package.

However, he was still well liked, and if they needed an extra pair of hands they would ring him and see how things were. If he felt OK he would go along and pitch in wherever he was needed; he was paid in cash, no questions asked.

Among other things, he made a significant contribution to the building of the new shed for the storage of summer visitors' boats. When the topping-out party was being planned, he was naturally invited. The building wasn't completely finished, but the frame and the roof were in place, and it was a long time since they had thrown a party, so a party it was.

They drank and chatted, and it grew late. Towards the small hours Johan said goodnight and staggered down to the harbour to sail his boat home. There was nothing strange about that, everybody knew he could sail to Domarö blindfolded if need be.

So they said *Good night* and *Safe journey* and *Try not to crash into any elks*, and they never saw him again.

Nobody knew exactly what happened, but it was thought that when Johan got down to the harbour in the darkness, he was overcome by tiredness, or decided not to sail home. Instead he dragged a few tarpaulins together and made himself a bed. A few tarpaulins to serve as a mattress, and a few to cover himself up.

He was still lying there at seven o'clock in the morning when a lorry carrying sand backed down into the harbour area. Torbjörn, the driver, had been at the party and it had been a late night. When he saw the pile of old tarpaulins in his rear-view mirror he couldn't be bothered to get out and shift them, so instead he reversed straight over them.

The back wheel went over something, and he kept on going. The front wheel went over something smaller, and he kept on going. Only when he had gone a couple of metres further did he glance back at the pile of tarpaulins. He could see something trickling out from underneath them. Then he stopped and got out.

Afterwards Torbjörn would curse himself for failing to notice that Johan's boat was still in the harbour. If he had, he might perhaps have suspected something, because Johan did have a tendency to fall asleep just about anywhere. But he hadn't thought about it, and instead he had reversed over him with five tons of sand. What Torbjörn saw when he pulled back the tarpaulins would never leave him.

Something had been mentioned about a bottle of schnapps found beside Johan's body. Anders knew better now.

That night, faced with the sea, with the depths he must travel across, his father had suddenly been afraid. He had fetched the bottle of wormwood from his boat and tried to give himself courage, tried to protect himself.

Whether it was down to poisoning or a fear that would not pass, he had curled up under the tarpaulins. Like a child.

Like me.

Curled up under the covers, hoping it would go away and leave him alone.

Anders could see it in his mind all too clearly. The sea, the night, the fear. Leaving the lights and the people behind and suddenly being overwhelmed by the fear with which there can be no negotiation and for which there is only one cure: *Hide! Don't let it see you!*

'Oh, Dad...poor Dad...'

The fishing spear

Simon was sitting up straight at the kitchen table, his hands neatly folded on his knee as Anna-Greta rummaged around in the hidey-hole. She was in the process of selecting her bridal gown, and he was waiting to be shown the shortlist.

The morning had been dedicated to preparations for the following day. They had rung around and invited the people they wanted to invite, the community hall had been booked for a small reception and a buffet had been ordered from a caterer in Norrtälje. In the morning, before the wedding, Anna-Greta would travel across to a friend in Nåten who used to work as a hairdresser, and still knew a fair bit about how to make a person look their best.

'So what shall I do, then?' Simon asked.

Anna-Greta had laughed. 'Well, I suppose you'd better make the most of your last few hours of freedom. Practise doing up your bow tie.'

Simon had called Göran to invite him and they had also decided that Simon would make use of his time to come over and sort out Göran's well at last. He had to do something, otherwise he would just end up wandering around and getting nervous.

Despite the way Anna-Greta had fast-tracked the whole process, as if she just wanted it out of the way, things had changed when it was clear it was really going to happen. First of all there was the reception, then the buffet and the invitations. Then this idea that she needed to go and get herself done up beforehand. And now the dress.

This sudden burst of activity was not without its effect on Simon. He was sitting here now worrying about whether or not he should wear patent-leather shoes, and whether they still fitted. And even if he should use pomade in his hair.

Everything went quiet out in the hidey-hole as Anna-Greta gathered things together. Then she emerged. Simon straightened his back. To be honest, he thought the whole thing was quite amusing. The wedding and everything surrounding it had brought out a new side of Anna-Greta, more feminine than her everyday persona. He liked it, as long as it didn't go too far.

She came into the kitchen with a pile of dresses over her arm and something in her hand, which she put down on the worktop. She held the dresses up in front of her one by one, and Simon expressed a preference for a beige one in a heavyish fabric, embroidered with white flowers. It turned out that this was Anna-Greta's favourite too, and so the matter was settled. When Anna-Greta had put away the rejected dresses, she picked up the item from the worktop and placed it on the table in front of Simon.

'Do you remember this? I found it out there.'

The object lying on the table was a small fishing spear made of metal. Simon picked it up and turned it over in his fingers.

Oh yes, he remembered it all right.

When Johan was eighteen, he and Simon had worked together to dig a herb bed next to Anna-Greta's house. While he was digging Johan had found the fishing spear. They had borrowed books to check it out, and had come to the conclusion that it was at least a thousand years old.

The find aroused Johan's interest, and during that summer he borrowed more books and read up on the subject. What fascinated him most was that their patch of land, the place where their house stood, had once been under water. Deep under water.

He had read about land elevation in school, of course, learned that the islands were rising out of the sea by about half a centimetre per year. But the spear made it real and concrete. A person in a boat, someone who was out spearing fish, had passed directly over their garden a thousand years ago, and dropped their spear. It was a thought that wouldn't let Johan be.

Reading had never been a passion for him, but all that summer he studied the history of the archipelago in general and of Domarö in particular. It went so far that he even considered applying to university to study geology or something similar, but when the autumn came he managed to get a place as an apprentice at the shipyard in Nåten, and his plans for higher education were abandoned.

The fishing spear was forgotten, and finally ended up in the hidey-hole.

Simon balanced the spear on his index and middle fingers. It weighed about half a kilo, and had probably been attached to a stick, which had rotted away long ago. The fish had been speared, lifted out of the water and eaten. The person who had been hunting the fish had probably made a new spear, hunted more fish and eaten them, but to no purpose. He too had eventually fallen to the bottom of the sea or on to the ground and rotted away. Only the spear still existed.

'Anna-Greta?' asked Simon. 'What actually happened to Johan?'

Anna-Greta folded the bridal gown carefully and placed it in a plastic bag to protect it. Simon didn't know if it was a stupid question, but in a way she had brought the topic up herself by bringing him the spear.

He had begun to think he wasn't going to get an answer when Anna-Greta laid the plastic bag on the kitchen sofa and said, 'Have you heard of something called Gunnilsöra?'

'Yes,' said Simon. 'It's that island you can only see sometimes. The one that appears and disappears. Why?'

'What do you think about it?'

Simon didn't understand where the conversation was going, but replied as best he could. 'I don't know that I *think* anything about it, really. I know it's been interpreted as everything from the shores of Paradise to the dwelling of the Evil One. But it's some kind of optical phenomenon, surely? Something to do with the weather.'

Anna-Greta ran her finger over the spear, which was clean and smooth after Johan had cleaned it. 'It called to him. He caught something he shouldn't have caught.'

'Called to him? What called to him?'

'He said it was an island over towards Gåvasten. But that it wasn't Gåvasten. That it kept moving. One night it was just off the Shack, he said. And it was calling to him. Don't you remember how frightened he was, Simon? How frightened he was all the time?'

'Yes,' said Simon. He remembered both the enthusiastic boy who had dug up the spear, and the increasingly confused and distant man the boy had become. 'But this sounds crazy. An island? Hunting a person?'

Anna-Greta leaned towards him and lowered her voice to a whisper. 'Haven't you heard the sea? Heard it calling?'

Only a week ago Simon would have been concerned about Anna-Greta's mental health if she had asked him a question like that with such quivering earnestness. A week ago he hadn't seen the depths, hadn't sunk a body into those same depths.

'I don't know,' he replied. 'Maybe. Have you heard it?'

Anna-Greta looked out of the window and her gaze reached far into the distance, to the outermost shipping lanes. 'Have I told you about Gustav Jansson?' she asked. 'The lighthouse keeper? On Stora Korset?'

'Yes. You knew him, didn't you?'

Anna-Greta nodded. 'It all started with him. For me.'

The keeper

Stora Korset is the last outpost facing the Åland Sea. The island is so remote that the lighthouse keeper there receives what is known as an isolation supplement in addition to his normal pay. A little bonus for enduring the loneliness.

From the end of the 1930s to the beginning of the 1950s, it was Gustav Jansson who ran the whole show out there. He originally came from Domarö, but found it difficult to get on with people, and when the post of lighthouse keeper became available he took it as an opportunity to be left in peace at last. Then he spent thirteen years there with four hens as his only company.

He did *not* like the war. The din of practice firing and drift mines that had to be rendered harmless was one thing, but the worst thing was that visitors came to the island. Military personnel knocking on his door and asking questions about this and that, boats mooring at his jetty on reconnaissance missions. For a while there was talk of some kind of fortification on Stora Korset, but fortunately the plan came to nothing.

How terrible would that have looked! A tower with a gun emplacement down on the rocks below, soldiers stomping around smoking and frightening the hens. No, if that had happened he would have demanded to leave forthwith.

However, the war did bring one good thing.

Gustav Jansson had never been married. Not because he had anything in particular against women, no, he disliked men just as much. He was a solitary soul by nature and not suited to the companionship of marriage.

However, the war brought a woman he was able to tolerate. Not that he would have married her even if the possibility had existed, but he could tolerate her company and gradually found himself looking forward to the days she came to the island with snuff and newspapers.

He was enough of a man to appreciate female beauty in spite of everything, but what he liked most about Anna-Greta was that she didn't talk unnecessarily. Gustav's taciturnity made other people nervous, and they would chat away even more as if there were some kind of quota that had to be filled.

Not Anna-Greta. It was only after they had been acquainted for a year or so that they said any more than was absolutely necessary to carry out their transactions. At that time Gustav had bought a jigsaw puzzle from Anna-Greta. When he had done that one he wanted to buy a new one, which led to a certain amount of discussion. What kind of picture, how many pieces?

He ended up being a subscriber, and was particularly fond of puzzles with a sea motif. Since he had neither the space nor the inclination to keep the puzzles once he had completed them, he would place the pieces carefully, then when he had finished he would take the puzzle apart and put the pieces back in the box. Once a month Anna-Greta would come and replace the completed puzzle with a new one. At half price, because she could sell the old one again.

Over the years they had the odd conversation that was unrelated to their business dealings. A certain level of intimacy grew between them.

A couple of years after the end of the war, the general view was that Gustav Jansson had lost his mind. He did his job as lighthouse keeper extremely well, there were no complaints on that score, but you just couldn't talk to the man. He had spent too much time reading the Bible.

Anna-Greta knew better. It was true that reading the Bible was Gustav's only diversion apart from jigsaw puzzles out on his little island. He knew it inside out, and would even conduct conversations with himself, where one party was an austere prophet and the other a free-thinker.

But he wasn't mad. Gustav had simply realised that the surest way of frightening away unwelcome visitors was to preach at them. People became strangely uncomfortable when they heard the word of the Lord being intoned as they were tying up their boats at Gustav's jetty, and visits were kept short. Gustav was left in peace with his lighthouse and his God.

One afternoon at the beginning of the 1950s, Anna-Greta arrived later than usual for her monthly visit. With the north wind blowing at twelve metres per second, Gustav was surprised to see her at all. As Anna-Greta unpacked Gustav's purchases in the lighthouse keeper's cottage, the wind picked up even more. Some gusts made the wind gauge shoot up to twenty.

It looked as if Anna-Greta was going to have to stay on Stora Korset overnight. Gustav managed to get in touch with Nåten via short-wave radio, and they promised to make sure that Torgny, Maja and Johan would be informed that Anna-Greta was fine and was waiting for better weather conditions before setting off for home.

Although Anna-Greta and Gustav had a working business relationship and could perhaps even be called friends, it was still slightly embarrassing for Gustav to have womenfolk in the house overnight. He didn't know what to do with himself, he felt like a spare part in his own cottage.

It was a relief to discover that Anna-Greta wouldn't say no to a drop of schnapps. They sat across the kitchen table from each other, looking out over the rough sea, the breakers picked out by the flashing light, and drank a few glasses. Their embarrassment melted away.

No one who hadn't heard it for themselves would have believed it, but as the evening wore on, Gustav became positively chatty. He built up the fire and, as the temperature rose, told tales of foundered ships, maritime maps scratched into flat rocks and birds that collided with the lighthouse during their autumn migration and died by the barrowload.

When he pulled off his woolly jumper, Anna-Greta noticed that he was wearing his vest inside out, and mentioned this to him. Gustav looked at her, his eyes half-closed. 'Well, you have to protect yourself as best you can.'

'Surely you don't believe that nonsense, Gustav.'

'No. But I do believe in this,' said Gustav, taking out a bottle containing a cloudy liquid. 'And so should you. If you're going to spend the night here.'

Just to be polite Anna-Greta drank a shot glass of the bitter brew. She knew that many lighthouse keepers grew wormwood to use as a spice for their schnapps, but Gustav's version was overdone to say the least. It tasted disgusting.

'It's not much of a pleasure to drink,' said Gustav as Anna-Greta slammed her glass down on the table, 'but it protects life, and that might be worth something after all.'

Anna-Greta wasn't prepared to settle for a statement like that. The schnapps had made her eager to ask questions and it had made Gustav communicative, and so it happened that Gustav explained for the first time what the situation was with the sea.

It wanted him, he said. It called to him. It showed him things and made him false promises. It threatened him. He had turned to the Bible and found some guidance, but if the wormwood hadn't been growing in such profusion around the lighthouse, he would never have got the idea.

And it seemed to work. The sea no longer dared touch him in a menacing way, and the whispers of the night had as good as fallen silent since he started thinning his blood with wormwood.

The next morning the wind had eased, and Anna-Greta was able to set off home. Before she left Gustav gave her a coffee tin in which he had planted a wormwood root in a little soil.

'Take good care of it,' he said, half-joking in his deep, prophesying voice, 'so that it may be fruitful and fill the earth.'

Anna-Greta waved goodbye to Gustav and headed away from Stora Korset. She had gone no more than one nautical mile when she heard a strange noise coming from the engine. She cut the power immediately, afraid of doing more damage, and started to check connections and gaskets.

But the noise was still there, even though the engine was switched off. It was a caressing, whispering sound. She turned this way and that, but was unable to locate the source of the noise. She leaned over the rail and looked down into the water. The water was soft and welcoming, like the open arms of a lover. That was where she wanted to be.

That was the first time she heard the call.

She managed to break the spell by starting up the engine and concentrating on its even throbbing, but behind the sound of the cranks and pistons working away she could still hear the wordless whispering that held such a promise of warmth and simplicity.

Gustav had maintained that there were people on Domarö who knew the secrets of the sea, but never spoke of them. Anna-Greta thought she now understood why. There was one important detail missing from Gustav's private insight.

You can't hear it if you don't know about it.

Anna-Greta continued with her trading around the islands for a few more years, but after meeting Simon she sold her boat to avoid hearing the siren call of the sea. As time went by it appeared to have lost interest in her, and the calling stopped.

She had planted Gustav's wormwood on the edge of the shore down below the Shack, and there it spread in silence without anyone asking any questions.

Together with Simon, Anna-Greta entered a different life where the sea had no access. And things would probably have stayed that way if Johan had not come to her one evening many years later and told her about the island that was nagging at him, the voices that spoke to him.

To cut a long story short, she eventually managed to get out of Margareta Bergwall what there was to know about the sea. She was holding a trump card, because she could also provide something that had been lacking until now: a defence. Within a few years the wormwood was flourishing in several gardens belonging to those in the know, and Anna-Greta went up in everyone's estimation.

She took care not to involve Simon. Even if the sea was capricious and sometimes selected its victims from those who knew nothing, it was evident that the more you knew, the greater the risk of hearing the call. Or being taken.

So what became of Gustav Jansson, then?

Nobody knew what had happened. Perhaps he ran out of wormwood, perhaps something else went wrong, but in the bitter winter of 1957 the lighthouse was suddenly dark. It was a night of heavy snowfalls, and it wasn't until the following morning that anyone was able to get out to Stora Korset.

Gustav's outdoor clothes and boots were not in the cottage, so therefore he must have gone out on to the ice. However, the snowfall during the night had obliterated any tracks.

It was not until spring, when the snow on the ice melted, that they were able to find an indication of what had happened to Gustav. On the shining ice off Stora Korset, footprints could be seen. The snow had been compressed where Gustav had walked, and was melting more slowly than the loose snow around it.

A line of ghostly white footprints led across the ice in the direction of the mainland. It was possible to follow them for over a kilometre. Then they stopped. In the middle of nowhere, with Ledinge barely visible, the last footprint could be seen. Then the trail came to an end.

Perhaps the wind had managed to sweep away the rest of the trail after all, perhaps Gustav had collapsed on that very spot and then been collected or dragged or lifted in some unknown way.

He was gone, at any rate, and the following year the lighthouse on Stora Korset was automated. The lighthouse keeper's cottage was rented out to an ornithology group who mounted warning lights around the lighthouse to alert small birds to the danger.

Correction

Anna-Greta had just finished her story when the outside door opened. From the way it was yanked open and the footsteps that followed, they could tell it was Anders. When he came into the kitchen his eyes were staring and he was rubbing his hands in a way that Simon recognised from Johan. Nervously, impatiently.

'Just wanted to let you know I borrowed your boat,' said Anders. 'And that I'll be there tomorrow. Congratulations.'

Anders seemed to be on his way out, and Anna-Greta said, 'Sit down. Have a cup of coffee with us.' Anders chewed his lips and rubbed his hands, but then took off his jacket and hat and pulled out a chair.

'You've been out in the boat, then?' said Simon, and Anders nodded. Anna-Greta poured him a cup of coffee and Anders drank with both hands wrapped around the thin cup, as if he were frozen. 'I was on Gåvasten.'

Anna-Greta laid her hand on his arm. 'What's happened?'

Anders shrugged his shoulder jerkily. 'Nothing. It's just that I'm possessed by my own daughter and she's somewhere out there in the sea and the gulls are keeping watch...'

'There are several people,' said Anna-Greta. 'Several people who have become...possessed.'

Simon was surprised that Anna-Greta was speaking openly

about something to do with the sea. Perhaps she judged that the information could not be kept from Anders, that it was better if he found out like this. Anders' foot, which had been drumming on the floor, suddenly stopped and he listened carefully as Anna-Greta told him what had happened to Karl-Erik, and to the children on the jetty.

'Why?' asked Anders when she had finished. 'Why does this happen? How can it happen?'

'I can't answer that question,' said Anna-Greta. 'But it does happen. And you're not the only one.'

Anders nodded and stared into the bottom of his coffee cup. His lips were moving slightly, as if he were reading an invisible text in the coffee grounds. Suddenly he looked up and asked, 'Why are they horrible? I mean, it seems as if they're just...horrible.'

Anna-Greta replied as if she were weighing every single word before she uttered it. 'It's...it's virtually only horrible people...who have disappeared. Over the years. Horrible. Or aggressive. Elsa Persson. Torgny. Sigrid. And so on, back through time.'

Anders looked from Anna-Greta to Simon. 'Maja wasn't horrible,' he said, seeking support in their eyes. It wasn't there. Both of them avoided meeting his eye and said nothing. Anders leapt up from his chair and flung his arms wide.

'Maja wasn't horrible! I mean, she was only a *child*. She wasn't horrible!'

'Anders,' said Simon, reaching for his arm, but Anders pulled it away.

'What are you saying?'

'We're not saying anything,' said Anna-Greta. 'We're just—'

'No, you're not saying anything. You're not saying anything. You're saying that Maja...that she was horrible. She wasn't. That's completely wrong. It's crazy, what you're saying.'

'You're the one that's saying it,' said Anna-Greta.

'No, I'm not! It's completely wrong!'

Anders turned and rushed out of the kitchen. The outside door

381

opened and slammed shut. Simon and Anna-Greta sat in silence at the kitchen table for a long time. Eventually Anna-Greta said, 'He's forgotten.'

'Yes,' said Simon. 'He's made sure of that.'

The way it was

Anders wandered around the village. He went over to Kattudden and looked at the devastation there, sat on the shore for a while tossing pebbles through the thin covering of ice closest to the shoreline, went back to the old village and stood for a long time on the steamboat jetty staring over towards Gåvasten.

It was starting to get dark by the time he got back to the Shack. There was a note on the door from Simon, saying that he should come up to Anna-Greta's so that they could have a sensible conversation. Anders ripped it off and screwed it up.

The house was cold but he didn't want to light a fire, they would see the smoke from the chimney and would come down wanting to talk. He didn't want to talk, he didn't want to discuss this matter at all.

He fetched a blanket from the living room, wrapped it around himself and sat down at the kitchen table. In the last of the fading light he studied the photographs from Gåvasten. Cecilia's smile, Maja's absent expression, her gaze turned to the east.

He had put everything from his apartment in storage, thinking that he would make a completely fresh start here on Domarö. He hadn't even brought the photograph of Maja, the photograph of that mask.

The devil troll.

Anders rubbed his eyes and shook his head. He knew the photograph off by heart, didn't need it there in front of him. Maja's expectant expression when she had scared them.

Father Christmess, Christmess presents...

'No!'

382

Anders got up from the table and put his hands over his ears, as if he could stop the memory of her voice from finding its way in. Her thin little voice as she sat next to the tree singing...

'I saw Daddy killing Santa Claus, I...'

All children do that sort of thing!

Anders tore open the door of the larder and found one last wine cask, which he ripped open and drank so greedily that it ran down the sides of his mouth.

It was a wonderful life, I loved her so much...

'Stupid stupid idiots! I hate you!'

He spun around and caught sight of the bottle of wormwood, took a swig and swilled down the burning nausea with more wine. His stomach churned in protest and he ran to the toilet to throw up, but when he leaned over the bowl he could manage nothing more than a couple of sour belches. He sat down on the floor with his back against the warm radiator.

It wasn't true that Maja was horrible. Yes, she got annoyed easily. Yes, she had a lively imagination. But she wasn't horrible.

Anders jerked his head and hit the back of his neck on the edge of the radiator; shades of red flickered before his eyes. He staggered into the kitchen and pulled the photographs towards him again, looking at his family. Cecilia's warm, kind eyes gazing into his. His lower lip trembled as he picked up the phone and keyed in her number. She answered on the second signal.

'Hi, it's me,' he said.

He heard a faint sigh at the other end of the line. 'What do you want?'

Anders dragged his hand through his hair a couple of times, rubbed at his scalp. 'I have to ask you something. I have to say something. Maja wasn't horrible, was she?'

There was no reply, and Anders scratched at his scalp so hard that he drew blood.

'That's what they're saying,' he went on. 'That's what they think. But you and I...we know that's not true, don't we?'

With every second that passed without a word from Cecilia, something was growing inside his head, something that was so big and hurt so much that he could have ripped off his entire skull.

'Anders,' said Cecilia at last. 'Afterwards…you turned her into something else. Something different from what she was.'

Anders' voice sank to a whisper. 'What are you saying? She was wonderful. She was just…wonderful.'

'Yes, she was. That too. But—'

'I never thought anything else. I thought she was terrific. All the time.'

Cecilia cleared her throat, and when she spoke again there was a sharp impatience in her voice. 'If that's the way you want it. But that's not the way it was, Anders.'

'How was it, then? I always thought she was…the best you could imagine.'

'You made that up afterwards. You couldn't cope with her. You once joked about swapping her for—'

Anders slammed the phone down. It was dark outside the window now. He was so cold he was shaking. He sank to his knees and crawled to the bathroom, where he sat down with his back to the radiator again, staring into the washbasin and gnawing on his lips until there was a metallic taste in his mouth.

His hands lay loosely, the backs resting on the floor. There was a faint smell of piss and his mouth was sticky after a day without any liquid apart from wine and wormwood. He was a dried-up little nothing, the shrivelled remains of something that had perhaps not even existed.

'I am nothing.'

He said it out loud to himself in the darkness and there was consolation in those words, so he said them again, 'I am nothing.'

The fact that his life had been shit for the past few years wasn't exactly news. He knew that. But at least he had believed he had his memories of a life lived in the light, those precious years together with Cecilia and Maja.

But that wasn't true either. Not even that.

He sniggered. He sniggered a little more. Then he lay down flat on his stomach and licked the floor around the toilet, carried on up the pedestal. It tasted salty. Odd hairs stuck to his tongue, but he went on licking. He cleaned along the edges, licked off the coating on the seat and finished off by swallowing the gooey mess that had gathered in his mouth.

So. That was that. So.

He hauled himself to his feet, took a couple of deep breaths and said it again, 'I am nothing.'

There, he'd said it. All done. On steadier legs he went and sat down at the kitchen table again, looked over at Gåvasten which had begun to send its signals out into the night. He was floating on a sea in a state of dead calm. No waves of expectation or false memories obscured his view.

You have left me.

Yes. He had not been able to put his finger on the feeling when it was there, but now it had left him he felt its absence. Maja was no longer within him. He had driven her out. She had left him.

Nothing.

He sat for half an hour with his head resting on his arms, chilled to the bone as he accepted the way things had been. Maja had been dreadful. He had often wished they had never had her. He had said it out loud several times: that he wished she would just disappear. That they could swap her for a dog, a well-behaved dog.

I wanted her to disappear. And she disappeared.

She wept and screamed and kicked as soon as she didn't get her own way. She immediately smashed things that didn't behave in the way she wanted. She had no boundaries. They didn't dare let her watch children's programs after she threw a vase at the screen when a cartoon character said something stupid. How many hours had they spent sweeping up beads after Maja had tipped them on the floor, how many hours dealing with ripped-up drawing pads and comics?

That was the way it was. That was the way it had been. Like having a monster in the house, you had to be wary of every step, constantly on the alert to avoid provoking its fury. They had been to the clinic, they had seen a child psychiatrist, but nothing helped. Their only hope was that it would pass as she got older.

Anders' teeth were chattering, and he pulled the blanket more tightly around him.

This was the reason behind his enormous burden of guilt, the one he had tried to get rid of by drinking, then managed to suppress with patient effort: the fact that it was all his fault. He had wished she would disappear, simply disappear, and that was exactly what had happened. He had made it happen.

'All parents blame themselves when something happens to their children,' the family therapist had said when Cecilia forced him to go along with her.

No doubt that was true. But presumably those parents were able to arrive eventually at the conclusion that it wasn't their fault their child had been run over, developed cancer or got lost in the woods. At least they hadn't *wished* for it to happen. And if they had wished for it to happen, then at least their child had disappeared in a natural way, insofar as such a thing exists.

Maja had ceased to exist as if she had never been there, as if she had been...wished away. That couldn't happen, and therefore the explanation that Anders had wished her away was just as reasonable as any other, and that was the one he was sticking to. Whichever way he looked at it, he always came to the same conclusion: he had killed his own child.

It was only when Cecilia had left him and he had drunk himself into oblivion that a last glimmer of hope had appeared in the darkness: he began reshaping his memories. Through drunken days and nights he crafted a new past. One where Maja had been wonderful all the time and he had just loved her, pure and simple.

He had never had a bad thought about her, and therefore her disappearance was incomprehensible. It was a great tragedy that had nothing to do with him, he who had loved his daughter more than anything else in the world.

That's how his past had looked. Until now.

Anders gave a start as the telephone rang. He couldn't cope with answering it, and after six signals it fell silent once more. He couldn't talk to anyone. He didn't exist, he was nothing.

He rested his head in his hands again and listed to the emptiness. A new thought occurred to him.

So if I wanted to get rid of her...why was it so terrible when she disappeared? I mean, I should have been...pleased. In the end. What I wished for happened.

He got up from his chair. His stiff, frozen knees creaked as he took a turn around the floor.

The answer was obvious: deep down, right down inside he had never wanted that to happen. However difficult she was there were better times, good times. And they had started to become more frequent, last for longer. The change they had hoped for was on the way. That last day, the trip to Gåvasten was an example. She had almost behaved like a normal child for several hours.

And he had loved that child, that questioning, intense, living child, he had been prepared to wait for her through the hysterical outbursts and the smashed possessions. Things had been heading in the right direction. Then she disappeared, and he could remember only his bad thoughts, until it tipped over in the opposite direction.

I never knew her.

No. As he stood here now in the middle of the kitchen floor with the blanket around him, he realised the heart of the matter could be expressed in those terms: he had never known who Maja was. There had been too much wheeling and dealing. If children can be horrible, was Maja horrible, really? He had no idea. He didn't know her.

And now she had left him.

Heaven

'Daddy? What happens when you're dead?'

'Well, there's…'

'I think you go to heaven, don't you think so?'

'…well yes.'

'So what's it like there? Are there angels and clouds and so on?'

'Is that what'd you'd like?'

'No. I hate angels. They're horrible and ugly and they look stupid. I don't want to be with them.'

'So where do you want to be?'

'Here. But in heaven.'

'Then I expect that's what will happen.'

'No it won't! It's God who decides what happens!'

'In that case I expect God can decide that everybody can have things the way they want them to be.'

'But that's impossible.'

'Why?'

'Because then everybody would have their own heaven, and God wouldn't like that.'

'Don't you think so?'

'No. Because God is an idiot. He's made everything bad.'

Home visit

It was getting towards eight o'clock and Anders was still sitting at the kitchen table with the fragments of his former life spread out before him, trying to piece together something that might help him to get up, when he heard the moped.

They're coming.

He had almost managed to forget Henrik and Björn. After his long sleep they had been reduced to a distant dream, something that had happened long ago and had nothing to do with him. But here they were. The saddest boys in the world who had decided to carry out the bidding of the sea. Now they were coming to get him.

Come on then.

The moped's engine was racing, as if it were stuck in first gear. Perhaps he'd managed to damage it with the fire. The roaring engine drew closer to the house, and he waited for it to be switched off and the outside door to be opened. He was resigned, and placed one hand on top of the other on the table, waiting for whatever was going to happen.

The engine didn't stop when it reached the house, but carried on along the outside wall and across the rocks until the revs slowed and it stopped outside the kitchen window, rumbling to itself. They were waiting for him. He leaned on the table and pushed himself up, with the blanket around his shoulders like a coat, and walked over to the window.

He could see them down on the rocks like dark shapes. Henrik was in the saddle and Björn on the platform. Anders undid the window latch and pushed it open. Henrik cut the engine, down to a muted chugging.

'What do you want?' asked Anders.

'We may be dead,' said Henrik. 'But we will be right by—'

'Stuff all that. What do you want?'

'We'd like to smash some teeth—every single one in your head actually—because you're *bothering* us. You have to stop *bothering* us. If I were you I wouldn't bother. Really.'

'Why?'

'Because something bad could happen to someone you care about. Or put it this way...' Henrik went on with his manic paraphrasing, but Anders was no longer listening.

He had turned away from the window and was looking for the torch. Björn had something in his arms, and it if was what Anders thought it was...

The torch was in the drawer where all the rubbish was kept. He grabbed it and switched it on, hurled himself at the window and directed the beam at Björn as Henrik droned on with esoteric references to 'Girlfriend in a Coma' and how there were times when he could have murdered, on and on.

The light fell on Björn. He was sitting cross-legged on the platform, and in his arms he was holding the body of a child dressed in a red snowsuit. The reflector strip along the side glowed white and it was Maja's snowsuit, the one she had been wearing that last day.

Anders may have spent hours doing nothing but thinking, but now every thought was swept away in a second, and there was only action. He ran through the kitchen into the living room as the moped engine behind him began to race once again.

The door to the veranda was stuck and he lost a couple of valuable seconds when it refused to open. He hurled himself at it shoulder first and stumbled out on to the veranda just as he saw the lights of the moped bouncing across the rocks, on its way down to the sea.

Now I've got you, you bastards. You've got nowhere to go.

If he had stopped to reflect for a moment he might perhaps have realised that Henrik and Björn weren't stupid enough to think that he would simply stand and watch as they rode off with his daughter. That the fact they were heading for the sea was rather strange.

But he didn't stop to reflect. He had seen that Björn had Maja in his arms, he had heard Henrik threaten to harm her and he was acting in accordance with those two facts. With only his socks on his feet he took the veranda steps in two leaps and saw that Henrik and Björn were down by the shoreline.

Anders' lips curled up in a predatory grin. They had nowhere else to go. Even if they were ghosts, the moped was an ordinary moped and a moped cannot travel across water. It didn't occur to him that he had met them before, that he had no weapons to use against them now either. The only thought in his head was: *I've got you now*, and the knowledge in his body, the wormwood's knowledge, that they couldn't harm him either.

He was only five metres behind them when they rode out on to the water. Anders' body continued moving forward of its own volition until he fell over on the shoreline. The moped moved across the surface of the water past the jetty, and Henrik waved goodbye to him. Anders was left standing on the shore with clenched fists and the blood rushing through his head.

That's impossible! They can't do that!

'Stop, you bastards! Stop!'

Henrik waved his fingers over his shoulder again, and in a blind fury Anders raced out into the water. Which was not water. He had travelled a couple of metres before he realised he was standing on ice. For a moment he stopped dead in sheer physical amazement. He was still holding the torch, and shone it around him, ahead of him.

The sea had not frozen yet, but behind Henrik and Björn stretched a causeway of ice just wide enough for the moped to run along, a bridge of frozen water extending from the point where they had ridden into the water and set off.

Anders ran.

Under different circumstances he would have been astonished at the fact that he was running past his jetty with little waves lapping on either side of him, but the only thing he could see was the straight line between his body and Maja's, the distance he had to cover before he had her in his arms.

He ran with long strides and with every step his wet socks froze on to the ice a fraction before they were pulled free, which give him an excellent grip, and he was gaining on them, he was gaining on them. Before he set off on the water they had been twenty metres ahead of him. Now the distance was shrinking a little with every step he took. The moped was not travelling fast, and he would be able to catch up with it.

And then?

He wasn't even thinking about that.

The moon was high in the sky, creating a silvery path that fell diagonally across the causeway of ice. The beam of the lighthouse on

Gåvasten was flashing directly towards him. That was where they were heading, but they weren't going to get there. He would take them. Somehow he would take them.

He had run approximately three hundred metres from the shore. He could no longer feel his feet, they were nothing but a pair of frozen lumps moving him forward. He was so close to the moped that he could see individual strands of Henrik's hair in the moonlight, and he was trying to urge his body to make one final spurt when something fell from the platform.

Anders slipped, stumbled, fell to his knees on the ice and shone the beam of his torch on the bundle in front of him as the moped continued on its way, out to sea.

Maja, Maja, Maja...

It was her, there was no doubt. When he shone the torch he could see the patch on the chest of her snowsuit. Maja had stuck a knife in it when she was having difficulty putting it on, and Cecilia had mended it with a patch with a picture of Bamse on it.

'Sweetheart? Poppet?'

He crawled over to her and pulled her close. When he had the snowsuit in his arms he screamed.

She had no head.

What have they done, what have they done, what have they...

Everything went black and he collapsed on top of the little body that was beyond all help. He fell right on top of her, and it didn't matter. She had no head, no hands, no feet.

As the darkness tied a knot around his head he heard the gulls in the distance. Gulls that were flying at night. Maja's body crunched beneath his, was squeezed together.

He curled up on the ice and raised his head slightly, shone the beam of the torch on the neck of the snowsuit. There was no body inside. He reached out weakly and touched what was there instead. Seaweed. It was filled with wet bladder wrack.

He lay completely still for a moment digesting this fact as the screams of the gulls drew closer. He felt something cold trickle over his ear and raised his head, drew his legs up under him and managed to get to his feet with the snowsuit in his arms.

A hundred metres out to sea he saw the moped swing around. The headlight was facing him like an evil eye, and it was getting closer.

A trap. It was a trap.

He turned and staggered a few steps towards the shore. The surface beneath his feet squelched and splashed. The ice he had run along earlier had begun to melt. He covered perhaps another ten metres, and then his feet were under water and the ice bridge was swaying beneath him.

He clutched the snowsuit tightly and kept going. After a few metres more the ice broke beneath him and he sank down into the water. He had no weapons, and only the moon could see him. He lay in the cold sea and the headlight kept on coming closer.

Clever. Clever of them.

One tiny, tiny detail they had overlooked. The bladder wrack they had used to fill the snowsuit was acting as a kind of a float. He didn't sink immediately. He gained another minute's respite before the cold and the water took him.

Movement was almost impossible. His body had been frozen already, now it felt as if his skeleton itself was clinking with splintering ice as he began paddling towards the shore out of a pure and meaningless instinct for self-preservation.

The moped passed him and Henrik and Björn braked, blocking his way. He saw them only vaguely, as if a film of ice had formed over his eyes. Behind them hundreds of thin silhouettes moved against the starlit sky.

The gulls want to join in, too.

A kind of peace sank into his body, a hint of warmth. It was over now. His efforts had been in vain, but it didn't matter any more. It had given him something. He had at least got to see her snowsuit once again. That was something. He would have it with him in his watery grave. The only sad thing was that the gulls would tear at him too, perhaps even peck out his eyes before he...

'Come out,' screamed Henrik as a cloud of birds enveloped him, 'find the one that…' The high-pitched screams of the gulls filled the night as they dived on the boys on the moped and ripped at their hair, pecked at their faces.

Björn stood up on the platform, hitting out at the savagely flapping birds, but for every bird he managed to chase away, there were five more who settled on him, stabbing at his clothes, driving their beaks into his inhuman flesh.

Anders' eyelids twitched and all he wanted to do was sleep, sink down. It was warm now, and a beautiful spectacle to watch. The white wings of the gulls shimmering in the moonlight, their ferocious defence of him, one small human being.

Thank you, beautiful birds.

His left hand was clutching Maja's snowsuit tightly and the movements of his legs stopped as Henrik and Björn shot away on the moped, disappearing in the direction of Gåvasten with the flock of seagulls after them. Anders paddled feebly with his right hand, just to stay afloat long enough to enjoy the beautiful sight for a little while.

Good night, little lapping waves. Good night little lapping waves…

He thought it was Henrik and Björn coming back, having shaken off the gulls. But the sound of the engine that was getting louder was different, somehow. His frozen thoughts moved slowly around in his head as he began to sink. The water had just begun to cover his eyes and run into his mouth when he worked out that it was probably Simon's engine.

The engine slowed and switched to neutral, and Anders just had time to take in a mouthful of cold water before a hand grabbed his hair and pulled him upwards.

Then he was lifted into the boat in a way that was impossible to understand. It was as if the water threw him upwards, away from itself, and he tumbled on to the deck.

He lay on his back looking up at the stars and Simon's face. A clenched fist was laid on Anders' brow and before he fainted he

thought he could see the water lifting from his body in clouds of
steam, could feel a wave of real heat sweeping through his blood. Then
he saw and felt nothing more.

Strange Ways

So carry me. Carry me all the way home.
Carry me up the path,
round the side of the house, over the threshold, into the house.
Lift me inside in your hands
opened gently like eyelids.

MIA AJVIDE — IF A GIRL WANTS TO DISAPPEAR

Another one to the sea

The boat was lying by the jetty and Anders was lying on the deck.
With the help of Spiritus, Simon carried on drying his clothes and
warming his body. He had asked the water to cast Anders away from
itself, but there was no help to be had in getting him ashore.

During the afternoon Simon and Anna-Greta had kept an eye on
Anders' house to see if the light came on, if Anders came home. They
had taken a walk around the village to look for him, they had phoned
but got no reply. When the evening came they had begun to think he
had caught the tender and left Domarö. Hopefully.

But Simon had a bad feeling as he went down to his house to try
on his clothes for the following day.

Since Anders came back to the island, Simon had never questioned his readjusted picture of Maja, had never seen any reason to do so. This was Anders' way of dealing with his grief, and as long as it worked for him he was welcome to carry on living under his illusions, as far as Simon was concerned.

But the situation had changed.

It had changed when Elin Grönwall started burning houses on Kattudden, when Karl-Erik and Lasse Bergwall ran amok with their chainsaws and Sofia Bergwall pushed the other children off the jetty. When the horrible people returned to Domarö.

Simon didn't know if you could actually call Maja horrible. He too had had his tussles with her, and she was definitely not a 'good' child. She was moody, hyperactive and quick to anger. Yes, she laughed if someone fell over and hurt themselves. Yes, she enjoyed crushing butterflies to dust between her hands. But horrible? Simon had also seen a fierce appetite for life and a vivid imagination which, in a best-case scenario, would stand her in good stead in the years to come.

But even so. Even so.

If Anders really was carrying Maja or a part of Maja inside him, it was not a good thing if he regarded himself as being pregnant with an angel. There was no guarantee that Maja wished him well, and he ought to be aware of that.

That was more or less Simon's reasoning earlier in the day when he had failed to give Anders the assurances about his daughter's goodness that Anders had sought. In the current situation it was no longer possible to do that.

Anders twitched on the deck and Simon placed his fist on Anders' forehead, sending another pulse of warmth through his blood. Anders was still clutching the red snowsuit tightly in his left hand, the suit that Simon also recognised.

How can this be?

Simon had been standing in front of the mirror in his bedroom holding items of clothing up in front of him when he heard the cry, 'Stop, you bastards! Stop!' He had thrown down the clothes and rushed to the kitchen window.

It wasn't easy to see in the moonlight, and what he saw down by the jetty flew in the face of reason. However, he recognised an emergency when he saw one and began to hobble as quickly as he could to the outside door, then down to the jetty.

By the time he got in the boat, Anders had stopped far out in the bay.

Spiritus, Spiritus...

Fortunately Simon had had the matchbox in his pocket, and as his fingers closed around it he thought he could see how things stood. Anders also had a Spiritus, but like Simon he hadn't said anything about it. How else could the strip of ice lying in a black line across the sea be explained?

Simon had pumped petrol into the engine, pulled out the choke and started her up. In his agitated state he had forgotten to push the choke back in when he accelerated, and the engine died. It had taken a while to get it going again, by which time Anders had turned for the shore and started sinking.

When Simon saw the headlight of the moped heading straight for Anders across the water, he had realised that another Spiritus might not be the right explanation. That nothing he knew applied any longer. He had managed to get so far in his thoughts before the mooring ropes were untied and he set off at full speed towards the flock of birds falling from the moon.

Anders coughed a couple of times and opened his eyes. He looked at Simon and nodded slightly. Then he pulled the snowsuit close and clutched it to his chest, saying, 'They tricked me.'

For a long time he said nothing more. He lay still on the deck, twisting and turning the snowsuit in his hands. Then he hauled himself into a sitting position and leaned his back against the central seat. He looked down at his body, pulled at his shirt.

'Why aren't I...wet?' He looked at Simon and frowned. 'How did you get me out of the water?'

Simon scratched his neck and studied the patch on the snowsuit. Bamse had a pile of honey jars. Presumably he was very happy but the moonlight wasn't bright enough for Simon to see what mood he was in.

Anders turned his head and looked back at the bay, towards the spot where Simon had picked him up. 'Didn't it happen? Was it just... didn't it happen?'

Simon closed his eyes tightly, opened them again, cleared his throat and said, 'Oh, it happened. And I think...you need to be told. Quite a few things.'

The television was on up at Anna-Greta's, even though she wasn't watching. This was an occasional habit, or vice, of hers, so it was against a backdrop of people yelling and shouting at each other that Simon sat Anders down at the kitchen table, wrapped a blanket around him and poured him a glass of brandy.

When Anna-Greta went into the living room to switch off the television, Simon followed her. A sweaty man standing in front of a steel-grey skyscraper vanished from the screen and Simon said quietly, 'He has to know. Everything.'

Anna-Greta's expression didn't change. She looked closely at Simon's face, then gave an almost imperceptible nod and said, 'Then he will also be—'

'I know,' said Simon. 'But that doesn't matter. It's already after him. He has to be told what it is.'

He told Anna-Greta very briefly what had happened out in the bay. Then they went into the kitchen together, sat down opposite Anders and told him the whole story.

Left

Tempered by fire. Anders had never really understood the concept, something being tempered by fire in order to change it. He still didn't really know what it meant, but he had an idea of how it felt.

He had despaired and been nothing, then he had chased after a burning hope. He had gone from the depths of cold to a rapid warming process in the course of just a few minutes, the opposite process to tempering steel, and that was just how it felt. He had been softened. Every nerve was on the surface, and his body was as loose as a rotten pear. If he didn't hang on to the edge of the table he would dissolve into a puddle. With every glass of water he drank, he felt more and more diluted.

Anna-Greta and Simon talked and told stories. Of Domarö's past, of the pact with the sea and the people who had disappeared. Of the island that had persecuted his father, and the recent change in the sea.

Anders listened and understood that he was being told astonishing facts. But it wasn't really hitting home, it was passing him by. His gaze returned over and over again to the red snowsuit, hanging up to dry in front of the kitchen stove.

He listened as attentively as he could, but it still seemed like any old story, a story in which he had no part. His story had been about Maja, and that story was over now. It was that thought which kept on going around and around in his head like the whine of a dentist's drill: *They tricked me. They. And Maja.*

Maja had been a participant in all of this. She had left him and gone back to them. She was one of the evil spirits now, one of all those horrible people who had been put to death, sacrificed, or gone to the sea of their own free will. Everything had been a game to trick him, to entice him.

To Gåvasten.

And he had gone. Presumably they would have taken him during the day if it hadn't been for the gulls. They hadn't been after him at all, they had protected him and formed a wall between him and the thing that wanted to take him.

You took me with you. And then you left me.

He had been aware of Maja's presence all the time. At first he had thought it was in the house, then he had realised it was inside his own body. It had left him now. He knew that. She had done what she had to do. And then she had left him.

The hours passed and he asked questions where necessary so that the narrative continued. He was afraid of being left alone with his thoughts.

Gåvasten.

Which means the stone of the gifts. Which gave. And took. And took.

Now it had taken everything. Anders could no longer hear Simon and Anna-Greta's voices. He stared at Maja's red snowsuit, and it really was the end now. There was, to put it bluntly, nothing to live for any longer.

Why should I live?

With the voices buzzing in the background he made an effort to come up with one reason why he should continue to crawl around between heaven and earth. He couldn't find one. A person is given a certain number of opportunities, and certain number of roads to follow. He had reached the end of every single one.

All that was left was the fear of pain.

He didn't notice that Simon and Anna-Greta had stopped speaking as he went through the alternatives.

The last thing he wanted was to drown himself. Hanging was horrible, and by no means foolproof. He had no tablets. Drinking himself to death would take too long.

For a brief moment he saw himself from outside, as it were, and found that these thoughts brought him peace. He had finally made his mind up, and it felt...not good, but less painful. There was even a hint of tingling anticipation deep inside.

Things will be better.

That last, faintly flickering possibility that something really did exist on the other side. A place or a state where there was joy, happiness. A place that was made for him. That wasn't his belief, but...

Anything is possible.

Yes, anything is possible. Hadn't that been proved during the last few weeks? We know nothing and anything is possible, so why not a heaven or a paradise?

And then it occurred to him. The shotgun. The one that had featured in the story of Simon and Anna-Greta. He knew that Anna-Greta found it difficult to get rid of things, so presumably the gun was in the house somewhere, possibly in the hidey-hole.

Anders nodded to himself. The shotgun was good. It would satisfy all his requirements. It was quick, it was certain, and there was a perverse beauty in using the gun that had saved his father's, and thus his own life. To end things with the same weapon.

So be it.

Once the decision was made and the method established, he became aware of the silence in the kitchen. He was worried that he might have been speaking out loud without being aware of it and, venturing a neutral little smile, he turned to Simon and Anna-Greta.

'Yes,' he said. 'There's a lot to think about.'

Anna-Greta gave him a penetrating look, and Anders followed his comment with a thoughtful nod, as if they really had given him something to think about, despite the fact that he had only heard fragments of what they had been telling him.

'Anders,' said Simon. 'You can't stay down there in the Shack while...all this is going on.'

Anna-Greta finished off, 'You're staying here.'

Anders nodded for a long time, then said, 'Thank you. That's great. Thank you.' He looked at Simon. 'Thank you for everything.'

Why didn't you let me sink?

When Simon continued to look at him suspiciously, Anders searched his memory for some detail that would make it sound as if

403

he had been listening. He found it and added, 'It's unbelievable, all that business with...Spiritus.'

'Yes,' said Simon, but the tense, watchful atmosphere did not ease. Anders realised he wasn't performing very well, and that it had been noticed. If this went on, the conversation would take a new turn and he didn't want that. He let his body slump and said, 'I'm absolutely shattered.'

That at least was true, and the reaction was exactly what he had hoped for. Anna-Greta went to make up the bed in the guest room and Anders remained in the kitchen with Simon.

'Is there any more brandy?' asked Anders, just for the sake of something to say, and Simon fetched the bottle and poured him another drink. Anders took note of where the bottle was kept, in case he might need a drink to help him carry out his plan.

He knocked back the contents of the glass and it had no effect whatsoever, it merely went down and was dispersed into the darkness of his body. Simon was still looking at him, he seemed to be on the point of asking a question but Anders forestalled him by taking up another of the threads he remembered from their story.

'It's strange about the Bergwalls,' he said. 'The fact that they all seem to have been...influenced.'

To his relief Simon took the bait. 'I've thought about that a lot,' he said. 'Why only certain people have been affected. Elin, the Bergwalls, Karl-Erik. And you.'

Before Anders could stop himself he had said it. 'She's gone.'

Simon leaned across the table. 'Who's gone?'

Anders could have bitten his tongue, but he shrugged his shoulders and tried to say it as casually as possible. 'She's left me. Maja. I'm free. Everything's fine.'

He heard Anna-Greta's footsteps coming down the stairs and stood up, folded the blanket over the back of the chair. Simon also got to his feet, and Anders precluded any possible follow-up questions by going over to him and giving him a hug. 'Good night, Simon. Thanks for this evening.'

Anders didn't feel remotely tearful as Simon patted his back and hugged him in return. The decision had been made with such clarity that he was already dead in every meaningful sense. It was merely a question of establishing the time and place for his death in the physical world.

Anna-Greta went through the arrangements for the following day and Anders nodded at everything. It was easy. Everything was generally much easier when you were dead, he noticed. It was the perfect solution, a miracle cure. Everybody should try it. On his way upstairs he glanced over at the door to the hidey-hole.

When?

As soon as possible. The vague euphoria currently floating in his chest wouldn't last long, he realised that. If he postponed the deed, the roaring, bottomless darkness would return. It had to happen soon, very soon.

He could hear Simon and Anna-Greta's voices downstairs as he went into the guest room across from Anna-Greta's room. She had put out some clothes for him to borrow for the following day. He undressed and got into bed, feeling as excited as a child the night before its birthday, he could see Maja in his mind's eye, jumping up and down in bed and ripping open her presents while she—

No. Go away. Go away.

He felt a stab of pain in his chest as he pushed away the picture of Maja and evoked the taste of metal on his tongue, felt his lips closing around the barrel of the gun, his finger on the trigger. He sucked on the image and was at peace once more.

A little while later he heard Anna-Greta and Simon come upstairs and go into the room opposite. By this stage he was so far into his own death that he really did slip away from this world, and fell asleep.

'You old fool, how did you come up with such a thing?'

'It just felt as if it was time.'

'Was it your idea?'

Simon hesitated. Göran laughed and patted him on the shoulder. 'No, I thought not. It's not like you at all. But it's very much like Anna-Greta!'

Simon pulled a face and said childishly, 'Yes, but I want to get married too.'

'Yes, yes, I don't doubt that,' said Göran. 'But I just found it difficult to picture you...going down on one knee.'

Simon glanced at Göran's stiff legs and awkward gait. 'I find it difficult to picture you going down on one knee as well.'

They emerged from the forest and headed down towards Kattudden. The worst of the devastation had been cleared away, but when they cut across the Carlgrens' garden, where the outhouse had been damaged by some of the trees that had had to be felled, they had to pick their way among lopped-off branches and rough wood that would presumably lie there for some time. Göran kicked an empty plastic bottle out of the way and said, 'I wonder if there's any point, really.'

'In what?'

'Well, we've tried to keep a bit of a watch out here at night. So that nothing else will happen. But I mean, we can't go on like this forever.'

'You're thinking about your own cottage?'

'Yes. If this carries on, I imagine that's bound to go as well, eventually. Unless we catch them, of course.'

Göran's cottage was at the southern end of Kattudden. A line of trees separated it from the area Holger's father had sold to the broker. However, Simon understood Göran's unease. With a big fire and the wind in the wrong direction, the flames would soon reach Göran's house. And in that case a newly-dug well wouldn't be much help.

'Let's see how it goes,' said Simon. 'I mean, you can always do the actual digging later.'

'True.'

They passed through the village and glanced over at what used to be the Grönwalls' summer residence. Simon's throat went dry as he thought about what had happened to the girl who had lived there. They took the short path to Göran's house.

'What's your take on all this?' asked Göran. 'Can you make any sense of it?'

'None at all,' lied Simon, taking out the divining rod made of rowan which he used for appearances' sake.

'Do you think you'll be able to find a pure source here?' asked Göran. 'I know there have been problems in the past.'

'Let's wait and see,' said Simon, starting to scan the ground as they moved towards the house.

Göran sat down on the porch and watched Simon as he moved slowly across the garden with the divining rod in one hand and the other hand in his pocket. He thought this was a strange technique. Twice before he had watched people using a divining rod, and they had held the forked branch steadily in both hands. He had neither seen nor heard of Simon's one-handed grip before.

Oh well, Simon was welcome to walk backwards with the branch in his mouth as far as Göran was concerned, as long as he found clean water. For what it was worth.

Göran sighed and looked sideways at the front of the little cottage his grandfather had built more than a hundred years ago. He thought what a dreadful waste it all was. One little spark, and the entire history of this part of the family would be wiped out.

When he looked back at the garden, Simon had stopped and was looking down at the ground.

So there was water after all.

Göran got to his feet to go over to him, but froze as Simon raised his head and their eyes met. Something was wrong. Simon's eyes were wide open and his mouth was gaping, the branch fell from his hands and he wobbled as if he had been dealt a powerful blow.

'Simon!'

Göran got no reply, and went over to Simon, who was swaying on the lawn with unseeing eyes. A couple of words forced their way out and Göran thought it sounded like:

'I…know.'

Old lead

Anders woke to a silent and empty house, inside and outside. Nothing was moving, and he could hear only the faint sounds of the house itself. He lay there for a while staring up at the white-painted wooden ceiling. Nothing had changed. The darkness was ready to pounce, only his decision was keeping it at bay.

He got up and dressed slowly and carefully in the clothes Anna-Greta had laid out. Then he crept down the stairs. The kitchen clock was showing quarter-past eleven, and Simon and Anna-Greta were out attending to their respective tasks. Everything was as it should be. He opened the door at the bottom of the stairs.

The hidey-hole consisted of two rooms, each approximately seven or eight metres square, and originally intended for children who never came. Now they were filled with all kinds of rubbish and long-forgotten memories, things that might come in useful but never did, and closest to the door more practical things, such as tools and painting equipment.

He passed a pile of old clothes and rags covered with a Swedish flag and went into the inner room. It was darker in here because the window was partly covered by an old table standing on end, and the smell of mould and age was more noticeable. He switched on the light.

The room was full of old nets, agricultural tools, spinning wheels and similar items. Someone from *Antiques Roadshow* would probably have been able to sniff out the valuable items amid all the rubbish.

The thing he was looking for was straight ahead of him, propped up against a broken chair as if it were waiting for him.

He crouched down and picked up the double-barrelled shotgun, turned it over and broke it open. The chambers were empty. Anders lowered his head. The darkness pricked up its ears and crept closer to him, he could feel it as a pain in his stomach, growing stronger by the minute.

He placed the barrels in his mouth, closed his lips around them and curled his finger around the trigger. The darkness halted, moved back a little way. He had gained some respite.

His hands were trembling as he put down the gun and started looking for cartridges. He looked on the floor, on tables, behind nets. His fear of the darkness made his whole body shake as he swept aside piles of old newspapers, pushed his hands behind a chest of drawers and felt granules of dried mouse droppings slip through his fingers.

He sat up straight, pulled out the bottom drawer and there, among old whetstones and keys to locks that no longer existed, he found the box. An unassuming brown cardboard box containing seven cartridges. He breathed out, a panting sound, then took out one cartridge and studied it.

This little instrument of death was considerably newer than the gun. A cylinder of thick, red cardboard enclosed a densely packed clump of lead shot. Right at the bottom sat the gold-coloured detonator with its charge of primer.

Anders picked at the little circle in the centre of the cartridge's base. One blow to that circle and the primer was ignited, exploded and hurled out the shot.

So simple, really.

He pulled the gun towards him, pushed the cartridge into the bore and snapped the barrels into place. He ran his finger over the hammer and pulled it back until it too clicked into place.

So simple.

The entire construction of the gun was nothing more than a loop around the thin hammer that would peck at the detonator with its beak and then…all over. In a few seconds it would all be over at last.

The best thing would probably be to prop the stock of the gun in one corner so that the recoil wouldn't displace the gun, with the risk that the shot would tear him to pieces without actually finishing him off. He looked around the room, and just as he established that it would be easy to clear the corner behind the nets, he became aware of his own selfishness.

It's their wedding day.

But he couldn't wait. He carefully put down the gun and lifted up the first of the nets.

You can wait. You can wait one day.

He stopped with the net folded over his arm and shook his head.

You have to. However hard it might be. For their sake. You can't do this to them.

He knew it was true. With the net pressed against his chest he waited for the darkness to pounce, to punish him for his hesitation. But it didn't come. It trusted him. It could wait.

Tomorrow.

He knew that Simon and Anna-Greta were going on their little honeymoon to Finland the following day. He could do it then. And he could also show them the consideration of not doing it *here*, in their house. That would be inestimably selfish, and besides he knew exactly where it should be done, the perfect place for gifts and sacrifices.

Gently he moved the cock back and hid the loaded gun behind the nets, went back into the kitchen and poured himself a cup of coffee while he waited for Simon.

Simon didn't come.

It had been agreed that they would catch the one o'clock boat together, but it got to half-past twelve, quarter to one and there was no sign of Simon. Anders thought he must have misunderstood in his preoccupied state the previous evening, and that they were supposed to meet at the jetty.

He would pretend to be alive for one more day, for their sake. Then that would be an end to his consideration for others. It was bad enough that they would find out when they came back from their trip, but it couldn't be helped. He couldn't carry on living just to make them happy.

But he would pretend for one more day, so while he smoked a cigarette he checked his appearance in the hall mirror to see if he would pass muster for a wedding. The white shirt and trousers were slightly too big for him, but the shoes were a surprisingly good fit. On the coat hooks he found one of Simon's old jackets and pulled it on.

When he closed the door behind him to be welcomed by yet another grey, overcast day, he thought he could probably get through this too. The gun was loaded and ready, it was only a matter of perhaps twenty hours before it would be put to use.

For the moment the darkness seemed satisfied that the preparations had been carried out, and it even took its eyes off him a couple of times as he made his way down to the steamboat jetty.

Simon wasn't there either. There were about twenty people gathered on the jetty, all dressed up in their best clothes and all on their way to Nåten and the wedding, but the bridegroom was missing. Anders went over to Elof Lundberg. He was wearing a very grand overcoat, which didn't go with the inevitable cap at all.

'Have you seen Simon?'

'No,' said Elof. 'Isn't he already there, then?'

'Yes. I suppose he is.'

Anders moved away and tried to remember what Simon had said. *He was going to look for water at Göran's place, wasn't he?*

Anders looked around, but Göran wasn't on the jetty either. He wasn't proud of it, but a terrible little hope flickered into life within Anders: something had happened. Something that would mean the wedding had to be postponed. Something that would allow him to go back to the hidey-hole today, after all.

The tender glided alongside and there was chattering and laughter as the wedding guests climbed aboard. As it reversed out Anders stood in the prow, looking over towards Simon's jetty. Perhaps he had taken his own boat over to Nåten?

But the boat was by the jetty, and there was no sign of the bridegroom anywhere.

Proof of eligibility

Anders stayed in the prow for the whole crossing and didn't speak to anyone; when they hove to he was the first one off, and walked quickly towards the church. Behind him came the wedding guests, chattering noisily.

Nåten church was in a beautiful spot on a small hill close to the sea, and the churchyard covered the entire slope down to the shore, where the emblematic anchor that adorned every written communication from the church lay like a brake, as if to stop the headstones and crosses from tumbling down into the sea.

The wedding ceremony wasn't due to start for half an hour. Anders guessed that those who were about to be married would usually wait for the exact moment in the community centre beyond the churchyard gate. He went up the steps and knocked on the door. When no one answered, he stepped inside.

Two long tables were laid for the guests, and an extravagantly decorated buffet was displayed on a smaller table in the middle of the room. He could hear women's voices from behind a door at the far end.

She has to be told.

The sound of the guests' voices was getting closer. Anders walked to the other end of the room, tapped on the door and opened it.

Despite the fact that he was committed to death and that nothing mattered any more, he couldn't help but be taken aback at the sight of his grandmother in her wedding finery.

Anna-Greta's long, grey hair had been arranged in a wave-like style that caught the pale light from the window, so that it poured down over her in cascades of silver. The white flowers on her beige dress reinforced the impression of a borrowed starlit glow that reached all the way up to her forehead. Her face had been skilfully made up to bring out the sparkle in her eyes.

Next to her, two women of the same age sat fiddling with something on her dress. Anders looked quickly around the room. No Simon.

'How do I look?' asked Anna-Greta.

'Wonderful,' said Anders honestly. 'Has Simon been here?'

'No.' The sparkle in Anna-Greta's eyes dulled a little. 'Hasn't he arrived?'

Anders shook his head and Anna-Greta made a move to go out and check for herself, but one of the women held her back and said, 'Don't worry, he'll come. Now stand still.'

Anna-Greta flung her arms wide in a helpless gesture as if to show that she was a captive. 'Go and wait with the others,' she said. 'I'm sure he'll be here.'

Anders backed out of the room and left her in the hands of her guards. He had done what he could. It was no longer his problem. And yet he felt sorry for Anna-Greta. So pretty, so dressed up, so full of anticipation. His little grandma.

Because he knew that Simon would not come. That somehow or other he had been captured by the forces that were on the move. End of story. Simon was gone, and Anders intended to catch the three o'clock boat back and put an end to all his sorrows.

It was quarter to two when Anders walked up to the church and looked in through the open door. Some thirty people were seated in the pews. The guests who had come over on the tender had been supplemented by people from Nåten and those who had come in their own boats. Up by the altar the priest was adjusting a bunch of white roses in a vase.

The slope drew Anders down to the churchyard, and he wandered among the gravestones. He stood for a long time in front of the family grave where both his father and his grandfather stood alone with their names beneath Torgny and Maja. Presumably Anna-Greta would make sure that his own name was added at the bottom of the column of lone men.

And Simon? Where will Simon end up?

At just after two, people started coming out of the church to see what was happening, or rather to see why nothing was happening. Anders carried on down to the water's edge to avoid being spoken to. He stopped in front of the huge anchor and read the plaque.

IN MEMORY OF THOSE LOST AT SEA

Anders ran his hand over the rusty cast iron, over the treated wood. It would be more fitting for him to be buried here, beneath the anchor, because he had been lost at sea and then wandered around pointlessly on dry land for a couple of years. He followed the chain that ran from the top of the anchor down into the ground.

Where does that go?

He saw the chain disappearing deep underground or out across the bottom of the sea; in his mind he hurled his body in the direction of the chain and followed it downwards…

…burrowing down into the slime on the seabed, down into the mud and the blue clay, down to the point where nothing can live, where there is complete silence…

His thoughts were interrupted by shouts from the direction of the church. People were pointing out to sea, and when Anders turned around, his lips curved into a smile in spite of everything. A boat was heading towards them from out in the bay. A rickety fibreglass boat with a twenty-horsepower Evinrude engine. Simon's boat.

The wedding guests poured down the slope like a flock of eager sheep and gathered on the shoreline as the boat approached. There were two people on board, and when the boat was about a hundred metres from land, Anders could see that it was Simon and Göran.

Göran was driving, and Simon was sitting up in the prow with his hair blowing around his ears. People clapped and cheered.

The magician's final entrance.

The boat didn't head for the harbour, but made straight for the incline below the anchor. Göran put the engine into neutral and floated the last few metres into the shore. Simon climbed out, and the guests combined their efforts to haul the boat safely ashore.

Simon's eyes sought out Anders and he started to say something, but the guests grabbed him by the arms and pulled him up towards the church, where Anna-Greta was now waiting for him, her arms folded across her chest. Without doubt the entrance was effective, but Anna-Greta could be forgiven for wishing that on this particular day there had been slightly less spectacle and slightly more solemnity.

Anders followed a couple of steps behind and waited until everyone else had disappeared into the church before he walked in and took a seat at the back.

Let love come

The description of the wedding has been omitted.

Strangely enough, descriptions of weddings aren't all that interesting. I mean, two people promising each other eternal commitment and fidelity before God really ought to be something enjoyable, but actually it isn't.

It's like a horror story, but in reverse. When the monster shows its ugly mug at the end, it's always a disappointment. It can never match up to our expectations. It's the same with a wedding. The journey along the winding paths of love is spine tingling, the lead-up in some cases is a real battleground and the basic idea behind the whole thing is beautiful and mind blowing.

But the ritual itself?

You would have to call in Marc Chagall, Wolfgang Amadeus

Mozart and David Copperfield's tech team to do the idea justice. People would hover above the ground, there would be flashes of lightning, waterfalls and a symphony that would make the plaster fall off the walls and swirl in flakes around the conjoined couple like confetti spiralling up to the ceiling.

Nothing like that occurred in the church at Nåten.

Suffice to say that Simon and Anna-Greta exchanged vows, that some appropriate music was played on the organ, and that many people were moved. However, there was one beautiful thing that happened. Anna-Greta was a radiant bride, and Simon was rather a mess. Despite the fact that he had managed to get into his wedding outfit, it looked as if he had done so in rather a hurry. His tie was crooked, his socks didn't match his trousers and his hair was tousled.

But let joy be unconfined nevertheless! Let love come! Let it be victorious!

Let the couple walk out on to the church steps and let Anna-Greta's two friends, who know how these things should be done, shower them with confetti, and let us hear the choirs of angels in the background and see the cascades of eider feathers that have been collected from the islands for months, let them fall from the heavens like snowy apple blossom strewn from the hands of God the Father as he opens his warm embrace.

Yes!

Yes, yes, yes!

And then let us go together to the community centre and help ourselves to the buffet. This day is not over yet. Not by a long way. Let us go.

The water

People spread themselves out around the tables and, to Anders' relief, Anna-Greta took him by the arm so that he ended up next to her, with no one on his other side. Opposite him sat Anna-Greta's two friends, and after Anna-Greta had introduced them as Gerda and Lisa, the two ladies concentrated on each other.

The guests filled their plates and helped themselves to beer or soft drinks. It certainly wasn't a showy affair, and it was almost fortunate that Simon's entrance had made it something to remember.

But Simon wasn't done yet.

After Anders had congratulated his grandmother and told her once again how lovely she looked, he leaned over to pass on his good wishes to Simon too, but Simon was preoccupied with something going on inside himself. He was staring down at the table with concentration etched on his face, his lips moving slightly.

Anders was about to say something to bring him back to reality when Simon suddenly got to his feet and tapped on his neighbour's bottle with a fork.

'Dear friends!' he said. 'There are certain things that...' He stopped and looked at Anna-Greta, who was looking at him questioningly. He cleared his throat and tried again. 'First of all I would like to say how happy I am. That you have come here today, that I have been given...the blessing of marrying the most wonderful woman ever to have sat in a boat. Or not sat in a boat.'

A few people laughed and scattered applause broke out. Anna-Greta lowered her eyes becomingly.

'And there was another matter...and I don't know how to...there's something I have to tell you, and I don't really know...there are so many...'

Simon looked around the room. There was total silence now. One person had their fork halfway to their mouth, and lowered it slowly as Simon groped for the right words.

'What I wanted to say,' said Simon, 'is that since so many people from Domarö are gathered here together…and perhaps this isn't the most suitable occasion and I don't really know how to put it, but…'

Simon stopped speaking again and Anders heard Gerda whisper to Lisa, 'Is he drunk?' Lisa nodded and clamped her lips together thinly as, under the table, Anna-Greta gave a hesitant tug at Simon's trouser leg in an attempt to get him to sit down.

Simon made a decision and straightened up, speaking more clearly, 'There is no sensible way of putting this, so I'm just going to say it and you must take it as you wish.'

Lisa and Gerda had leaned back in their seats, folded their arms, and were looking at Simon with distaste. Other guests were looking at each other and wondering what was to come. Eyebrows were raised when Simon seemed to be starting on a completely different tack.

'The wells on Domarö,' he said. 'I know that several people have had problems with salt water getting in, that the drinking water is contaminated by the sea seeping in.'

There were nods here and there. Even if it was impossible to understand why Simon had brought up this issue, at least what he said was a well-known fact. When Simon started to speak again, his eyes flickered over towards Anders from time to time.

'We have also had a number of other problems recently. People suddenly being odd or even…wicked. People who don't seem to be themselves, if you see what I mean.'

There were nods of agreement here and there. They could go along with that too. Before long he would probably mention that the cod had been fished out as well, another tedious but incontrovertible fact.

'What I wanted to say,' said Simon, 'is that I've worked out that these two things are connected. This…illness or whatever we ought to call it, affects those who have salt water in their wells. So…those of you who have salt water in your well, don't drink it!'

If Simon had hoped for gasps of amazement and recognition from his audience, he was disappointed. Most of them were looking at him with expressions ranging from scepticism to incomprehension. Simon flung his arms wide and raised his voice.

'That's how the sea gets in! Don't you understand? They're in the sea and they...find their way in through the water in the wells. If we drink it they get inside us and we...change.'

When Simon still didn't get the reaction he was looking for, he sighed and said in a more resigned tone of voice, 'I'm just asking you to believe what I say. Don't drink water that has become salty. Let's say it's poisonous, just for simplicity's sake. Don't drink it.'

Simon slumped back down on his chair and there was a long silence. Gradually murmured conversations sprang up around the table. Anna-Greta leaned over to Simon and said something. Lisa and Gerda still had their arms folded, and looked as if they were waiting for the next instalment.

And Anders...

It was as if he had heard only snatches of a melody until now. Sometimes faintly, as if it was coming through the wall from another room. Sometimes louder but quickly fading, as if from a passing car with its stereo turned to full volume. Sometimes just a note or two in the soughing of the trees and the dripping of the water during the night.

With Simon's words, the entire orchestra stepped forward out of the darkness and crashed into life, deafening him and silencing his whole body.

The water. Of course. The drinking water.

Despite the perception that Maja was running through his body, it had never occurred to him that that was actually the way it *was*. He had been going around knocking back wine from plastic bottles, sometimes several litres per day. Wine diluted with water from the tap. He had woken feeling thirsty and hungover, and had drunk lots and lots of water.

And what really made him almost slide off his chair as he sank further and further into the music: Maja had not left him at all. He just hadn't been drinking water. During the whole of the previous day he had drunk only undiluted wine and wormwood concentrate. It was only when he got to Anna-Greta's house that he had taken in liquid in the form of water. And their water wasn't…infected.

Anders felt a hand on his back and Simon leaned over him. 'Do you understand?' he whispered.

Anders nodded vaguely as the music of all the connections continued to reverberate in his head. The eternal sea, always one and the same, that could work its way into every crack, could spread and extend but always returned to itself. One vast body with billions of limbs, from thundering waves to rivulets as thin as a spider's leg that found their way in, found their way through. The sea. And those who existed within it.

Simon pulled at his arm and Anders got up and followed him as if he were in a trance.

No one has such long fingers.

In his mind's eye he could see the sea groping its way across the rocks on the islands, through fissures in the bedrock, down into the ground, into the wells, and it was like a mantra running through his head as Simon led him outside: *No one has such long fingers. No one has such long fingers.*

'Anders, are you still with us?'

Simon waved a hand in front of his eyes, and with an effort Anders managed to bring himself back, to discover that he was standing on the porch of the community centre. His right hand was resting on the cold iron railing; he gripped it tightly, holding himself firmly in place.

'How did you work it out?' he asked.

'When I was looking for water for Göran,' said Simon, 'and I felt all the brackish water coursing through the rock—'

'Felt?'

'Yes.' Simon pulled the matchbox out of his pocket and showed it to Anders, then put it away again. Anders nodded. He did actually remember that part of the story.

'And then I thought about what your water is like,' Simon went on, 'and above all what Elin's water was like. After the fire I was by her well, there was something that drew me to it, there was something there. I didn't pick up on it at the time, but I tasted the water and it was salty. More salty than yours. Since then that thought has been in the back of my mind and…today I caught sight of it.' Simon sighed and glanced at the closed door of the community centre. 'Although I don't really think I managed to convince anybody.'

'Why were you so late?'

Simon shrugged his shoulders. 'I had to check. Karl-Erik's well and the Bergwalls' well. It was the same there. Salt in the water. When they were sawing they probably had flasks of water with them, and drank as they worked. I think it reaches some kind of critical point and then…it breaks out. The other person.'

Anders leaned on the railing and looked down towards the harbour. It was an hour until the next tender crossed the sea. Was permitted to cross the sea.

No one has such long fingers. No one has such strong fingers.

Unannounced, a memory popped into his head. He was perhaps ten years old when his father put out a hoop net for fun and caught one solitary eel. Anders had stood on the jetty watching his father trying to grab hold of the eel to get it out of the boat. It had been impossible.

Eventually his father managed to push the eel into a plastic bag. It slithered out. He got the eel into the bag once again and held the top closed with both hands as he climbed out of the boat with great difficulty.

When he got up on to the jetty he stopped and stared at the bag and laughed out loud. Despite the fact that his hands were strong and he was clutching the bag as tightly as he could, the eel had still managed to brace itself against the bottom of the bag and was slowly and inexorably forcing its way past his clenched fists and out of the bag. It fell on to the jetty, hurled its body forward and slid into the water.

'Well, there's a thing,' said his father with a kind of admiration in his voice. 'That one certainly wanted to live.'

Afterwards they had laughed about it. His father so big and strong, the eel so small and tough. And yet the eel had won.

No one has such long, such strong fingers.

And yet it is still possible to slither through. If you just want to live enough.

Come in

At half-past six the tender moored at the jetty on Domarö, and a man who no longer wanted to die left the group of cheerful people getting off. He ran to the west. When he drew level with the ramblers' hostel he had to slow down, since a renewed desire to live does not bring with it new lungs.

Anders jogged to the point where the track divided in two. He was forced to walk the last stretch because his windpipe was whistling and he felt as if he was breathing through a straw. He passed the straight pine tree, pulled open the door of the Shack and went straight into the kitchen without taking off his shoes. He leaned over the sink, turned on the tap and drank like a man who has walked across the desert. He panted, breathed in deeply, drank again. Straightened up, panted, drank again.

He drank until his stomach was distended and the cold water was threatening to come back up through his throat. Then he lay down on the floor. When he rocked from side to side he could hear the water lapping in his stomach.

Come in. I will carry you.

He closed his eyes and listened, checked what he was feeling.

He had promised Simon and Anna-Greta that he would go back up to Anna-Greta's house as soon as he had done what he had to do at home. But still he lay there on the floor, waiting as the water in his stomach gradually ceased to be a cold, separate clump, as its temperature rose to body heat and became a part of him.

Are you there?

There was no answer, and doubt sank its claws into him. What if Simon had been wrong? What if Simon had been right, but it still didn't mean that Maja was on his side? The snowsuit. How had Henrik and Björn actually got hold of the snowsuit?

This was the last chance. He was balancing on the edge of a precipice, and only a touch as light as a feather, the right touch, could save him. If it didn't come, there was nothing but the downward plunge and the darkness.

Come. Touch me.

Inside his body was a hollow space that was much bigger than his body. A summer breeze off the sea wafted through the room, bringing with it a single fluffy dandelion seed that floated around on the air currents until it finally landed on the inside of his skin. It tickled and settled down. That was what it felt like. So faint. But he knew.

You are here.

After that first, microscopic touch it grew stronger. What the water had carried with it spread through his blood, into his muscles, and the tickle became a soft caress and a greater presence, as if the downy seed really had brought with it other seeds that had now taken root in his flesh, causing small dandelions to bloom. He couldn't see them, but beneath the horizon they lit up his world, and his eyes filled with tears.

Hello, sweetheart. I'm sorry I…forgive me. For everything.

He looked in cupboards and drawers and got out every bottle he could find, then filled them from the kitchen tap. He ended up with about ten litres of water in large and small bottles, which he stuffed into two carrier bags. He found room for the bottle of worm-wood too.

Finally he fetched some Bamse comics from the bedroom and slipped the photographs from Gåvasten into his pocket. Then he left the house. Before he even got to Anna-Greta's house he fished out one of the bottles and took a couple of swigs.

The newlyweds were sitting in the kitchen, and had changed into their everyday clothes. Everything was as usual, and everything was different. New bonds had been formed without anything changing on the surface. When Simon caught sight of the carrier bags, he asked, 'Is that…water?'

'Yes.'

'Can I have a look at one of the bottles?'

Anders dug out one of the bottles and placed it on the table in front of Simon. It was an old plastic bottle; the label had fallen off, and the slightly cloudy water was clearly visible through the plastic. All three of them gathered around the bottle as if it were a relic, a sacred object.

There was nothing special to see, Anders had already established that when he was filling the bottles. The water in the Shack had always been cloudy because of methane gas or chemical deposits, it had always had that misty, slightly ghostly appearance; it needed to stand in an open container for a while before it cleared.

Simon pulled a glass towards him, looked at Anders and asked, 'May I…?'

A pang of…a protective instinct ran through Anders, but before he could open his mouth Anna-Greta had said what he was about to say, 'You're not going to drink that?'

'I've drunk it before,' said Simon. 'But this time I was only intending to pour it out. Is that OK?'

Anders nodded, finding the situation slightly absurd. Simon was asking for permission to pour water out of a bottle. But it wasn't absurd. Not anymore.

Anders felt uncomfortable as Simon unscrewed the cap and poured the water. Maja was in that water, and Simon knew that, which was why he had asked for permission. It was like handling someone's ashes. The relatives must be consulted.

She isn't dead. She isn't gone. She…

Anders suddenly thought of something Simon had told him a long time ago, or was it just a few days ago? Time had lost its meaning as days and nights, hope and powerlessness slipped in and out of each other in strange ways.

He was about to ask, but Simon's experiment caught his attention. Simon had picked up the matchbox and tipped the insect into his left hand. He now moved his right hand towards the glass, glanced at Anders, then dipped his index and middle finger in the water. Closed his eyes.

There wasn't a sound in the kitchen as Simon waited. Thirty seconds passed. Then Simon removed his fingers from the glass and shook his head.

'No,' he said. 'There is something there. Particularly now that I know. But it's too faint.'

For a moment Simon didn't know what to do with his wet fingers. He was about to dry them on his trousers purely as a reflex action, but stopped himself and allowed them to dry on their own. Anders raised the glass to his lips and drank the water.

'Do you really think that's a good idea?' asked Anna-Greta.

'Grandma,' said Anders. 'You have no idea how good it is.'

It couldn't be helped, all that drinking had made him desperate for a pee. Presumably all the fluid that left his body, tears, sweat, urine, somehow made what was in the water...evaporate from him, but there it was. He would just have to drink some more afterwards.

On the way to the toilet he passed the closed door to the hidey-hole, and through the wall he waved goodbye to the shotgun inside. He made a mental note to take out the cartridge when he had the opportunity, so that nobody would come to grief.

He emptied his bladder while contemplating the framed picture above the toilet. A classic motif: a little girl with a basket over her arm is walking along a narrow footbridge across a ravine. Beside her hovers an angel with great big wings and outstretched arms, as if to catch the girl if she should fall. The girl is completely oblivious to both the danger and the presence of the angel, she is simply the roses in her cheeks and the sunshine in her eyes.

That's what it's like, thought Anders, *that's exactly what it's like.*

He had no idea what he meant, what this particular picture had to do with his story, but one thing he did know: the great stories were true, the timeless pictures portraying need, beauty, danger and grace were meaningful.

Everything is possible.

When he got back to the kitchen Anna-Greta was busy lighting a fire. Simon was still staring at the bottle as if he were gazing into a crystal ball, where a glimpse of something might appear at any moment. Anders sat down opposite him.

'Simon,' he said. 'What happened with Holger's wife? With Sigrid?'

Simon looked up from the bottle. 'I know,' he said. 'I've been thinking about that too.'

'What have you come up with?'

'Don't you remember what happened?'

Anders grabbed the bottle and drank deeply. 'No,' he said. 'There's so much that I...a lot of things have just disappeared. Those first days here on the island are very...foggy.' Anders smiled and had another drink. 'And I probably haven't...been myself, not really. If you know what I mean.'

'How does it feel now?'

Anders ran his hand over his chest. 'It feels...warm. And less lonely. What about Sigrid?'

Anna-Greta placed a steaming pot of coffee on the table and sat down between them.

'I have to say one thing,' she said, looking from Anders to Simon, then back at Anders. 'Bearing in mind what we know and what has happened, this might sound...harsh. But what I want to say is...don't try to do anything. Don't try to...challenge the sea. It's dangerous. It could go wrong. It could go very, very badly wrong. Much worse than we can imagine.'

'What do you mean?' asked Simon.

'I just mean that...it's bigger than us. Infinitely bigger. It can crush us. Just like that. It's happened before. And this is not

426

just about us. Other people live here too.'

Anders thought about what Anna-Greta had said, and it certainly made sense, but there was one thing he didn't understand.

'Why are you saying this now?' he asked.

Anna-Greta's hand was unsteady as she poured coffee into her saucer and reached for a sugar lump. 'I thought it might be appropriate,' she said. 'To remind you.' She pushed the sugar lump into her mouth and slurped a little of the boiling-hot coffee.

'Sigrid hadn't been in the water for very long when I found her,' said Simon. 'Just a few hours. Despite the fact that it was a year since she disappeared.'

'But she was dead, wasn't she?' said Anders.

'Oh yes,' said Simon. '*Then* she was dead.'

Anna-Greta held the coffee pot out to Anders, and he waved it away impatiently. She put it back on the tablemat, ran her hand over her forehead and closed her eyes.

'What are you saying?' said Anders. 'I thought she'd…been dead for a year, but only in the water for a few hours. That was the odd thing about it.'

'No,' said Simon. 'She'd been gone for a year. But she'd died from drowning just a few hours before I found her.'

Anders looked at his grandmother, who was still sitting with her eyes closed as if in pain, a deep furrow of anxiety between her eyebrows. He shook his head violently and said, 'So where was she, then? All that time?'

'I don't know,' said Simon. 'But she was somewhere.'

Anders sat motionless as goose bumps covered his entire body. He twitched. Stared straight ahead. Saw the picture. Twitched again.

'And that's where Maja is now,' he whispered. 'Without her snowsuit.'

Nobody said anything for a long time. Anna-Greta pushed away her saucer and looked anywhere but at Anders. Simon sat there fiddling with his matchbox. Outside and around them the sea breathed, apparently asleep. Anders sat still, twitching from time to time as yet another horrible picture pierced his breast like a cold blade.

Something inside him had known this. Perhaps he had actually remembered what had happened with Sigrid, somewhere right at the back of his mind. Or perhaps he simply knew. That a part of Maja existed inside him, and another part existed…somewhere else. Somewhere where she couldn't reach him and he couldn't reach her.

Anna-Greta broke the silence. She turned to Anders and said, 'When your great-grandfather was little, there was a man in the western part of the village who lost his wife to the sea. He would never talk about how it had happened. But he never stopped searching for her.'

Anna-Greta pointed to the east.

'Do you know about the wreck? On the rocks on Ledinge? There were bits left when I was young, but it's all gone now. That was his boat. I don't know what he did to…annoy it. But at any rate his boat was found there eventually. Way inland, up on a hill. Smashed to pieces.'

'Sorry,' said Simon. 'Did you say he was from the *western* part of the village?'

'Yes,' said Anna-Greta. 'That's what I'm getting at. His house and all the houses around it…disappeared. A storm came from the west. And as you know perfectly well: storms don't come from the west, from the mainland. It's not possible. But this one did. It came in the night, blew up to hurricane force in a moment. Eight houses were… smashed to kindling. Five people died. Three of them were children who didn't get away in time.'

She uttered the last sentences with her gaze firmly fixed on Anders. 'Plus the man who set out in the first place. The one who started it all.' When Anders didn't say anything she added, 'And you know what happened to Domarö even further back in the past. We told you that yesterday.'

Anders grabbed the bottle and took another couple of swigs. He didn't respond. Anna-Greta's face was distorted into an expression somewhere between sympathy and rage—more of a grimace, really.

'I understand how you feel,' she said. 'Or at least...I can guess. But it's dangerous. Not only for you. For everyone who lives here.' She reached across the table and placed her hand on the back of Anders' hand, which was ice cold. 'I know this sounds terrible, but...I saw you standing looking at the anchor yesterday. In Nåten. There *are* many people who have drowned, who have disappeared...naturally, if I can put it like that. Maja could have been one of them. You *could* look at it like that. And forgive me for saying this, but...you *have* to look at like that. For your own sake. And everyone else's.'

The handover (we are secret)

Anders was sitting on the edge of the bed in the guest room. Among all the pictures that had flashed through his mind during the course of the evening, there was one that wouldn't go away, that left him no peace.

She hasn't got her snowsuit.

He had brought it up from the kitchen and hung it carefully over the back of the wooden chair by the window. Now he had it in his arms as he rocked back and forth.

She'll be freezing, wherever she is.

If he could only dress her in her snowsuit, if he could only do that. He caressed the slightly worn fabric, the patch with Bamse and the jars of honey.

Simon and Anna-Greta had gone to bed an hour ago. Anders had offered to sleep on the sofa downstairs if they...wanted to be alone on their wedding night, if they didn't want anyone nearby. The offer had been met with an assurance that it was absolutely fine to have someone nearby, that as far as the wedding night was concerned, this was a night like any other. A quiet night.

Anders hugged the snowsuit, torn between two worlds. A normal world, where his daughter had drowned two years ago and become one of those lost at sea, a world where you could talk about sleeping on the sofa and receive an indulgent reply, where people got married and put on a buffet.

And then there was the other world. The one where Domarö lay in the arms of dark forces that held the island in an iron grip. Where you had to watch every step and be prepared to be torn away from relationships at any moment. So that not everything will disappear.

Bamse, Bamse, Bamse…

That was probably why Maja had always liked the stories about Bamse so much. There were problems, there were baddies and there were those who were stupid. But it was never *really* dangerous. There was never any real doubt about how you ought to behave. Everybody knew. Even Croesus Vole. He was a baddie because he was a baddie, not because he was splintered and anxious.

And Bamse. Always on the side of good. Protector of the weak, unfailingly honest.

But he really loves fighting…

Anders snorted. Bamse was much more interesting in Maja's version. A bear who means well, but can't help getting into a fight as soon as he gets the chance.

Just like Maja.

Yes, perhaps. Perhaps it was because she broke the songs that she broke things as well. They had to become splintered, to become like her. But more interesting.

Anders took out one of the Bamse comics he had brought with him and found that the story was ridiculously appropriate for what was going on. Little Leap wins a holiday in a ski resort. The hotel turns out to be haunted. The ghost seems to be after Little Leap, but Shellman understands, as always.

He builds a machine that makes a Little Leap costume drop down over the invisible ghost. The ghost sees himself in the mirror and stops being horrible. He wasn't after Little Leap at all. He just wanted to be like him.

Anders felt something switch off inside his head while he was reading the story; he came back to himself only when he put the comic down.

I am the costume. The apparition.

He wanted to sleep. He wanted Maja to take over and give him some kind of guidance. Before he undressed he placed the chair next to the bed. On the chair he placed a pen and an open notepad. Then he drank three gulps of water, got undressed, climbed into bed and snapped his eyes shut.

It didn't take many minutes of keeping his eyes screwed tightly shut to realise that he was wide awake. There was absolutely no chance of falling asleep, however much he wanted to. He sat up and leaned back against the wall.

What shall I do? What can I do?

The paper on the chair glowed white, and his eyes were drawn towards it. The clarity of his vision shifted. He was seeing in a different way. For a fraction of a second he managed to think: *I am seeing through my eyes*, and then he was no longer a part of himself.

A creaking sound brought him back to his body. He didn't know how much time had passed, but he found himself sitting on the floor with the Bamse comic in front of him and the pen in his hand. The quilt was in a heap on the bed.

The comic was open at a short story, just two pages, which was called 'Brumma's Secret Friends'. Brumma hid in the cupboard under the sink and made friends with the brush and shovel. When Mummy shouted for Brumma, the brush was terrified; it said, 'We are secret, secret', and turned back into an ordinary brush.

There were drawings on the pages. Lines and shapes on every available surface. No letters. The only thing Anders could in any way interpret as meaningful was a zigzag line across several frames, which looked more like a temple than anything else.

Was there a reason why this particular story had been chosen, or was it just a coincidence, like the story of the haunted hotel? Had Maja just been reading and drawing, as she used to do sometimes?

The creaking sound came again, this time just outside the door. Anders gave a start and pulled the quilt towards him, threw it over his head and curled up, lay as still as still could be. The handle was pushed down tentatively and the door opened. Anders stuck his thumb in his mouth.

'Anders?' Simon's voice was no more than a whisper. The door closed behind him. 'What are you doing?'

Simon was standing in front of him in his dressing gown as Anders crawled out from under the quilt. 'I was scared.'

'Can I come in?'

Anders waved in the direction of the bed, but stayed where he was on the floor with the quilt round his shoulders. Simon sat down on the bed and looked at the comic. 'Have you been drawing?'

'I don't know anything,' said Anders. 'I don't know anything about anything.'

Simon linked his hands together and leaned forward. He took a deep breath. 'It's like this,' he said. 'I've been thinking things over. There's a lot to say, but I'll start with a question. Would you like Spiritus?'

'The insect? In the matchbox?'

'Yes. I thought it might protect you. The thing is, Anna-Greta and I are going away tomorrow. I don't like the idea of you being... unprotected.'

'Didn't you say it involved some kind of pact?'

Simon took the matchbox out of his dressing-gown pocket. 'Yes. And I don't know what that really means. But I think something pretty awful happens when you die.'

'And you want to give it to me.'

Simon turned the box over in his hands. A faint sound of scraping

432

and ticking could be heard from inside as the larva shifted its position.

'I have been afraid. You enter into some form of pact with what is deep and dark in the world. I have regretted doing so. But I couldn't help myself. I was stupid, to put it mildly.'

Simon fingered the unfamiliar wedding ring and went on, 'But I wouldn't suggest this if I didn't believe it could help you. Whatever is after you has something to do with water, and this…can tame water.'

Anders looked at the box in Simon's hand; his eyes moved up over the green towelling of the dressing gown and stopped at Simon's face, which suddenly looked immensely old and tired. The hand holding the box was almost touching the floor, as if the insect weighed a hundred times more than its appearance suggested.

'What shall I do?' asked Anders.

Simon drew the hand holding the box towards him and shook his head. 'Do you know what you're getting into?'

'No,' said Anders. 'But it doesn't matter. It really doesn't matter. At all.'

Now Simon had got what he wanted, he seemed to be struck by remorse. Perhaps he didn't want to expose Anders to the risks involved after all. Perhaps he didn't want to be parted from his magical Spiritus. He ran his thumb distractedly over the boy on the box.

'You have to spit,' he said eventually. 'Into the box. You have to give it saliva. And you have to keep on doing that every single day for as long as you live. Or until you…pass it on.'

Anders gathered saliva in his mouth. After a while he nodded to Simon and took the box from him, pushed it open. Anders allowed the gob of saliva to emerge from his lips, to drip down…

'No, wait!' said Simon. 'Let's not—'

But it was too late. The tear-shaped, bubbling gob had already left Anders' mouth and fell straight on to the insect's leathery skin just as Simon's hand reached out.

Anders had thought nothing could taste more disgusting than the wormwood concentrate. He was wrong. Whatever penetrated his mouth now and spread throughout his body had a non-physical dimension that a taste could never match. As if he had bitten into a piece of rotten meat and at the same moment *become* the meat.

He opened and closed his mouth in a series of dry retches and his body shook in small convulsions, causing the box to fall from his grasp. Simon sat on the bed with his hands covering his face as Anders slumped sideways, clutching his stomach. He vomited and vomited without anything coming out of him.

The box was lying roughly twenty centimetres in front of him. A round black shape appeared over the edge, and the next moment the whole insect was out of the box. It had grown. Its skin was shiny and its body was moving smoothly across the floor, heading for Anders' lips. It wanted more of this manna, directly from the source.

Even though he felt so ill, Anders managed to sit up so that the insect couldn't find its way into his mouth. With trembling hands he placed the box over it and slid it shut without harming the insect.

There was a great deal of activity inside the box, and it moved across the floor in jerks and thrusts. Anders swallowed a bubble of vileness and asked, 'Is it angry?'

'No,' said Simon. 'Just the opposite, I should think.'

He looked into Anders' eyes. For a long time. Something happened between them, and Anders nodded.

Before Simon left the room he said, 'Take care of yourself.' He pointed at Anders, at the matchbox. 'That only happens the first time. The taste.'

Anders sat on the floor watching Spiritus bounce around in his little prison like some kind of morbid toy.

He still didn't know what he was going to do or how he was going to do it, but one thing he did know: during that long look, Simon had given his approval. *Do what you have to do.*

Anders conquered his revulsion and cupped his hand over the box. The insect calmed down as it felt the warmth of his body, his presence, and he became aware of everything that *flowed*.

His body was an immense system of larger and smaller channels, where water ran in the form of plasma. He had learned about this in school: the plasma carried corpuscles, thrombocytes, but he could neither see nor feel those, he could see only cloudy water being pumped around by the heart, out into his arteries, and he saw and knew that he was a tree, all the way out to the most fragile twigs. A tree made of water.

He was also able to feel very clearly all the water flowing or standing still in the house, although this feeling did not have the same intensity of revelation. The network of water pipes was visible through the walls, just like an X-ray, and the bottles of water he had brought with him...

Now...now...

He curled his hand around one of the bottles on the floor as he held his other hand over the matchbox. Yes, he could feel the water in the bottle. But nothing else. It was just the same as with his blood: he could feel only the water, but he felt that all the more strongly.

He looked at the hand cupped over the box and a couple of lines by the poet Tomas Tranströmer came into his mind. He didn't really read much poetry, but he had made a start on Tranströmer's collected poems so many times that he knew the first one by heart.

In day's first hours consciousness can grasp the world
As the hand grips a sun-warmed stone.

That was exactly how it was, with the reservation that the world his consciousness grasped was the part that consisted of water. He could follow it through the cold-water pipes, feel the drips from the leaking kitchen tap where he lost contact with it for half a second until it joined the thin film of water finding its way into the waste pipe and continuing downwards, out and eventually into a larger body of water that lay outside his range.

He let go of the box and the perception faded as he moved his

435

hand away, centimetre by centimetre. When the hand reached his face and moved across it, the feeling was gone. He was a person, not a tree.

It would take less than this to make you lose your mind.

Once when he was about twenty he had been at a party and had ended up next to a guy who had just swallowed a blue pill. They were sitting at a glass table, and the guy had stared at that table. After a couple of minutes he had started to cry. Anders had asked him why he was crying.

'Because it's so beautiful,' he had replied, his voice thick with emotion. 'The glass. I can *see* it, do you understand? What it's made of, what it really is. All the crystals, the strands, the tiny, tiny bubbles of air. *Glass*, you know? Do you understand how beautiful it is?'

Anders had looked at the table and had been unable to discover anything special about it, apart from the fact that it was an unusually ugly and clumsy glass table, but he had decided not to mention this. The guy might well have taken something else, because he was found later in a snowdrift into which he had dug his way. The reason he gave was that his blood had begun to boil.

You could lose your mind.

Perhaps a human being has the ability to see through glass, as it were, to experience water if we have a tool to help us use our brains and sensory perceptions to the full. But we don't do it, because of the toll it takes. We refrain, so that we may live.

Anders took a couple of swigs of water and got back into bed. The powerful experience of becoming aware of the water's secret life had made him feel exhausted but not sleepy, and for several hours he lay curled up, staring at the wall opposite where the pattern on the wallpaper formed itself into the molecular structures of unknown elements.

Only when the first light of dawn began to seep in through the window, painting the wallpaper grey, did he begin to drop off. As if from far away he heard the alarm clock ring in Simon and Anna-

Greta's room, and he could see them in his mind's eye, getting up and dressing for their short honeymoon.

Enjoy yourselves, my darlings.

There was a faint smile on his lips as he fell asleep.

Those Who Have Turned Away

Staircases that go upwards although in fact they're going downwards...

KALLE SÄNDARE

Maja

'Let go of me! Let go of me!'

I don't like him. He looks horrible. I scream. The other one comes and puts his hand over my mouth. I bite him. It tastes of water. Why don't Mummy and Daddy come?

They're carrying me somewhere. I don't want to go. I want to go to Mummy and Daddy. I'm too hot. My snowsuit is too hot. We're going down some steps. I scream again. Nobody can hear me. That's when I start crying. There are a lot of steps.

I try to look so that I can remember the way back. There is no way back. There are only steps. And they don't work.

I'm crying. I'm not as frightened anymore. I don't want to scream any more. Just cry.

Then it gets warmer and something smells nice. They're not holding me as tightly any more. I'm not struggling. I stop crying.

The moped

Anders was already sitting up in bed when he discovered that he was awake. His body was drenched in sweat and his heart contracted; he thought for a moment that he was in a cell. Then he recognised the walls, the pattern on the wallpaper, and realised he was still in the guest room at his grandmother's house.

But he had been there, inside Maja's memory.

He had felt the fear, the heat, and screamed from the depths of own lungs. He had seen the incomprehensible flight of steps and he had seen Henrik and Björn. Henrik had carried him and Björn had put a hand over his mouth when he screamed.

A dream. It was a dream.

No. Elin too had been tormented by memories that were not her own. Pictures she could not possibly have known about. The memories of others. This was the same thing.

Henrik and Björn. Hubba and Bubba.

He knew what he had to do. The clothes he had worn to the wedding were hanging on the bedpost, but he rejected those and picked up his own clothes, which lay in a heap in the corner. Despite the fact that they had been accidentally rinsed by the sea, the fluffy Helly Hansen top and the scruffy jeans still smelled unpleasant. They were impregnated with the smell of smoke, spilt wine and the sweat of fear, and it would take a proper wash to get rid of all that.

But still. This was his uniform. He pulled it on with the intention of wearing it until the whole thing was over. He gathered up his bottles and comics from the floor. When he looked at the lines on the Bamse cartoon, he could see that the zigzag line he had taken for a temple could just as easily be a flight of steps.

He took a few gulps of water. The perception of Maja's presence in his body was once again so familiar that he didn't even feel it, he simply knew that it was there. When he had swallowed the water, he opened the matchbox.

The insect had grown, and was now so fat that it only just fitted in the box. When Anders let a heavy gob of saliva fall on to it, it came to life and began to writhe in its narrow confines. Anders pushed the box shut and closed his hand around it, once again feeling that all-encompassing awareness of the water around him, within him.

He could feel the movements of the larva through the thin cardboard and felt a little sorry for it. But this was not the right moment to reflect on cruelty to animals and the rights of insects. In any case, Simon had said at the kitchen table that it wasn't an insect. It had no will of its own, no purpose other than to be a source of power for its bearer. A kind of battery. Spiritus.

Anders tucked Maja's snowsuit under his arm and went down to the kitchen. It was just after eleven o'clock. There was a note in Anna-Greta's handwriting on the table. He was to take care of himself, and everything he needed was there in the house, there was absolutely no need for him to go out.

There was coffee in the machine, and Anders poured himself a cup. As he drank it he could feel every tiny movement of the liquid passing through his body. When he had finished he fetched a plastic bucket from the cleaning cupboard and half-filled it with water from the tap. He sat down on a chair with the bucket between his thighs, held the matchbox firmly in one hand and dipped the fingertips of his other hand in the water.

He simply knew.

As if the hand in the water were holding a remote control, or rather had *become* a remote control with which he was so familiar that he no longer needed to look at the buttons, he was now able to direct the water. His hand did not exist, the signals went directly from his brain to the contact surface.

He asked the water to move clockwise, anti-clockwise. He asked it to climb up and run over the top of the bucket so that his legs were soaked. Then he put down the bucket, placed his hand on the wet fabric and asked the water to leave it. A burst of steam rose up towards his face.

I can do it.

When he had emptied the bucket and put the matchbox in his pocket, he went and fetched the shotgun. He stood for a while weighing it in his hands, wondering whether it might be of any help to him. Its metallic weight was reassuring, its polished wood; a weapon.

But it wasn't a weapon he needed, at least not one like this. He removed the cartridge, replaced it in the drawer where he had found it and rubbed his hands. He was clean.

A pair of Simon's well-worn boots from the army surplus store stood in the hallway. They were only slightly too big for Anders. He pulled them on, fetched Maja's snowsuit from the kitchen and went out.

Regardless of what kind of creatures Henrik and Björn might be these days, whatever they were composed of, however they lived, one thing was clear: the moped was an ordinary moped. It had weight and solidity, it could be damaged or destroyed. And it had to be somewhere.

When Anders reached the village road he could feel how cold it was. The air was raw, the temperature around freezing. He wrapped Maja's snowsuit around his neck and tucked the ends down inside his top to keep himself warm.

He looked around. The ramblers' hostel was on his right, the path down to the jetties on his left. Unlikely.

A place where nobody goes.

The western side of the island was more or less uninhabited, with just a few isolated, newly built villas on the side facing the mainland. It struck him that he had virtually never gone that way, not since he was little. At that time he and the others in the gang had occasionally embarked on an expedition into the unknown. The western part of the island was simply not part of their world, because no one they knew lived there.

Anders pushed his hands into the front pockets of his jeans, and was immediately aware of the water as his hand brushed against the matchbox; he moved his hands to his back pockets instead. It wasn't the most comfortable way of walking, but he could only cope with that heightened awareness for short periods at a time. It was there anyway, because the box was so close to his body.

He passed the Bergwalls' house and stopped. There was no sign of life from inside the house; perhaps the family had been moved to the mainland. The outside tap was shining.

Who's there?

The house lay on top of a little hill and had a view of the sea, but it was a hundred metres or more to the water's edge. Anders lit a cigarette and tested his feelings. He couldn't see the water down inside the rock, but it must be there, must have found its way with its long fingers until it was able to look out through shining taps and enter into the people.

He made his way along paths where people seldom went, he found some of the overgrown foundations of the houses that had once made up the western village. He finally reached the rocks and looked over towards Nåten, almost indistinguishable in the fog over the sea. He continued on into the forest, walked across uncultivated agricultural land. When he found an old barn that was even more crooked than the Shack, with the roof on the point of collapse, he thought he had found the right place, but the barn contained nothing but rotten wood, rusty tools and a few piles of slates meant for a roof that had never been built. Anders sat down on one of the piles and blew out a long breath.

Where are you? Where the hell are you?

His plan was simple. If he found the moped, he would also find Henrik and Björn. He would wait for them, and when they turned up he would...that was where the plan came to an end. But he had Spiritus, and something would be done.

He was exhausted and hungry after searching for many hours. He would have to go home for something to eat if he was going to be able to carry on.

When he reached the village road again he considered going back down to the Shack to wait, after all they might come looking for him again. Yes, that's what he would do. He would spend the night at the Shack and wait for them, whatever happened.

Since there was more food in his grandmother's house he went there first and made himself a couple of roast beef sandwiches, which he ate gazing out across the sea. It was almost twilight, and he was waiting for the lighthouse at Gåvasten to start flashing.

He took a few swigs of what he had started to think of as Maja-water and ran his fingers absent-mindedly over the telephone dial. Anna-Greta had never bothered to get a phone with a keypad, despite the fact that this made any contact with computerised organisations so much more difficult. She wanted to talk to a real person, that was how she put it.

Before he had even considered how and why, he found himself dialling Cecilia's number. Just because it was such fun to use a phone with a dial, and he couldn't think of another number to ring.

He didn't think Cecilia would be at home, and as the signals rang out an immense desolation began to echo in his ears. He felt so horribly and irrevocably *lonely*. This wasn't a feeling of panic, or the fear that had seized him so many times in the past; this was a great sorrow, and the overwhelming feeling that he was totally alone in the world.

'Hello?'

Anders took a deep breath and forced back the sorrow as much as possible, but his voice was weak as he said, 'Hi, it's only me. Again.'

There was the usual pause as Cecilia switched from anticipating a pleasant chat to expecting a difficult conversation.

'You shouldn't call here, Anders.'

'No, I don't suppose I should. But at least I'm sober.'

'Well, that's good.'

'Yes.'

There was a silence between them, and Anders looked down towards the Shack, waiting in the twilight.

'Do you remember that time when you gave me a lift on

your bike? After I bought you an ice cream?'

Cecilia gave an exaggerated sigh. However, when she replied her voice was slightly less dismissive than in previous conversations. At least he was sober, as he had said.

'Yes,' she said. 'I do.'

'Me too. What are you doing?'

'Now?'

'Yes.'

'I was having a little sleep.' She hesitated before adding something a little more personal, 'I didn't really have anything else to do.'

Anders nodded and looked out over the sea; his gaze had just reached Gåvasten when the first flash came.

'Are you happy?' he asked.

'Hardly ever. What about you?'

'No. What happened with that bloke you met?'

'I don't want to talk about that. How about you?'

'What do you mean?'

'What are you doing?'

One flash, two flashes, three flashes. It was still much too light for the intermittent beam to build a pathway across the sea. Four flashes.

'I'm looking for Maja,' he said.

There was no reply from Cecilia, just a click in Anders' ear as she put the receiver down. He waited. After a while he could hear her crying some way off.

'Cilia?' he said, and then louder, 'Cilia?'

She picked up the receiver, her voice thick, 'How...how can you be looking for Maja?'

'Because I think I can find her.'

'You can't, Anders.'

He had no intention of starting to explain everything, it would take hours and Cecilia wouldn't believe him anyway. One flash, two flashes. Something happened. He suddenly felt as if the flashes from the lighthouse were warm. And good. A light found its way inside

445

him and a terrified little pocket of joy leapt in the air.

'Do you remember that song they sang at Dad's funeral?' he asked. 'As long as the little boat can sail, as long as the heart can beat, as long as the sun sparkles on the blue billows?'

'Yes, but…'

'That's how it is. That's exactly how it is. It doesn't end. Everything is still here.'

Cecilia sighed again, and he could picture her slowly shaking her head.

'What are you saying, sweet—'

Cecilia swallowed the last word. Out of habit she had been about to end the sentence with 'sweetheart'. Just the way they used to talk to each other. She cleared her throat and said in a controlled voice, 'I don't think we should talk anymore now.'

'No,' said Anders. 'You're probably right. But I wish you well. I might not ring you again.'

'Why do you say that?'

'Do you want me to ring you again, then?'

'No. Well…but why did you say that?'

'Just in case.' Anders swallowed a lump that had started to grow in his throat and said quickly, 'I love you,' then hung up. He sat for a long time with his hand resting on the receiver, as if to prevent it from jumping up in the air or ringing.

He hadn't known before he said it out loud. Perhaps it wasn't even true. But after hearing her voice, her more-friendly voice in his ear for several minutes, it had suddenly come over him. Perhaps it was just the longing for another person, or nostalgia evoked by happier memories, perhaps he idealised her now that he no longer saw her, perhaps it wasn't true.

But love? Who can say what is just a mire of dark needs and desires, and what is true love? Does such a thing exist? Can't it be that if we say, 'I love you' to another person and know that we mean it, then that is love, regardless of the motive?

Maja or no Maja, he loved the person sitting at the other end of the

446

line far away from him. What the reason might be, what had changed, he had no idea. That was just the way it was.

It was almost dark over the bay now, and when Anders rested his elbows on the windowsill he could see the beam of the lighthouse on Gåvasten flickering like a golden street across the water, disappearing for five seconds and then reappearing, disappearing.

Where the streets are paved with gold.

He blinked a couple of times then shook his head at his own stupidity. Why should the moped necessarily be on Domarö just because that was where they used to ride around? It could be anywhere, on any island, he of all people ought to know that. The sea was their highway.

The sea is so big, the sea is so big...

But they couldn't just go riding around whenever they felt like it; if that were the case, then somebody would have spotted them. It must be somewhere that wasn't too far away, a place where there weren't too many people...

Anders went into the kitchen and fetched the big torch, checking that the batteries were working. Then he pulled Simon's jacket on over his Helly Hansen top and zipped it up with Maja's snowsuit tucked inside, with the result that he looked pregnant. He moved Spiritus to the jacket pocket.

When he got outside it wasn't quite as dark as it looked from inside, but in about half an hour it would be evening. He quickened his steps down to the jetty, keeping his fingers crossed that Göran would have brought back Simon's boat, as he had promised.

He had. The scruffy boat that had been involved in so much over the past few days lay scraping gently against the jetty and Anders climbed aboard, untied the ropes and started the engine.

It seemed perfect, almost too perfect, and he didn't know whether Henrik and Björn had a feeling for such coincidences, but he suspected that they did. You can't idolise Morrissey and The Smiths without nursing a longing to go back to the beginning, to the times and places where everything started, for good or evil.

Anders swung the boat around half a turn, opened the throttle and set off, heading straight for Kattholmen.

Back to the old place

The trees felled by the storm lay here like long-necked, thirsty dinosaurs, stretching out all the way to the water's edge. A general amnesty had been declared. If the sea froze in the winter, anyone who was interested could make their way over to Kattholmen and chop up as much wood as he or she wanted; the main thing was to get it cleared.

But there were only these enormous fir trees, which were very hard to handle. Difficult to saw up, tough to chop, and the wood wasn't much good either. There was very little interest. If it had been birch, which is fairly easy to work with, there would have been no need to wait for the ice; people would have come over in boats to grab what they could, and Kattholmen would have been cleared in no time.

But the fallen fir trees were still here, dark, gloomy tree trunks lying across the rocks, with the odd branch sticking up out of the water here and there like the arms of skeletons pleading for help, ignored and rejected by one and all.

The moon had begun to tire and shrink, balancing helplessly on the branches of the few firs still standing. Veils of cloud drifted past, and as Anders drew closer Kattholmen was bathed in a light with no luminosity, like aged aluminium. He rounded the northern point where a concrete buoy marked a shipping lane that was no longer used, and continued along the rocky shore on the eastern side of the island.

The boathouse was still there. It would be hundreds of years before wear and tear took its toll on its walls, built with horizontally placed logs, and none of the trees had fallen on it. Anders slowed down and drifted the last few metres, turning off the engine and folding it inboard to avoid damaging the propeller. When the keel scraped along the seabed he clambered into the water, which immediately seeped into his boots. He pulled the boat ashore and switched on the torch, directing the beam towards the boathouse.

Nothing had changed. It looked exactly the same as the last time he had been here. The place where the fire had been was still there, the fire from which glowing coals had been kicked at Henrik's naked back. But the grass flattened by Henrik and Björn's bodies had long since grown tall again. It glittered wetly in the beam of the torch.

Anders looked over at the door and could almost hear the fanfare behind it, the voice singing, 'It's the final countdown...' but the only sound was the whispering of the wind in the dry pine needles.

He took a few steps to the left, shone his torch along the side of the house, and there it was. The wooden platform had been damaged by the fire but was still in one piece, the petrol cap gleamed as Anders swept the torch over Henrik and Björn's moped. There were tyre tracks in the grass leading down to the water.

So here we are...

Anders sat down on the bottom step and looked out across the water. Simon's boat rocked gently as a wave hit the stern. The aluminium light of the moon made the world frozen and metallic. A dry tree trunk creaked behind his back and he found himself at the beginning of everything and the end of everything. The fixed point. The final countdown.

Ten, nine, eight, seven, six...

He counted backwards slowly from ten to zero perhaps thirty times while nothing happened, still staring out across the water as he waited for those who had the key. The ones who knew, and were going to help him whether they wanted to or not.

He pushed his hand inside his jacket and rubbed the smooth fabric of the snowsuit with his fingers. The moon hauled itself laboriously away from the tops of the fir trees, looking down at him as he sat there on the step. Ill at ease, he stood up, pulled the peg out of the door and pushed it open, shone his torch inside.

It was obvious that people had been here since his last visit. A different generation had taken over where theirs had ended, a more careless generation. A wooden chair had been smashed and a pack of cards lay scattered across the floor. In one corner there was a pile of empty bottles, and there were no mattresses or covers on the beds.

Anders went over to the table and sat down on a chair that wobbled under his weight. Through the little window he could see the moped up against the wall. He bent down and started gathering up the cards, thinking he might play a game of solitaire, but gave up. There seemed to be some cards missing in any case, he could only see about twenty.

While he was still leaning forward he heard a splash from outside. It sounded different from the water slapping against the boat, and he stiffened. Immediately afterwards he heard Henrik's voice. 'Don't come here tonight,' he yelled. 'Someone here's going to put a hatchet in your head!'

Anders slowly straightened up and dropped the card he was holding in his hand. It was the five of diamonds. He stared at the rhomboid symbols and found no meaning, nothing to interpret. He got up from the table, adjusted Maja's snowsuit so that it lay like a band around his stomach, and went to the door.

Henrik and Björn were standing at the foot of the steps. The ridiculously long blade of the knife was sticking straight out from Henrik's raised hand.

'This old house,' said Björn. 'Too many bad memories.'

Anders sat down on the top step and looked at them. They hadn't really changed much since that time after all. The place where they found themselves made him see them through a filter of memories, and he no longer saw two vengeful ghosts, but two miserable boys who had no one but each other. And he knew the song, so he said, 'I really liked you and I meant to tell you. But I never did.'

Henrik lowered the knife and the scornful expression left his eyes. Anders extended his hand towards them, palm upwards, and said, 'It was me who gave you the tape, do you remember?'

Björn nodded and began to speak, but Henrik silenced him with a gesture. 'What do you want?' he asked.

Anders ran his hand over his stomach, over the snowsuit. 'I want my daughter back. And I think you two have the key.'

The distorted smile returned to Henrik's lips. 'The key?'

'You're the ones who can help me.'

Henrik and Björn looked at one another. The knife swung to and fro in Henrik's hand. Anders couldn't work out what silent decision had been reached between the two of them as they sat down side by side on the step below him. Since it had worked the last time, Anders thought quickly and said, 'Please, please, please...

It was like a game in a minefield. Once again Henrik's face relaxed. The three of them sitting close together, huddled on the steps, passing Smiths' references back and forth. It could be normal, it could be tender. Anders didn't know if it was.

Close together...

He tried not to let it show on his face as a cold shiver of fear ran down through his chest, filling his stomach with anxiety. His eagerness had made him miss out an essential part of the plan, to say the least. He hadn't drunk any of the wormwood. Not today, not yesterday. And they knew it. Otherwise they wouldn't be sitting so close to him.

Björn was looking at Henrik as if waiting to see what he would say. Henrik remained silent, looking at a point just below Anders' chin. Then he raised the knife and brought it slowly towards Anders' face. Anders jerked back a fraction.

The wormwood. How could I...

'Wait,' said Henrik. 'Wait.' The corners of his mouth twitched. 'Chill out and wait.'

Anders sat still and tried to summon up an expression of friendly interest as Henrik rested the blade against the left side of his neck. He looked into Henrik's eyes, but could read nothing through the thin, gelatinous film covering Henrik's iris and pupil. The cold metal was resting on Anders' skin just a few centimetres below his chin, on the carotid artery.

451

'I can see your face,' said Henrik. 'And it's kind, in a desperate way. But that thing in the back of your mind…what *is* that?'

A pulse of black emotion came from Henrik, and Anders realised that he had lost, that perhaps he had never had any chance of winning. The pulse passed into his body like a spasm, a command to his muscles to *flee*, but before he had time to leap up or hurl himself to one side, Henrik had made the cut.

A burning thread seared Anders' skin and before he had time to react, his blood began pumping out of his body. The blood came pouring out in a series of powerful spurts, splashing over Henrik's face and hands, the steps and Anders' legs. An artery had been sliced open and as he instinctively pressed his left hand to the wound, he realised he was beyond help.

His lifeblood was forced out in time with the rhythm of his heart-beat, squeezing out beneath his fingers with an incomprehensible force. Only now, when his heart was working against him, could he feel its full power. He could feel every beat beneath the palm of his hand like a blow, as fresh blood found its way out of the circulatory system. It ran down under his jacket and soaked his top in a matter of seconds.

His eyelids fluttered and he was vaguely aware of Henrik getting up and positioning himself in front of the steps as if he were about to give a speech. Björn and the dying Anders were to be his audience.

'So, the end of the world. Night time?' asked Henrik, and Björn replied, 'I really don't know.'

'Day time then?'

'I really don't know.'

Anders slipped to one side and his right hand landed on top of his jacket pocket. He felt the hard box through the fabric, and just as Henrik said, 'And what about having children? Any point?' Anders pushed his hand into his pocket and took hold of the box. His fingers were stiff and cold as if they were frozen, and his nails scrabbled help-lessly over the smooth surface. The blood from his throat was coming in weaker pulses now, but they were still powerful enough for a faint cascade to splash up into his eyes. And he saw the water, saw the water in the blood plasma leaving him, but he didn't have the strength to do anything about it. Then he felt a tickling movement against his skin as the box opened by itself and Spiritus crawled into the palm of his hand, as Henrik said, 'So...no debate. Just chill out and wait.'

It's flowing. The water is flowing.

He asked it to stop. The prayer shot up from his hand and spread throughout the tree that was his veins and arteries. When it reached the cut the prayer stopped, drawing towards itself everything in the flowing blood that was water, until only solid, coagulated elements remained around the wound. In order to compensate for the loss of fluid, the artery on the right hand side of his neck began to throb so strongly that it could be felt as spasms beneath the skin.

Anders closed his hand carefully around Spiritus, and through a veil of red he could see that Björn was now sitting right in front of him, with his back towards him. Henrik was searching for a suitable final comment. His face lit up as he found it. He flung his arms wide and he was about to start declaiming, but at that moment Anders jumped on Björn from behind and wrapped his arms around him.

Water.

He could see it. A cucumber. It is somehow incomprehensible that a cucumber can consist almost entirely of water and yet still have a solid form, and that's exactly how it was with Björn. His blood, his internal organs, his skeleton were all made up of water in varying degrees of inertia, and Anders had this water in his hands.

Björn tried to stand up and shake himself free, but Anders asked for heat. He asked for all the heat that could be summoned, he asked the water in his arms to *boil*.

Boil, you bastard!

Björn fell back on the steps as a wave of heat washed through him. Within a couple of seconds he was transformed into a mass of boiling water, scalding Anders on the arms and chest. Henrik ran towards the steps, and just as he got there Björn opened his mouth to scream.

No scream came, but out of his mouth spurted a fountain of

bubbling, boiling water which hit Henrik in the face and chest, so that he staggered backwards and fell over in a cloud of steam. Björn collapsed on the steps and vomited one last shower of boiling water over Henrik before he fell headfirst to the ground and rapidly shrank. In just a few moments he was reduced to a pile of wet, steaming clothes.

Henrik writhed around on the grass, rolling back and forth as if to try and extinguish his burning body. Then his movements slowed and he lay still.

Anders leaned forward and tried to stand up. It was impossible. His legs had lost all their strength when the blood left him. He was a wrung-out rag, and like a rag he allowed himself to tumble helplessly down the steps, only just managing to put out his hands to save himself as he landed.

He crawled forwards. The steam from Björn's clothes rose up and evaporated into the night sky, and as Anders crawled past them he could feel the heat from inside the heap, like a little dormant volcano. Henrik was lying flat on his back on the grass, staring up at the sky. Anders crawled over to him as quickly as he could, feeling Maja's snowsuit sliding over his stomach.

Don't die. Don't die.

Henrik's face was in the process of melting away. His chest was collapsing. The thin skin around his eyes had already dissolved into liquid, and his eyeballs looked like painted porcelain marbles placed in a hollow of inflamed flesh. Henrik's fingers were moving slightly over the grass, as if he were stroking it.

As Anders made his way over to Henrik, the process of disintegration slowed down as the heat of the boiling water diminished. A few final curls of steam rose from what was left of Henrik's face, and the attack was over.

It was not a human being lying there on the grass. A human being cannot fall apart in the way that Henrik had done. The water had sliced through him without distinguishing between the hard and soft parts of a human body. The left side of his chin and neck were gone, his cheeks were perforated with a series of large and small holes that went right through his head.

A human being who had recently sustained such injuries would give off a stench of blood or burnt skin, but there was no smell coming from Henrik. A face sculpted in sand that had had a bucket of water thrown over it. Some parts had been washed away or fallen off, others were intact.

'Henrik...'

Anders leaned on his elbow so that he could look into Henrik's eyes, which were still there, but were staring in an insane, pop-eyed manner since the skin around them had disappeared. Henrik's pupils moved in his direction. It was impossible to tell if Henrik was smiling, since his lips had more or less gone.

'Can I see...' said Henrik. His voice was unclear, gurgling, as if he were speaking through a film of liquid. 'Can I see...what you've got...'

Anders didn't know what he meant, but just at that moment Spiritus moved in his hand, twisting like a finger trying to escape from his grasp. He held his hand up in front of Henrik's eyes. Opened it and closed it quickly.

Henrik's head moved almost imperceptibly. 'Thought so—' he said.

'Henrik,' said Anders. 'You have to tell me—'

Henrik interrupted him with his inhuman, bubbling voice. 'Are you feeling bad for me? Don't. Deep down, you know, I really want to go.'

'Asleep,' said Anders. 'I know. We listened to it in your cottage. We were sitting on your bed. Please, please, please, Henrik. Tell me.'

'The key...' said Henrik.

'Yes. What do I have to do?'

Henrik emitted a puff of steam or air that was transformed into steam by the cold, it was impossible to tell which. His chest collapsed a few centimetres more. His voice was now no more than a faint hiss, and Anders placed his ear close to Henrik's mouth so that he could hear.

'It's in your hand.' There was a brief silence, then Henrik added, 'Dickhead.'

Anders' extra finger was burrowing and bumping against the palm of his hand as if in response, and he pulled himself forward so that his mouth was right next to Henrik's completely undamaged ear, but before he had time to ask anything more, Henrik let out a final, whispering sigh, 'There must be another world. A better one. '

Then he said no more. Anders gave in to his neck muscles, which were insisting on rest, and sank down with his forehead on the grass next to Henrik's head.

Farewell. Dickhead.

The loss of blood and the exertion had finished him. All he could do was lie there, just managing to turn his head to one side so that he could breathe. The minutes passed and the chill of the ground began to make the right side of his head go numb. Spiritus was crawling around in his hand but not trying to escape. Anders could feel the streams and veins of water in the ground beneath him, and was barely able to distinguish them from his own weakened circulation.

I am…sinking…

The only heat that existed was coming from the burning, agonising wound in his throat. The warm wound remained on the surface, while he sank down into the coolness of the earth and it grew dark around him. He lost contact with his body and fell.

Sing me to sleep…

He no longer knew what was up or down, he was in freefall, unaware of anything beneath him or any approaching conclusion. He was floating. He was in dark waters, and he was drowning.

His lungs contracted as he tried to breathe in air that did not exist. He had only seconds left to live. But the seconds passed and still his consciousness drifted in the formless darkness, refusing to die away and thinking: *I have been here before. I know what happens next.*

The horror of what was to come made a heart begin to beat more quickly somewhere out in the darkness. It could be his own heart, but such distinctions were meaningless here. There was a heart beating in fear, and there was something coming closer.

It's coming…

The darkness grew thicker, a shadow began to form inside a shadow. He was nothing against this shadow and he was being sucked towards it like krill about to be strained through the baleen plate of a whale. It wasn't interested in him, it was too immense to bother about him, but he was in its way and he was being drawn into it.

Come with me…come with me…

A hand crept into his, a little hand. It tugged and pulled. Maja's hand.

You have to come now!

No. I am Maja. Daddy's hand is so big. When we go for a walk I just hold on to his forefinger. His forefinger is in my hand. Why doesn't he come?

Daddy, come on!

Her hand is in mine, it's so tiny and slender, it's as if I'm holding a finger, come on Daddy, now Daddy, we have to go!

I'm coming.

He followed the hand that was pulling him, he pulled on the finger that was following him and the darkness shifted in shades of aluminium as the finger and the hand turned into an insect and the salt-laden sea air was drawn into his lungs in a single deep breath.

I'm coming.

He was able to see once again. He was able to breathe. His body was lying on a grassy slope. The wind sluiced across his face. Beside him lay wet clothes, as if laid out to dry in the moonlight. Judging by the position of the moon in the sky, he had been gone for a long time, perhaps several hours. Ten metres away from him lay the boat, pulled up on the shoreline.

I can't do it.

He saw before him the effort required to push the boat out into the water, to get the engine started. He didn't think he could do it. He wanted to carry on sleeping, but without dreams.

Come on!

'Yes, yes…' mumbled Anders, getting unsteadily to his feet and tottering over to the boat. The wind had picked up and was helping him. The little waves had been working on the boat, and had started to draw it towards them. In a little while longer it would probably have drifted away. He only had to give it a gentle nudge, and it was floating out on the water, then he followed it, scrambled up and fell over the rail.

He tried to open the hand holding Spiritus, but his fingers were locked. With the help of the other hand's slightly more flexible fingers, he managed to force the hand open and tip Spiritus back into the matchbox. He stared at the engine.

One pull. I can manage that.

He was on the point of giving up again when the engine didn't start first time, but he gritted his teeth, prayed a wordless prayer and tried again. The engine started. Before he grabbed the controls he checked that he still had the snowsuit inside his jacket.

To no purpose.

Slumped on the seat in the prow so that he could barely see over the rail, he left Kattholmen and headed for Domarö. He knew what he must do, but he had to rest first, regain a little of his strength.

He was almost unconscious when he reached his jetty and it wasn't until he was halfway up to the Shack that he caught sight of himself for a brief moment and asked himself a question:

Did you make the boat fast?

He didn't know, he couldn't remember, and he didn't even have the strength to turn around and check. If he *hadn't* tied the boat up, he wouldn't be able to do anything about it anyway. A while later he was vaguely aware of opening the outside door, closing it behind him, finding a bottle of diluted wine on the bureau and knocking it back. Then he collapsed on the floor and knew no more.

The first

Anders will be the last. Let him sleep and rest. He will need it. Meanwhile, let us listen to the tale of the first one.

It is a kind of fairy tale, and as in all fairy tales, the details have drifted away on the tide of time and we are left behind on the shore with at best part of a keel, a ship's figurehead or a log book damaged by the water.

Something happened. It happened at some point. That is all we need to know. At the time when the inhabitants of Domarö made their living from herring fishing and an unholy alliance with the powers of the deep, the tale may have been better known. Now only fragments remain, and we must let our imagination build the ship.

Because the story is about a ship. Or rather the wreckage of a ship. It might have been a small cog, that is of no importance. The ship had been transporting salt, presumably between Estonia and Sweden, following some route or other.

The crew could have been Swedish or Estonian, but in any case we have only one survivor to take into account. We will assume he is Swedish, and we will call him Magnus.

We find him on the Åland Sea. His ship has drifted off course and has foundered in an unusually thick October fog. Terrified and frozen to the marrow, Magnus has managed to scramble up on to part of the stern, which has broken away. He calls to his shipmates, but there is no reply. The fog lies like a blanket around him, preventing him from even seeing the size of the piece of wreckage that is carrying him.

But he is floating. He has been lucky in the midst of the disaster. The piece of the ship on which he finds himself is shaped in such a way that no part of his body is in the water. He has been lucky. If only he were not so dreadfully cold!

We do not know how long Magnus drifts in this way. It could be days, but it is probably only hours, since the fog does not lift. He is floating through a milk-white world and he cannot hear anything, apart from the sounds he himself makes when he changes position or cries for help out into the emptiness.

The first thing he becomes aware of is not a visual impression or a sound. It is a smell. And the smell alone, the aroma is enough for him to feel that warmth is beginning to seep into his body. It is the smell of animals.

Once before he got lost in the fog at sea. On that occasion they reefed the sails and waited for the mists to disperse. But before that happened they made contact with the land through that smell. Manure, animals' bodies, land! Animals mean people, and rescue. They rowed in the direction of the smell and found their way into the harbour.

Hence the spark of hope in Magnus's terrified guts. He grabs hold of a loose plank of wood and paddles in the direction he thinks the smell is coming from. He must be heading in the right direction, because the smell grows stronger.

He can hear a cow lowing. The fog begins to dissolve into veils and separate sections. The cold diminishes, and the light breeze carrying the smell is warm, a summer breeze, no less.

Presumably Magnus is a believer. Presumably Magnus is praising God as the fog lifts and he can see land at last. But he can hardly believe what his eyes are seeing.

Paradise.

It is the only possible explanation. That he has drifted so far off course that he has ended up in paradise. He has heard that the Garden of Eden could well have been on an island. It seems as if he has found that island.

A few more strokes with his improvised paddle bring him to a beach with fine, pale sand. Where the beach ends, a meadow of lush grass takes over. A number of well-fed cows are grazing there. On a slope he sees sturdily built houses, surrounded by fruit trees in blossom.

And it is warm, pleasantly warm. For a long time Magnus does nothing but sit on his piece of wreckage, staring open-mouthed. He hardly dare step ashore, he is afraid that this paradise will melt away like the fog if he touches it with his feet.

There is a freshness about everything. Everything is sparkling and gleaming as if it were new, created just for him. Yes, that is exactly how it feels. There is a film of moisture over everything and water drips from the leaves of the trees, as if this island has risen from the sea just to meet him.

Tentatively he lowers his foot into the water and discovers that the sandy seabed is firm. He wades ashore, he walks across the beach, up towards the meadow and the houses. He disappears from history, never to be heard of again.

Time to start a fight

When morning came, Anders no longer had a body. He had a wound. All his limbs were aching after a night on the hard floor, his head hurt, and his throat was pulling and throbbing. His fingers were stiff and his bladder made its presence felt, joining in the chorus of pain.

When he opened his eyes, which had managed to gum themselves shut during the night, he felt the pain deep inside the pupil itself as the daylight stabbed its way in. He lay still, looking over towards the toilet door and trying to find one part of him that wasn't hurting. He flicked his tongue around inside his mouth and discovered that his tongue was uninjured, that neither the inside of his mouth nor his teeth had been damaged over the past few days. It felt sticky in there, and it tasted disgusting. But it didn't hurt.

He rubbed his eyes and bits of dried blood came away, colouring the tips of his fingers pale red. He had lost all feeling in the ear that had been pressed against the rag rug during the hours of the night. He sneezed, and snot mixed with blood shot out of his nose.

Today is the first day of the rest of your life.

He managed to sit up, and grabbed hold of the door handle. Using the handle for support, he got to his feet and staggered to the toilet, where he drank from the tap until he could drink no more. White spots were dancing in front of his eyes, and he had to sit down to pee. He sat there for a long time with his head in his hands.

When the worst of the dizziness had passed, he stood up and pulled out Maja's snowsuit. It was no longer wet, but it was blotchy with patches of dark, dried-in blood. He threw it out on to the hall floor and got undressed.

The Helly Hansen top was stiff, and his jeans and T-shirt were stuck fast to his skin. He pulled them off and felt a searing pain as the cut on his right thigh opened up again and began to bleed. A smell of putrefaction rose from his body, and he didn't dare look at himself in the mirror.

The boiler wasn't much good, and he turned up the heat on the shower to maximum. Then he stood beneath the running, lukewarm water with his face upturned. From time to time he drank a couple of gulps. The blood that had flowed out of his body must be replaced. When the water began to cool he soaped himself and carefully cleaned the gash in his thigh.

He closed his eyes and moved his soapy fingers to the wound in his throat. The skin was split in a gash half a centimetre wide, and the flesh was sore when he touched it. He could feel his pulse beneath his fingertips. The artery had repaired itself during the night, but was almost exposed in the absence of protective skin. He cleaned the area carefully and rinsed it with clean water, which was now almost cold.

He stood there until the water was ice cold, letting it sluice over his face, and drank and drank. He turned off the shower and when he had rubbed and patted himself dry with a hand towel, he found that the white spots had disappeared, that he could see clearly.

The bathroom mirror had steamed up; he cleared a patch with his hand and inspected the wound in his throat. It didn't look too bad, but he could see the artery moving beneath the connective tissue like a small fish in a net. He found a couple of pressure bandages and some surgical tape, and dressed his wounds as well as he could. His throat really needed stitches, but to go all the way to Norrtälje, wait in the

462

Emergency Department, try to explain to a doctor…it just wasn't going to happen.

And besides…

When he was fighting with Henrik and Björn, and afterwards when he was wading through the water to get into the boat, he had acquired a kind of knowledge. It could be down to his own traumatised state, but he didn't think so, and Simon had said something along the same lines: it was weakened.

There was a weakness in the sea. That was why Sigrid had floated ashore, and that was why some element of the people who had disappeared had managed to escape and penetrate the wells. There was a tiredness, a lack of attention, and he intended to make the most of it. If he could. If it was there at all.

He walked through the hallway naked, picked the snowsuit up off the floor and continued into the bedroom. The cold was giving him goose bumps, and he put on some clean clothes out of the suitcase he had brought from the city. Underwear, a pair of black corduroy trousers and a blue and white checked shirt. In the wardrobe he found his father's thick green woolly jumper, and pulled it carefully over his head. The polo neck made his throat itch, but it was good because it held the dressing in place.

He felt as if he were getting dressed up, smartening himself up for his own execution, and it was a good feeling. That was the point he had reached. He ought to have cleaned the house as well, left it tidy, but he had neither the time nor the energy.

He examined Maja's snowsuit and decided that the stains wouldn't come off without washing it, and he had no time for that either. He wound it around his stomach and managed to knot the sleeves and tuck in the legs so that it ended up like a very large waist bag.

He went into the hallway and picked up Simon's jacket. His fingers found the matchbox, half hidden in the torn lining of the pocket. He took it into the kitchen, sat down at the table and looked out of the window.

Evidently he had made the boat fast after all, at least at the stern end. The prow was facing away from the jetty at a right angle and the engine was scraping against the stonework, but the sea was almost dead calm, and there was nothing to worry about. Beyond the jetty, out in the bay he could see the lighthouse on Gåvasten, a white dot in the morning light. A reflector suddenly glinted like a beckoning flash.

Don't you worry. I'm coming.

Spiritus was moving slowly around the sides of the box when Anders opened it and let a gob of saliva fall. When he tried to push the box shut, the skin wrinkled, because the insect had grown so fat there wasn't really enough room any more.

He could poke it with his finger and push it in, but it was too much. After all, it had saved his life the previous night. In the junk drawer he found a box of matches for lighting the fire, which was slightly bigger. He tipped the matches out and moved Spiritus into the bigger box.

Anders couldn't tell whether the insect was happier in its new prison, but at least he could close the box without resistance. He stood up and put the new box in his trouser pocket.

He should have been hungry, but he wasn't. It was as if his stomach had solidified around its own emptiness, and was unwilling to let in any food. And that was fine. In any case, he couldn't begin to imagine what he might eat.

He filled a glass with water from the kitchen tap and drank it, *cheers, sweetheart*, filled it up again. And again. His stomach, already stiff, contracted around the cold liquid.

On the worktop stood the bottle of wormwood. Without weighing up the pros and cons, Anders raised it to his lips and took a couple of deep swigs. His mouth tasted like shit and the dizziness went straight to his head, making him sway where he was standing.

With his back to the sink, he slid giggling to the floor. When his bottom hit the linoleum with a hard thud, the giggling turned into gasps of laughter. He slapped the palm of his hand on the floor but couldn't stop laughing, he just had to get it out, so he sang in a loud voice:

'*Thunder honey, Grandma's thunder honey, that's what he eats when it's time to start a fight.*'

Still giggling, he staggered into the bedroom and found Bamse. He pushed the bear underneath the knotted sleeve of the snowsuit so that Bamse's head was sticking up above his hip and the short legs were dangling down his left thigh. He patted Bamse's hat, said, 'How lucky I am to have such a friend!', and by leaning on the walls and the furniture, he managed to make his way through the house and on to the porch.

His head cleared slightly once he got out into the fresh air. He rubbed his eyes hard with his knuckles and stopped giggling, blinking in the sunlight. It was a beautiful, calm day, a wonderful autumn day not unlike the winter's day almost two years ago that had brought him to this point.

His legs carried him steadily down towards the jetty. He could see the natural world around him with exaggerated clarity, he could feel the water inside, beneath and in front of him. He was an oversensitive consciousness transported in a fragile body, an infinitely complex organic computer inside a shell of rusty metal.

And the strongest bear in the world!

He loosened the mooring rope and clambered down into the boat, sat down and picked up the fuel can, gave it a shake. The liquid splashed to and fro ominously. He looked up and gazed over towards Gåvasten.

Well, I'm only going in one *direction, aren't I? I'm hardly likely to be coming back.*

He looked at the bubble of air that marked the level of the fuel. It sank to the bottom when he put the can down, and at the same time something sank inside him. The fatalistic calm that had filled his spirit since he got dressed faded in the face of this practical fact: there was no need for him to fill up with fuel, because he wouldn't be coming home.

Slowly, slowly the boat drifted south, while he sat with his arms resting on his knees, staring towards Gåvasten. Then he nodded briefly, pumped up the petrol, pulled out the choke and yanked on the starter.

As long as the little boat can sail...

The engine started and he shut down his mind against any questions, engaged the clutch and set off as slowly as possible. Gåvasten was gliding towards him across the sea and he was thinking about nothing at all, he just kept his eyes firmly fixed on the lighthouse and watched the distance diminish. When he was about halfway he could see that the birds were still out there. Hundreds or perhaps thousands of little white dots swarmed around the glowing white walls of the lighthouse like moths around a bright light.

With only a few hundred metres to go, the engine coughed. He was running out of fuel, but the strange thing was that the boat seemed to be moving *even more slowly*. When he had travelled another hundred metres or so, he heard a cracking noise.

Terrified, Anders looked along the sides of the boat, because it sounded as if the old fibreglass were splitting. There was no sign of anything, but the noise grew louder and the boat began to vibrate.

What the fuck...

The engine coughed again and when it got going once more it felt as if it were struggling into a headwind. It was roaring for all it was worth, but the boat was barely moving forward. The vibrations became jolts and jerks and the engine began to cough.

'Come on! Come on!'

Anders turned around and slapped the engine as if to stop it from falling asleep. When his hand flew back from the cowling, he saw something that made him realise his efforts were pointless. He could whip the engine until it bled, he still wouldn't get anywhere.

The whole bay had frozen. He was surrounded by ice in all directions. The engine gave a couple of final coughs, then died.

No lapping of the waves, no wind, no engine humming. The only sound was the screaming of the gulls as they moved around the prayer wheel of the lighthouse like white-clad pilgrims. Anders tilted his head to one side and looked at them. They were moving in a clockwise direction.

The central axis.

It wasn't difficult to see, alone in the stillness on the desolate sea, where the only sound and the only movement was coming from the gulls. They were the ones keeping the world in motion by circling around the central axis.

His thoughts were about to fly away, but were interrupted by a fresh cracking sound. This time it was not the boat's progress through the freezing water that was creating the noise. This time it was what he had first thought. The fibreglass hull of the boat was cracking as the ice grabbed hold of it and squeezed. Anders shook his head.

Sorry. It's not going to be that easy.

If there was some form of thinking entity behind what was happening, it wasn't particularly intelligent. It had certainly managed to bring the boat to a standstill. But it wasn't so easy to bring him to a standstill. Anders patted Bamse tenderly and clambered over the rail.

The ice bore his weight. He left the boat and set off across the water towards the lighthouse.

The honeymoon

The ferry was a floating microcosm of pleasures. You walked a few steps to eat, a few more to enjoy duty-free shopping. You went around the corner to dance and up or down a flight of stairs when it was time for bed. Simon usually thought this was a pleasant change from all the difficulties caused by the distances on Domarö, but on this voyage the ship was inducing a feeling of claustrophobia rather than freedom.

And yet he and Anna-Greta had a bigger and better cabin than on previous trips. It wasn't exactly a suite, but it was above deck and had windows. Simon was usually quite happy in a cabin below deck as the throbbing of the engines lulled him to sleep, but the previous night he had lain awake with Anna-Greta beside him and a lump in his chest.

Did I do the right thing?

That was the question that was tormenting him. He had given Spiritus to Anders, and had done it in a way that could only be interpreted as encouragement to tackle things as he saw fit. Had it been the right thing to do?

Simon lay awake in his bunk, listening to the sea surging along the sides of the ship and feeling weightless with doubt and anxiety. He had committed himself to following his fate, together with Spiritus, to whatever the bitter end might be. He had not been particularly afraid.

Or had he?

Had he in fact been afraid, and made use of Anders to get rid of his fear? He could no longer say for sure. He had lost his foundation and his ballast when he gave away Spiritus, and it was not relief he felt now, but an unpleasant weightlessness.

Thus Simon's night passed as the ferry ploughed through the darkness, reaching the outer rocky islets of the Roslagen archipelago towards morning. When Anna-Greta woke up, they got dressed and went down to breakfast.

When they had helped themselves to rolls, various spreads and coffee, and settled down at a window table, Anna-Greta looked searchingly at Simon and asked, 'Did you sleep last night...' she smiled, '...husband?'

Simon smiled. 'No...wife...it was a bad night.'

'Why?'

Simon rubbed the palm of his hand with his forefinger and stared at the scrambled egg quivering on his plate with the vibrations of the ship. It looked like his brain felt, and he couldn't come up with a good answer. After he had remained silent for a while, Anna-Great asked, 'Isn't there something you have to...do?'

'Like what?'

Anna-Greta nodded towards his jacket pocket. 'With the box.'

The movement of the forefinger became more frantic, and the

palm of his hand started to hurt. Simon looked out of the window and saw that the rocky islets had become islands. They had just passed Söderarm. In an hour or so they would arrive in Kappellskär. The finger stopped rubbing and he placed his hands on the table, palms down.

'Well, you see...I gave it to Anders.'

'Gave?'

'Yes, or...handed it over. Passed it on.'

Anna-Greta frowned and shook her head. 'Why?'

'Because...'

Why? Why? Because I'm a coward, because I'm scared, because I'm brave, because Anders...

'Because I thought he might need it.'

Anna-Greta's eyes were fixed firmly on his. 'For what?'

'For...for what he had to do.'

As Simon had feared, Anna-Greta was lost for words. Her hands dropped to her knees and she gazed open-mouthed out of the window at the islands, which seemed to be spooling past on a slow film. Simon picked up his fork and put a small amount of scrambled egg in his mouth. It tasted of ash. He put down the fork again just as the ship gave a jolt and the egg lurched towards the middle of the plate like an amoeba.

Anna-Greta looked at him. Simon's eyes darted away. The ship jolted again, more sharply this time, and when he finally made the supreme effort to look into Anna-Greta's eyes, he found something else there.

They looked at each other. The engine's revs increased and all around them they could hear clinking and clattering as glasses and cutlery trembled and collided. A faint lurch ran through the entire ship; Simon was pushed forward slightly, but didn't take his eyes off Anna-Greta.

The engines roared and everything shook. Raised voices from the tables around tried to make themselves heard above the rattling and roaring. There was a more powerful jolt and Simon's stomach hit the table. Anna-Greta was almost tipped backwards off her chair, but managed to save herself by grabbing hold of the windowsill. They had stopped.

Their eye contact had been broken during the ship's last convulsion, and they both looked out of the window. Simon thought he could just make out Ledinge and Gåvasten in the distance, in a sea that had frozen solid. The ship was trapped in a thick layer of ice, and Simon was intelligent enough to understand.

What have I done? What have I done?

People had got up from their tables and were conducting loud conversations as they ran to the windows to see what was going on. A man and a woman pushed in at their window, obscuring the view and exclaiming incredulously, 'This is just ridiculous…this just can't be happening…how can this happen, we were in open water a few minutes ago…'

Anna-Greta caught his gaze once more. She nodded slowly and said, 'So there we are. Whatever will be, will be.'

She reached out and placed her hand on the table between them, palm upwards. Simon grabbed it and squeezed it.

'I'm sorry,' he said. 'I couldn't do anything else.'

'No, I realise that,' said Anna-Greta. She let go of his hand and looked at it as it lay there open on the table. With her forefinger she traced the lines on his palm. 'I realise that. My husband.'

A better world

The screams, the racket of the gulls had become part of normality by the time Anders set foot on the rocks of Gåvasten for the third time in his life. He hardly noticed them, they were merely a carpet of sound, a part of the place, now that he no longer feared them.

He climbed up from a sea covered in ice on to an islet where it was still autumn. Where there was no snow, and where odd bushes still had leaves, and the tufts of grass in the crevices were green.

The place he was heading for was on the eastern side of the island. He had seen it the last time he was here, and it was just visible in the background in the photographs, but he hadn't *noticed* it until now, hadn't dared to formulate the thought.

Standing on the rocks on the eastern side, he couldn't understand how he had been so blind. Maja had tried to show him with the beads, with the lines in the Bamse comic, and it had been right there in front of him all the time: the flat rocks on the eastern side led steeply down into the sea in a broken step formation.

But it wasn't a step formation. It was a *flight of steps.*

From where he was standing, the top four steps were clearly visible, disappearing down beneath the ice. He recognised them from the dream-like vision when he had been Maja. They were just about three metres wide, and each step was more than half a metre deep. They were so worn down by the water and wind that you could be forgiven if you didn't see immediately what they were.

But it was a flight of steps. Steps leading downwards. Once upon a time, many hundreds of years ago, they must have been completely underwater, but the land elevation had brought them up into the light. Or perhaps they had been there *before* the ice pressed down the land. Anders stood with his arms wrapped around him and looked down the steps.

Who goes there?

He had to use his hands to help him clamber down the first step. These steps had not been built for human beings, or even by human beings, in all likelihood. Who could possibly have carried out this work in prehistoric times *under water?*

He moved down another step. It was perhaps slightly less deep than the first one.

Who?

Someone or something beyond the scope of his imagination. Once upon a time, long long ago, it had used this route to make its way up and down, but then stopped because it had grown too old or too weak. Or too big. Now only the route remained.

Another step. And another.

Anders was standing on the ice at the foot of the visible section of the flight of steps. The sky was teeming with white birds on the edge of his field of vision. He pushed his hand into his trouser pocket and took out the box. Then he sat down on the step above with his feet dangling just above the ice.

He opened the box and tipped Spiritus into his hand, closing his fingers around the insect in a gentle fist. The knowledge of the water flowed through him, and with it came a fresh insight. He opened his hand again, looked at the black insect, now as thick as his middle finger, writhing around on his palm.

You belong here.

The wound in his throat was chafing, and Anders scratched it cautiously as he stared down at the semi-transparent layer of ice. Spiritus was tickling his palm as it sleepily moved around in circles.

This is where you come from.

The insect was a part of what was beneath the ice, at the bottom of the steps. Why else would it have turned up on Domarö, a godforsaken—in the true meaning of the word—a godforsaken island in the southern Roslagen archipelago? Because this was where it came from, of course.

He raised his hand to eye level and studied the black, shining skin, the vestigial segmentation of the body that was like a single small, dark muscle. He breathed on it.

'Are you mine?' he whispered, but there was no reply. He kept his mouth close to the insect and breathed warm air over it. 'Are you mine?'

He allowed a thick blob of saliva to drop, and the insect rolled around, hugging itself like a contented cat in the viscous liquid until its skin shone.

I know nothing.

But still he shuffled off the step so that he was standing on the ice once again. He crouched down and touched it with his fingertips, asked it to melt. A layer of water formed on the surface, and the next moment he sank through ten centimetres and was standing on rock.

The water seeped into his boots, chilling his feet. A semi-circle of open water extended two metres from where he was standing. Through the clear water he was able to glimpse three more steps, disappearing down into the darkness.

The ice was easily a metre thick at the edge, and Anders' chest contracted. The power that must be required to cover an entire sea with such thick ice. He felt as if his chest were being compressed by strong hands, and he could hardly breathe. He looked up at the sky.

The birds were going crazy. It seemed as if every single bird was desperate to occupy the space directly above his head, and it was barely possible to distinguish individual bodies among the flapping, screaming lid of feathers and flesh hovering above him.

He closed his eyes and ran his fingers over the tuft on Bamse's hat, the tuft Maja used to suck on as she lay there listening to her tapes. The deep sea lay beneath his feet, the birds screamed and yelled above his head. He was standing on the brink of something, and as a little man he was incapable of grasping its proportions.

Where's the little man? No sign! Not there! Blood will flow, ho ho ho...

Ronia the Robber's Daughter had been on TV and by mistake Maja had happened to see just as the wicked fairies arrived. She had run sobbing out of the room.

Anders grasped the tuft on Bamse's hat in his left and, closed his right hand around Spiritus and asked the water to part.

There was a swell and a slapping around his feet. The water spurted over the edge of the ice in cascades, cold water spattered his face. A V-shaped wedge formed diagonally below him, as if the water had been sucked down into a hole rather than being forced over the edges. However, the wedge was not deep enough to free the next step.

Part!

The power from Spiritus flowed like a low-voltage current through his body, down into his feet and out into the water, but nothing happened. He tightened his hand around Spiritus as much as he dared. He knew that the power to achieve what he wanted was there. He just couldn't quite manage to pass it on. Expelling a breath he let the prayer go, and the water swirled over his feet once more.

A blob of bird shit plopped on to his head and ran down his forehead. His left arm had been hit too, and a milky white stream of excrement was working its way along his ribbed sleeve. He shook his arm before the shit reached Bamse, wiped his forehead, tipped his head back and yelled, 'So what am I supposed to do? Tell me, instead of shitting on me! Tell me what to do!'

The gulls had no answer for him. They tumbled towards each other in a rustle of feathers, still screaming at the top of their little lungs and dropping strands of slimy waste into the water, on to the ice.

Disgusting. It's disgusting.

Anders looked at Spiritus. The insect resembled a lump of excrement as well.

It should be beautiful. But it's just revolting.

The feeling of physical revulsion sank its claws into him, because he knew what the next step was. What he could do to provide the power source with a better connection, create a stronger contact between himself and...the battery.

It's a battery. I am a machine and it is a battery. Nothing else.

His stomach did not accept this argument and curled up, twisting away as if from a threatening blow as Anders moved his right hand towards his mouth. A wave of resistance rose from his frozen feet and up through his body, aiming to stop him, prevent it from happening, protect itself.

Anders screwed his eyes tight shut and opened his mouth wide, slapped his right hand to his mouth as if he were terrified. Spiritus flew into his mouth and crawled over his tongue. Before he had time to change his mind, before his body had time to come up with any further resistance, he swallowed.

Making a decision is one thing, seeing it through is something else entirely. The fat, slippery body got stuck before it had gone very far, and his throat closed up, refused to let it go down. Anders swallowed again as Spiritus' movements tickled his soft palate, threatening to trigger the vomiting that was lying in wait.

He cupped his hands and scooped up a handful of sea water, tipped it into his mouth and swallowed again. The pressure in his throat eased, and Spiritus slipped down.

He stood with his arms dangling by his sides and breathed deeply in and out several times. All the sounds around him slowly quietened, and the world in front of his eyes stratified and flickered, as if he were looking at it through layers of cobwebs.

Then it came.

Earlier he had felt as if his hand were a remote control; now that feeling spread throughout his whole body. And it wasn't just that he could exercise control. He *was* whatever he controlled. When he looked down at the surface of the water, he no longer saw water, he saw what he himself was made of, what he was a part of.

He ran his hand over his face. It was still there. He pinched his cheek. The skin resisted and it smarted a little. He was a person made of flesh and blood, but a *different* person. Someone whose body was a space he inhabited. Outside that space he could hear the screaming of the birds, through the windows of his eyes he saw himself, and he was the sea.

He asked for safe passage for his carrier, and began to make his way down the steps. No water foamed over the edges, it was as if the sea were *actually parting*, gathering on either side of him, and he walked down the steps between two shimmering walls of water.

The steps were slippery with seaweed, and the bladder-wrack bubbles popped quietly as he cautiously moved downwards. He slipped and grabbed the step above to save himself.

It isn't meant for humans...

The feeling of being the sea remained, but his former consciousness came to the fore and began to talk through the ease with which he was walking down a flight of steps into the depths.

475

It isn't meant for humans. You're going to die.

Yes. But he'd already accepted that, hadn't he? He didn't even have enough fuel to take him back to the normal world, he no longer needed fuel. He was going to go down these steps and see where they led. Then there was nothing more.

Maja.

He was going to see Maja.

He had walked down six steps. His left hand closed around the tuft at his hip and brought him even closer to his human body and consciousness. There was the sound of flapping and fighting above his head, and almost all the light disappeared. He turned around.

Only faint dots of light from the sky penetrated through the furiously fighting block of birds that had crowded down into the passageway to follow him. The flapping of their wings fanned air across his face, and as if the birds' lungs were being compressed, or the acoustics had altered, all he could hear was whistling and croaking from their throats as they struggled to keep their distance from him, while still following.

The odd gull was forced out along the edges, passed through the walls of water and was sucked up to the surface. An injured bird dropped two steps away from him, hit the rock and lay still.

This is impossible…

Anders asked the water to close slowly around the gulls. The passageway shrank, and the birds hurled themselves up over the edges or dived out into the water, swam a short distance and then rose to the surface. Silence fell. Anders was standing on the sixth step in a bubble of air, and it was as dark as late twilight. He could sense the next step, but nothing more.

He carried on downwards.

After seven more steps it was almost completely dark around him. The seaweed and bladder wrack thinned out and disappeared. If he raised his head he could still see the surface up above, dark blue like a summer night sky, but hardly any light penetrated. He kept on going.

The steps became shallower the deeper he went. When he had covered thirty or forty metres in total darkness, they had the same dimensions as a normal staircase. He had no concept of time or space, he was merely a body moving downwards. To avoid losing contact with himself and being swallowed up by the darkness, he began to count the steps.

He conjured up the numbers in yellow against the graffiti wall of the darkness. He embellished them with flowery touches and had little animals hopping around them, to fend off the final separation from the essence of himself, a thinking being. He walked. He walked.

Seventy-nine...eighty...eighty-one...eighty-two...

He was so busy creating flourishes and colours around his numbers, asserting his humanity in the great darkness, that he didn't notice when it happened. He was just considering whether to have a squirrel or a magpie on the branch sticking out from step eighty-two when he noticed that the steps were no longer heading downwards, but upwards.

He stopped. Looked around. Pointlessly. He was in total darkness. He could swear he hadn't reached any kind of landing, any place where the steps leading down had stopped and the steps leading up had begun. At some point the flight of steps had just...changed direction.

He tried to picture it, to see how such a construction might be possible. He couldn't do it. The only idea that came close was a flight of steps that turned itself inside out, becoming an upside-down mirror image of itself.

There is no way back. There are only steps. And they don't work.

These were Maja's words from the dream. Now he understood them. The steps didn't work. They were all wrong. But he kept on going. Upwards.

After twenty more steps he could just make out the summer night sky above him. Ten more and it became an ordinary sky, seen through water. The steps had become deep once more, and when he tried to climb up on to the next one he stumbled and banged his knee on the edge.

He sat down and looked up at the sky. The air in his bubble was beginning to run out, and he asked the water to part all the way up to the surface. The passageway opened up as if he had used unnaturally long arms to draw back a pair of curtains. What he saw made him lower his head in despair.

No, no, no! All this, and now...

The windows of Gåvasten lighthouse were glittering in the sunlight far above him. Now he understood what the impossible behaviour of the steps meant. He had been led back to his starting point. Spiritus had allowed him to slip through, but he was not allowed to slip *inside*. The only thing he had got for his efforts was a sore knee.

He leaned back against the next step and pulled up his trouser leg. The jagged edge of the step had gashed his skin, and a small amount of blood was seeping out. He grinned scornfully at it and tipped his head back. The sky was clear, and what he could see of the lighthouse over the edge of the rock was shining white. He wondered what would happen if he simply asked the water to close around him. Presumably he wouldn't die, but there was always that possibility.

Exhausted, he blinked at the bright light up above and decided to wait a while after all. It was beautiful anyway. There was nothing to hope for, but...

The gulls.

Where had the gulls gone? His field of vision was limited, but at least one bird should have been visible. But nothing was moving across the sky except thin veils of cloud, and he could hear nothing of the birds.

He got to his feet and climbed up the next step. And the next. He had to heave himself up the last step, and once again he was standing on the rocks of Gåvasten.

It was late spring.

The air was pleasantly mild, and flowers were growing in every crevice. Mayweed and chives danced in a gentle breeze coming off the sea. The lighthouse glowed chalk-white beneath an afternoon sun that was just warm enough. A wonderful day.

Anders looked around. No gulls on the water, no gulls in the sky. Not a single bird as far as the eye could see. His woolly jumper was making him itchy in the warmth, and he pulled it off and knotted it around his waist, over the top of Maja's snowsuit.

He wandered dumbstruck over the rocks. When he caught sight of Simon's boat, neatly pulled up on to the shore instead of lying abandoned out at sea, he sat down and rested his chin on his hands.

Where am I? When am I?

He squinted into the sun, sparkling on the sea, and studied the boat. It didn't look the same, somehow. It looked newer, or…healthier. There were no scratches or cracks in the hull, and the engine cowling shone. Anders was seized by a sudden sense of unease, and turned his head to the south.

Domarö was exactly where it should be. A tangled thickening of the horizon, a brushstroke of fir trees against the pale sky. But it was just the same as with the boat, it somehow looked more…newly made. Healthier. Stronger.

He felt a movement in his stomach, like the first perceptible movements of a foetus. He stuck his hand inside his shirt, placed it over his stomach and, with a feeling of disgust, realised that the black larva in there was living its own life. They had moved apart and were no longer one and the same. He was Anders, and an insect was crawling around inside his stomach.

He stood up and walked down to the boat. The mooring rope lay neatly coiled up on the prow; the freshly varnished oars shone. He pushed off and the boat slipped easily off the pebbles as he climbed in.

He pulled the string and coolant sprayed out through the little hole beneath the cowling. He felt the engine. It was vibrating. It was running. It just wasn't making any noise. He engaged the gear lever and the boat moved smoothly forward. He accelerated and the boat moved more quickly, still without a sound.

He turned the prow towards Domarö and picked up speed. The

mild air should have been cold against his face as he moved faster, but it maintained exactly the same pleasant temperature whether he increased his speed or slowed down. Everything was perfect, and the fear inside him grew stronger and stronger.

The trip across to Domarö passed with incomprehensible speed, as if the distance had contracted while he was travelling. After no more than a minute he swung in alongside one of the smaller jetties next to the steamboat jetty, tied up the boat with the soft, white cotton rope and climbed out.

The boathouses were prettily painted Falun red, and looked as if they were made of velvet in the soft afternoon light. Anders looked around and noticed someone up on the steamboat jetty, with their back turned towards him.

He walked along the shoreline and when he looked up in the direction of the village he could see that the shop was open and the pennants advertising ice cream were fluttering gently. Giant Cornet, Pear Split. Neither of those was available nowadays, as far as he knew. Someone was standing up there studying the advertising posters.

MINCE 7.95/KG, GHERKINS 2.95/KG.

I know what this is, thought Anders, as he climbed up on to the steamboat jetty and went over to the person standing with his back to him. *I know where I am.*

'Excuse me,' said Anders, and thought he had uttered the words only in his mind, as they didn't come out of his mouth. The person in front of him was a man dressed in blue jeans and a checked shirt, not unlike the one he himself was wearing. The man did not react to the inaudible words. Anders moved closer.

'Excuse me?'

Anders felt at his lips, licked his index finger. Yes, his mouth was there, his tongue was there. It was so quiet here. Not a sound from machines or voices, no birdsong from the trees.

When the man still showed no sign of hearing, Anders walked around so that he would be able to look him in the eye or give him a shake. He passed the man's side and his stomach flipped over, everything flickered before his eyes as the whole thing turned into its opposite.

Anders was standing where the man had just been standing, staring at the man's back as he began to walk up towards the shop. Anders ran up to the man and around him, and the same thing happened again. Something switched over in his head, and he was following a man on his way down to the jetty, once again able to see only the man's back and the back of his head.

He stopped. The man resumed his previous position down on the jetty, gazing out to sea. Anders turned around and walked up to the shop. He half-expected to see his own herring box up there, his own hand-written sign.

Because it was that day. The day when a man had walked out into the water, and Cecilia had given him a lift on her bike. The best moment of his life. The same weather, the same signs, the same feeling. Apart from the fear bubbling inside him.

You want me to stay. You want me here. You're showing me what you think I want to see. My heaven. That's what you're doing.

The man who had been looking at the adverts was just walking away. On the village road to the south, a woman in an old-fashioned summer dress was also walking away. A woman in a skirt made of rough homespun fabric with a scarf around her head was standing on a slope picking lily-of-the-valley, facing away from him.

No one is seeing the same thing.

The woman picking flowers belonged neither to this century nor the last one. Presumably she couldn't see a shop, and she certainly couldn't see any adverts for ice cream. She might possibly be seeing the bakery that Anders knew had once stood on the spot where the shop was nowadays. In her eyes the steamboat jetty was probably no more than a fairly small wooden structure.

Nowadays. What is nowadays? Where are we?

Anders closed his eyes and rubbed them so hard that he squashed the eyeballs back into his head. When he opened them, he saw the same thing as before. A beautiful landscape, a beautiful day, and people moving away or with their backs turned towards him.

He kicked at the gravel and little stones rolled away without making a sound. He took a deep breath and yelled 'Maja!', but didn't. The air came out of him, his vocal cords vibrated, but nothing could be heard. The silence was so dense that it deafened him, as if he were deep under water.

Which is exactly where I am.

He turned on to the southern village road and walked towards the ramblers' hostel. Like all the buildings on this version of Domarö, it was lovelier than ever. It wasn't that it looked *newly built*. Brand new buildings are seldom particularly attractive. No, it was more the fact that everything was so perfectly aged that it merely emphasised the beauty of the building.

Skansen. The Swedish folk museum.

Something along those lines. Every building, every object, every plant looked as if it was part of an exhibition. As if they *represented* something rather than actually *being* something. Themselves. Life-size models.

A woman in a white dress with black spots and a man in trousers, a waistcoat and a shirt with the sleeves rolled up were playing croquet in the hostel garden.

The mallets hit the wooden balls silently, inaudibly, and they rolled through the hoops or past the hoops. Apart from the lack of sounds, the only strange thing about this scene was that the man and woman never looked at each other and were never facing him. The match continued until the woman's ball hit the wooden peg at the end of the course.

The man and the woman picked up their balls without attempting to say anything to one another, and turned back towards the hostel as if in a choreographed pantomime, where the only requirement was that their eyes must never meet.

Just as the man's body turned towards the hostel, towards Anders, he felt that powerful surge in his chest and found himself standing at the bottom of the steps watching the man and woman walk up them, open the door and disappear inside the building.

It's just me.

Everyone else on board this unreal island was caught up in the pantomime, and was behaving exactly as they should. Only he was a deviation, a disturbance that Anders had to be moved around with force so that the dance would not be interrupted, or collapse.

It must be that way.

If all the people who were walking around here really were seeing different things, different worlds, then it was also essential that they never looked at each other, because then they would see something *different*, and the illusion that was being presented only to them would shatter.

The narrow gravel track leading down to the Shack was edged with lily-of-the-valley. Anders crouched down and grabbed a bunch, stuck his nose into them. Nothing. There were no smells here either. He put one of the poisonous berries in his mouth and chewed. Nothing. He could feel the berry on his tongue, so that sense was still intact, but there was no taste.

He came out onto the rocks and there stood the Shack, just as in the other world.

No...

Anders closed one eye and looked along the length of the straight pine tree. The house was no longer crooked and warped. He had always thought the house looked ugly with its uneven slant, wished he could do something about it. Now he had his wish. The house was straight, and of all the things he had seen so far, this frightened him the most. The fact that the Shack was no longer the Shack. It was a well-constructed summer cottage situated in the most beautiful location.

Cautiously he walked up to the door and opened it. A colony of fly pupae hatched in his chest and began to fly around, searching for a way out and making his chest quiver inside. It was no longer the day when Cecilia had given him a lift. The interior of the Shack came from the time when he and Cecilia had lived here and been happier than ever.

Because that's what I want it to be.

Trembling, he walked across the rag rug Cecilia had bought for ten kronor at an auction, or the image of it. Everything he could see was taken from inside his own head. He walked into the living room, and as he noticed that the door leading to the bedroom was ajar, there came the first sound he had heard in this place: an irregular ticking that seemed to be coming from inside his ears.

He put his hand over his mouth and realised his teeth were chattering. Not even this silence could swallow internal sounds. He crept across the floor of the living room, even though creeping was meaningless here.

The ticking changed to an agitated knocking as he reached the door and looked in.

There she was.

On the floor next to her bed sat Maja, digging into the bucket of beads. In front of her lay small piles of different coloured beads which she was busy sorting. He heard her humming to herself without actually hearing it. He knew she always hummed when she was preoccupied with something.

A few strands of her thin brown hair lay across the back of her neck, some were tucked behind her slightly protruding ears. She was barefoot, and had on the blue velour tracksuit she had been wearing under her red snowsuit.

Anders' legs gave way and he fell silently and helplessly to the floor. The back of his head hit the thick floorboards, and flashes of white seared his retinas. Before the flower of pain had time to come to full bloom, he raised his head so that he could carry on looking, afraid that the image would be ripped from his grasp, torn away from his eyes if he lost concentration for even a second.

The pain filled his skull, but Maja was still there. His head throbbed as he turned over so that he was lying on his stomach, with his face only two metres from her back. The small fingers picked out the beads, sorting them neatly one by one into the right pile.

I am here. She is here. I am home.

For a long time he just lay there looking at her as the headache eased. His teeth were no longer chattering. He had travelled such a long way to see exactly this. And now she was sitting there, two metres away from him.

And he couldn't reach her.

'Maja?' he said. There was no sound. She didn't react.

He wriggled across the floor, over the threshold until he was right next to her, he could see the milk stain on the knee of her tracksuit. He sat up and placed his hand on her shoulder.

He felt the soft curve beneath the fabric, not much bigger than an egg. He stroked her shoulder, enjoying the sensation in his hand, and squeezed gently as silent tears poured down his face. He stroked her upper arm, and the tears ran into his mouth. They tasted of salt. They were coming from him.

But she didn't turn around. She didn't know he was there. He was just a pair of mute, weeping eyes, watching her.

'Sweetheart. Maja, sweetheart, little one, I'm here now. Daddy's here. I'm with you. You're not on your own anymore.'

He hugged her back, rested his cheek on the back of her neck and carried on weeping. She should have turned around, she should have complained: *Daddy, your stubble's all scratchy and I'm getting wet,* but nothing happened. As far as she was concerned he didn't exist.

He sat like that until the tears dried up, until he could weep no more. He let go of her and shuffled half a metre backwards, letting his gaze roam over her back, the contours of her spine protruding beneath the material.

I will sit here forever. When she gets up, I will follow her. Like a ghost. I am with her, as she was with me.

He closed his eyes. He felt brave enough to close his eyes now.

Would she experience it the same way? Like the vague, elusive presence of another person, following her wherever she went? Would it frighten her? Could she be frightened? Could he have any effect on her at all?

With his eyes still closed he reached out and touched her back. It was there. The feel of the soft velour against the palm of his hand was there, even though he had his eyes closed.

Can I…

He shuffled forward and to the right as his hand slid over her back, over her shoulder. He moved around her on his knees, still with his eyes closed, felt her collarbone beneath his fingertips. He sat directly in front of her and followed the line of her throat up to her face. There it was. Her face. The round cheeks, the snub nose, the lips that moved as she hummed.

He opened his eyes.

His hand was resting on the back of Maja's head, and he was sitting exactly where he had been sitting before he started shuffling around. He had run his fingers over her lips and she hadn't noticed a thing. He didn't exist. He wasn't even a ghost to her.

He leaned back, stretched out on the floor and looked up at the ceiling, which was not stained with smoke or marked by cobwebs, but was a beautiful white ceiling of carefully laid tongue and groove. Exactly the kind of ceiling he liked best.

He could sit next to Maja, he could look at her and touch her, but he couldn't reach her. Their worlds were not permitted to meet.

But she came to me. I knew she was there. She came to me. Through the water.

Everything within him became still. The disappointment and frustration faded away. He tried to see it, tried to think.

She came to me…

He raised his head and looked at the little blue figure next to the bed who had now picked up a heart-shaped bead tile and was busy pressing beads into place. Maja.

But this was not Maja. The person who was Maja, who had memories and pictures and who could talk, had come to him, had somehow managed to escape into the sea. What was sitting by the bed was only her body, or that part of her that was necessary to enable him to see what he wanted to see.

Maja?

There was a point where both worlds collided and mingled together. That point was himself, since she existed within him. He closed his eyes and searched for her.

We're not playing hide and seek any more, little one. You can come out. Out you come! The game is over, it's safe now.

He concentrated on what had happened with Elin. The thing that had been in the bucket, that had been forced out of her and had to be returned to the sea. Somewhere inside him was something similar. He called to it now, searched in the darkness of his own body.

Where are you…where are you…

Like the silvery flash of a fish in the net far below the surface, he caught sight of it. It was dispersed throughout his entire body, but he approached it from all directions at the same time and made it come together, gather into a formless, hovering mass that he could take hold of and localise with his consciousness. It was in his stomach now, circling around the insect down there that was floundering and thrashing about in a panic.

Everything around him was gone, was unreal. His strength and his thoughts were focused on one single thing: holding on to something intangible. As he moved towards Maja's body on the floor, his eyes closed, he had to divert a minute amount of his attention to his own movements, and the other thing threatened to slip from his grasp like the eel had slipped through his father's fingers.

He pushed away the eel, couldn't think about the eel, couldn't think about his own knees as they slid across the floor, couldn't hope or wish for anything as his fingers once again moved over Maja's body until he was sitting right in front of her. He still hadn't lost his grip, she was still there in the darkness in his hands, in his mind as he leaned forward and placed his mouth over hers.

Come. Out.

He pushed it in front of him, up from his stomach, up through his throat, and he really could feel it like a little body, a stream of silky liquid sliding over his tongue, out through his lips and into her mouth.

He gasped and collapsed. Part of him had left his body. He didn't dare look. There was nothing more now. He closed his eyes, and there was only silence. Then he heard Maja's voice:

'Daddy, what's the matter?'

Slowly he opened his eyes. Maja was sitting there looking at him with a puzzled frown.

'Are you sad? Why have you got Bamse?'

He looked into her eyes. Her hazel eyes that were looking enquiringly at him. A large body shifted position, and a shudder ran through the world.

The rattle that emerged from his throat told him that he too was now capable of producing sound. Maja's concerned expression was on the point of tipping over into fear, because he was behaving so oddly. He swallowed down everything that wanted to come spurting out of him, pulled Bamse free and held him out to Maja.

'I brought him for you.'

Maja grabbed Bamse and hugged him, rocking back and forth. Anders could hear a faint rustling as her elbows moved across her knees, he leaned towards her and smelled the familiar scent of her shampoo. He stroked her cheek.

'Maja, sweetheart...'

Maja glanced up, looked at him. Another shudder passed through the house and he felt it as a powerful vibration in the floorboards. Maja screamed.

'What's that?'

'I think...' said Anders, taking her hand and getting to his feet, '...I think we have to go now.'

Maja was pulling away. 'Where are we going? I don't want to go!'

The house shook, and Anders saw the poker fall over next to the fireplace. Maja's piles of beads collapsed and mixed together, and she freed herself from his grasp so that she could start sorting them out again.

He bent down and picked her up. She kicked and protested in his arms, but he took no notice, he held her close to his body and ran through the house, towards the front door.

He was through the garden and running down towards the steamboat jetty when Maja relaxed in his arms and started to laugh.

'Gee up, Daddy!' she screamed, clicking her tongue.

He heard the sound of his own feet moving along the track, but he was no longer running on gravel. The gravel was disintegrating, collapsing in on itself, and the lilies-of-the-valley along the edge of the track wilted, were drawn down to the ground and disappeared.

He took the shortest route across the rocks, but they had become dark and slippery. The sky was dissolving like a cloud in a storm. Down by the jetty, two people in old-fashioned clothes stood screaming at each other as they looked around in terror.

Everything except the people was shrinking and imploding in slow motion, and as Anders ran out towards the boat with Maja in his arms, he saw for a fraction of a second what he was not permitted to see. What this world actually consisted of. He would have fallen on his face in terror or adoration if he hadn't—

'Gee up, Daddy!'

—if he hadn't had to get Maja away from here.

When he jumped down into the boat and placed Maja on the seat, he realised the run had taken no more than a few seconds. He had come out on to the rocks and thought that they looked slippery, and then he was past them without even noticing how it had happened.

He started the engine and just about managed to turn the boat, and then they had reached Gåvasten. Distances were being drawn in on themselves, and everything was getting closer to everything else.

Gåvasten was still there. The white lighthouse still extended up towards the sky, which was now as dark as night, but when Anders turned around towards Domarö, the island was only a few dozen metres away. The perspective had shifted. Domarö was the same size as when he had seen it from a kilometre away, but he understood that it was closer because he could see the people. Could see their waving arms, their running bodies.

And the height of Domarö continued to diminish. The island was sinking.

'Come on, sweetheart! Quick as you can!'

Maja crawled out of the prow and jumped down on to the rocky shore. She had seen what he could see, and was frightened. 'Where are we going?'

She lifted her arms up to him; he picked her up and ran towards the eastern side of the island.

Let it still be there, let it still be there...

The steps were still there, but when he got to the rocks on the eastern side, the sea too had begun to drop the mask, and was in the process of dissolving into a leaden mist with the flight of steps running down through it.

Anders put Maja down; she was hugging Bamse tightly. He crouched down and said as cheerfully as he could manage, 'Up you come. You can ride on my shoulders.'

Maja stuck her thumb in her mouth and nodded. Anders moved down from the top step, and with some difficulty Maja climbed on to his shoulders with her legs around his neck. She didn't want to take her thumb out of her mouth, or let go of Bamse. He held on to her knees tightly so that she wouldn't fall, and started the downward climb.

They were moving in their narrow corridor of air, and the downward climb became an upward climb without him even noticing. Somewhere along the way the steps changed direction and the mist around him turned into water. The sweat was pouring into his eyes; it didn't occur to him to ask it to stop. His legs were aching, his back, the back of his neck, but he clutched Maja's knees and kept on moving upwards, constantly afraid that he would trip and fall on the uneven steps.

His lungs were burning by the time he was standing on the rocks on the other Gåvasten once again, and every gasping breath brought with it puffs of ingrained tobacco smoke, loosened during his flight. When he crouched down to let Maja slide off his shoulders, he fell over. Maja shrieked and tumbled sideways on to the rocks, but landed on Bamse.

She neither cried nor screamed. She sat there curled up with her eyes open wide and her thumb in her mouth, hugging Bamse. Anders reached out a feeble hand and touched her foot, as if to check that she was really there. She looked at him with those same wide eyes, but said nothing.

The inside of his body was blasted as if it had been in a furnace, he had used up the very last of his strength in running and climbing, and all he could do was lie there full length on the rocks, gasping for breath and looking at his terrified daughter.

She'll be fine. She doesn't understand. She'll be fine.

It wasn't Anders who was shaking, it was the rock itself. A roaring rumble was rising from the very bowels of the earth, and it was growing in strength. He was lying with his ear to the ground, and he could hear it.

It's coming…

For a brief moment he had caught sight of it through the webs of illusion in which it concealed itself. The thing that held the people captive, the thing that needed their strength in order to live and grow. The threat from the underworld, the spirit of the sea, or the creature whose presence gave rise to legends. The monster.

There was no point in trying to describe it. It was great power and many-headed vision, a black muscle with millions of eyes, blind and without a body. It did not exist. It was all that existed.

The vibrations in the rock were transmitted into Anders' skull. His little brain splashed around inside trying to frame an idea of what he had been through, but without success. The important thing was not to be here when it came.

Anders rolled over on to his back and sat up, placed a hand on Maja's knee. He didn't really have the strength, but as some sergeant had said to him during his military service, 'You're going to run until even your own mother thinks you're dead, and then you're going to run a little bit more.'

His mother was out of the picture, he had only himself to rely on, and he didn't think he was dead. So there must be something left inside him. He wiped the sweat from his eyes and looked out across the ice-covered sea.

The birds...

They were no longer circling around the island, but they had not disappeared completely as in the other place. The whole flock had now gathered in an area about a hundred metres to the east. Many were flying around as before, but even more were standing on the ice, walking restlessly to and fro as if waiting for something.

There was no time to think. They were back in this world now, where it was October. His body was still steaming with heat, but...

'Here, little one.'

He untied the snowsuit from around his waist and moved closer to Maja, who was still sitting with her knees drawn up, sucking her thumb. Her eyes were staring in a way that made him uncomfortable. He tried to ease Bamse from her grip so that he could put the snowsuit on. She wouldn't let go.

'Sweetheart, it's cold. You need to put this on.'

Despite the fact that it impeded what he was trying to do, he was relieved when she shook her head violently. He tugged at Bamse's hat to get the bear away from her. The vibrations in the ground were getting stronger, and he had to make a real effort to speak calmly.

'Come on now, poppet, you'll catch a cold...'

He pulled at Bamse's hat and Maja held on tight. He felt a kind of cough in his chest, and a laugh burst out of him. He was laughing. His stomach was bubbling with sheer joy, and he carried on laughing. It was just so stupid.

He had fetched her from the other side, an earthquake was approaching from somewhere beneath them, and he was sitting here tugging at Bamse's felt hat while she held on tight and shook her head.

Maja tilted her head on one side and took her thumb out of her mouth, 'I'm not cold, Daddy. Just my feet, a little bit. Where's Mummy? I want her to come too.'

'OK,' said Anders, swallowing the laughter. 'OK. Mummy's coming later.'

Maja looked critically at the snowsuit in his hands. 'And that's *dirty*. Really dirty.'

The fabric was stained with patches of dried blood, which in places had become sticky with the heat of his body during their flight. Yes, it certainly was *really dirty*.

Maja looked around her. 'What's that noise?'

'I don't know,' he lied. 'But we have to go now.'

He picked Maja up in his arms again and she let go of Bamse so that she could wrap her arms around his neck, while Bamse lay safely pressed between them. The rumbling was growing louder, and by the time they reached the shore on the south side, the layer of ice covering the sea had broken away from the island. He had to leap across a strip of open water so that he could run to the boat, which was still stuck fast in the ice out there.

By the time he reached the boat and put Maja down, the ice had begun to crack and explode. Deep cracks were beginning to run through the shining surface, and all the birds rose into the air, screaming excitedly as the ice broke and dark strips of water appeared.

I am the sea.

He turned the ice in front of the boat into water, he grabbed hold of the boat and pulled it along. Maja almost fell as the boat shot through the passageway of open water appearing ahead of the prow. She clung to the rail and laughed.

'Faster! Faster!'

Anders shook his head. She wasn't interested in how this was possible. The important thing was that it was *fun*, that they were going *fast*. He was the sea and he thrust the boat ahead of him with greater power. Maja's hair fluttered in the wind as she held on to the rail, bobbing up and down with her upper body as if to help, to urge the boat on.

A loud bang echoed through the air, and Anders turned. East of Gåvasten a black shape rose up, smashing the thick ice to pieces along its edges. It was already about a metre high and twenty metres wide, growing in size as it rose.

They were so far away that Anders could barely make out individual birds, but he could see the flock diving at the thing that was rising from the sea, attacking it, doing no more damage than a mosquito bite with their little beaks.

He turned to face Domarö, which was coming up rapidly. A mosquito was tiny, nothing compared with a man, who could squash it with his little finger. But a thousand mosquitoes was another matter. Perhaps the gulls' battle was not as hopeless as it seemed.

The ice had broken up into huge pieces as Anders steered the boat in towards the same jetty where he had moored it in the other world. He helped Maja up on to the jetty and turned to face the sea once again.

Next to Gåvasten there was now a new island, the same height as the rock on which the lighthouse stood, and at least five times as wide.

Gunnilsöra. Gunnil's ear. Gilded ear. The island of dreams.

A shudder ran through the sea and the jetty rocked beneath his feet. Both Gåvasten and the other island disappeared, and Anders blinked in bewilderment. The line of the horizon was moving, undulating like tarmac in hot sunshine.

He understood. Once again he picked Maja up and carried her ashore. As he was running towards the steamboat jetty he saw Mats, the shopkeeper, standing up there looking through a telescope. His wife Ingrid was next to him. Mats lowered the telescope and shook his head, said something to her.

'Hello!' yelled Anders. 'Mats! Hello!'

Mats caught sight of him. 'Anders, what...' He stared at the blue bundle in Anders' arms and pointed. 'Is that...?'

Anders made it on to the jetty.

'Yes,' he said. 'Sound the fire alarm, now!'

'But how…I mean…'

'Please Mats, just trust me. It's all going to hell. Sound the fire alarm and…' Anders glanced out to sea. The horizon had risen a little further towards the sky. '…get out of here. Right now!'

Mats looked out to see and his jaw dropped as he too saw what was coming. With Ingrid beside him he raced up to the shop. Anders followed them with Maja in his arms, and arrived just as Mats was opening the cupboard. He pressed the alarm button and it sent its mournful wail out across the island.

'People aren't at home,' said Mats, locking the cupboard again out of habit.

As they ran uphill Anders thanked some lucky star that the children were still in school, and that those who had jobs on the mainland were at work.

He turned around.

The wave was now only a few hundred metres away. Despite the fact that Anders was now on higher ground, the wave was so tall that it obscured the view of Gåvasten and the thing beside it. Maja saw it too.

'Daddy, are we going to die?'

'No, sweetheart,' said Anders, following Mats and Ingrid as they moved higher still. 'We're not. Not after all this. No way.'

'Is Mummy going to die?'

'She isn't here. She's a long way away. She's fine.'

'Why is she a long way away?'

An elderly couple whose names Anders couldn't recall, who lived a couple of blocks up from the shop, opened their front door and looked out. 'Where's the fire?' asked the old man. Mats stopped and pointed out to sea.

'A wave is coming. Get out of here.'

The old man peered out to sea and his eyes opened wide. He grabbed his wife by the hand. 'Come on, Astrid.'

By the time the old couple had put on their clogs and got down their front steps, there was a deafening crash from the harbour, and a blast of air made Anders wobble forwards. Maja squealed, thinking he was going to fall on top of her, but he managed to regain his balance and staggered on towards the forest.

He could hear a thundering sound like a waterfall behind him, and a few seconds later sea water was swirling over his feet. A sharp pain shot up his leg as a shard of ice hit his right foot. He gritted his teeth and limped along, picking his way between large and small pieces of ice that were floating on the water as it was sucked back towards the sea.

Fortunately the old couple were of tough archipelago stock, and they plodded along with their clogs splashing through the water a couple of metres ahead of him, just behind Mats and Ingrid. Maja hauled herself up and looked over his shoulder.

'Daddy, there's another one coming!'

He looked back. The boathouses down by the harbour were gone, and the shoreline had risen by several metres, as if Domarö too had shaken itself up and risen from the sea to meet the threat. Unfortunately this was not the case. It was the wave sucking the water towards it. The next wave.

Mats noticed that Anders was limping, and offered to carry Maja, but Anders shook his head. He had carried her this far, he would carry her all the way. The only problem was that he could hardly walk.

'Wait, just hang on a minute!' the old man shouted to Anders, waving the others on. Anders stood with Maja in his arms as the man ran back to his house. Now he remembered the man. He used to buy herring from Anders; he was already an old man in those days, and Anders thought he had such an unusual name for an old man.

Kristoffer, Anders thought. *His name is Kristoffer Ek. Torgny's dad.*

Kristoffer disappeared out of sight and Anders looked anxiously at the sea. It would take a while before the next wave reached them, but when it did...

I am the sea.

He was still standing with his feet in water and the water linked him directly to the wall of sea water that was approaching from out in the bay. He rose against it and Spiritus burned in his stomach as he left his consciousness and became one with the hurtling wave.

Stop! Stop!

He was in the wave and the wave was in him, its insane power ran through Spiritus and out into his fingers, clenching into fists around Maja's body as he tried to restrain, to brake. The insect in his stomach tensed like a muscle strained to breaking point, and this was not meant for humans.

He knew it was pointless. Like trying to hold back a bolting horse with a fishing line. And yet he resisted until it all became too much, and something burst inside him. He felt a searing pain in his stomach. His contact with the water was broken.

'Ouch, Daddy! You're pinching!'

He returned to the solid world, where his arms were squeezing his daughter tightly. He relaxed; he had to concentrate to stop his legs giving way beneath him. Close by his ear, Maja asked, 'Why is Mummy a long way away?'

'We'll ring her later, sweetheart. Afterwards.'

The wave shimmered like a gigantic mirror being dragged across the surface of the sea, the broken pieces of ice were like cracks and marks on its shining surface. It was not within human power to stop it. Anders had turned and started to run once again when he heard the sound of an engine starting up, and the next moment Kristoffer pulled out of his drive on a bright blue platform moped.

'Jump on!' he shouted.

Anders clambered on to the platform with Maja in his arms, and as Kristoffer accelerated along the forest track, she whispered in his ear, 'Who's *that*?'

'That's Kristoffer,' said Anders. 'He's helping us.'

Maja nodded. 'He looks nice. A bit like Simon.'

Anders hadn't given Simon and Anna-Greta a thought since this

497

all started, he had just registered the fact that they were *out of the way* and therefore safe. Either at sea or in Kapellskär.

Domarö. It only wants to get at Domarö.

They caught up with the others. Kristoffer braked and Astrid perched gratefully on the edge of the platform. Kristoffer waved to Mats and Ingrid, but Mats shook his head and kept on running with his wife. Presumably the moped would lose so much speed with them on board that it was quicker to keep running.

'To the rock!' shouted Anders. 'The erratic boulder. That's the highest point.'

Kristoffer nodded, and they shot off along the track. As they passed Mats and Ingrid, Anders shouted the same thing to them. After a hundred metres Kristoffer turned off and they bounced along over roots and stones. But they were moving upwards, climbing all the time.

It was impossible to ride along the last bit, and despite the fact that his feet were hurting so much it brought tears to his eyes, Anders clung to Maja and she clung to him as they got down from the platform and began to climb.

They reached the boulder just in time to see the wave come crashing in over Domarö. Like a dark blue fifteen-metre wall with a crown of ice shards, it came down over the community. Anders sank down at the edge of the rock and watched as what the first wave had left of the Shack was swallowed up by the mass of water.

The chunks of ice flew off the crest of the wave and destroyed the roofs of Anna-Greta and Simon's houses just seconds before the alarm bell tower collapsed under the pressure and the wall of water smashed the whole thing to driftwood dancing in the foam, and then were was nothing left. The six refugees were standing on a tiny island a dozen or so metres above a rushing, roaring sea, with wreckage swirling around them.

Anders looked up. Gåvasten lighthouse could no longer be seen. The little island was still out there, but the lighthouse itself had disappeared, swept away by the wave. A shudder ran from the sea through the earth, continued into their bodies through the rock, and the island that had appeared next to Gåvasten began to sink.

The water beneath their feet ebbed away. Above his head, Anders heard Mats say, 'There were people there…'

Anders leaned back and saw that Mats was looking through his telescope. He lowered it and shook his head as he gestured out towards the sinking island. 'There were people out there. On the island. Lots of people. They're gone now.'

Anders hugged Maja and buried his nose in the hollow at the back of her neck. The water sank down, exposing a village that was no longer there. Beneath them lay nothing but a muddy mess of fallen trees and the wreckage of houses and outbuildings. Here and there lay large or small pieces of smashed boats. The only thing that was left was the lump of concrete that formed the steamboat jetty.

It's dangerous. Not only for you. For all those who live here.

This was what Anna-Greta had meant, what she had wanted to prevent. Anders pushed his nose harder into Maja's neck, rubbing his cheek over her back.

'Ouch Daddy, you're all prickly. Stop it.'

Anders smiled and turned her to face him, stroking her cheek gently with one finger. Maja clamped her lips together in a way that meant she was thinking.

'Daddy?'

'Yes.'

'I dreamed I was calling to you. A lot. Was I?'

'Yes, you were.'

Maja nodded grimly, as if this confirmed something she had suspected for a long time.

'What did you do then?'

Anders looked into her serious, worried eyes. He tucked a strand of her hair behind her ear and kissed her forehead.

'I came to find you. Of course.'

499

In the churchyard in Nåten there is an anchor. An enormous anchor made of cast iron, with a memorial plaque:

IN MEMORY OF THOSE LOST AT SEA

After the incomprehensible storm, the anchor was no longer there. From the spot where the anchor had been, a fresh trench ran down to the shore. As if the anchor had been dragged along by its chain, dragged through the earth like a plough, leaving the furrow behind it before it disappeared into the sea.

Whatever had been fastened to the anchor had torn itself free. Or been set free.